About the Authors

Cat Schield lives in Minnesota with her daughter, their opiniated Burmese cats and a silly Doberman puppy. Winner of the Romance Writers of America 2010 Golden Heart® for series contemporary romance, when she's not writing sexy, romantic stories for Mills & Boon Desire, she can be found sailing with friends on the St. Croix River or in more exotic locales like the Caribbean and Europe. You can find out more about her books at www.catschield.net

Charlene Sands is a *USA TODAY* bestselling author of thirty-five contemporary and historical romances. She's been honoured with *The National* Readers' Choice Award, *Booksellers* Best Award and *Cataromance* Reviewer's Choice Award. She loves babies, chocolate and thrilling love stories. Take a peek at her bold, sexy heroes and real good men! www.charlenesands.com and Facebook

Sarah M. Anderson won *RT Reviewer*'s Choice 2012 Desire of the Year for *A Man of Privilege*. *The Nanny Plan* was a 2016 *RITA*® winner for Contemporary Romance: Short. Find out more about Sarah's love of cowboys at www.sarahmanderson.com

D0808338

Irresistible Bachelors

Irresistible Bachelors:
Bachelor
Undone

CAT SCHIELD

CHARLENE SANDS

SARAH M. ANDERSON

MILLS & BOON

First Published in Great Britain 2021
by Mills & Boon, an imprint of HarperCollins*Publishers* Ltd,
1 London Bridge Street, London, SE1 9GF

www.harpercollins.co.uk

HarperCollins*Publishers*
1st Floor, Watermarque Building,
Ringsend Road, Dublin 4, Ireland

ISBN: 978-0-263-30245-5

MIX
Paper from
responsible sources
FSC
www.fsc.org
FSC™ C007454

Printed and bound in Spain
by CPI, Barcelona

THE BLACK SHEEP'S SECRET CHILD

CAT SCHIELD

For my Desirable sisters, Jules, Sarah and Andrea.
You inspire me everyday with your fabulousness.

One

Savannah Caldwell bypassed the line of partygoers held in a queue by velvet ropes and headed for the burly linebacker with the crooked nose guarding the nightclub's front entrance. Club T's was only open Friday through Monday. Without a table reservation, the average wait for general admission on a Monday night was one to three hours. Savannah had no intention of standing around that long to get in to see her brother-in-law.

A driving beat poured from the club's mirror-lined doorway. At one o'clock in the morning, Club T's was in full swing, and Savannah was actively second guessing her impulse to hunt down Trent to discuss business at this unorthodox hour. But she'd been turned away from his office earlier when she'd tried to make an appointment with his assistant, and so coming here seemed the only way she could get him to acknowledge her.

A wave of melancholy caught her off guard. She'd been fixated on Trent since age eleven when she'd left Tennessee and moved to LA to live with her aunt Stacy, the Caldwell family's live-in housekeeper. At first Savannah had just wanted him to like her. As she entered high school, she'd developed a full-blown crush on him. But it wasn't until she'd moved to New York City at eighteen and began modeling that Trent finally noticed her as a woman.

When she'd married Trent's brother, Rafe, sixteen months ago, Trent had severed all contact with her. The loss had been devastating. To cope she'd buried her sadness. But suppressing her emotions had turned her into a poorly crafted replica of who she used to be. She spoke less. Dressed and acted like a matron twice her age. She'd lost all touch with the optimistic young woman who dreamed of a loving family, and a husband who adored her.

Savannah stepped up to the blond bouncer with the well-defined cheekbones. In four-inch heels, she stood six feet tall, yet the top of her head came no higher than the second button of his snug black polo with Club T's logo. Where ten minutes ago she'd been truly determined, she was suddenly awash in hesitation. Even if Savannah was comfortable with confrontation, she was no match for this man. He was accustomed to subduing intoxicated, belligerent troublemakers twice her size.

WWCD. What would Courtney do?

She drew in a breath to counteract her rising anxiety and ran through the centering exercises her acting coach had drilled into her. Playing the part of wealthy mean girl Courtney Day on a soap opera for three years had enabled Savannah to summon the demanding character at will, even two years after she'd stopped acting.

In the early days of working on the show, Savannah had struggled in a role as foreign to her as Courtney. While she'd certainly encountered enough rich, entitled and manipulative women during her years of living in the Caldwell household to draw from to create Courtney, Savannah hated the sort of conflict the socialite thrived on. Savannah would rather retreat than stick up for herself and had a hard time acting as if everyone should rush to do her bidding.

She'd landed the role because of how she'd looked in Courtney's designer clothes, with her hair and makeup done by professionals, not because she could act. Within the first two days, it was obvious she was going to be fired unless she learned to embrace Courtney's mean-girl persona. A fellow actor recommended her acting coach. Bert Shaw was tough and smart. He convinced her to live the persona 24/7 until she was more familiar with Courtney than Savannah. It had taken two weeks, but once she surrendered to Courtney's strengths, her flaws were easier to accept.

With a slow blink, Savannah wrapped herself in her alter ego once more. "I need to speak with Trent," she told the gatekeeper.

To her shock, the man nodded. The smile he gave her was surprisingly gentle for one of his imposing bulk. "Of course, Mrs. Caldwell. He said to let you right in."

Savannah wasn't sure whether to be delighted or worried that Trent had at long last made himself available after ignoring her phone calls for the last seven days. What sort of game was he playing? Knowing Trent the way she did, it could be any number of things.

"He'll be in the VIP section upstairs." The bouncer unhooked the rope from the stanchion and gestured her toward the entrance.

Courtney treated most people as if they existed only to serve her. Savannah should have sailed through without giving the bouncer another glance, but she sent him a grateful smile as she went by.

Once upon a time she might have enjoyed being here, but not tonight. Club T's catered to twentysomethings who favored short dresses that bared long tanned legs and impressive amounts of cleavage. As she eased through the press of bodies, she was feeing positively archaic.

She'd had fun taking in the LA and New York City nightlife at Trent's side. But that was before she'd entered a loveless marriage, given birth to her son and become a widow all in the space of a year and a half. Not what she'd hoped for herself.

When she thought about the girl who'd dreamed of living happily ever after, she missed her a lot. Naive and very foolish she might have been, but she'd also been brimming with optimism. Undaunted by a lonely childhood where she'd been more burden than someone's pride and joy, she'd craved a traditional family lifestyle, with a husband and children, a cozy house with a dog, and a white picket fence. Instead, she'd fallen for Trent Caldwell and picked the one man who would never make her dreams come true...

Handsome and confident, with an irresistible charm, Trent could also be difficult and moody when things didn't go his way. His family brought out the worst in him, something Savannah had often witnessed during the years she'd lived with them.

When Trent's father, Siggy, went after his younger son for his wild nature and reckless behavior, the whole house had resonated with his denigrating monologues. Siggy saw himself as the head of a dynasty and viewed Trent as the bad seed. During the seven years Savannah had lived with her aunt, it became clear that while eldest son, Rafe, could do no wrong, younger son, Trent, did nothing right.

In the aftermath of those arguments, Savannah had always gone to Trent. In him she saw reflected the loneliness and isolation that defined her situation. Believing they were kindred spirits fanned her girlish crush on him. She supposed that Trent acted the way he did because it was expected of him rather than because it was his nature. Just as she was confident that if he'd been raised by a father who'd been supportive and kind, rather than a tyrant, he would have ended up totally different.

She paused at the edge of the dance floor and searched for the stairs that would take her into the VIP section. Since Savannah had never visited Las Vegas before, she had no idea where she was going. The photographs she'd seen of Club T's didn't do the enormity of the place justice. The club occupied forty thousand square feet in Cobalt, one of the premier hotels on the Strip. In addition to the enormous dance floor inside, the club boasted a sprawling outdoor patio and pool area.

The club was owned by three men—the T's that made up the club's name. Trent Caldwell, Savannah's brother-in-law, who managed the day-to-day business, had a 50 percent stake. The other half was split between Kyle Tailor, former Cubs pitcher and part owner of the LA Dodgers as well as the boyfriend of Trent's sister, Melody, and Nate Tucker, Grammy-winning singer/songwriter, Free Fall's lead singer, producer and owner of Ugly Trout Records.

Before Savannah could start moving again, a medium-size man with brown hair snagged her arm. "Hey, there, beautiful. If you're looking for someone, here I am. Let me buy you a drink."

"No, thank you."

"Come on. One drink."

"I'm meeting someone."

"I'm sure he won't mind."

She'd had too many encounters with men like this. She didn't need a basket filled with cookies or a red cape to attract the wolves. Something beyond being blonde and pretty made her prey. And all too often she had a tendency to trust when she should question instead.

"I mind."

The bodies around them shifted, allowing Savannah to slip away without further confrontation. She angled away from the bar and the dance floor. Sheer luck allowed her to blunder in the right direction. Another mammoth guarded the VIP entrance, but he let her in without challenge. Noting the earpiece he wore, Savannah assumed he'd been warned to expect her.

She wound her way past plush, curved couches loaded with celebrities from the music industry and Hollywood. Her brother-in-law was easy to locate. She just needed to look for the most beautiful women.

Trent was completely in his element. Like an emperor accustomed to being adored, he sat on a curved couch, arms spread wide to allow the brunettes flanking him to snuggle close. Each girl had a drink in one hand and rested the other hand possessively on Trent. If they hoped to pin down this elusive bachelor, Savannah wished them luck. From the look on his face, he wasn't into either of them. Not that that would stop him from showing them a good time. And from their blatant pawing, it appeared that's what they were looking for.

Savannah stepped up to Trent's table and spoke his name. The DJ picked that second to talk over the loud music and drowned out her voice. Nevertheless, whether he heard his name or just noticed her awkwardly standing there, Trent turned his attention to her.

As his eyes met hers, longing slammed into her, as inescapable as it was four years ago when he'd kissed her for the first time. Strong emotions bumped up her heart rate and released butterflies in her stomach. Squaring her shoulders, she ignored her body's disloyalty. She couldn't let Trent get to her. She'd come to Las Vegas with a business proposition and that's what she needed to focus on.

"Savannah, what a surprise." A welcoming smile curved

his lips, but to someone who'd seen Trent unguarded and truly happy, it looked fake. "Come join us."

She shook her head. "I'm not here to party."

He mimed that he couldn't hear her and waved her closer. Savannah held her ground, not relishing the idea of becoming one of his groupies. If she'd felt out of place downstairs, that was nothing compared to the humiliation of standing on display for Trent's fashion-forward friends. Pity, boredom and mockery made up their expressions as they judged her.

In the year and a half since she and Rafe had become a couple, she'd adapted to his preferred style. Her husband had dictated that she wear her hair sleek and fill her closet with elegant clothes worthy of a CEO's wife. Tonight, she'd been thinking along the lines of business rather than clubbing when she'd left the suite wearing a sheath of red satin and sheer checkerboard squares over a nude lining. It covered her from collarbone to knee and made her stand out from the crowd in the worst way possible.

"I need to speak to you." As much as she hated raising her voice, the loud dance music required her to shout to be heard.

"Just one drink." He signaled the waitress. "One drink and we can talk right here."

She was not going to go sit beside Trent and pretend that the way he'd treated her this last year and a half hadn't bothered her. Because it had. She'd been angry with Trent for refusing to even consider making a commitment to her and tormented by guilt for marrying his brother for all the wrong reasons.

Savannah crossed her arms over her chest. She might have to beg for Trent's help, but she wouldn't let him see her humiliation at needing to do so.

"I'd prefer our conversation to be a private one."

She'd never negotiated with Trent and won. The man

never seemed to care whether or not he got what he wanted. He was always ready to walk away from the bargaining table, which gave him an advantage.

They stared at each other—each determined to have their way—until the music and the lights faded to insignificance in the background. Trent's gaze toured her body with lazy intensity as he waited for her to surrender to his will. It bothered Savannah how much she wanted to give in to him.

His power over her hadn't faded one bit. Her thoughts were jumbled as she was overwhelmed by the urge to taste his sexy mouth and feel his hands roaming all over her. Their lovemaking had always been hot and satisfying. He'd spent an exceptional amount of time getting to know her body's every sensitive spot. An ache blossomed inside her. It had been nineteen long months since she'd last been with him, and her every nerve was on fire with anticipation.

Coming here tonight had been a bad idea. She should have held out for a civilized meeting in his office. Instead, she was filled with a recklessness inspired by the dance music's heavy beat and her own dangerous desire.

She had to go.

As a child Savannah had coped with her father's temper and her grandmother's frequent illnesses by hiding somewhere she felt safe. By the time she'd become a teenager, the habit of fleeing difficult situations was fully ingrained in her psyche. Retreat and regroup. Now that she was a mother, she'd grown better at standing her ground, but when overly stressed she fell back on what was familiar. Which explained why she turned away from Trent and headed for the exit.

The club seemed busier than it had five minutes earlier. Savannah wormed through the press of undulating bodies, familiar tightness building in her chest. The ever-changing lights and the hammering beat of the music combined to batter her senses. Her legs shook as she wound her way past the dance floor, and she wrenched her ankle during an awkward sidestep. Her head began to spin. Pressure built until she wanted to scream. She had to get out of the club. But which direction was the exit?

"There you are." The man she'd escaped earlier sneaked his arm around her waist and breathed alcohol at her. Her brief encounter with Trent had stripped away her Courtney armor. Locked in her panic attack, she was vulnerable to the man's boldness. "Thought you could get away from me, didn't you?" His lips met her cheek in an untidy kiss.

"Let me go," she said, but her voice lacked energy and the man was too drunk to hear her even if she'd shouted.

"Let's dance."

"No." She tried to squirm away but found nowhere to escape as the crowd pressed in on them.

All at once a large hand landed on the man's shoulder and tightened. With a yelp, the guy set her free.

"Hey, man. What are you doing?"

The drunk might have been a wolf, but Trent was a ferocious lion. "Leave this club before I have you thrown out."

If she hadn't been so rattled, Savannah might have enjoyed the way her assailant scrambled away from Trent.

Despite the heat being generated by a thousand dancers, Savannah's skin prickled with goose bumps. The urge to turn tail and run seized her, but before the impulse worked its way into her muscles, Trent slipped his arm around her waist.

Through modeling Savannah had gained an understanding of her physical appeal. Training to become Courtney Day had shown her how to act more confident. By the time Trent had come to New York to visit his sister, Melody, at Juilliard, Savannah was no longer an insecure girl, but a confident, sensual woman he desired. And more importantly, one he could have.

Falling back into old patterns with Trent was easy and comfortable, and she didn't resist as he drew her away from the crowd. He led her to a nondescript door, used a key card to activate the electronic lock and maneuver her through.

As the door clicked shut behind them, leaving them alone in a brightly lit hallway, Trent brushed her ear with his lips. "I see you still need someone to watch over you."

Being in his debt before she'd asked for his help wasn't a successful approach. "You didn't give me the chance to handle him."

"Would you like me to fetch him back?"

Savannah fought to control a shiver, knowing that to give in was to let him know how much she appreciated being rescued. "No."

Trent smirked at her. "You said you wanted a private conversation. How private do you need it to be?"

"Somewhere we can talk uninterrupted." She glanced up and down the twenty-foot hallway, seeing no one but hearing voices and laughter from around a corner.

"My office is quiet," he said, fingers sliding along her spine in a tantalizing caress. "Unless you're afraid to be alone with me?"

She twitched as his touch sent a lance of pleasure through her. "Why would I be?"

"You're quivering." He nuzzled her hair, voice deep and intimate. "Makes me think of the last time we were alone together."

"That was almost two years ago." But already the increased agitation in her hormones signaled that the chemistry between them remained as combustible as ever. *Damn.* She hadn't counted on lust being a factor in her negotiations with Trent.

"In the past, we've had a hard time keeping our hands off each other."

"That explains why you stayed away from me. Why did you stop taking Rafe's phone calls? It really hurt him."

His blue eyes narrowed. "Ask me if I'm worried how Rafe felt. He was my older brother, yet he never once stood up for me against Siggy. Not when we were kids or when Siggy refused to bring me into the family business. Rafe was the golden child and he liked it that way. So, what? I'm supposed to forgive and forget because he has a change of heart on his deathbed?"

There it was. That chip on his shoulder. The one he'd developed in response to every slight his father had delivered. Trent had been the second son. The spare heir. The boy with eclectic musical interests and strong opinions.

She couldn't disagree with his perception of his relationship with his brother and father. She'd heard the arguments. They didn't appreciate just how brilliant he was. The only opinions Siggy Caldwell entertained were his own. Rafe had learned about the business at his father's knee, never challenging Siggy's decisions.

"Still want to talk?" Trent asked. Had he noticed something in her manner that led him to believe she regretted coming here tonight?

"Yes."

"Good. I'm dying to hear what brought you to Las Vegas."

"I need your help."

"You must be pretty desperate if you came to me." Trent scrutinized her expression for a beat before taking her by the arm and leading her down the hall. "Let's go to my office. You can tell me all about it."

As soon as Trent escorted Savannah into his office and closed the door behind them, he knew this was a bad idea. He blamed curiosity. She'd been trying to get a hold of him for a week.

Yet, he could've picked up the phone at any time and discovered what was on her mind. But he'd resisted. What had changed?

Long-buried emotions, aroused by the familiar scent of her perfume, provided the answer. His fingers itched to slide over her smooth skin. From his first sight of her in the club tonight, he'd been fighting the longing to back her against a wall and ease his mouth over her quaking body.

He released her arm and turned his back to her. Picturing her naked and moaning his brother's name reminded him why he'd been keeping his distance.

He slipped behind a wet bar that ran perpendicular to the wall of floor-to-ceiling monitors tuned to various key areas in the club. Fixing her a drink gave him something useful to do until the urge to crush her mouth beneath his abated. Trent gave himself a hard mental shake. Obviously he hadn't thought through this scenario when he'd suggested they use his office for their private conversation. Being alone with Savannah shouldn't trigger his libido. He thought he'd gotten over her the instant she'd said "I do" to his brother. Damn if he'd been wrong.

Disgusted, Trent pulled a bottle from the fridge and surveyed the label. "Champagne?" When she shook her head, he arched an eyebrow. "Aren't we celebrating?"

Her frown asked, *Celebrating what?* "You know I don't drink."

"Oh," he drawled. "I thought perhaps after being married to my brother, you might have started."

Savannah made a face at him but didn't rise to the bait. "I'll take some sparkling water if you have it."

Amused, Trent dropped ice into a glass and poured her a drink. Fixing a lime to the rim, he pushed the glass across the bar toward her. As much as he could use a scotch to settle his nerves, he refrained. Dealing with Savannah was complicated enough without a fuzzy head.

A familiar mixture of fondness and rage filled him as he watched her sip the drink.

From the moment the naive eleven-year-old with the big blue eyes had moved into the servants' quarters of his family's Beverly Hills home, he'd been drawn to her. Unlike his twelve-year-old sister, she'd exhibited none of the gawkiness of preteen girls. And her lack of street smarts had driven Trent crazy.

As a kid he'd slipped into rebellious and resentful mode pretty early. Being a troublemaker came easy. He wasn't anyone's hero. But he'd come to Savannah's rescue more times than he could count. She'd been a magnet for anyone eager to take advantage of a young girl from some backwoods town in Tennessee. To look at her you'd think she would turn to smoke if you touched her, but in fact there was supple muscle beneath her soft skin, something he'd discovered firsthand when he'd taught her a couple self-defense moves.

In some ways, she was still the same ragamuffin who'd needed protection from the mean girls in school and the boys who thought to take advantage of her naïveté. But being on her own in New York had given her a new set of skills. For one, she'd learned how to go after something she wanted. And for a while it was pretty apparent that what she'd wanted was him.

Which was why it had come as such a surprise that she'd chosen to marry his brother. Despite the years she'd spent in LA and New York, she remained a small-town girl at heart. She had no lofty dreams of fame and fortune. She'd never known stability growing up, so as an adult, Savannah craved marriage and children, a secure, safe life.

Her vision of a traditional family situation was completely foreign to Trent. His father was an ambitious tyrant who'd married late. His misogynistic behavior had driven his wife away not long after Melody was born. The prenup their mother had signed granted her nothing if she fought for custody of her children. Trent had never been surprised that she'd chosen the money.

Was it any wonder he had so little interest in marriage and family? But knowing how important it was to Savannah should've warned him to keep his distance. He might have, but she was irresistible to him.

No matter how many times he'd cautioned himself to stay away, he couldn't stop coming to her rescue. Only once had he abandoned her to trouble—the day she'd declared her intention to marry Rafe.

"Widowhood becomes you," he said. If he'd hoped to shock her, he failed.

Reproachful blue eyes fixed on him. "That's a terrible thing to say."

"Perhaps, but it doesn't stop it from being true."

Young Savannah had possessed a guilelessness that left her open for the world to read. And take advantage of. He'd expected her to be eaten alive in the cutthroat world of modeling and acting in New York City, but she'd figured out a way to survive. When he'd visited Melody during her junior year at Juilliard, he'd been checking in on Savannah, as well. At first he'd been surprised. The naive girl wasn't gone, but she'd become a little wiser. She'd also gained an air of mystery. He'd been intrigued.

He still was.

"Perhaps you should tell me why you're here, dear sister-in-law."

Her lips formed a moue of distaste at the specific emphasis he put on the last three words. Trent took no pleasure in highlighting the chasm between them, but it needed to be done.

"I have a proposition for you."

Trent had been dodging her for a week, assuming something of this sort. For sixteen months he'd been waiting for her to admit that marrying his brother had been a mistake. It irritated him that she hadn't. And now she wanted something from him.

"I'm not interested."

"You haven't even heard me out."

"We have nothing to talk about."

Her facial muscles tightened, lending her expression a determined look he'd never seen before. She'd always seemed untouched by demons that drove most people, unfazed by success or obstacles. What had changed? Marriage to his brother? Motherhood?

These were questions best left alone. Trent didn't need to venture down the rabbit hole of turbulent emotions conjured whenever he spent time with Savannah. Better to speed her on her way back to LA and be done with temptation.

"Maybe we don't have anything to talk about, but *I* have a great deal to say."

"Why don't you make an appointment with my office for some time next week." He knew he was taunting her but couldn't help himself. She'd become another in a long list of people who brought out his bad side.

"I've already been here five days and you've been avoiding me. I'm closing on the sale of my house tomorrow afternoon, so Dylan and I are leaving in the morning. I had hoped to have everything settled before we returned to LA."

Against his better judgment—because he was playing directly into her hands—Trent asked, "What exactly did you intend to have settled?"

"When Rafe died, he left his shares of West Coast Records to Dylan. That means until Dylan's eighteenth birthday, I'm in charge of the business." She shook her head. "I need help."

Now Trent was starting to see where she was going.

"You've got Gerry." Gerry Brueger had been Siggy's second in command for twenty years. Passed over for president when Siggy stepped down and installed Rafe as the head of the company, Gerry would jump at the chance to take over.

"It's not that simple. I need a CEO I can trust. Someone who gets the business and can turn things around."

"So hire someone."

"That's what I'm trying to do." She cocked her head and scowled at him.

"Me?" This was not at all what he'd expected. Trent shook his head. "Not interested."

"It's your family's company."

"It's my *father's* company." And his brother's. They'd never wanted him to be a part of it. "Besides, my father isn't going to welcome my interference." He noticed that her gaze shifted away. "Have you talked to Siggy about this?"

"It's my decision." But she sounded less confident than she'd been moments earlier.

"So you haven't mentioned any of this to Siggy?"

"He sold a majority of his shares in the business to Rafe. Dylan inherited them. Siggy isn't in control of the company anymore."

Her naïveté was showing. She might think she was in charge, but she was in for a huge battle if she thought she could bring Trent into the record company. He almost felt sorry for her.

"Sell the company back to Siggy and wash your hands of it."

"It's not that cut-and-dried." She set her untouched glass of water on a nearby table and squared her shoulders. "He won't buy back Rafe's shares, but I know he's planning to control things behind the scenes. Siggy intends for Dylan to run the company someday." Savannah paused and compressed her lips into a thin line. With a sigh, she continued, "In the meantime, I can't run it and I don't trust your father to be able to turn things around."

"Turn things around?" Trent had heard rumblings that West Coast Records was having financial problems. No surprise there—Siggy Caldwell's approach to the music industry was uninspired and his eldest son had been a chip off the old block. "What's going on?"

"I'm not exactly sure, because I've been getting the runaround from Gerry, but I think they're behind on paying royalties to their artists."

"When did this start?"

"I don't know. Shortly after we were married, Rafe confided to me that the company was struggling financially before your father retired." That had occurred three years earlier. "And after the cancer started eating away at Rafe, he wasn't making the best decisions. I'm sure things got much worse then."

Trent ignored the compulsion that demanded he step in and fix everything. "While this is all fascinating, what does any of it have to do with me?"

"The company needs you." Her big blue eyes went soft and concerned in the way that always kicked him hard in the solar plexus.

Trent's first impulse was to laugh. He never got the chance. Questions crowded in. He didn't give a damn about the company. But did *she* need him? Trent crossed his arms over his chest and regarded her through half-closed eyes. She was beautiful. Poised. But not happy. He should've felt triumphant. Instead there was a dull ache in his gut.

"You know, better than most, that isn't going to sway me. Try again."

She gazed at the blank walls that made up his office. If she was looking for some clue about how to appeal to him, she wouldn't find it there. He was a man who didn't give a damn about anything. Or that's the face he showed the world. It made it much harder for someone to hurt him if he showed no vulnerability.

"Prove to your father you're a better businessman than he is."

He should be gloating. Trent—not his father or brother—would be the one to save the struggling West Coast Records, but his only emotion was bitterness.

"He would never believe that." The great Siggy Caldwell never owned up to his mistakes. He sure as hell wouldn't admit that his pitiful excuse for a second son was a better anything. "If that's the best you have, I'm afraid I'm going to have to disappoint you."

She let the silence fill the space between them for a beat before speaking. "I need your help."

He resisted the urge to sweep her into his arms and pledge his support. She was staring at him in desperate hope, as if he was her knight in shining armor. That was the farthest thing from reality. Sure, maybe he'd helped her out a time or two in the past, but she wasn't his responsibility anymore. The time for rescuing her had ended sixteen months earlier when she'd promised to love, honor and cherish his brother.

"And just like that, you expect me to drop everything and rush to your aid?" It cost him, but he gave his words a sardonic twist and hardened his heart. "It's not going to happen."

Two

Despite all the times he'd rescued her in the past, Savannah knew she shouldn't have counted on Trent helping her. She'd committed the ultimate sin. She'd married his brother.

And now she was stuck in an untenable position. Her one-year-old son had inherited stock she couldn't sell to a third party without her father-in-law's permission. This meant as an asset it held no value for her. And because of the way the record label was hemorrhaging money, the stock would be worthless in no time.

Begging to be rescued was too humiliating and probably wouldn't work anyway. Negotiating was a much more palatable option. Once again, she channeled Courtney Day. Relaxing her shoulders, she spoke in her alter ego's confident tone.

"What can I say or do to change your mind?"

"I don't know." Something flickered in Trent's eyes. "What are you offering?"

"I have nothing to bargain with."

Cards on the table, she maintained her poker face while his gaze raked over her. Heat rose to her skin. It wasn't humiliation she felt, but desire. If confronted, he would deny that he wanted her, but the flare of his nostrils and the way his pupils dilated hinted that the chemistry between them hadn't faded.

"You have something."

Savannah shook her head, unsure if what she was picking up off him was real or wishful thinking. "Rafe burned through all our cash chasing alternative medical treatments that didn't work," she said. "After he died, I had to sell the house to pay off his debts."

And she'd come up short by a million. She'd counted on selling Rafe's shares back to Siggy for enough money to clear the debt and maybe have a little bit to start over somewhere new.

But Siggy didn't want his shares back. He wanted Rafe's son.

"The only thing of value left is Dylan's shares in the company," she continued. "But I can't touch that."

"I don't want money," Trent said.

No, of course not. He could buy West Coast Records three times over. "What do you want?"

That she was putting herself in his hands occurred to her the instant the words were past her lips. But what else could she do? Siggy was willing to clear her debt but insisted she and Dylan move in with him. Her father-in-law's opinion of her was low. He hadn't approved of his son marrying her and he'd let her know that on several occasions. The thought of living in that toxic environment made her panic.

"Why did you marry my brother?"

The question came out of nowhere, and for several seconds Savannah didn't know what to say. Discussing her marriage with Trent was fraught with too many complications. Trent would never understand or approve of what she'd done, because he couldn't understand how her circumstances had left her feeling vulnerable and alone.

"You knew what I wanted. What was the most important thing to me."

Something Trent was never going to give her—a family. They stared at each other while her unspoken answer hung between them. Speaking of her longing would open up old wounds and she couldn't bear that.

I can't give you what you want.

Her heart had shattered when he'd uttered those words two years earlier.

At last she sighed. "I wanted to be married. To have children."

"I don't understand why you chose Rafe. Was it because you were pregnant?"

Savannah noticed he didn't ask her if she'd loved his brother. Why bother when the math was obvious? Dylan had been born six months after Savannah and Rafe had promised to love, honor and cherish each other until death.

"That played into it." She'd been devastated that the man she loved couldn't give her what she wanted and terrified of raising a child on her own.

Why had she chosen Rafe? Because he'd wanted her.

"Rafe was excited about being a father. Family was important to him."

More important than she'd initially understood. And he'd been very persuasive. At the time she'd believed she could trust him. She wouldn't have married him if he'd been like Trent. But he'd never once made her doubt his desire to be a father, and he'd been over-the-moon excited that she was carrying a boy.

"Rafe and Siggy were exactly alike," Trent scoffed. "People mean no more to them than as a means to an end."

It was humiliating to know just how right Trent was about that. She'd thought Rafe was her friend. Growing up he'd been the nice one, always upbeat and well mannered. He'd never hurt Savannah's feelings when she'd tried to cheer him out of a bad mood. He'd been the one to lift her spirits.

From when they were kids, he'd known how she felt about his brother. A couple times he'd come upon her crying in the midst of teenage angst over Trent. And he'd made her feel less unwanted.

Rafe had been the one who'd encouraged her to take the modeling job in New York. And after she quit the soap opera and returned to LA, he'd been the one who'd helped her find a rental.

She'd never questioned why Rafe was so accepting about the circumstances surrounding her pregnancy. Nor had her suspicions been aroused by the fact that he'd been the one who'd handed her a box of condoms and sent her to Las Vegas to visit Trent and get him out of her system once and for all.

It wasn't until after Dylan was born, when Rafe collapsed and she discovered the illness he'd been hiding, that she'd learned how he'd tricked her. That he'd sabotaged the box of condoms. Gambled that she would get pregnant.

He'd bought into his father's notions of a dynasty. Wanted a son, but his cancer treatments had left him impotent and sterile. So he'd taken a chance and tricked her into getting pregnant by his brother.

At first she'd been shocked and appalled at being manipulated by someone she trusted. But in the end she couldn't hate a man who'd made such poor decisions with a death sentence hanging over his head.

"That last time we were together," Trent began, his voice pitched low. "Were you and Rafe already involved?"

Savannah came out of her musing to find Trent standing

within arm's reach. Closer than she'd expected. He stood with his head cocked, his manner watchful, as if waiting for a sign from her. Suddenly she was having trouble catching her breath.

He hadn't touched her. He showed no inclination that he wanted to. So why was she suddenly craving his kiss?

"Does it matter?" She should back away. Put the width of the room between them. A table. A chair. Better yet, a door. Several corridors. A couple dozen floors.

"Not to me." His tone was light but his gaze was intense. "But my brother might have appreciated knowing you were cheating on him with me."

"I wasn't cheating on him. With you or anyone else."

In her rush to vindicate herself in his eyes, she neglected to remember that little matter of math. Would Trent realize that nine months after they had been together in Las Vegas, she'd given birth to Dylan? The thought terrified her. What if he wouldn't help her after discovering she'd kept the truth about his son from him? It was a practical concern, but not her bigger fear.

It hadn't taken a lot for Rafe to convince her that once Trent learned the truth that he would still reject her and his son.

Which is why she hadn't told him about Dylan when she'd discovered she was pregnant. Was it cowardly of her to hide the truth because she was assuming the worst outcome? Of course, but nothing Trent had ever said to her gave her reason to hope that he'd miraculously alter his way of thinking because he was going to be a father.

"I don't want to talk about my marriage."

"Then we've run out of things to say to each other." Trent gestured toward his office door.

"That isn't necessarily true," she countered, snatching at something to keep the conversation rolling. If she kept him talking, he wouldn't be able to throw her out of his office and maybe she could get the topic back around to the record label.

"What else did you have in mind?"

"You could ask me about Murphy."

He'd gotten her the French bulldog as a Christmas present three years ago. At the time she'd thought he'd bought the cream-colored snore monster because he was starting to get ideas of taking their relationship to the next level. She'd been in heaven.

Having Trent all to herself for those two weeks had been magical. They'd snuggled on the couch and opened presents at midnight on Christmas Eve. The week leading up to New Year's, they'd walked the puppy, browsed through Chinatown and the East Village, taken in a couple Broadway shows. They'd rung in the New Year with a bottle of champagne and the most perfect lovemaking of Savannah's life.

Then, six weeks later, he'd canceled on her last minute, and she'd spent Valentine's Day crying into Murphy's soft puppy coat. She'd realized that the long-distance thing wasn't working for her and she'd decided to quit the soap opera and move back to LA.

"How is he?"

"Wonderful. He's devoted to Dylan. Follows him everywhere. Curls up with him at nap time."

"How did Rafe enjoy sharing his bed with the dog?"

Questions like these were a minefield. How did she answer? She couldn't reveal that she'd entered into a loveless marriage and had never shared a bed with her husband.

"He didn't." Which was at least true.

"I'm not surprised. Rafe was never an animal person."

Unlike Trent, who'd fostered several rescues over the years. He liked helping out—something he'd deny—but the temporary nature of providing a home for dogs who after a couple months moved on to permanent situations demonstrated his unwillingness to commit and his distaste for being tied down.

She'd been so hurt by his refusal to move their relationship forward, even though she'd known that's how he was when she'd gotten involved with him. She kept hoping that he'd change. That she'd be the one he'd fall in love with and would be unable to live without.

Instead, in her sorrow and loss, she'd let his brother manipulate her. In her heart she'd known Trent was a better man than his brother, and a small part of her had expected him to save her one more time.

Only he hadn't. And she couldn't blame him for leaving her to rot.

"I'm sorry," she murmured.

"For what?"

"It was wrong of me to get involved with Rafe."

"I've been waiting a year and a half for you to admit that."

Trent's arms were around her, his lips descending, before she could guess his intention. Fire flashed along her nerve endings at the first touch of his hot mouth against her skin. She gasped as his lips trailed down her throat. In the space of one heartbeat, she transitioned from wary to wondrous. His teeth grazed the sensitive joining of neck and shoulder and her toes curled. He knew her weaknesses. Every single one. Obviously he intended to capitalize on her bad judgment.

So what?

It had always been like this between them. Hot. Delicious. Inescapable. She groaned, surrendering to pleasure. Why not? They were both consenting adults. She was no longer married to his brother. This had nowhere to go. She'd discovered the folly in trying to create a traditional family. Failing at that, what more did she have to lose by giving in to this rush of desire? And if she convinced Trent to help her in the process, what was the harm in that?

All these thoughts flashed through her head in the instant before Trent's hand slid over her butt and pulled her pelvis into snug contact with his arousal. She fisted her hands in his hair and tugged to bring his mouth to hers. She wanted him, needed this—why deny it? Later she could chastise herself for this rash act.

Trent captured her mouth in a hot, sizzling kiss. The ache between her thighs pulsed with more urgency as his tongue plunged past her teeth. She met the thrust with ardent fervor. A growl vibrated in her throat. That they could be discovered at any second should have bothered her. On the other hand, maybe Trent had entertained enough women in here to make his staff wary of interrupting their boss.

That thought too should have disturbed her. But Savannah was beyond logic and reason.

She drew him toward the couch and pushed him onto it. He bounced a little as the cushions gave beneath him. With a sassy grin, she hiked up her skirt and climbed onto his lap. Settling her hot center against his erection caused them both to shudder. She wasn't sure when the Courtney Day persona had fallen away. What she was doing now was pure Savannah.

Breath ragged, palms gliding up her thigh, he regarded her. His guards were up. He'd tightened his lips into an unyielding line and a sharp line appeared between his strong, dark brows. Questions gathered in his eyes. Savannah rocked her hips in a sultry move that caused him to exhale sharply in a low curse.

He started to speak. She shushed him and captured his face between her hands to keep him still while she flicked her tongue against his lower lip and then pulled it between her teeth and sucked gently. Strong fingers dug into her thighs hard enough to leave bruises. She smiled as she kept up the tantalizing seduction of his mouth.

Earlier when he'd pulled her against him, she'd felt the familiar square of tin that held breath mints and a little something extra in his suit coat pocket. Now she reached for the box and slipped it free. Trent heard the familiar rattle and leaned away from her kiss.

Savannah sat up straight and held the tin between them. "I see you haven't changed your habits."

"I like being prepared."

She popped the lid and slipped a mint into her mouth. Sharp and cool, the peppermint flavor exploded on her tongue, making it tingle. "Want one?"

Eyes locked on hers, he opened his mouth and let her feed him one. While the mint dissolved, they regarded each other in silence. His gaze held challenge, but curiosity, as well. He wanted to know if she intended to get to what else the tin held. Savannah savored his anticipation. He liked being in charge. It's why he hadn't stuck around to be a part of his family's business, but had struck out on his own.

No one was going to boss around Trent Caldwell.

But Savannah had found him to be a wonderful partner in bed. For as often as he'd swept her into his passion and demanded her surrender, there had always been opportunities when he let her take the lead. Because of this, her confidence had flourished, not only with regard to her sexuality, but also in her worth as an individual.

The heavy pulse of desire between her thighs hadn't diminished one bit during this exchange. In fact, as she grew more committed to this next step, her hunger for him had only increased.

Savannah plucked out the square foil package and held it up. "Only one? You used to carry at least two." She might have sounded confident, but she wasn't. Courtney

Day might not have thought twice about a quickie with her sexy ex, but Savannah was rapidly losing her nerve.

"What makes you think I haven't used one already today?"

Trent had a healthy sexual appetite, and she wouldn't be surprised if he'd already had sex with three other women. She shouldn't care. But it hurt all the same. Several deep breaths later she'd pushed down panic and dismay. This couldn't become about what she'd had and lost. She needed a brief interlude to escape her troubles and there was no better man to rock her world than Trent.

But why was he baiting her? She could see from his flat stare that he expected her to back off.

"For a second I forgot who I was dealing with." She closed the tin with a metallic snap and tossed it aside.

Aware that he was scrutinizing her every move, she placed the wrapped condom between her teeth and set her hands to loosening his belt. Up until now she'd been doing a good job of appearing confident. But beneath Trent's unreadable gaze, she felt a tiny fizz of nervous energy dance along her spine, making her fingers clumsy. Trent made no attempt to help her. In fact he didn't move at all, except for the unsteady rise and fall of his chest.

At long last Savannah slid down his zipper and freed him. His erection sprang into her hands, eager for her attention. Overwhelmed by joy at what they were about to do, she paused for a moment, fingers coasting along his hot silken length. With a half smile she tore open the wrapper and unrolled the condom, sheathing him. His head had fallen back against the couch while his breath hissed out between clenched teeth. He squeezed his eyes shut and held perfectly still, every muscle in his body tense beneath her.

In her stylish but conservatively cut dress, Savannah might not have appeared as if she'd planned for a hot night at the club, but she'd chosen a red lace bra and thong set to wear underneath. Had she thought in her wildest dreams she would be in this position? Perhaps her subconscious had wanted this all along.

Before she could change her mind about what she was about to do, Savannah cupped Trent's erection in her palm, slid aside her thong and brought his tip into contact with her wet heat.

For the first time in several seconds Trent shifted. He cupped her butt in both hands and moved her forward and down until he was sheathed inside her. They groaned simultaneously as she came to rest, fully seated on his lap once again. Savannah put her hands on his shoulders, needing him for balance as her head began to spin.

This wasn't just sex. It had never been just sex between them. But there were no words of love or affectionate looks exchanged. This was a crazy, impulsive interlude that she desperately needed. Her goal was oblivion, and being with Trent always enabled her to forget her problems. Even when what was troubling her was Trent himself.

They rocked together in a familiar rhythm, maintaining a steady, relaxed pace.

"Take your hair down," Trent demanded, his voice an unsteady rasp.

Happy to oblige, she reached up and pulled out half a dozen pins and demolished the smooth, controlled hairstyle with a languid shake of her head. Long blond waves tumbled around her shoulders and tickled her cheeks. Trent had always loved her hair. He sank his fingers into the thick silky mass and brought her lips back to his.

Trent wasn't sure how he'd come to be on his couch buried deep inside Savannah, her tongue dancing with his in a passionate kiss, her manner every bit as wild as he remembered. Another woman might have pleaded with him for help or screamed abuse when he refused to fall in with her plans. He'd had only the briefest suspicion that Savannah intended to seduce him into helping her before he rejected the idea. Her hunger for him was as all-consuming as his for her.

That didn't make this a reunion between lovers. Not in the traditional sense. Sixteen months of bitter silence lay between them. Part of him didn't want to open the door to her. The part of him that did was in charge at the moment. Maybe what they were doing was saying goodbye. But as her teeth nipped at his lower lip, driving him closer to orgasm, he knew this brief taste of her had only revived his unquenchable desire.

Trent fought to make the moment last. But he was only able to hold on until he could determine that she hovered on the brink of a climax.

Her soft keening and the accelerated rhythm of her hips pushed him over the edge and they came together. Heart thundering, Trent sat perfectly still, his body drained, his heart twisted wreckage. *Damn her.* She'd made him do what he promised he wouldn't. He'd let her back in. His first instinct as he labored to breathe was to kiss her long and deep and never let her go. His second instinct was to remove her from his lap and kick her out of his office.

He did neither.

Instead, he sank his fingers into his hair, let his head fall back and stared at the ceiling. It was the pose of a man wondering what the hell he'd done.

Displaying no regret, Savannah pushed off the couch and got to her feet. Hips swaying in unconscious allure, she crossed to the bar and found a towel, bringing it back to him. By the time Trent had cleaned up and disposed of the condom, she was putting the last hairpin into her impromptu updo. The only signs of how she'd spent the last ten minutes were her flushed cheeks and smeared lipstick.

He glanced up and down the length of her as she stepped

back into her tall heels, and all he saw was a tranquil, confident woman. Gone was the femme fatale. Trent couldn't decide if he was glad or sorry.

"This doesn't change anything." His tone was brusque, his words more clipped than he'd intended. "I'm not going back to LA to bail out West Coast Records."

She looked at him askance, her eyebrows lifted in disbelief. "That's not what this was about."

"No?" But he knew she wasn't lying. Savannah frequently ended up in trouble because she wasn't calculating. The fact that he'd just accused her of unscrupulous behavior demonstrated that their unexpected sexual encounter had thrown him off his game. He hated that. It was time to take the situation back in his hands. "Where are you staying?"

His question surprised her. Something flickered in her eyes. "I'm not taking you to my hotel suite, if that's what you're thinking."

It wasn't what he'd been thinking, but now that she'd mentioned it, that sounded like a great idea. He'd like to strip that conservative dress off her and make love to her properly. But it was too late for that. Two years, one marriage and his brother's son too late.

"Where are you staying?" he repeated, letting her see that his patience was waning.

"Upstairs."

Cobalt had been Trent's first choice of location when he and his business partners decided to open Club T's. The hotel's owner, JT Stone, was a brilliant businessman with a great reputation and solid ethics. The rent was high for this exclusive real estate, but the hotel drew a chic crowd with deep pockets who liked to party and could easily afford Club T's high-end table service.

"I'll walk you back to your suite."

"There's no need."

Savannah wouldn't meet his eyes, and it was the first indication Trent had that the encounter had ruffled her composure.

"It's two in the morning." And Trent had no intention of returning to the club tonight. He'd lost his taste for partying the instant Savannah had appeared at his table. All he wanted was to head home, pour himself a liberal amount of scotch and brood. "And you've already had one run-in with a man you couldn't handle."

She gave an offhand shrug. "I think I handled you just fine."

He fought back an admiring smile. "I meant the guy in the bar."

"Oh, him." She shook her head. "I was on the verge of crushing his toe with my heel."

Unsure if she was kidding, Trent caught her by the elbow and turned her in the direction of the office door. He led the way through the back halls of the club and hotel to a service elevator. Once inside he turned an expectant expression on her. Rather than tell him her floor, she reached to push the button herself.

"It's no good, you know," Trent said as the car began to move upward. "If you try to bring me in at West Coast Records, Siggy will fight you with everything he has."

"But you're exactly what the company needs. You're brilliant. Your father and Rafe never understood that."

Trent stared at her in bemusement. She'd always been on his side. How had two people who only had each other's best interest at heart failed so miserably at being together?

Because he didn't want what she did. Family for him meant nothing but heartache.

"You're wasting your time and mine. Let the company fold. You and Dylan will be fine without it. I'll make sure of that."

Three

Savannah turned Trent's words over and over in her mind as he escorted her to the suite. His offer made no sense.

At her door, she stopped and faced him. "You'll make sure how? I don't intend to take your money."

All she'd ever needed was for him to love her. She'd wanted to be his wife and raise his children. To make a secure life for her family and feel safe in turn. Being shipped between her father and grandmother for eight of her first eleven years had never allowed her any sense of belonging. That wasn't to say she didn't have good memories of the small town in Tennessee where her grandmother lived.

"You said you sold your house to pay Rafe's debts. Where are you going to go and what do you intend to live on?"

"I'd hoped to return to Tennessee." California was expensive and she wanted to start a new life far from the Caldwell family.

She never should have settled in LA after leaving New

York. Originally she'd intended to move to Las Vegas to be close to Trent. He'd not been thrilled at having this plan sprung on him. It had been the first time she'd asserted herself and made her longing for marriage and a family clear to him. The fact that she'd pushed had caused their breakup. With her future up in the air, she'd gone to LA and reached out to Rafe.

He hadn't hit her with *I told you so* or made her feel worse about herself. He'd been supportive and friendly. A hundred times since then she'd wondered how her life would've turned out if she'd done any one of a dozen things differently.

"What's in Tennessee?" Trent asked.

Not a single thing, but at least it was somewhat familiar. "It's home."

He didn't look convinced. "And with no money, what are you planning on doing there?"

She'd considered returning to acting, but that would require relocating to New York or staying in LA. But with the terrifying load of debt hanging over her head, she was slowly coming around to the idea.

It meant giving up her dream of raising Dylan where neighbors knew each other and pitched in to help. At least for the time being.

"I had thought to move to Gatlinburg. The population is small, but it's a big tourist destination and I'm sure I can find something I can do."

"You didn't deserve to be put in this position by my family. You want to move to Tennessee, I'll help you with some cash to get you started."

She was okay with the idea of moving away, but Trent's offer of help made her feel as if he wanted her gone. Ridiculous. One brief sexual encounter with him and she was on her way to becoming emotionally attached again. *Damn.*

This was not why she'd come here. She needed him to save the record label so Dylan would have something to inherit.

"The only help I need is for you to take over West Coast Records." Despair swept over her, but she couldn't let Trent see her distress. "Beyond that, there's nothing I need from you." She used her key card and let herself into the suite. "Good night, Trent. It was nice to see you again."

With a cheeky Courtney Day smile, she waved at him and slipped through the open doorway. She thought she'd gotten the final word in, but Trent had one last parting shot before the door closed.

"Take the night and think about my offer."

Savannah opened her mouth to tell him he was wasting his breath, but he'd already turned and walked away. She resisted the urge to call after him. She was tired of arguing.

With her plan to escape her current predicament amounting to a major failure, Savannah sought solace in the one spot of light. Her son, Dylan. She entered her bedroom, found him sleeping peacefully in his crib and turned off the baby monitor so as not to wake Lori, the babysitter Savannah had used on and off in the months since Rafe's death. Dylan was a sunny, healthy baby who'd begun sleeping through the night by the time he was six months old.

Having never known her mother, Savannah hadn't known what to expect when her son came along. Although she'd long craved a family of her own, reality was never the same as daydreams. In Dylan's case it was so much better.

Savannah left her sleeping son and crossed to the bathroom. She stripped off her dress and examined her bare thighs. Sure enough, a bruise was forming where Trent's fingers had bitten down. She brushed her fingertips across the spot. Letting her body dictate the encounter with Trent hadn't been the best idea, but she didn't regret what had happened. Yet she knew her impulsiveness would have emotional consequences.

Maybe she should take Trent's help to get out from under Rafe's load of debt. Let Siggy destroy the company. What did she care as long as she and Dylan were free? Besides, even if she could convince Trent to take on the leadership of the record label, she might be inviting more trouble from her father-in-law. He was leveraging her situation to keep Dylan close. What if he came after her with some ridiculous legal ploy that she couldn't afford to fight?

Savannah changed into pajamas but doubted her ability to sleep, so she turned on the television and sat on the couch in the living room to watch a show about tiny-house hunting. Her mood lightened somewhat as she considered the idea of finding a four-hundred-square-foot house where she and Dylan could live a simple life.

The sort of life she might have had with her mother if she hadn't been killed while deployed in the Middle East when Savannah had been three. She'd give anything to recall even the blurriest image of her mother, Libby. Instead, all she had were the stark memories of being passed back and forth between her father and maternal grandmother like an endless tennis volley.

Her parents had indulged in a brief fling that resulted in Savannah being conceived. And despite her resolve never to follow in her mother's footsteps, she'd done exactly that. From what she'd gathered from her grandmother, Libby hadn't planned to tell Chet Holt he was a father. Nor had Savannah's dad been thrilled to be saddled with the responsibility of a daughter he'd never expected.

When her father's bad decisions landed him in prison for burglary, and with her grandmother's health making it too hard for her to care for Savannah, she'd been shipped off to LA to live with her aunt, who worked as a housekeeper for the Caldwells.

Savannah closed her eyes and recalled the discomfort of her first few months in LA. The Caldwells' house was not a happy place. Siggy's second marriage was on the rocks, and Melody fought with her stepmother nonstop. At sixteen, Trent was raising hell at school and driving his father crazy at home. Only Rafe seemed above the fray. He'd been breezing through his senior year of high school and was on track to finish in the top 10 percent of his class.

With those unhappy days filling her thoughts, it was no wonder that when she fell asleep in front of the TV she had a nightmare about her and Dylan living in the Caldwell home with Siggy. She woke to the sounds of her son stirring in his bedroom and stumbled in a fog of lingering dismay to get him changed before Lori woke. Savannah loved these quiet early hours with Dylan.

Snuggling him enabled her to escape her worries for a little while. His smiles lit up a room. He was such a happy, inquisitive child and since he'd begun to walk two weeks ago, she had to keep a close eye on him at all times.

Both Savannah and Dylan were still in their pajamas when the babysitter emerged from her room. Savannah had given him breakfast and was on the couch reading to him from his favorite picture book.

"What time is it?" Savannah asked Lori, standing with Dylan in her arms.

"It's a little after eight."

"Why don't you order us some breakfast," Savannah said. "I'd like an egg-white omelet and toast."

The closing on her house was at two thirty that afternoon. Their flight back to LA was at eleven. Savannah handed over her son and headed to the bedroom to get ready. She didn't linger over her morning routine and had her bag packed in short order. By the time she emerged, a waiter was pushing a room service cart toward the large window that overlooked the Strip. Savannah signed for the breakfast, and the man headed for the door. When he opened it to leave, Trent was standing in the hall outside her suite.

"Good morning," he said, not waiting for an invitation to enter the room.

Trent's abrupt appearance threw her for a loop. She'd considered he might call. But never in her wildest dreams did she think he might actually show up in person this morning. Dressed in an impeccable navy superfine wool suit with a crisp white shirt and cobalt tie, Trent looked ready to do business.

Savannah shot a quick glance toward her son. He sat on the floor surrounded by books and toys, happily gnawing on a plastic key ring. Lori had seated herself at the dining room table and was removing the metal domes from the plates of food. She seemed uninterested in Savannah's visitor.

In the dark hours of late-night Vegas, reconnecting with her ex-lover had been relatively uncomplicated. In the cold light of day, with her son—Trent's son—less than ten feet away, she was feeling overwhelmed by her past mistakes and future missteps.

"What are you doing here?"

"You aren't really planning on moving to Tennessee, are you?"

After her troubled sleep and her dream about living in Siggy's house, Savannah was feeling less confident than she had been the night before. Despite what she'd told Trent, the truth was she had no place to go once she signed the papers on her house. She'd been so convinced she could get Trent to help her she hadn't focused at all on what would happen if she failed.

"I…" Her chest grew exceedingly tight. She couldn't get any words out.

"Are you okay?"

"Fine." The word had very little conviction behind it. Where was Courtney now? Savannah had lost her connection to her confident alter ego.

"Where are you planning to go, then?"

Misery engulfed her. "I don't have a plan." He'd never know what it cost her to admit that. Too many times he'd viewed her as helpless. "My only option was for you to help me with the company."

"But that doesn't help you with your immediate problem of where to go once you close on your house."

She knew he was right.

"I called Melody last night," Trent continued. "She's in Australia at the moment, and with the time difference it was afternoon. She told me Siggy wants you to move in with him. You're not planning on doing that, are you?"

Not if she could help it. Even as a temporary measure, becoming beholden to her father-in-law was a bad idea. Savannah exhaled in frustration but didn't respond to Trent's question. She couldn't blame Melody for telling Trent what was going on. Melody was just as upset as Savannah about the situation. Trent's sister had worked hard and suffered much to get out from beneath her father's weighty expectations.

"It's a bad idea."

"It's not what I want to do." She crossed her arms over her chest and stared past his shoulder. "I'd prefer to move to Tennessee and buy a small house there."

But was it really the place for her and Dylan? Savannah had latched on to Gatlinburg because her grandmother's house had been in a town twenty miles away, and she'd built it up in her mind as a great place to raise Dylan.

As if aware of her thoughts, Dylan gave a happy gurgle and stood. Trent's attention swiveled toward the toddler as Dylan began his ungainly waddle toward them.

"He's walking already?" Trent regarded the boy impassively. "I didn't think he was quite a year."

Savannah's pride shone through as she answered, "He's a little ahead of the curve." Seeing his mother's smile, Dylan came at her in a rush. With her heart thumping painfully hard, Savannah scooped him off the floor and settled him on her hip. He wrapped his hand around her three-tiered strand of pearls that complemented today's collared black sweater dress with three-quarter-length cuffed sleeves.

"Dylan, right?" Trent was inspecting the boy through narrowed eyes.

"Yes."

Father and son stared at each other while Savannah waited for what would happen next. She'd been dreading this encounter since the day her son had been born. Part of her hoped to see recognition in Trent's eyes. She wanted him to claim Dylan. Then she could stop feeling guilty for denying her son his father.

"You can't do this to him."

Savannah wasn't sure what she'd expected Trent to say, but that wasn't it. "Can't do what to him?"

"Let my father get his hands on him."

"You make it sound so ominous." She'd become an expert at appearing more confident than she was. "What can Siggy do?"

"He could ruin his childhood the way he did Rafe's and mine."

From the expression on Savannah's face, she'd already considered this, and Trent's irritation grew. How could she even consider putting her son into such a toxic environment even for a few weeks? And then he realized her finances had to be in rough shape. What hadn't she told him?

"All right," he said, "let's stop dancing around."

Her eyes went round with apprehension. "What are you talking about?"

"I want to know exactly what's going on with you."

Savannah turned away and carried her son back to his toys. She then took her time pouring a cup of coffee and offering it to him. Trent shook his head.

"Dylan and I are returning to LA on an eleven o'clock flight. I have a closing on my house this afternoon. There's nothing else to tell."

Trent glanced around at the young woman working her way through a thick Belgian waffle and understood that Savannah would prefer not to air her business in front of the young woman.

"I was planning on heading to LA on business tomorrow. There's no reason why I couldn't go a day earlier. Perhaps you and I could celebrate after you close on your house and then tomorrow morning you could give me a tour of the company."

Savannah grimaced. "I'm not sure closing on my house is a reason to celebrate."

"Then just consider it an opportunity for the two of us to get reacquainted."

"Do you really want a tour of the company?" She sounded uncertain.

He hoped she was worried about how his father would react to her bringing Trent into West Coast Records. Her notion that he could do something to help her save the company was crazy.

"Absolutely. Why don't you give Gerry a call and tell him you're bringing by your financial adviser to look over the books."

Savannah gave him the first genuine smile he'd seen. "He's not going to be happy about that."

"Do you really care?"

"Siggy isn't going to be happy about that, either." It

didn't appear as if that bothered her, but Trent suspected it did a little. His father was bound to make her life miserable if he discovered she'd teamed up with Trent. "Are you going to help me with the company?"

"No." His intention was simply to let his father think that's what he intended to do. Perhaps then Siggy would buy back his company from Savannah, allowing her and Dylan to head off to her new life in Tennessee.

She looked confused by his answer. "Then why do you want to see the books?"

"Something has to be going on," he said. Overnight his curiosity had been aroused by what she had told him. While he'd heard West Coast Records was struggling, things didn't sound as if they were bad enough for them to stop paying their artists. "It doesn't surprise me that profits are down, but something more serious must be happening if things are in the state you say they are."

"What if Gerry refuses to give me the information?"

"Then we'll have our answer as to who is at the center of what's going on there, won't we?"

"You think Gerry has something to do with this?"

"With Siggy retired and Rafe sick, he was in the perfect position to mismanage the company." And Trent had never been particularly impressed with the man's business savvy. "So let's go see what's going on, shall we? I've chartered a plane. I'll pick you up downstairs at ten thirty."

"We're already scheduled on a flight to LA."

"It will be easier if I'm not chasing all over LAX looking for you." He softened his tone. "And it will be more comfortable for you."

Trent felt a tug on his pant leg and looked down. His nephew was standing, looking up at him. The boy's blue eyes, so reminiscent of Rafe's, were fixed on Trent's face. Something in his chest tightened. All at once he couldn't breathe.

This was Rafe's son. Savannah's son. Like a man drowning, Trent saw his past with Savannah flash before his eyes. The joy on that Christmas morning when she'd woken up to Murphy's sweet puppy face and adorable snuffles. What had he been thinking? He'd bought her a dog. She'd been feeling gloomy about spending the holidays alone. So he bought her something to take care of and flown to New York to give it to her. Making a woman happy had never been as easy as it had been with her.

And then because she'd misinterpreted his gift, he'd felt compelled to distance himself for months after.

When the toddler continued to stare at Trent, he bent down and picked the boy up. He didn't have much experience with children, but something about his nephew made it a simple thing to settle the child against his chest as if he'd done it a hundred times before. The amount of curiosity in the infant's eyes intrigued Trent. What could possibly be going on in that developing brain of his?

Dylan latched on to Trent's tie the same way he'd grabbed Savannah's pearls, and Trent heard her soft cry of dismay.

"He's going to ruin your tie," she said, stepping toward them with her hands outstretched as if to take her son.

"It's just a tie." Trent pivoted away from her advance. He couldn't explain his sudden reluctance to give the child up. "It looks like your breakfast is getting cold. Why don't you sit down and eat? Dylan and I will be just fine."

The distress in Savannah's eyes made no sense. It wasn't as if he was going to spirit the infant out of the suite. He had no interest in his nephew outside of satisfying a brief bit of curiosity about him.

Rafe had died within months of his son being born. Having a father like Siggy, Trent had little positive experience when it came to father-son bonding. Would Dylan suffer never knowing his dad? On the other hand, once

Savannah settled in Tennessee, she might marry again and Dylan would be raised by a stepfather. Either way, at least he would grow up dearly loved by his mother. That much was clear.

Trent picked up one of the picture books from the floor near Dylan's toys and sat down on the couch with the boy.

"That's his favorite," Savannah said, sitting with an untouched plate of eggs before her. "He'd love it if you read it to him."

Left on his own with the boy, Trent opened the book and began reading while Dylan patted the pages with his fat little hands and wiggled. Trent found himself smiling. For the last year he'd avoided thinking about his nephew. Although he'd never intended to saddle himself with a wife and children, the fact that Savannah had given his brother a son ate at him.

Rafe had gotten everything. Their father's love and approval. The family business. And Savannah. The first two Trent had come to terms with. The last one had blasted a hole in his heart big enough to drive a semi through. But it was his own fault. He could've had her. Dylan could have been his son. Except the conventional family Savannah craved wasn't what he wanted.

The idea that anyone would rely on him was a suffocating weight. Sure, he'd helped her out several times in the past, but those had been random acts when it had been convenient for him. He had to do things on his terms, not on anyone else's. Even now, stepping up to help her with the label, he wasn't doing it for her. He was doing it to piss off his old man.

Trent wanted to see if Siggy hated him enough to bankrupt the record label before he would let his son be in charge. To Trent's recollection, his father had never shown him anything but disdain. Rafe had been the favorite son. Siggy's firstborn. He'd taken after his father in appearance and mind-set: a businessman mired in ego and lacking vision.

Like his sister, Melody, Trent had inherited his mother's voice and musical talent. Not that he had any interest in pursuing a career in the business. He left the songwriting, piano playing and singing to his younger sister. Trent could not be more proud of Melody.

She'd struggled to find her wings in a household that didn't appreciate what she could do. Forced to attend Juilliard as a classic violinist when what she really wanted to do was compose pop songs for others to perform, Melody had dropped out of school midway through her junior year of college.

The gap in their ages had kept Trent from knowing Melody as well as he could. But when he'd gone to visit her in New York City and she'd come clean about her passion for writing music, he'd been behind her 100 percent about quitting school. She needed money to rent studio time to make a demo of her music and he'd happily provided it. He'd also put her in contact with the people in the music industry who could help her get started.

This bit of assistance and support had only added to the acrimony between Trent and his father. It was shortly after this that Siggy stopped speaking with Trent. The owner of West Coast Records had a vision in his head regarding his daughter, and it had nothing to do with her lowering herself to being someone else's songwriter.

Trent hadn't understood his father's perspective. Melody was immensely talented. She could have become an incredible star if she'd been interested in the spotlight. But she preferred being behind the scenes and having her music developed by others. At least that's the way it'd been until his friend and partner in Club T's, Nate Tucker, had convinced her to bring her violin on tour with Free Fall. Seeing a star in the making, Tucker had pushed her to sing one of her songs during his set. It had gone so well that she was now opening for him.

And as far as Siggy was concerned, this was Trent's fault, too.

"How are things going?"

Trent looked up from the book and spied Savannah standing before him. Although her makeup was flawless, he thought she looked pale. Was that brought on by stress or lack of sleep? He'd had a hard time settling down after walking her to her suite. Although he was no stranger to spontaneous encounters, usually the moments lingered in his mind for a short time and then faded away.

With Savannah everything was different.

He couldn't just revel in a quickie with his brother's widow, chuckle at the irony and move on. There was too much history between them. Too much he couldn't stop himself from needing.

"Great," he said. "You're right about him liking this book."

"He enjoys being read to." She smiled fondly at her son. "I guess what kid doesn't."

"I don't remember anyone reading to me, do you?"

Savannah shook her head. "My grandmother used to tell me stories about when she was a little girl. She grew up on a farm in Kansas and talked about milking the cows and barn cats having kittens. She described what it had been like to be in the cellar while a tornado took out the chicken coop but missed the barn and house."

Her distant gaze and fond smile clashed with Trent's attitude about his own upbringing. His childhood memories mainly consisted of watching TV and playing video games. His mother had never read to him. She'd been busy maintaining her appearance and chasing her own happiness. Personal trainers, self-help quacks and an assortment of assistants had kept Trent's mother lean of body and calm of spirit. Or at least they had tried to. Living with someone as critical as Siggy Caldwell was debilitating for anyone without sufficient self-esteem.

These days Naomi was a very different person. She laughed all the time and allowed herself to age gracefully. After leaving Siggy, she'd moved to New York and gotten some off-Broadway work. It was there she'd met and married her second husband, investment banker Larry Fry.

"I'm going to get Dylan ready to leave."

"I have to check out a couple things at the club before I go."

Trent gave up the boy, surprised at his reluctance to do so. Despite the fact that Dylan was a baby, he'd enjoyed the child's company more than he'd expected. But there was a huge difference between playing the part of fun uncle who spent ten minutes reading a book and a lifetime of caretaking as a father.

Savannah settled her son on her hip and spoke in a light voice. "Dylan, can you wave goodbye to your uncle Trent?"

The nearly one-year-old child did as he was bidden and followed it up by blowing a kiss. Trent was impressed by the boy's tricks and wondered if this was average for kids his age.

He didn't want to like his nephew any more than he wanted to get embroiled in Savannah's problems. But something was going on with West Coast Records, and his curiosity wouldn't let him turn it aside.

Besides, there might be an opportunity here and he'd be a fool to pass that up.

Four

While Trent negotiated the LA traffic, Savannah sat like a stone beside him. As of twenty minutes ago, she was officially homeless. Sunshine poured through the car window, but Savannah enjoyed neither the soothing brightness nor the warmth.

"Are you okay?" Trent had been casting glances her way since he'd picked her up from the closing.

"Dylan and I have nowhere to go." Her vision blurred as her eyes filled with unshed tears. She blinked them away. What was wrong with her that she stumbled from one desperate situation to another? "I'm a complete failure as a mother."

"Don't say things like that."

"I haven't done a good job providing for him or protecting him."

"This isn't a problem you created."

While she appreciated Trent's attempt to make her feel better, she couldn't ignore the string of bad decisions that had led her to this place. On the other hand, one of her choices, foolish or not, had given her the light of her life, her son.

"Maybe not a problem I created, but when I discovered how bad things were financially, I should have gone back to work and found us a place to live." She dug her fingernails into her hands to keep a grip on her anxiety. "Instead I stuck my head in the sand."

"Stop being so hard on yourself."

"Tell me you would've acted the same and I won't say another word."

"We don't come at problems the same way."

"Ha." To her surprise, arguing with Trent was making her feel better. She might be down, but she certainly didn't have to be out. "What do you think we're going to find at the label?"

Trent's expression darkened. "This is probably the wrong thing to say to you right now, but you probably should brace yourself for some unpleasantness."

"Too late," she said. "I called Gerry this morning before leaving the hotel, and he was not pleased by my request. So I'm completely convinced we will have a fight on our hands."

"Did you tell him I was coming?"

Savannah smiled. "And lose the element of surprise?"

Ten minutes later, Trent entered West Coast Records' parking lot and pulled into a visitor's spot. She put her hand on his arm as he made to open his door.

"Thank you," she said, seeing Siggy's car parked in Rafe's spot. "I know coming here isn't easy for you."

"It doesn't bother me."

From his expression, she couldn't tell whether or not that was true. She indicated her father-in-law's car. "Have you spoken to Siggy since Rafe's funeral?"

"No. We have nothing to say to each other."

To Savannah's relief, there'd been no father-son blowup at Rafe's funeral. The two Caldwell men had stood apart from each other the entire day and never indulged the ongoing animosity between them. She might not have loved Rafe, but Savannah had wanted his family and friends to mourn him uninterrupted by squabbling.

As much as Savannah longed to take strength from Trent's solid presence at her side, she kept her chin up and a respectable distance between them as they entered the building and strode across the bright, open lobby. West Coast Records had been located here since the '50s. Siggy had bought the company in 1976.

It had done well for a lot of years, but with the shift into digital, the label had been too slow to evolve and hadn't developed a solid plan of action to make money in the age when people didn't have to download an entire album but could pick and choose which songs they wanted.

From what Savannah had come to understand from her own research and what Trent had explained during the flight, West Coast Records had signed a bunch of artists and flooded the marketplace with mediocre music. They were trying to re-create the huge revenues they used to enjoy instead of spending the time it took to develop real talent and accepting that they were going to make smaller amounts than they used to.

Savannah led the way past the unoccupied reception desk toward Rafe's office. She hadn't been here more than a half-dozen times, but she knew the way well enough. As they moved through the halls, she noticed an abundance of empty desks. The whole building had a stillness to it that made her uncomfortable. At four in the afternoon, it was possible that the staff had gone for the day, but the lack of personal items at the desks made the office feel like a ghost town.

"Where is everyone?" she asked Trent, slowing down to peer around her. "It looks deserted."

"Maybe they've laid off some people."

The anxiety that had plagued her for months increased. What if she'd brought Trent in too late? If the company failed, the stock would be worthless. Right now she was using a small income she received from the company to pay the minimum on the debt until she could figure something out. If the label failed, that would dry up. Then, her only recourse would be to declare bankruptcy to get out from beneath Rafe's massive debt.

On the way to Rafe's office, they passed Gerry's.

"Any idea where Gerry is hiding?" Trent asked, arching one eyebrow. His reaction to being here was the polar opposite of hers. The worse things appeared, the more relaxed he became.

"I haven't been here since I found out Rafe was sick. Maybe Gerry took over Rafe's office."

When they entered the president's office, they found not only Gerry, but also Siggy. The old man was seated behind the desk as if he was still in charge. At the sight of him in her dead husband's executive chair, Savannah's anxiety became annoyance.

"What are you doing here?" Sigmund Caldwell demanded, getting to his feet in an explosive movement. Palms planted on the desk, he scowled at his younger son.

"Hello, Siggy." Trent took a step past Savannah, positioning himself like a protective guard dog. "I'm surprised to find you in the office." Thanks to the amusement in his tone, he didn't sound surprised.

"Trent is here because I asked him to come." Savannah held her expression neutral as her father-in-law's sharp gaze shifted to her. "I need to know what's going on with the company's financials."

"You don't need to know anything," Siggy said.

"That isn't true. With Rafe's death Dylan inherits his shares, and I'm his mother. It falls to me to make sure his inheritance survives." Savannah knew immediately she'd gone too far.

"Nothing falls to you. You are just a grasping woman who took advantage of my son's illness. If you think I'm going to let you make decisions about this company, you are sadly mistaken."

"Fine. Then buy the shares back." She was shaking, but the confrontation with her father-in-law was not as bad as it would have been without Trent at her side. She could never have done this without him.

Siggy looked her over, his disdain apparent. "I have a better idea. Why don't I pay you to go away? You leave the boy with me, and I set you up somewhere far away."

It was the deal he'd made with his first wife, Naomi Caldwell. "I have no intention of giving you my son."

The way Siggy smiled broadcast his skepticism. And given his ability to manipulate both his former wives, that didn't really surprise her.

"As you said, this company will belong to my grandson one day. The shares are his. I will manage it until he is ready to take over."

"But you are no longer the managing partner, nor are you the majority shareholder," Trent pointed out in a reasonable voice.

The instant he spoke, his father's attention swung back to him once more. "You do not belong here. If you don't leave now, I'll have security throw you out."

"Security? Word on the street is you can't afford security anymore."

Siggy's face grew ruddy. "Get out," he spat.

"Not without the financials," Trent retorted. He was as calm as his father was upset. "As guardian of the majority shareholder, Savannah needs to see what's going on."

Observing the exchange between father and son, Savannah almost felt sorry for her father-in-law. If Siggy hadn't been such a domineering bastard, perhaps they could've work through their differences amicably. But Siggy wanted to maintain control of his company, and to do so he needed control over her son.

With the four of them staring each other down, Savannah wasn't sure what would happen next. Without access to the computers, she had no idea how they could force Gerry or Siggy to open up the books.

But apparently, Trent knew exactly what he was doing. "Things will not go well for you if we get lawyers involved," he said ominously.

As a privately held company, West Coast Records was not required to file any public documents regarding its finances. The board membership was composed of six of Siggy's cronies but Savannah doubted they would be interested in being on the receiving end of any legal action she might take against them on behalf of her son.

"Gerry, give them access." Siggy slid from behind the desk, stalked up to his son and glared at him. "You might have won this round but I'll burn West Coast Records to the ground before I'll let you anywhere near this company."

Bold words, Savannah thought. But as she watched her father-in-law exit the room, she wasn't completely sure if it was bravado or a touch of madness that drove him where Trent was concerned.

Gerry did something with the computer and then left the room, as well.

As Trent slid behind the desk and began tapping away, Savannah sank into a guest chair opposite him.

"How do you do it?" She sat with her hands clasped tight in her lap and exhaled to calm herself. "How do you face him down so calmly? Doesn't he get to you?"

"Years of practice have taught me to cope." But stress

lines had appeared beside his compressed lips and his eyes were guarded.

Long minutes ticked by while Trent looked through the computer records. Savannah had a hard time containing her restless energy. Any second she expected Siggy to reappear and begin to berate her once more. If before this she'd been determined to keep Dylan out of his clutches, now she was even more convinced she couldn't let her son be anywhere near him.

She paced around the room, paying special attention to the photos and awards that lined the walls. From the look of things, the label hadn't had any great success since the early '90s. And she had a hard time finding Rafe's stamp on anything. This made her sad. In many ways her husband had been trapped by his position as eldest son.

Could he have done as Trent had and made his own way? Savannah wasn't sure Rafe had it in him to break free of his father's hold. Rafe was firstborn. His father's pride and joy. The weight of expectation had turned him into a mini Siggy.

"Finding anything?" She came to stand behind Trent and peer over his shoulder at the monitor.

Despite the seriousness of her situation, the stressful confrontation with Siggy and her fears for her son, she couldn't stop herself from snatching a lungful of Trent's familiar cologne. Her head spun as her senses came alive. His long fingers darted across the keyboard and she couldn't help herself from remembering how they'd felt biting down on her skin as she came the previous night.

His thick, wavy hair enticed a woman's fingers to roam. Not a speck of lint dotted the shoulders of his dark blue suit, but that didn't stop Savannah's craving to sweep her fingers across the material. Last night's reckless encounter had stirred up a beehive of longing. She hungered to touch him again and was willing to make up lame excuses to do so. Before she succumbed to temptation, she put her hands behind her back.

"What are you doing? That doesn't look like financial records."

At her question, Trent didn't glance up. "A friend of mine lent me a program." He removed a flash drive from the computer's USB port and slipped it into his pocket.

"What sort of program?" Savannah stepped back as he got to his feet.

"I'll tell you in the car."

"Is all this really necessary?" She wasn't sure what to make of Trent's cloak-and-dagger routine. Was he behaving this way for her benefit? Acting as if the trip to West Coast Records' offices was more productive than it had been?

Trent spread his fingers across the small of her back and nudged her toward the hallway. "Let's go."

Obviously he wasn't going to say another word while they were still in the building. As badly as she wanted to know what was going on, Savannah was enjoying the warmth of his palm far too much to be hurried.

As on the way in, they encountered no one, but the boardroom door was closed as they passed. Once in the parking lot, Savannah couldn't restrain her curiosity one second longer. "What's going on? Were you able to determine anything from the financials?"

"They gave us only the most rudimentary access."

"What does that mean?"

"That means they were ready for us. We got a year-to-date profit and loss statement and balance sheet. It shows that the company is profitable."

"How profitable?"

"Enough that they should be paying their artists. But you say they aren't."

"That's the impression that I was given. Maybe they are paying some but not all."

"Money is going out," Trent said, opening the passenger door so she could slide in. "I just can't determine if it's actually going to the artists." Without saying another word, he shut the car door, leaving her to mull over his last statement.

She waited until he'd slid behind the wheel and started the engine before repeating her earlier question. "What was with the USB drive?"

"I figured we wouldn't get much. So I came prepared. A friend of mine in Vegas runs a security company. And he wouldn't want it spread around, but he's a gifted hacker. I called him this morning, explained the problem, and he gave me a worm to implant in their system."

"A worm?" Savannah had watched enough TV to know what he was talking about. But she had never considered that real people used them. "Are you telling me you planted some sort of spy software in the company's computer system?"

"As good a hacker as he is, he could've cracked their system from the outside, but why bother when it's so much easier to do it from the inside?"

Savannah was starting to feel hopeful. "So what does this get us?"

"Full access to their system."

Leave it to Trent to come to her rescue once again. Savannah would never have conceived of something so clever and potentially illegal.

"So you'll be able to see what's actually going on?"

"That's the idea."

"Is it illegal?"

"I'd say it's a gray area. Dylan is the majority shareholder in the company. They are denying you access to the books." Trent backed the car out of the parking spot. "But it doesn't matter. Logan assures me his software's untraceable. They'll never know what hit them."

* * *

Adrenaline buzzed through Trent's veins as he negotiated the LA traffic on the way to the hotel Savannah had chosen until she found a more permanent place to settle. The fight with his father had gone as expected. Trent glanced at Savannah. She hadn't reacted well to Siggy's vicious attack. It had taken a great deal of willpower to keep from acknowledging her distress and comforting her back at the label. He didn't want either her or his father to get the idea something was going on between them.

In the old days when he and his father had fought, she had often come to him with comforting words. Initially he'd rebuffed her attempts to make him feel better, not understanding what she needed was reassurance that he was all right.

He glanced at her now. She stared out the passenger window. Her face was impassive, but her hands, clasped around the purse in her lap, were rigid with tension. He recognized that she was stressed. He gathered breath, refrained from speaking. What was he going to say? That everything was going to be fine? He didn't know that. And what was he doing getting more deeply involved in her problem with his father when he'd determined a decade earlier that he was done with the family drama?

"Dealing with Siggy isn't going to be fun or easy," he said, stating the obvious. "Are you sure you don't want me to help you get back on your feet somewhere besides here?"

When he made the offer the night before, he hadn't done so as an ex-lover or a brother-in-law. They'd been friends long before either of those things, and whether he'd always been able to admit it or not, she'd been there for him during some very dark days.

"I told you last night that I'm not going to take your money."

"You could think of it as a loan."

Her features relaxed into a wry expression. "I've considered that," she explained in an overly patient tone. "My answer is still no."

When had she become stubborn? Trent caught himself frowning. She wasn't the same woman he'd broken up with two years earlier. And he wasn't sure what to make of the change.

"Why are you so opposed to letting me help you?"

"I wouldn't be in the car with you if I was opposed to letting you help me."

"Then why won't you take money from me? It's not as if I'd notice it was gone."

She cocked her head and stared straight forward. "I can't explain it. Getting you to help me sort out what's wrong at West Coast Records isn't personal. I could hire a lawyer to do that."

"I thought you were broke?"

"I might be able to afford a really bad attorney," she retorted with a trace of a smile. And then she sighed. "To be honest, I wasn't thinking straight before last night."

"Last night? What changed last night?"

"Have you forgotten already?" Her voice packed just the right amount of sultry amusement to stir his lust.

He tightened his grip on the steering wheel to keep his hands from wandering across the space between them and slipping beneath the hem of her dress to find her bare knee. It drove him crazy that ever since she'd been married his brother she'd started dressing to repress her sensuality. A beautiful woman shouldn't hide the way Savannah did.

"Hardly." But after glancing in her direction, he wasn't sure if they were referring to the same thing after all. "You are talking about what happened in my office, aren't you?"

"You sound worried that I'm not."

"I don't sound worried." What was going on that he wanted last night's encounter to have changed her somehow?

It had been an interlude between ex-lovers. Nothing more. It certainly hadn't changed anything going on with him. So why did he expect her to be any different? Trent ground his teeth together, disliking his uncertainty. To his relief, Savannah chose to elaborate without his prompting.

"Being around you reminded me of the girl I used to be. You taught me how to take care of myself. I'd forgotten how to do that in the last year and a half."

As long as he could remember, he'd lectured her on the need to question people's motives before agreeing to something. She'd lost much of her naïveté while living in New York, but obviously she sometimes forgot to be wary of people eager to take advantage of her.

"Why didn't you take care of yourself while married to my brother?"

"In a lot of ways, your brother was like your father. He wanted a particular kind of wife. One who did as he asked and never argued. I didn't realize our marriage wasn't going to be a partnership until too late."

For the first time, it occurred to Trent that she hadn't been happy. Again came that urge to comfort her. Again he resisted. She wasn't his to worry about. Helping her sort through what was going on with the label was about getting back at his father. She'd hit the nail on the head last night when she'd encouraged him to demonstrate to Siggy that he was a better businessman.

"I'm sorry things didn't work out the way you'd hoped."

"I'm not sure I had an idea what I was hoping for."

Again her remark prompted questions, but Trent refrained from diving in. Last night she'd said she didn't want to talk about her marriage. He sure as hell didn't want to hear about it today.

He parked the car in the hotel parking lot and they went in the front entrance together. She'd chosen a budget chain, with none of the bells and whistles she might have enjoyed if his brother hadn't left her in debt. Whatever else had changed with her, she remained fiscally responsible.

Trent had booked himself into the Wilshire for the night. Although he could very easily have dropped Savannah off and headed to his hotel, he felt as if he owed her some idea of what he had planned.

Her standard hotel room was empty when they arrived. A crib had been set up by the window, but Dylan wasn't in it and the babysitter was nowhere to be seen.

"Shouldn't they be here?" For some reason the sight of the empty hotel room alarmed him. Maybe it was the way Savannah had tensed.

"I told Lori not to go anywhere until I got back." Savannah fumbled in her purse for her phone and scrolled through her contacts. "She didn't send me a text and she's not answering her phone. Where could they be?" The pitch of her voice registered anxiety.

"How long have you known this girl?"

"I first hired her to babysit Dylan right after Rafe's death. I knew there would be a lot to do and that it would disrupt Dylan's routines too much if I brought him everywhere I needed to go."

"And you checked her out?"

Savannah shot him a dark look. "I hired her through a reputable agency that had her thoroughly vetted."

"And she hasn't done anything like this before?"

"If by *like this* you mean taken Dylan somewhere without telling me, not to my knowledge."

Trent could tell his interrogation of Savannah wasn't helping the situation, and she was looking more upset by the minute.

"What is it you aren't telling me?" Trent demanded.

"Nothing really."

"I don't believe you."

"It's just that your father…"

Savannah had been dialing as she'd begun her explanation. Now she spoke to the person who'd answered. "Aunt Stacy," Savannah said into the phone. "I was wondering if Lori is still there with Dylan?" She paused and her entire body slumped with relief. "No, that's fine. I wasn't expecting him to be gone. Lori didn't say anything about heading over there." A pause. "Oh, he did? No, he didn't say anything to me about it."

Fury rose in Trent while he waited for her to finish chatting with her aunt. The part of him that wasn't plotting his father's downfall admired Savannah's ability to remain calm and think under pressure.

"No need to mention I called," Savannah was saying, her voice showing no stress at all. "I'll be by in a bit."

When she disconnected the call, she sank onto the bed and put her face in her hands. Her body shook as she gasped in a ragged breath. Trent put his hand on her shoulder. She jerked away as if burned. Her blue eyes were hot as she gazed up into his face. But as quickly as her temper flared, she calmed down.

"Sorry. That wasn't directed at you." She waved her hand in a random gesture. "Lori took Dylan over to Siggy's."

"Without saying anything to you or asking if it was okay?"

"He told her he'd cleared it with me." She rose, her movements stiff and slow as if every muscle in her body ached. "I guess I messed with him so he messed with me."

"I should have anticipated something like this."

"Neither of us had any way of knowing." Her neutral tone was at odds with the fear and anger she'd demonstrated moments earlier. "I'm sorry to ask for another favor, but do you mind driving me over there? It looks as if Lori helped herself to my car."

"Whatever you need."

Five minutes later, they were back in the LA traffic. Savannah's fierce demeanor invited no conversation. Trent kept his focus on the road. The drive to his father's house took over an hour. It was a tense sixty minutes. He couldn't imagine what she was going through, the panic she must have felt coming back to the hotel and finding her son gone, the roller coaster of emotions when she figured out the nanny had taken Dylan to his grandfather.

Trent wanted to be there when she faced down Siggy, but when they pulled up to the enormous Beverly Hills mansion, she shook her head when he shut off the car.

"I need to do this on my own."

"Are you sure that's your best option? My father will try to bully you."

"He's gone too far this time."

"Call me when you're on your way back to the hotel." Everything in him was clamoring to accompany her into the mansion and act as her champion. "I need to know you're okay."

"I'm going to be just fine."

"Regardless. Call me."

With a nod, Savannah got out of the car and Trent stared at the mansion's front door long after she was lost from view.

Five

Savannah's heels clicked against the travertine tile of the wide entryway as she let herself into Siggy's mansion. The earlier heat of anger had been replaced by icy determination. Ever since she'd come to live in this house at age eleven, she'd been intimidated by the man who lived here. She'd seen how he criticized his sons, dominated his staff and intimidated his business associates.

But today he'd stopped being someone to fear. Today, he'd interfered with her son, and she would do whatever it took to make sure that never happened again.

Set on a half-acre lot, the modern house had a wide-open floor plan that was perfect for entertaining. As a child, Savannah had witnessed hundreds of parties, and when she was old enough, she'd served at many.

The backyard had enough space for a large pool with a broad black-and-white marble surround, a pool house and a separate outdoor dining area for twelve beside an expansive fire feature.

Although the house was fifteen thousand square feet, there were only six bedrooms, and the way the public spaces opened onto each other, it was easy for her to find Siggy and Dylan in the main living room.

Lori was the first one to catch sight of her. Siggy was on the phone near the middle set of French doors that opened onto the backyard, his back to her. Dylan toddled along the espresso-toned hardwood floors that flowed into the dining room. Savannah made straight for him and snatched him into her arms. Pausing for a brief second to hug him and breathe in his familiar scent, she then turned to her babysitter.

"Give me my car keys and get out of here before I have you arrested."

The girl backed away from Savannah's advance, obviously terrified. "I didn't do anything wrong," she protested. "He asked me to come by with the baby. He said it was okay. He told me you knew."

"I don't care what he said. I hired you. You only answer to me." Savannah felt no remorse at scaring the girl after what she'd done. She put her hand out and stared daggers at Lori until she put the car keys in Savannah's palm.

"How am I supposed to get home?"

"I couldn't care less."

Savannah turned her back on the girl and headed for the foyer. While a part of her wanted to confront Siggy, she knew she would lose the battle. However, before she could reach the foyer, a tall broad-shouldered man in a black suit stepped in her path.

"I can't let you leave."

A little dazed by what he'd just said, Savannah was momentarily stumped for a response. Was she to be a prisoner? Savannah considered the surge of independence with which she'd turned down Trent's offer of support. Never in a million years had she thought Siggy would prevent her from leaving.

First she scowled at the man blocking her way, but seeing he had no intention of moving, she glanced over her shoulder at her father-in-law. He was still on the phone and didn't acknowledge the standoff happening twenty feet away. The righteous fury that had carried her this far had started to subside, but mounting panic gave her an adrenaline boost. She'd prepared herself to reclaim her son and fire Lori. She hadn't planned on having to save herself, as well.

"Step aside," she told the man and silently cursed when she heard the slight tremor in her voice. The entranceway he blocked was ten feet wide, leaving plenty of room to go around him, but with Dylan in her arms and four-inch heels on her feet, she doubted she could move fast enough on the marble floor to make a break for it.

"I can't let you go until he says it's okay."

Unwilling to argue with the man further, Savannah turned her back on Siggy. Frustration and helplessness washed over her. She hated feeling this way. It was how she'd felt from the moment she'd slid Rafe's ring onto her finger. Why had she let him talk her into marrying him? She should have toughened up and trusted she could handle being a single mom.

Siggy concluded his call and headed in her direction. Savannah barely let him take three steps before venting her outrage.

"How dare you try to keep us here." She didn't care if this was the wrong tack to take with her father-in-law. "Call off your gorilla. Dylan and I are leaving now."

"We need to talk."

"There is nothing to talk about. Dylan and I are leaving."

"To go where?" He might have sounded reasonable, but

his eyes flashed with disdain. "You have no money and you are deep in debt."

"Thanks to your son."

"He was sick."

"Yes, and he made a lot of bad choices. It left me with a huge financial burden and barely anything for Dylan and me to live on. You know he would hate that."

"I know that he would like for me to take care of his son."

His son. But not her. Instinctively, Savannah tightened her hold on Dylan and shifted so that her body was between her son and the two men who flanked her. Would they try to take him by force? Savannah pushed down dismay. She would not leave here without her Dylan, but couldn't bear the thought of staying. They would be prisoners.

"Then please buy back the stock Rafe left Dylan. Give us the chance for a fresh start."

"A fresh start? What sort of fresh start are you looking for?"

"I thought I would find a small house for just the two of us, and go back to work."

"You mean acting." He said it with a great deal of derision. "That wouldn't be necessary if you moved in here."

Around and around the argument went. She and Siggy had been wearing out this topic since shortly after Rafe's death nine months ago.

"I want Dylan to live in a neighborhood filled with children who come over after school to play."

She had this idyllic image in her head of small-town living, where her house was the most popular one on the block with the kids. Siggy's Hollywood home was a showplace and not one bit kid friendly.

"He's not old enough to go to school."

And by the time he was, she'd be well and firmly trapped. "Do you plan on keeping me here by force?"

"Of course not. You're free to go whenever you wish."

"Thank you." She turned to go, but her way was still blocked. "I wish to go now."

From behind her came Siggy's smooth voice. "Dylan stays."

Savannah fought down panic. "We're both leaving."

For a span of several heartbeats, no one moved. Then the front door opened and Trent stepped inside.

Trent left the front door open as he crossed the expansive foyer. The man barring Savannah's path had two inches and thirty pounds on Trent, but he didn't see this as a problem.

He looked into Savannah's eyes and hoped she'd follow his lead. "We have a plane to catch. And you know how the traffic is."

"Yes, of course." Her gaze searched his.

"She's not going anywhere." Siggy actually appeared to think he could get away with compelling Savannah to stay by bullying her.

"That's not true," Savannah stated, her relief obvious. She took the hand Trent held out to her and came to stand beside him. "Dylan and I were trying to leave, but your father was threatening me."

"Is that true?"

Siggy didn't answer Trent's question but instead asked one of his own. "So you're cheating on your husband with him?"

"Rafe is dead. She can't cheat on his memory."

"And it's no business of yours who I'm with." Savannah shook her head. "Trent is family and he's helping me. Something you should be doing."

"Neither one of you is going to get anywhere near the company again."

"Dylan owns a majority share. That means I'm in control until he turns twenty-one. You have nothing to say about it."

"It's my company. I built it. I have everything to say about it."

"Not unless you buy the shares back."

"I don't have to buy the shares back," Siggy said, his eyes burning with malice. "All I need is control of my grandson."

Beside him, Savannah stiffened. Trent stepped forward. "Do not threaten her."

Siggy sneered. "Or what?"

Trent wasn't a reckless teenager anymore, but his father continued to treat him with contempt. Since striking out to make it on his own, Trent was less and less bothered by his father's low opinion. He'd come to accept that no matter how successful he was, nothing diminished Siggy's disapproval.

"Try me and see." Trent gave his father a cold smile, set his hand on Savannah's back and guided her toward the front door.

She was trembling as they crossed from the cold foyer into the bright afternoon sunshine, but as they headed across the driveway to her car, she released a shaky smile. "I've never been so happy to see anybody in my entire life."

"That's probably not something you would've said yesterday."

She opened her car's back door and settled Dylan into his seat. "You might be surprised."

Trent waited for her to say more, but she simply buckled her son in and closed the door. At last she faced him, and her gorgeous smile hit him like a two-by-four. Unfortunately it was gone as fast as it had arrived.

"I don't have to tell you how frightening that was. He wants to take Dylan away from me."

"You need to contact a lawyer and get ahead of this."

"You're right." Her shoulders slumped. "But right now I need to get out of here."

While Trent followed her back to her hotel, a plan began to form in his mind. He parked next to her in the hotel's large lot and intercepted her as she was getting out of her car.

"You can't stay here."

She didn't look happy as she gazed toward the hotel's shabby facade. "But it's only temporary."

The longer he was with Savannah, the more he felt driven to fix things for her. It was an old pattern. One he thought he'd abandoned when she'd married Rafe. "I don't mean the hotel. I mean LA."

"I don't want to, but with everything that's going on with the company, I can't leave until things are settled." She wasn't acknowledging how dire her situation was. Alone in LA, she would be at Siggy's mercy.

"You and Dylan are coming back to Las Vegas with me."

Trent didn't second-guess his decision to get further entangled with Savannah and her son. A week ago, he'd been avoiding her, refusing to get involved in her troubles. But what was going on between her and his father kept him from being neutral. She might have been foolish to marry his brother, but she didn't deserve to lose her son because Siggy had lost his.

"I can't."

"What's stopping you?" The question came out with a sardonic spin. "You have no ties to LA. In Vegas you have me."

She opened her mouth and looked ready to refuse. He could almost see the wheels turning. Was she trading one bad situation for another? He could have reassured her, but no matter what else had happened between them, he'd always been honest with her.

"I don't like the idea of you and Dylan alone here." Trent couldn't imagine returning to Las Vegas and leaving her to fend for herself. "And I don't trust Siggy."

She gripped her keys tight and looked a little like a defendant awaiting a verdict. "How long will it take to sort out what's going on with the company?"

"I don't know. It will depend on what Logan finds in the company's files."

"I suppose I could find an inexpensive rental in Vegas."

"I think you and Dylan would be better off staying with me."

"Absolutely not."

"I live in a gated community, on an estate with two acres of land and a guesthouse. My housekeeper loves children and is completely trustworthy. Rhoda can watch Dylan whenever you need her to."

Although he thought he'd made a terrific pitch, Savannah looked unconvinced. "I don't understand."

"What's there to understand?"

"We haven't spoken since I married Rafe. Just yesterday I had to hunt you down in the club because you wouldn't answer any of my calls. Now you're bending over backward to help me out. I don't get it."

He didn't want to dig too deep into his motivations. "Don't look a gift horse in the mouth."

"You'll have to do better than that."

"What do you want me to tell you?"

She cocked her head and regarded him through narrowed eyes. "What changed? Why are you suddenly my knight in shining armor again?"

"I'm not." But he could see where she might be misinterpreting his helpfulness. "My motives are purely selfish."

"How, exactly?"

"Didn't you see the look on my father's face?" The memory of it made Trent grin. "He is beyond frustrated that I'm helping you."

"So this is about you and your father?"

"Yes." And in the spirit of honesty, Trent continued, "I also feel responsible for you getting involved with my brother and in this mess."

"Why do you think that?"

"You obviously were in a vulnerable place after we broke up, and Rafe took advantage of that."

She stared at him for a long moment before nodding. "I'd better go get Murphy and our things."

"Does that mean you're coming with me to Las Vegas?"

"It makes sense for the time being." She didn't appear happy or relieved.

"Why don't you stay here with Dylan and I'll take care of collecting your stuff?"

She shook her head. "Is it weird that I'm uncomfortable waiting in this parking lot alone?"

Trent realized then what a good job she'd been doing hiding her anxiety. "Not weird at all. Grab Dylan and we'll do this together."

Ten minutes after she'd checked out and left the babysitter's suitcase with the concierge, they were headed back to the Van Nuys airport. Both she and Trent had been driving rental cars. They dropped them off at the agency before heading to the chartered plane.

All through the day, from the plane ride to their confrontation with Siggy and now a second flight, Dylan had proven to be a sunny, spirited child. Trent sat across from the boy and regarded him in bemusement. "He takes after you."

"He definitely has my nose."

"Yes, but that's not what I was referring to. I meant his temperament."

"What about his temperament?"

"Dylan is a happy baby. Rafe was a fussy child. At least that's what my mother says. And he turned into a difficult adult."

"Your brother had his moments." Savannah kept her attention fixed on Dylan. "I don't know how I got so lucky with Dylan. He's been easy since the day he was born." She laughed. "Makes me want to have several more."

Whenever she'd made statements like this, Trent visualized her surrounded by little girls with heart-wrenching blue eyes and blond ringlets. For some reason, he'd never pictured her with boys. Yet here sat a handsome lad with dark brown hair and curious blue eyes, and Trent wondered how many more sons were in her future.

"You're an excellent mother. Of course, that's no surprise to anyone."

"It was a surprise to me," she said. "As much as I've always wanted a family, I really wasn't sure if I was capable of taking care of one."

Her confession surprised him. "But you've always seemed so determined…"

How had she been so eager to do something when she wasn't sure if she could? Trent had always been confident in everything he did. He couldn't imagine taking on something he knew he couldn't handle. With her inability to stick up for herself, she'd always struck him as insecure and unwilling to take chances. Maybe she was braver than he'd ever realized.

"Just because I'm scared of something doesn't mean I won't do it. If that had been the case, I never would've gone to New York City. Never modeled. And I sure wouldn't have acted on a soap opera." She gave him a melancholy smile. "I didn't believe I could do any of it. Especially after I saw how beautiful the other girls were and heard the stories of how hard the modeling business was."

"When you left LA, I never imagined you doubted yourself. Why would you? You were beautiful."

"I was short."

"You're five-eight."

"Most models are five-ten and taller. I didn't book a lot of jobs because of that. And it kept me off the runway. Which made me feel inadequate. It's why I traded modeling for acting."

"How did I not know you felt this way?"

"I saw the girls you dated. Not only were they beautiful, but they were also over-the-top confident. They had to be to keep up with you."

But none of those girls had stuck. None of them lingered in his thoughts like Savannah had. Like she still did.

"What do you mean, keep up with me?"

"You know, your party lifestyle. The clubs, the celebrities you hang with. All that can be pretty intimidating for a girl with small-town roots, raised in the servants' quarters."

"I never saw you like that."

"I saw me like that." She tickled her son and made him giggle.

Trent let her words sink in. Why, in all the years they'd known each other, had she never spoken of this? She made it sound as if she didn't think she was good enough for him. That wasn't true. The trouble in their relationship had been that they wanted different things.

Besides, she'd considered herself good enough for his brother. Or was it that Rafe had never made her feel less than utterly desirable and truly wanted? A vise clamped down on Trent's chest.

"Well, you shouldn't."

He checked his watch and then turned his attention to

the darkening sky outside the aircraft. They would be on the ground in twenty minutes. Trent could feel Savannah watching him, sensed her desire for him to elaborate, but he had no more to say.

An hour later, he was carrying his sleeping nephew through his house. Before taking her out to the guest-house, Trent gave Savannah a tour of the wide-open first-floor living area.

Despite her years in his father's mansion and her year and a half living in her own enormous house, for some reason she was goggling at Trent's nine-thousand-square-foot spread.

"You live here?"

He wasn't sure what to make of the laughter in her voice. "Obviously."

"It's a little over-the-top, don't you think?"

"I bought it for the outdoor space," he explained, feeling slightly peevish at her criticism.

While the traditional French country style wasn't his cup of tea, the amenities more than made up for the elaborate plasterwork on the fireplaces and overabundance of pillars and crown molding. Floor-to-ceiling windows and French doors filled the house with light. The place had come furnished with faux antiques that complemented the builder's vision of a French château.

"I can't wait to see it."

Trent guided her through a set of French doors that let out onto a wide, covered terrace. In addition to the guest-house, his backyard hosted a large pool with a swim-up bar and a pool house, an outdoor movie screen and a putting green. Savannah put on the brakes as soon as she stepped outside.

"Is that a slide?" She pointed out the towering water slide that spiraled from the second-floor terrace to the pool. "I'm not sure this is going to work out for Dylan and me."

"Why not?"

"It's a big boy playground." And from the way she was looking at him, he was the big boy.

"What does that have to do with anything?"

"Don't you think having your sister-in-law and her infant son living in your guesthouse will cramp your style?"

"I'm not planning on throwing any wild parties while you're here, if that's what you're insinuating."

She sighed and gave him her full attention. "We'll stay just a couple days. Long enough for me to get my feet back under me and to find a place we can rent for a little while."

"Stay as long as you want," Trent said and meant every word. "Now that that's settled, are you ready to see the guesthouse?"

Six

Shaded by the palm trees that dotted the landscape, Savannah sat beside Trent's pool with her feet dangling in the lukewarm water. No breeze stirred the air and sweat trickled down her skin. She was ready for the break in the heat the forecasters promised for later in the week. Apparently in the weeks leading up to Halloween, the highs in Las Vegas dropped from upper nineties to low eighties.

Beside her on the terra-cotta tile sat a plate with half a tuna sandwich and a glass of iced tea. Nearby, Dylan slept peacefully in a portable crib and Murphy snored happily on a shaded lounge chair. They'd been living in Trent's guesthouse for four days. With his backyard as gorgeously landscaped as any five-star resort, Savannah felt as if she was on vacation, not in the midst of a personal crisis.

She felt safe for the first time since she'd found out that Rafe was sick. Already her guards were coming down. Which troubled her because she hadn't only been motivated by fear of what Siggy might try next when she let

Trent talk her into returning to Las Vegas. She'd also been swept up in a giddy euphoria that he'd cared enough to worry about her. In short, Savannah's reasons for coming to Las Vegas were more about what might happen with Trent than what had happened with Siggy.

Today she would stop procrastinating and corner Trent about what was going on with the label. She knew he and his friend had been digging into the company's files, and she needed to know what they'd found. But given the way he'd avoided answering her inquiries so far, she worried that what they'd found was really bad.

Just then, Trent came out onto the patio from the main house. Over the past few days, Savannah had noticed more and more that if she thought hard enough about Trent, he either appeared or called. In the old days she might have thought this meant they were in sync. These days she chalked it up to her infringement on his bachelor lifestyle.

"You look happy," he said, keeping his voice low as he approached. Today he wore a pair of khaki pants and a white polo that brought out his tan. His blue eyes flicked toward Dylan's crib. "I think Vegas agrees with you."

"I think what agrees with me is feeling safe for the first time since Rafe died and I found out how bad our financial situation really was."

"It's going to be okay."

She studied his features and felt reassured by his sincerity. "Can you tell me what you found out about the business?"

"It's as you expected. The financials are not in good shape. They haven't been paying their artists everything they're owed. One or two probably won't sign another contract."

"What can we do?"

"West Coast Records has several strong artists. But there are too many who've done nothing. It's not their fault. They weren't well managed. A few of them could be kept on, provided their next albums are better produced."

"But who's going to do that? I don't know anything about the music side of things. I might be able to run the business side with help, but when it comes right down to it, the label needs someone like you who can do both."

"I know what you're thinking, but it's not going to happen. My father will never allow me to take over the company."

"Not even if you can save it from going under?"

"From the correspondence between him, Gerry and Rafe, Siggy doesn't believe the company is in trouble."

"How is that possible? Surely even if Rafe kept how bad it was from him, Gerry would have told Siggy the truth."

"And been the one to shatter the old man's vision of his perfect firstborn son?"

Savannah heard the bitterness in Trent's voice. No matter what he said to the contrary, it still stung that his father showed him so little respect.

"Besides," Trent continued, "Gerry has had his own agenda these past couple of years."

Not liking the sound of that, Savannah asked, "What sort of agenda?"

"Some of the company's troubles stem from Gerry's embezzling."

"Embezzling?" Savannah shook her head, unable to believe what she was hearing.

"Apparently he's been stealing money from the company for years. He's been in the perfect position to steal and hide it. I'm sure as years went on and he wasn't caught he grew bolder. And when he was passed over for CEO in favor of Rafe, he probably figured he'd get whatever he could and get out."

"What do we do? Do we call the police?"

"Unfortunately Gerry is a lot cleverer than my father

ever gave him credit for. Not only did he steal money, he made it look as if Rafe took it. Only by digging into Gerry's finances was Logan able to find out that Gerry's spending outpaced his salary and bonuses."

Savannah's hopes plummeted. Nothing they'd found helped her situation. The company was likely on the verge of bankruptcy and so was she.

"Come on," Trent said, stripping off his shirt as he headed toward the pool house. "Let's go for a swim."

When she'd packed for Vegas the first time, she hadn't planned to be vacationing. "I don't have a suit."

The most she'd done in the last few days was to wade in the shallow end of the pool so that she could let Dylan frolic in the water. Given how hot the last few days had been, this hadn't been satisfying, but she'd been reluctant to venture off the property and go shopping for herself.

"I keep all sorts of suits in the pool house," Trent replied, disappearing into the building. Less than a minute later, he was back wearing swim trunks, his glorious chest and abs bare to the sun. "Try one of these."

It did not surprise Savannah one bit that the bikinis Trent held up were on the tiny side. "I don't suppose you have a one-piece in there somewhere."

He shook his head. "The last thing you need is a one-piece. You have a gorgeous body. You should show it off."

She'd had a gorgeous body. Now she carried a little extra weight on her hips and knew Trent liked his girls lean and fit. Almost as soon as the thought arrived, she dismissed it. What did it matter how Trent liked his women? She wasn't one of them. With a heartfelt sigh, Savannah got to her feet and took the bikinis Trent held out.

"I know he's sleeping, but could you keep an eye on Dylan while I change?"

After what had happened in LA, she was having a hard time letting Dylan out of her sight. If Trent had noticed her paranoia, he hadn't said anything. Savannah knew she would have to eventually leave her son in someone else's care, but for right now she was more comfortable keeping him close by.

Trent was peering at a sleeping Dylan when Savannah returned. In this unguarded moment Trent's expression captivated her. With his features softened in wonder, he looked younger and happier. Even though he didn't realize Dylan was his son, he was growing attached to the boy. This made Savannah's stomach tighten in an uncomfortable knot. Part of her wanted to tell Trent that he was Dylan's father. But would he believe her? Or would he see this as a ploy to manipulate him?

Better that the secret remain hidden. Trent liked his bachelor lifestyle and his freedom. No reason to disrupt either. She appreciated his help with the company and wouldn't burden him with the one thing he never wanted—a family.

"What?"

"Hmm?"

She came out of her thoughts and found him staring at her.

"You are looking at me funny. I'm not a complete idiot when it comes to kids, you know."

"You're not?" She retreated into friendly banter. "And where did you get all your experience?"

"For a couple months last year, I dated a woman who had two."

"Two what?"

"Two children. Agnes and Theo. They were four and eight. Great kids."

This news caused Savannah's confidence to implode. After everything he'd said about not wanting a family, he'd dated a woman with children. It felt like betrayal, which was ridiculous. He could date anyone he pleased. It was no business of hers. After all, she'd married his brother.

"That's nice." The urge to run over, pick up her son and hug him close was almost painful in its intensity. Savannah recognized her need for comfort.

"She was great. The kids were great."

"Sounds great."

"Aren't you going to ask me what happened?"

Savannah shook her head. "Are we going to swim or talk?"

Without waiting for his answer, she dived into the pool. The tepid water felt refreshing after the afternoon heat, and Savannah swam beneath the surface until her lungs burned. She rose, snatched a quick breath and dived again. Not until her fingers touched the pool's far wall did she come up again. Sucking in huge gulps of air, she turned and pushed off to stroke back the way she'd come.

Damn Trent for making her feel jealous. She had no right to the emotion where he was concerned. Most of the women she pictured him with were young party girls. She'd never imagined him dating someone with baggage. In the back of her mind a distressed voice called, *Why not me?*

At some point during her frantic swim, Trent had entered the pool. He stood near the center, his expression unreadable as she approached. Savannah stopped several feet away and gazed toward the portable crib. Through the mesh sides, she could see Dylan sleeping peacefully.

"She didn't mean anything to me."

Savannah couldn't believe Trent was continuing the conversation. "Really, it's none of my business."

"It was six months after you and I broke up. I wanted to see what dating a woman with kids was like." Obviously, Trent was not going to let it go.

"And what was it like?"

"Not bad. Different. We didn't really date. More like hung out. Right off the bat she told me she wasn't interested in someone like me."

"A party boy?"

"She wanted someone she could build a future with."

Savannah knew what that was like. "But she dated you anyway."

"She'd been divorced about a year and was looking to getting her feet wet in the dating pool." Trent ran his fingers through his hair, making it stand up in all directions. "I met her at the club. We went out once and both of us knew right away it wasn't going to work out."

"But you kept seeing her."

"There was no pressure."

Savannah had tried to keep things free and easy while they'd dated, but she hadn't always been successful. In her heart, she'd longed for a future with him. A life filled with children and happiness.

"Why are you telling me all this?"

"I don't know."

"That's not like you. You always have a reason for what you do."

"I usually have a reason for what I do. Except when it comes to you."

"Trent—"

Before she could finish whatever it was that she'd been about to say, his arms went around her and his lips found hers. Held tight against his strong body, Savannah gave herself to the powerful emotions surging through her. With her fingers buried in his hair, she hung on for dear life as he devoured her mouth. The water gave her buoyancy and she floated in a bubble of joy.

She wanted him. She wanted this.

The privacy offered by the lush landscaping around the pool eased Savannah's doubts as Trent released the clasp holding her bikini top in place. She gasped as his lips drifted down her neck and settled over the wildly beating pulse in her throat. She wrapped her legs around his hips, feeling his erection hard against her stomach. His right hand came between them and settled over her breast while his other hand cupped her butt, lifting her partially out of the water.

She reveled in the sweep of his tongue over her nipple. It tightened into an aching peak as he laved it once more before pulling the hard bud into his mouth and sucking. She closed her eyes and let the delicious sensations wash over her. After the first time they'd made love, the passion she and Trent shared left Savannah convinced that they belonged together. But no matter how overpowering and all-consuming the connection was between them, Trent wasn't about to settle down and give her the life she craved.

Over the heartbeat thundering in her ears, she heard the soft sounds Dylan made as he stirred to wakefulness. Her hands had worked their way down Trent's torso to the waistband of his swim shorts. Desire clouded her mind, but Savannah's maternal instincts were stronger. With a shudder she broke off their kiss and pushed against Trent's shoulders.

"Dylan," she gasped, shuddering as Trent's fingertips grazed the edge of her bathing suit bottoms, tantalizing inches from where she ached. "He's waking up. I need to get to him."

Without a hint of reluctance or disappointment, Trent set her free. As she swam to the pool's edge, she wasn't sure whether to feel relief or regret that he was being so understanding. With conflicting emotions churning in her gut, Savannah quickly toweled off and went to check on her son.

Dylan was rubbing his eyes, but when she spoke his name, he looked up at her with a wide grin. Savannah's heart melted. How lucky she was to have such a wonderful baby boy. Hearing Trent emerge from the pool, she glanced over her shoulder at him. If she couldn't have the love of her life, at least she had his son.

"I'd better get back to the guesthouse so I can change him."

"Savannah, about what just happened…"

"There's no need to say anything." Her heart contracted at his need to make excuses. "It's always been like this between us."

"And that's it?"

"What more is there? Nothing else about our situation has changed. We're the same people who broke up two years ago because I wanted a family and you didn't."

"I guess we are." His neutral expression told her nothing. "It's just always been easy to forget our differences when I'm kissing you."

He was certainly right about that. And the more time she spent around him, the more likely they would be to indulge in their passion for each other. But there was no future in that. She needed to start thinking about where she was going and what she was going to do.

"Do you have some time this afternoon to start coming up with a plan for straightening out the company?"

"I have a couple of meetings at the club that should take me into early evening. How about we do a late dinner here?"

"Seven?"

"Sounds about right."

Savannah wrapped herself in a dry towel and then picked up Dylan. She offered Trent a bright smile that hid her heavy heart. "I'll see you then."

As soon as Savannah disappeared in the direction of the guesthouse, Trent dived back into the pool. To burn off some of his sexual frustration, he swam hard for several laps before levering himself out and flopping onto a nearby lounge chair. For the last four days he'd been tormented by Savannah's proximity. Night was the worst. Knowing she slept mere steps from his big empty bed had summoned every memory of their time together. To keep himself from acting on his fantasies about her, he'd taken to spending long hours at the club and not returning home until the sky lightened toward dawn.

All of which had simply stoked his hunger, making him unable to keep his hands off her moments earlier. And now he'd agreed to a late dinner under the guise of talking business.

With a growl, Trent got to his feet and headed inside. She would expect him to have answers, and if he couldn't provide any she might get frustrated enough to head back to LA and take Siggy on by herself. He needed to sort through their options. Just as important, he needed to chat with one of his partners in the club, Nate Tucker.

Trent showered and dressed in gray slacks and a bright blue shirt. His impulses pointed him toward the back of the house, where he might run into Savannah again. Cursing his weakness, Trent headed for his garage.

The gated community where he lived was a twenty-minute drive from the Cobalt. Negotiating the heavy Las Vegas traffic gave him plenty of time to ponder what had led up to that fantastic kiss in the pool. What had possessed him to tell Savannah about Karen? He wasn't the type to dredge up past romances. And to belabor the fact that he'd dated a woman with children could only hurt Savannah.

Had he hoped to reiterate that he wasn't a guy who wanted to be tied down with kids? An observer of the conversation might have wondered if Trent was trying to give the impression that he'd at least experimented with being a family guy.

When Trent got to Cobalt, instead of heading to his office at the club, he headed for the hotel's executive offices. JT Stone, owner of the hotel, was a brilliant businessman and would have solid advice about how to deal with the failing record label. The two men had bonded over similar experiences growing up with difficult fathers and running family businesses. In JT's case, he'd fought to regain control of the company that had been in the family for years and won. But in the end, he'd sold the family's overleveraged hotel chain to his cousin in order to own Cobalt free and clear. That JT's father had ended up in prison for fraud had been icing on the cake.

Trent approached JT's executive assistant. "Is he around?"

Nina nodded. "He has a meeting in half an hour, but he's free until then."

"Thanks." Trent stepped into the doorway that led to JT's office and knocked on the frame. "Nina said you have a couple minutes."

"Sure, come on in." JT stood and came around his desk to shake Trent's hand. "What's up?"

"I have a little business dilemma I'd like to talk to you about."

JT's expression lit with interest. He'd dealt with more than his share of business dilemmas in the last two years. Gesturing toward the comfortable sitting area near the large windows that overlooked Cobalt's extensive grounds, JT grabbed a couple bottles of water and joined Trent.

"What's going on?"

"You know how things are with me and the family company."

"Sure."

"My sister-in-law came to me a few days ago wanting my help. When my brother died, he left his controlling interest in the business to his son. That puts Savannah in a position of overseeing the majority shares."

"Let me guess—she asked you to step in as CEO."

"Not exactly. Both of us know there's no way my father would go for that. But she needs my help sorting out the company's various problems."

"Such as?"

"For one thing, they're not paying their artists all the royalties owed to them."

"Because they don't have the money?"

"The company has been doing poorly for years, but things got worse once my brother got sick." Trent cracked the seal on the bottle of water and drank. "Then there's the problem of embezzlement. West Coast Records' general manager has been stealing for quite a few years."

JT arched an eyebrow. "And you know this how?"

Trent gave a little shrug. "I might have had Logan digging around in their computers."

JT and Logan were related through marriage. Their wives were two of the three Fontaine sisters, who ran resort and hotel properties on the Strip. Trent had often wondered what it was like for JT to be married to his competition. His wife, Violet, managed two of the three Fontaine properties.

"Did Logan find anything else troubling?"

"I haven't spoken with him in a couple days, but it's possible." Trent rubbed his eyes, noting a mild twinge in his temple as he considered what else might be going wrong. "In the meantime, Savannah is deep in debt thanks to her husband's reckless spending, and the only asset she has is her major stake in a failing company."

"She should try to dump the company now before the word gets out."

"Unfortunately the way the corporation was set up, she has to get approval from the board in order to sell. And since my father controls the board, he's making things difficult for her."

"Why?"

"He wants control of his grandson and Savannah out of the picture."

JT nodded his understanding. "She's not willing to let that happen."

"Siggy isn't going to let Dylan go without a fight. He already made an attempt to kidnap his grandson."

"You're kidding, right?"

"I wish I was." Trent went on to share the details of their visit to the company and how they'd come back to find Savannah's hotel room empty. "She and Dylan are staying with me at the house. The whole thing really spooked her. She hasn't left the property since she arrived."

"But he can't actually force her to give up her son."

"No," Trent agreed, his mind running through all the things Siggy could do. "But he knows how to play dirty, and I wouldn't put it past him to take her to court over some sort of manufactured evidence that makes her appear as if she's a bad mother."

"But she could fight him."

"She doesn't have the resources for a prolonged battle."

JT was assessing him through narrowed eyes. Trent could read his thoughts easily enough. The owner of Cobalt was wondering why Trent wasn't doing everything in his power to help his sister-in-law fight.

"I've offered financial help," he explained, preempting the man's question. "She's being stubborn about taking money from me. I don't think she'd be living in my guesthouse if Siggy hadn't spooked her by having the nanny bring him Dylan without Savannah's permission."

"You guys go back a ways, don't you?"

"We dated." As much as Trent liked JT, he wasn't about to open up about his complicated relationship with his brother's widow.

But that didn't stop JT from asking. "And yet she married your brother?"

"Yeah." Trent would've liked to leave it at that, but JT was staring at him and didn't appear as if he was going to take Trent's brief response as a hint to drop it. "She wanted family. Kids. You know."

"Seems pretty cold of her to take up with your brother after you two stopped seeing each other."

Trent would never describe Savannah as cold. "I don't know that she chose my brother to spite me. She'd always liked Rafe. And she got pregnant."

None of this showed Savannah in a flattering light, which didn't strike Trent as being fair. And yet, wasn't this exactly what he'd been thinking about her for the last year and a half? What was with his sudden urge to defend her?

"She's been through a lot," he concluded.

"She's pretty lucky to have you." JT's demeanor went from curious to brisk and businesslike. "So it sounds like the problem you're facing is this. Her son owns a majority share of a company that's going under and she has no way of selling the shares and raising the money she needs to pay off her husband's debts."

"You summed it up perfectly."

"But if I know you," JT said with a smile, "you've plotted half a dozen ways to get her out of her predicament."

"Actually, I've only come up with three. And I wanted to run them by you to see which you think might work out the best."

"Fire away."

Seven

Courtney Day's unflappable smile concealed Savannah's disappointment as she carried a glass of wine across Trent's enormous living room to Scarlett Fontaine. All afternoon Savannah had been alternately nervous and giddy about the upcoming alone time with Trent. Instead of an intimate dinner between just the two of them, Trent had shown up a half hour late with Logan Wolfe and his wife in tow. To hide her disappointment, Savannah had donned her alter ego and was playing the perfect hostess, the way she'd done a hundred times as Rafe's wife.

"It's really nice to meet you," Savannah said, in awe of Scarlett's beauty. She'd seen her dozens of times on TV, but the real woman was so much more charismatic. "I'm a huge fan."

"Ditto." Scarlett gave a little laugh at Savannah's expression. "What? You don't think I know who you are? I'll have you know *Loving New York* has been a total obsession of mine for years. I thought you were great on it."

"Thanks. It was an interesting three years."

"Do you miss it?"

"Sometimes. I thought about getting back into acting, but I'm not sure LA or New York is where I want to be." Savannah recognized she might not have a choice.

"I totally understand where you're coming from. I'm lucky I've been able to coordinate my filming schedule so I only have to be in LA once a week. It's been a bit of a challenge balancing the management of Fontaine Richesse with my acting career. Fortunately I have an amazing husband who supports me one hundred percent." Scarlett shot a heated glance toward the two men standing out on the terrace.

"Fontaine Richesse? You mean the hotel on the Strip?" Savannah's admiration for the woman went up several degrees. "You manage that and have an acting career?"

Scarlett's husky laugh echoed around the two-story living space. "I have excellent people in place to help me with the hotel, and my sister Violet is always on call if something comes up when I'm not around."

"Still." Savannah was feeling woefully inadequate. What had she done in the last year and a half? "I'm feeling overwhelmed and I'm not even working at the moment."

"But you have a baby to take care of, and you just lost your husband. Plus from what Logan tells me, the company your son inherited is having all sorts of problems."

Savannah wasn't surprised Scarlett knew some of her background. After all, Logan was helping Trent. Obviously the couple would have talked on their way here, and Logan would've explained what the meeting was about.

"It's a bit of a mess," Savannah agreed. "I don't know what I'd do if Trent hadn't agreed to help me."

"How long have you two known each other?"

"My aunt is his father's housekeeper. I moved in with her when I was eleven."

"So you grew up with him?"

"Sort of. It's weird living in someone else's house and being separated by the whole employer/employee thing. I probably shouldn't have gotten to know Trent and his siblings as well as I did."

"Had you always been in love with his brother?"

"No." It was an awkward situation to try to explain. "Actually, Trent and I dated for a few years while I was living in New York." Perhaps *dated* was not quite the right term for what they had done. She knew he'd seen other women when they were apart. But every time they got together, he'd made her feel like she was his only one.

Scarlett's eyes widened a little at Savannah's confession. "That explains a lot. You sure know how to make things complicated."

"I don't try to complicate things," Savannah said, "but they often seem to end up that way. I'm not very good at getting what I want."

"Maybe you just don't believe that you deserve to get it."

"You might be right." She'd never really believed that Trent would give up his bachelor ways for her. And that had kept her from fully committing to their relationship, as well. "I've always shied away from disappointment. It's kept me from going after what's really important."

"It's not too late."

"No, I suppose it's not." But she was lying.

Savannah glanced in Trent's direction once again. She'd really blown it with him when she'd agreed to marry his brother. If she'd chosen any other man, Trent might have been willing to give their relationship another chance. But Trent's resentment of his brother ran deep and her desperate decision had built an insurmountable wall between them. There was no going back from that.

Trent might be willing to help her, but that was because he had his own agenda when it came to West Coast

Records. The chemistry between them might be as hot as ever, but in her heart she knew what had happened in his office last week and had almost happened today was more about looking backward than moving forward.

"I was planning on moving to Tennessee once I found someone to run West Coast Records," Savannah said. "But lately I'm not sure I belong there or that I belong anywhere." Her gaze drifted toward Trent.

"You should give Las Vegas a try. If you're still interested in acting, it's a short plane ride to LA."

"When I left New York, I intended to continue acting, but then Rafe and I got involved and he didn't want his wife to work."

"Do you have an agent?"

Savannah shook her head. "I had one in New York, but we parted ways when I moved to LA. I wasn't sure if I wanted to work in film or TV and figured I would do something about representation once I got to there. Only... things happened and I never did."

"I'll put you in touch with a couple agents I know. Either one would be great to represent you."

"Thank you."

To her surprise, she felt a flutter of excitement in her chest. She'd connected working as an actress with living in LA. Savannah had opened her eyes to other possibilities. If she worked in film, she might go on location anywhere in the world. Lots of actresses balanced children and careers. No reason why she couldn't.

"I'll bet Trent would like it if you stuck around Las Vegas."

"Once we get things sorted out with the company, I'm not sure he'll notice if I stick around or not." But was she being honest with herself or was this another attempt to protect herself from getting hurt again?

"You don't believe that." Scarlett regarded her somberly.

"When my sisters got involved with JT and Ashton, I knew before anyone else that they belonged together. I get the same vibe when I look at you and Trent."

Savannah shook her head. "You've seen us together for less than a minute. How could you possibly tell anything about our relationship?"

"I've known Trent for two years, and Logan and I have been to his club a lot. I've never seen him look at any woman the way he looks at you."

Afraid of how much she wanted to believe Scarlett, Savannah gave a little laugh but decided not to argue. It didn't really matter how Trent looked at her. Two years ago, he hadn't wanted a future with her. In the meantime, she'd married his brother and given birth to Dylan. Trent might desire her—and that's probably what Scarlett was picking up on—but he most certainly was not going to give up his lifestyle and ask her to marry him.

And since that's what she wanted, wasn't she a fool to let herself get caught up in him once more? She needed to move out. That meant she had to stop burying her head in the sand, get a job and a place for her and Dylan to live.

"I'm really glad I met you," Savannah said. "I need to get back to work, and I'm thinking the sooner the better."

"I'm heading to LA in a couple of days. If you'd like to come along, I'd be happy to introduce you to some friends who could get you started on the right path."

Maybe by the time she got herself reestablished in LA the situation with Siggy would be less stressful. And if not, a new source of income meant she could afford to fight him and keep her son safe.

Savannah smiled at Scarlett in appreciation. "That would be terrific."

Trent glanced over his shoulder and saw the two women engrossed in their conversation. "You were right," he told

Logan, delighting at the rare smile curving Savannah's beautiful lips. "Savannah looks a lot more relaxed."

"My wife is like that. She has a knack for making people feel better. And if Savannah wants to go back to acting, Scarlett can help her out. She has some great contacts in Hollywood."

That made Trent frown. He hadn't considered that Savannah might return to LA so soon. It had only been a week since Siggy had pulled his stunt, and there was no reason to think he wouldn't try something equally despicable if Savannah and Dylan returned to LA.

His concern grew over dinner as Scarlett and Savannah chatted about the industry. It was apparent that his sister-in-law intended to return to work.

The two couples lingered over the meal and then moved outside for dessert. Trent hadn't done a lot of this sort of entertaining. A low-key evening with another couple was a nice change from the sort of parties he usually threw here. Between the game room in the upstairs loft that overlooked the living room and the big backyard with the pool, slide and outdoor movie screen, he usually hosted groups that liked to dance, drink and get a little crazy.

Savannah had taken a couple minutes as everyone moved outside to go check on her son. She came back with the baby monitor and explained she'd sent Rhoda home. The conversation between the women changed then to talk of babies and future plans for children.

Scarlett patted her husband's knee and shot him a sly smile. "We've decided to put off having children for at least another year. He's not happy about it, but I don't think my husband has any idea how demanding I'm going to get when I'm pregnant."

"It can't possibly be any worse than you are right now." Logan's words didn't match the tenderness in his eyes as he gazed at his gorgeous wife.

"Then you're in for a rude awakening. Violet was the sweetest thing until she got pregnant with Rowan. Poor JT was beside himself." Scarlett rolled her eyes in dramatic fashion.

"Beside himself with joy, maybe." Trent recalled JT being nothing but thrilled in the months leading up to becoming a father. He laughed at the sharp look Scarlett shot at him. "And Logan will be no different."

"You're not helping," Scarlett said, turning to Savannah. "I suppose you're going to side with them, too."

"I used to want a big family," Savannah said, not letting her gaze stray anywhere near Trent. "But now that I have Dylan, I'm content."

Trent felt an awkward *whump* in his chest. If he hadn't known better, he would've thought it was his heart breaking. Savannah was trying hard to spin her situation into something positive, but Trent had known her a long time and didn't believe for one minute that she would give up on her dreams unless they'd been crushed by disappointment.

"Melody and I are your family, too," he reminded her.

"I haven't forgotten. Which is why I've decided not to move to Tennessee."

"That's great."

"I'm glad you're okay with it," Savannah said, giving him a weak smile. "And if I can swing a few acting jobs in LA, I can afford a little house for Dylan and me here."

She made it sound as if she was intended to move out as soon as possible. "No need to rush. You can stay here as long as you want."

"I appreciate your generosity, but I think I've relied on you far too much already."

How did he explain to her that he liked it when she relied on him? When he came to her rescue she always gazed at him as if he was larger than life. In her eyes he was a hero, not the troublemaker everyone had to watch out for.

Trent kept an eye on the clock as the evening wound down. He'd hoped for some alone time with Savannah before she turned in, but the hour grew later and later. At long last, Scarlett patted her husband on the knee.

"I think you mentioned needing to get some more work done this evening," Scarlett said, standing up. "A security expert's job is never done."

"I think everyone here can sympathize," Trent said, trying to keep his relief from showing as everyone made their way to the foyer. "All of us have been known to work some pretty unorthodox hours."

"Thanks for the invite," Logan said. "Next time, let's do it at our house."

The two men shook hands while the women hugged. Minutes later, Trent and Savannah stood alone in his empty house. He wasted no time pulling her into his arms and kissing her. From her passionate response, she'd been feeling the same sensual pull. Her fingers tugged his shirt free from his pants and dived beneath the hem.

He groaned at the pleasure of her palms skating along his bare back. Lifting her into his arms, he made for the guesthouse, instinctively knowing she would want to be nearby if Dylan needed her. His frantic heartbeat made it hard for him to take things slow, but as he lowered her feet to the floor beside her bed, he sucked in a calming breath, pushed her out to arm's length and closed his eyes.

"Tonight we're going to take our time," he said, opening his eyes and peering at her.

She was flushed, her expression slightly dazed. She backed away and put her hands to her cheeks for a moment. Trent thought for sure she'd come to her senses. To his relief, instead of ordering him to leave her room, she stripped her asymmetrical tank over her head and cast it aside. Standing before him in a nude bra and khaki leggings, she threw her hands wide as if in surrender.

"I don't know if I can."

Trent loosened the buttons on his shirt and sent it sailing to join her top on the floor. "We have the rest of the evening to get it right."

Her pale eyebrows rose. "That's a relief, because I'm pretty sure we're seriously out of practice." She stuck her thumb inside the elastic waistband of her leggings and stretched them away from her body. "Would you like me to take these off, or do you want to do the honors?"

Trent's mouth went dry. He stepped into her space and bracketed her waist just above the material. Her smooth skin was warm beneath his palms. Moving with slow deliberation, he dipped his fingertips below her waistband. His hands rode her curves downward, taking her leggings with them. She was trembling as he helped her step out of the snug pants.

While she unhooked her bra and slipped it free, he dropped a kiss on her stomach. Eager to revisit every inch of her, he trailed his fingertips from her instep to her knee. Her breath grew shallow, uneven. She set her hands on his shoulders and leaned on him for support as her legs shook. Still kneeling, he hooked his fingers into her cream lace panties and eased them down her thighs.

"I don't know how much more of this I can take," she gasped as his mouth grazed down from her belly button.

"Let's see about that, shall we?"

Getting to his feet, Trent eased her back onto the bed and quickly divested himself of his clothes. She lifted onto her elbows to watch him, and he was aware of every greedy flicker in her blue gaze.

She propped one foot on the bed and waggled her knee in an enticing manner. "Come get me."

He hesitated only long enough to fish several condoms out of his pants pocket. She raised her eyebrow as he dropped them onto the nightstand.

"It's been too long," he said, setting his knee on the bed.

Her hands slid up his ribs and across his back as he covered her with his body. "Too long since what?"

"Since I've had you all to myself."

He kissed her then, stopping any further conversation and distracting her from the anguish behind what he'd said. She was all supple limbs and hot, welcoming mouth. Her tongue danced with his as they rediscovered each other with lips, teeth and hands. Nibbling his way down her neck, he found the sensitive spot made her writhe. Last time in his office, he'd been denied her beautiful breasts. He intended to make up for that.

A breathy moan broke from her lips as he swirled his tongue around her breast, making her back arch. She dug her fingers into his shoulders. Knowing exactly what she liked, he moistened her hard nipple and released a puff of air across the sensitive nub. Once again he was rewarded as her hips lifted. Her every moan, gasp and cry caressed his senses, the familiarity erasing their almost two-year estrangement.

Where once she'd been flawless, her body had now gained character. Motherhood had brought changes that he found vastly intriguing. He appreciated how her stretch marks testified to her maturity. And the extra weight she carried on her hips and butt lent her figure a lushness that enhanced her sensuality.

She protested when his fingers trailed across a stretch mark on her belly. "Motherhood isn't kind to a woman's body."

He resisted when she tried bringing his hand back to her breast. "You are more beautiful than ever."

"Next you'll be telling me it's okay that I packed on the pounds."

"You've hardly done that. And I love every inch of you. I always have."

He slid his shoulders between her thighs and filled his palms with her round backside. Her whole body trembled as he grazed his lips along the hollow beside her hipbone, and a ragged laugh escaped her.

It had been too long. Far too long. He licked her then. Her hips bucked in reaction, so he put his palm flat on her belly to keep her still. Her trembling increased as he tasted her excitement and found her ready for him. He flicked his tongue the way she liked and she moaned. At the sound he smiled. Then, he hummed against her, knowing it made her crazy.

"Yes!"

He needed her to remember how it was between them. To be the only man she thought of. Pulling out every trick in the book, he made love to her with his mouth, hands and voice.

"I want to hear that noise again," he said, looking up to watch her expression.

"What noise?" She was almost too breathless to be understood.

"The one you make when I do this." He repeated his action and wrenched a soft yelp from her throat. "Yes," he purred, "just like that."

In the past, he'd utilized his expertise to bring her to the edge of orgasm and keep her there. Once, he'd even drawn this out for an hour. But tonight she came the instant he slid one finger inside her. With her lips parted on a strangled cry, her body bowed. The length and intensity of her climax caught him by surprise.

"Words cannot describe how amazing you are at that." A single tear slipped down the side of her face, and she brushed it away with the back of her hand before extending her arms to him. "Come up here and kiss me."

He obliged, but kept the contact light and sweet despite

the temptation of her parted lips and the fingers she'd tunneled through his hair.

"I'm going to return the favor, I promise," she said, grasping his bicep with surprising force. "As soon as I've recovered."

"Later."

Trent reached to the nightstand and after two futile attempts managed to grab a condom with his shaking fingers. He caught the wrapper between his teeth and carefully tore it open. Hollowed out by the longing to be inside her, he sheathed himself in the protection and suckled her breasts as he settled between her thighs.

If the tantalizing movement of her hands down his body was intended to drive him mad, it worked. And based on the look she cast from beneath her lashes, she knew just how well. He didn't care. His level of arousal was almost painful as she wrapped her long fingers around him. A groan tore from his throat.

Fighting the urge to drive into her heat, he unclenched his teeth long enough to gasp, "I promised we'd take our time." He pulled her hand away from his erection. "I'm too close for much of that."

"Not close enough." Her pout made him smile.

Their lips came together again. The kisses were slow and sweet, a blending of tongue and breath. The mood shifted from frantic hunger to wrenching emotion. It was easy to forget the distance and hurt that had separated them.

Savannah slid the sole of her foot over Trent's muscled calf and let her hands roam over his chiseled torso. Each rise and dip of his glorious body was imprinted on her memory, but the real thing was so much better.

With her body building slowly toward another mind-blowing orgasm, Savannah stormed Trent's mouth with her tongue and nipped at his lower lip. She rocked against him until he flexed his fingers on her hip and shuddered. His erection lay trapped against her belly, hot and eager for her. Her hands dived between them and stroked him.

"I can't wait another second. I need you inside me."

"I need that, too." His voice rasped against her neck. "It's been too long."

When he shifted over her, she spread her legs and lifted her hips. Her head fell back and her breath caught as he positioned himself and thrust.

Stars exploded behind her eyes. "Magic," she murmured, closing her eyes to glory in how her body stretched and adapted to accommodate him. The fit was always perfect. He was her match in this.

"How I've missed this." Trent seized her mouth and began to move.

It wasn't like the night in his office when they'd both been hungry and frantic. This time Trent stared into her eyes and laced his fingers with hers. The emotion shading his expression was so raw it threatened to rip her heart out. Savannah wanted to turn aside and not get sucked into the whirlpool of longing for things that could never be.

Trent would never want more than this. She'd learned to accept that, but at moments like these when he gave her everything he was, her foolish heart hoped that maybe this time it would be different. Shutting the door on such thoughts, she closed her eyes and let her other senses take over.

His ragged breath fanned her hot skin as he kissed her shoulder. They were both close. She recognized the tension in his muscles and the rising intensity of his low murmurings. He wanted her to come and wouldn't let himself go until she did. Her climax waited, just out of sight. She was holding back, unwilling to reach for her pleasure, wanting to prolong the intimacy of the moment just a little while longer.

But her body wasn't about to be controlled. The first sharp bite of her orgasm stopped her breath. Her eyes snapped open. She caught Trent's satisfied smile as he watched her. The sight of him was enough to send her over the edge. Pleasure reared up and slapped her hard. Savannah exploded.

Trent's muted exclamation came a second later. Savannah had a moment to appreciate that he'd kept his voice down in consideration of Dylan sleeping in the room next door before a second wave of pleasure rolled through her.

She was sunk. The pressure in her chest told her that what had happened tonight had opened a rift in her defenses she'd be helpless to patch. It would take time and space to heal, and she wasn't sure she had the willpower to let either do its work.

In the aftermath of their lovemaking, Trent rolled over so that she was lying on top of him. He sent his fingertips skating along her spine in long, soothing caresses. She loved this part. The moments when Trent's guard was still down and she could talk to him about anything. But tonight she had trouble thinking of a subject that wouldn't lead to trouble.

Trent was the first to speak. "I'm sorry I was so angry with you for marrying Rafe."

"We'd been broken up for months. And it had ended so badly. But I shouldn't have started seeing Rafe."

"I couldn't believe how fast you got over me."

She was surprised by his admission. "I didn't get over you." She frowned. "You were the one who didn't want me."

"That's not true."

Trent shifted them until they lay on their sides facing each other, legs tangled to maintain their connection. Savannah put her head on the pillow while he caressed her cheek. Her heart thumped erratically as she took in his somber expression.

"You told me you had no interest in getting married and having children," she reminded him.

"That didn't mean I didn't want you. I just didn't want the same things you did." He kissed her forehead. "You were the one who decided to end our relationship. Not me."

Savannah remembered how she'd ached the day she'd told him they were done. "I guess in the end, it doesn't matter which of us called it quits. The fact is, we wanted different things and neither of us would be happy long term."

"I don't believe that's true. I would've been happy with you." The simple words sounded as if they came straight from his heart.

"But you didn't want…" *Children. Marriage.*

"I felt backed into a corner by your expectations."

"By my…?" She was horrified. If she could have put her dreams aside and been satisfied to just love Trent, would they have stayed together? She grew lightheaded at the thought of all the heartache she could've avoided. "How is that possible? I never put pressure on you."

"No, you didn't. At least not intentionally. But you had such an idealistic view of how you wanted your life to be." His fingers toyed with a strand of her hair, tickling her shoulder. "Were you happy with my brother?"

"Our marriage was more about an understanding than passion." She read no tension or hostility in his body as his hands played over her skin with lazy contentment. "He didn't love me."

"Did you love him?"

"Not the way a wife should. As I said, we both went in with our cards on the table. He wanted Dylan to carry on your father's dynasty." She shifted her head and kissed Trent's bare shoulder.

"And you were okay with that?"

"I was scared and alone and pregnant. I didn't know what I was going to do." Remembering that time, Savannah winced. That woman had been forlorn and in desperate need of saving. "I auditioned for anything that came along, but no one wanted to hire a woman who was three months pregnant. And I was sick. All the time. They talk about morning sickness. I had all-day sickness."

"I'm sorry it was such a hard time for you. And I'm glad my brother was there to help."

Rescuing her had always been Trent's thing. She could hear the regret in his voice and lifted her head to gaze into his eyes.

"He would have loved to hear you say that."

Trent scowled and gave her hair a fond tug. "You always see the best in people." He sounded like a weary big brother. "That's what gets you into trouble."

"I know you and Rafe never got along because of how your father favored him, but he wasn't a villain." Savannah wasn't sure why she needed Trent to recognize an alternate view of his brother. "He was as hurt and frustrated as you were. Siggy dumped the entire burden of his expectations and the weight of West Coast Records' legacy on Rafe. I'm not sure you realize how lucky you were to escape."

From his closed expression, she could tell he didn't believe her.

"Rafe wanted the business and he got it."

One thing marrying Rafe had done was give her a front-row seat to the dysfunction of the Caldwell household. During the short months she'd been Rafe's wife, she'd learned how much he'd been bothered by the rivalry Siggy had created.

"You're right, but he didn't want to be in it alone. He recognized that he needed your ability to scout new talent and Melody's talents as a songwriter and producer. Siggy ruined his dream as much as he destroyed yours."

"If you're trying to convince me to like my brother, you're wasting your time."

"It's not about you liking Rafe." Savannah laid her cheek against his chest once more. "It's about how the bitterness you carry for him keeps you stuck in the past."

If Trent understood that Rafe had been Siggy's tool, he might one day release some of the resentment that made him keep people at a distance. Maybe he'd stop running from love.

From her.

From being a family with her and Dylan.

Hopelessness swept over her. But could Trent ever see her son as anything other than his brother's child? And what would happen if he learned the truth? Would he hate her or could he understand why she'd chosen not to tell him?

Savannah kissed Trent, letting her love for him ignite her passion once more. His ardent response pushed her anxiety to the far reaches of her mind. She had time to sort everything out. Now all she wanted to concentrate on was this moment and this man.

Eight

"It's so good to see you," Savannah said, hugging her sister-in-law.

Because of Melody's touring schedule, Savannah hadn't seen her since Rafe's funeral. For the past year she'd been traveling around the country opening for Nate Tucker and his band. Melody had lost weight but gained a little rock 'n' roll flair. Dressed all in black, she wore a flared leather skirt and lacy T-shirt with ankle boots. Formerly happy to write songs and stay in the background, she'd resisted when Nate set out to convince her to open for his band. But the singer/songwriter/producer was nothing if not persistent when he recognized talent—in addition to being part owner of Club T's, Nate had started his own record label and had a recording studio downtown.

"I'm excited to be in Las Vegas and can't wait to get into the studio to put the finishing touches on my first album."

"When do I get to hear some of it?"

"Soon," Melody promised, her gaze darting to one side.

"I wrote a couple more songs that I want to get into the studio and record. After that I'll go through what I have and see what might work for the album."

"I'm sure they're going to be fantastic. All of them."

"Where's my nephew?" Melody asked. "I thought after what my father did you'd have a hard time letting him out of your sight."

"Trent has him in the pool." Savannah kept her expression as neutral as possible beneath Melody's wide-eyed regard. "He's teaching him how to swim, if you can believe it."

"I can't believe you're here," Melody said. "At Rafe's funeral, you and Trent were on opposite sides of the room from each other the entire day. What changed?"

"Your brother and I have sort of come to an understanding. I can thank your father for that. I wouldn't be here if there wasn't trouble with West Coast Records. And if Siggy hadn't threatened me with taking Dylan away."

"It seems like there's more going on here than just a simple understanding." Melody put special emphasis on the last word and gave Savannah a knowing look. "I mean, you're living with him."

"In the guesthouse," Savannah explained. "And you're right—there's more going on. Rafe's and my finances were really bad. I'm almost a million dollars in debt. And until I'm working again, I have no income to live on."

"What are you going to do?"

"My plan is to go to LA tomorrow with Scarlett Fontaine. Thanks to her, I've set up three interviews with agents."

"Who's watching Dylan while you're interviewing?"

"I'm leaving him with Trent's housekeeper. She's been terrific."

"Oh, good. Since you're leaving him here, then I can pitch in. I need a little practice taking care of a baby."

Savannah stared at Melody in confused silence, unsure if she should voice the first thing that popped into her mind. "I'd love for you to spend some time with Dylan. But why do you need practice?"

"I'm pregnant." Melody offered up a tremulous smile. "Yikes."

"That's great. I'm so happy for you and Kyle."

"Well, you can be happy for me."

From the tenor of Melody's response, Savannah sensed not all was well. "Kyle isn't happy? How is that possible? He adores you."

"I haven't told him yet."

Savannah closed her eyes briefly, recalling the confusing muddle of uncertainty and joy when she realized she was pregnant.

"You know he's going to be great about this."

"I don't know that. We haven't been together that long and haven't talked about marriage. I don't know where he stands on the whole kid thing."

"How far along are you?"

"Barely six weeks. I took a long weekend off from the tour and flew to LA for his birthday. It was a fantastic three days." Her eyes glowed with heartbreaking fondness for several seconds before dimming. "And then Nate called to say that they'd added an extra two weeks to the tour and Kyle got so mad. He complained about how much time we'd been apart and told me to quit. We had a huge fight." She trailed off, looking miserable.

"But he was all for it. He's been one hundred percent behind your career from the very beginning."

Melody gave a little shrug. "I don't think either one of us realized how hard it was going to be to be apart." She sat down and put her hands in her lap. "He's been so distant these last few months. I don't know what's gotten into him. I'm worried he doesn't love me anymore."

"That's impossible. I've seen you two together. He adores you."

Melody pressed her lips together, shifted on the couch and heaved a huge sigh. "A month ago, he practically accused me of cheating on him with Hunter Graves."

Savannah understood why Kyle might be worried. "Because of that photo of the two of you holding hands as you left that New York club?" She'd wondered what was up after seeing the image, even though she knew without a doubt that Melody would never risk her relationship with Kyle. "Okay, I'm sorry, but I could see where he might have gotten the impression that you and Hunter were together."

"But we're just friends. Nothing more. It was a madhouse as we left. Hunter grabbed my hand so we wouldn't be separated on the way to the car."

"You dated him on and off for a year and a half before you and Kyle got together."

In fact, at one point Melody had tried to use Kyle to make Hunter jealous. The plan had backfired, but in the best way possible. The ruse had awakened Kyle's true feelings for Melody and made her realize the man she was meant to be with had been right under her nose.

"And I was miserable," Melody said. "Why would Kyle think I would go back to that?"

"Maybe you should talk to Kyle about all this. Tell him how you feel."

Given her own situation, Savannah wasn't the best person to be offering relationship advice, but she felt compelled to say something that might ease her friend's mind.

"I don't know, but we haven't spoken more than a half-dozen times in the last three months."

And Savannah knew that wasn't like them. "You need to talk to him about this."

"I will. I promise. But I really need to get the album finished first."

"How long do you think that's going to take?"

Melody had been living with Kyle three months before going on tour with Nate. They'd been dating for six months before she moved in with him. And before that, they'd known each other and been friends since high school. Kyle had been Trent's best friend since they'd met freshman year, and Savannah had known Kyle from all the times he'd hung out with Trent. She hadn't been surprised when Melody and Kyle finally got together.

Melody looked uncomfortable. "I don't know."

"The longer you wait, the worse it's going to be." Since Rafe's death, at least once a day Savannah regretted not telling Trent the truth about Dylan when she first learned she was pregnant. She'd kept quiet because she'd been afraid to get hurt again. Which had been silly, because she'd lost Trent anyway.

"You're right. But if I go to LA and tell him, I'll know how he reacts. If I stay here and finish the album, I can pretend for a while that when he finds out he's going to be thrilled."

Melody was operating with the same faulty logic Savannah had used. It had backfired for her; she could only hope that the same didn't happen to her good friend.

"He is going to be thrilled," Savannah assured her, trusting that truth. "He loves you."

"Sometimes love isn't enough." Melody stared at her hands.

Savannah's voice rang with conviction. "And sometimes it's all you need."

Their conversation was interrupted by the appearance of Trent and Dylan, with Murphy trotting along beside them. As always when Savannah saw father and son together, her heart gave a big bump.

"How'd his swimming lesson go?" she asked, holding her arms out for Dylan's towel-wrapped body.

Trent showed no inclination to give up Dylan. "He's already learned how to hold his breath when he goes underwater." He leaned forward to kiss Melody on the cheek. "It's good to see you."

"It's good to see you, too." She looked a little startled by her brother's sunny demeanor and shot a sidelong glance in Savannah's direction. "I hope it's okay if I crash here for a couple weeks while I finish my album. Unless it's too crowded?"

"I have plenty of room. When is Kyle coming? I'll make a couple tee times to get him out of your hair."

"He's not going to come this trip." Melody made a stab at looking undisturbed, but couldn't quite pull it off.

Her brother frowned. "Why not?"

Savannah decided it might be easier for Melody to have this conversation with her brother if they were alone. "I'm going to change Dylan."

With Trent focused on his sister, Savannah had an easy time making her escape. She dressed her son in dry clothes and wondered what Trent would make of his sister's situation. He had demonstrated the same sort of protectiveness with Savannah as he had with Melody. Especially when it came to her relationship with his best friend.

While he and Kyle had always been the best of friends, Trent hadn't been wild about Melody dating him. But since she was a strong-minded woman in her twenties, with a successful career and clear idea of whom she was getting involved with, Trent's warnings had been unwelcome.

To distract herself from what was going on in the main house, Savannah took stock of her limited wardrobe and began planning for the upcoming interviews in LA. She was still operating with the same suitcase of clothes she'd brought to Las Vegas the first time. While preparing to sell the house, she'd packed up the bulk of her wardrobe and put it in storage with the idea that she would sort through it as soon as she'd gotten settled.

Dylan's swim had taken the edge off his energy, and he was content to sit on the floor in her closet and play with his musical bear. By pushing on the bear's right paw, he was able to scroll through the playlist until he found his favorite song. Then he waved his hands and sang along in his cute baby way while Murphy barked and growled at the noisy toy.

"Why am I not surprised that he's musical." Trent's voice came from the doorway. "I hope you don't mind that I let myself in."

"I don't mind. This is your house. And that's why I've been thinking that maybe Dylan and I should move out."

"Move out? Why?"

"Melody needs the peace and quiet of the guesthouse in order to finish her album."

"Where are you thinking about going?"

"I thought something nearby." She paused. "Or LA."

Trent's eyebrows crashed together. "Have you forgotten the reason you moved in here in the first place?"

"I haven't forgotten."

Trent thought she'd come to Las Vegas to keep Dylan safe, but that wasn't the only reason. She'd foolishly hoped that once Trent spent time with her and Dylan that he'd miraculously decide that being a family with them was all he wanted.

"But things are different now," she continued. "And depending on how my auditions go in the next couple days, I might need to be closer to make the most of the opportunities."

"That's not the tune you were singing two days ago, and don't give me the excuse about Melody. You knew she was coming. Why the sudden change of heart?"

Savannah couldn't explain the real reason to him: the

awkwardness of living in his guesthouse and wanting to be more than just a convenient fling. Falling in love with him all over again wasn't good for either of them. For a second, Savannah's chest became tight and her lungs refused to work. She searched for calm.

It was good for Dylan that she and Trent were getting along, but keeping things friendly and uncomplicated would be best. In addition, she needed to stop relying on Trent to save her and stand on her own two feet.

"I guess it comes down to not having a plan and not having much in the way of options because of my financial situation. What Siggy did spooked me. I reacted before thinking everything through."

"There's no reason to believe he won't try something again."

"That's why I'm leaving Dylan here while I meet with agents. I know he'll be safe with you."

"I don't understand why you're so determined to get back to work. You're more than welcome to stay here as long as you want."

"That's generous of you, but I really need to move forward with my life." And if it wasn't going to be with Trent, then she needed to put some distance between them as soon as possible. "And speaking of Melody, have you spoken with her about what's going on between her and Kyle?"

"She said they're having a little trouble." He ran his hand through his hair and his mouth tensed. "She warned me to leave things alone and mind my business."

"She's right. Melody's a big girl. She doesn't need her brother messing in her love life."

"So what am I supposed to do? Sit by and let her be miserable?"

"Why don't you focus on what we're going to do about West Coast Records and let Melody sort out her own problems? If she wants you to step in, she'll say so."

"Fine. I found a guy who can take over running the company. I'll text you his number so you can meet with him while you're in LA. I think you'll like him."

"That's wonderful. I'll look forward to talking with him. And if I want to hire him, do you have a plan for how to get him past Siggy and Gerry?"

"If things go the way I think they will, you won't have to."

Savannah shook her head. "Will it do me any good to ask you what you have planned?"

"Grab dinner with him at Cuts Beverly Hills."

"So your father will get wind of the meeting?"

"Exactly. The restaurant's practically in his backyard, and he's sure to hear if you show up."

"And then what? We sit around and wait?"

"If I know my father, we won't have to wait for long."

Pushing a stroller that contained his sleepy nephew, Trent sauntered into the recording studio of Nate Tucker's indie label, Ugly Trout Records. Since Savannah had left for LA this morning, Trent had been feeling edgy and out of sorts. While he knew it was important to her that she get back to work, he couldn't help but feel as if it was a huge mistake for her to think about returning to LA. After what had happened the week before, he'd assumed she would hide out in Las Vegas with him at least until they figured out how to handle Siggy. Trent's intention was to untangle Savannah from his father's company. Today, he was going to present to Nate an idea for how to go about that.

The receptionist directed Trent to studio B, where Melody and Nate were doing some recording for her album. When Trent entered the studio's production booth, Nate's gaze flicked over his two visitors before returning to Melody.

Trent leaned against the wall and listened to his sister.

Accompanied by a guy in a knit cap playing the guitar, she sat at an electric piano, her strong, pure voice pouring out a song of heartbreaking angst. The uncomplicated arrangement allowed her songwriting to shine. Trent felt the hairs rise on the back of his neck at the emotion resonating through the lyrics. What was going on with his baby sister?

As she finished the song, Nate blew out a breath and rocked back in his chair. "She sounds amazing. This album is going to be a knockout."

A little dazed, Trent nodded. "It sure sounds like it."

Although Trent had seen his sister perform in several large venues, he continued to be amazed at her talent. Unlike Trent, who'd dabbled a bit here and there, Melody had embraced her musical side. As soon as she could pick up a violin, she'd started taking lessons. At eight, she'd taught herself how to play the piano and had begun composing silly little songs that her friends sang all the time, driving her two older brothers mad.

All this had ended one day when she was ten. Melody had written her first serious piece, and Trent had suggested that she record it. What was the point of having access to your very own recording studio and not using it? Trent had set up a one-hour session as a surprise for her, suspecting that if he told her in advance she'd never go through with it.

As it was, encouraged by Trent's confidence in her, she'd reluctantly agreed to record her song. She'd been struggling with the start of it when their father walked in. Or perhaps *stormed in* was a better description. Siggy had been furious at what Trent had done. He didn't want the expensive studio time wasted on his daughter. Melody had been so upset she never finished recording the song and stopped singing altogether.

From that point forward, she concentrated solely on her

violin and piano, in her own way trying to please her father, just as Rafe did. Trent had gone the complete opposite direction, aggravating his father at every turn.

"Nate," Melody said from the booth, "can you play the song back so I can hear it?"

"Sure." Nate cued the song before turning to Trent. "She's such a perfectionist. I think she's recorded fifty songs."

"And I'm sure each one is better than the last. She just doesn't think she's any good. We have our father to thank for that."

Dylan was awake, his eyes bright as he listened to Melody's song. Trent unbuckled him from the stroller and lifted him so he could see his aunt. She grinned and waved. Dylan blew her a kiss and wiggled in Trent's arms.

"I've told her she has a month to whittle her album down to fourteen songs. I'm just afraid that in that time she's going to record a dozen more."

"A month? Is she planning on sticking around that long?"

"I don't know." But Nate looked troubled. "Originally I gave her two weeks, but she asked for more time."

"Is there something going on between her and Kyle?"

The way Nate's expression shut down told Trent everything he needed to know. "It's none of my business. And it's none of yours."

"She's my sister. He's my best friend."

"Stay out of it."

"Fine." He ground out the word, taking his frustration out on the wrong person.

In truth, Trent didn't want to meddle in his sister's love life, but focusing on her distracted him from fixating on Savannah. His initial intention to keep his distance had been shattered in his office the night she'd come to Club T's. Since then, he'd involved himself in her struggles with his father and had tumbled back into her bed and under her spell.

"Melody and I agree that the album could use a duet," Nate said, unaffected by Trent's bad mood. "What would you think about recording 'She's the One' with her?"

"Me? Sing?" He preferred to make music with a guitar.

"Melody said you're pretty good."

Trent felt his face grow warm. Singing was something he enjoyed doing in the privacy of his car or shower. "I'm not professionally trained."

"You think I am? I'm just a poor kid from North Dakota who happens to like playing in a band."

Nate might be from North Dakota and he might have grown up without money, but his talent and ambition as a singer, songwriter and producer made his statement laughable.

"I'll sing," Trent said, surprising himself. "As long as you promise not to put it on the album."

"Let's record it and see how it goes."

"She'd be much better off doing a duet with you. She needs someone established to kick-start the album so she can make a pile of dough."

"You know she'd really love to put the album up for free, right?"

Trent wasn't surprised. Melody had always been about the art, not the money. "But you talked her out of that, I hope."

"Not exactly. She's pretty adamant, and she's making enough money from touring and her songwriting royalties not to worry about a paycheck."

"But to give it away?" As a businessman, the idea pained him.

"I'll see how she feels once the whole album is done. In the meantime..." Nate leaned forward and pushed the button that would let him be heard in the recording booth.

"Trent is here and he's agreed to record 'She's the One' with you."

Trent groaned as his sister's face lit up with a broad smile. "After I do this, we have some business to discuss," he said to Nate.

"Is something going on with the club?"

"Club T's is doing great. This matter is as much personal as it is business."

Nate gave him a curious look. "Does it have something to do with your sister-in-law living with you?"

Trent wasn't surprised that Nate knew about Savannah. Melody had likely mentioned that she was spending time with Dylan. "It has to do with my nephew's ownership of West Coast Records."

The two men had been friends as well as business partners for several years. Nate knew all about the family business and the difficult Siggy Caldwell.

"The shares he inherited from Rafe?"

"The company isn't doing well, and Savannah needs a large influx of cash to pay off the debt my brother stuck her with."

Nate gave a solemn nod. "Sounds like the lady needs our help. Why don't you get in there and do a little singing, and then we'll talk."

"Is Dylan okay in here with you?"

Nate took the boy and set him on his lap. "I've been dealing with temperamental artists for the last ten years. I think I can handle a one-year-old."

Grinning, Trent headed into the recording booth. The guitarist had left his instrument behind, and Trent picked it up. "Think he'd mind if I borrow this?"

"Jay's pretty cool about that sort of thing," Melody said, a half smile on her face as she watched Trent settle onto the stool and test the strings. "Are you really going to do this?"

Trent might not have been interested in a music career, but that didn't mean he couldn't have had one if he'd wanted it. Back in high school, he and a few of his buddies had formed a band and even played a few gigs. It had enhanced his bad boy mystique and got him as much action as the school's jocks. Plus, he hadn't been all banged up from playing sports.

"Nate has promised me it will never make the album," Trent said, "so I don't see what harm there is."

"We'll see." Melody gave him a sly smile. "Do you remember how it goes?"

"I think I can manage." And he started to play.

Nine

Savannah hummed as she descended in the hotel elevator, eager to head to LAX for the flight back to Las Vegas. She'd spent an eventful three days in LA and couldn't wait to get home to Dylan.

The dinner the night before at Cuts with Fred Hammer had given her a sense of what Trent was trying to provoke his father to do. It was obvious that the man knew the music business and would be a fantastic CEO for West Coast Records. The fact that he'd stolen several of the label's best artists over the last five years was a testament to his business acumen. It wasn't hard to imagine just how much it would upset Siggy to have this guy in charge of the company.

Morning sunlight poured through the lobby windows as Savannah crossed the marble floor in the direction of the exit. She was so preoccupied with thoughts of her son, she was completely caught off guard by the woman who stepped into her path.

"Savannah Caldwell."

"Yes?" She didn't recognize the brunette in snug jeans and a white T-shirt and at first thought she might have been an assistant to one of the agents she'd spoken with the day before.

The woman held out an envelope. "This is for you."

Reflexively, Savannah took it. "What is this?"

"You've been served." Without another word, the woman headed for the hotel's front entrance with the confidence of someone who had done this a thousand times before.

With her mind blank with astonishment, Savannah opened the envelope and pulled out a legal document. It didn't take her long to get the gist: contesting Rafe's bequeathing the company stock to Dylan, citing the fact that he wasn't Rafe's biological son. Every bit of optimism Savannah had gained over the last seventy-two hours vanished. Instead of leaving the hotel, she made her way to the nearest chair and dropped into it.

How was she going to explain to Trent what his father was up to? Savannah had stopped worrying about the stock and the money since she'd decided to return to acting. She would figure out a way to restructure the debt and be able to pay it off eventually. But if Trent discovered Dylan wasn't Rafe's child, he would despise her for lying to him. She needed to talk to Siggy. At least one good thing had come of this—she didn't need to fear losing her son to her father-in-law.

Savannah got in her car and headed to Siggy's house. Half of her thought she'd be denied entrance, but Siggy obviously expected her, because she was ushered right in. He was sitting behind his large desk in his office and didn't get to his feet as she entered the room.

"You're suing me?"

"I'll not have you pass off your bastard as my grandson."

Savannah resisted the urge to tell the old man that Dylan was *still* his grandson. "Dylan is Rafe's son."

"Not his biological son."

Savannah went cold. She stared Siggy down, utilizing every bit of Courtney Day she possessed to keep her panic from showing. Did he know something? Or was he guessing? She had no way of knowing without tipping her hand.

"You have no idea what you're talking about."

"I know exactly what I'm talking about. You tricked my son into marrying you and into making that boy his heir."

"That's not at all what happened." Even as she said the words, Savannah knew she was wasting her breath. "And you have no way of proving that it did."

"But I can prove that Dylan isn't Rafe's biological son. The last time he was here, I took a sample of his DNA and had it tested."

What after all this time could have prompted Siggy to do something like that? Was it because she and Trent had joined forces and were threatening his business? Her relationship with Trent while she lived in New York had never been a secret, but Siggy rarely paid attention to his son's activities. Would he have been aware that they were romantically linked? Or because he'd never viewed Savannah as being good enough to be Rafe's wife, had Siggy merely been grasping at straws?

"It doesn't matter what you can or can't prove. Rafe wanted a son and he got one."

As she spoke, Savannah began to calm down. Siggy would have a hard time contesting the will. Rafe never specified that he was leaving the stock to his biological son, and Rafe's name was on Dylan's birth certificate as his father.

"But I can drag this issue through the courts for a very long time. And when the DNA tests come back, you'll get to explain to Trent why you've been lying to him all this time." Siggy looked pleased with himself, leaving Savannah to wonder what he knew or what he thought he knew. "Meanwhile, I'll be taking back control of my company."

Now Savannah understood what Siggy was driving at. She'd helped Trent provoke his father and this was the result. And she knew Siggy was right about Trent. He'd be furious that she'd lied about Rafe being Dylan's father all this time. The only thing Savannah could do to salvage the situation was to figure out how to negotiate so Dylan's paternity never became public knowledge.

"You want your company back? I want to be out from under the debt your son created."

Siggy's eyes narrowed. "What are you offering?"

"I'll sign the stock back over to you if you'll give me the million I owe. It's Rafe's debt, not mine, and you and I both know the stock is worth way more than that." At least until the company went under.

"If we go to court, I'll get my stock and I won't have to pay you a cent."

"Are you sure? Because if you take me to court, I'll make sure everyone knows how badly the company is doing. Including the royalties not being paid to your artists and how close you are to bankruptcy. In the meantime, I've hired Fred Hammer to take over as CEO, and his first act will be to fire Gerry and have him arrested for embezzlement. Think about it."

Leaving behind an uncharacteristically speechless Siggy, Savannah made her way out of the house. Head held high, but knees wobbling with each step, she made it to the driver's seat of her car before deflating with an enormous exhale. Determined not to break down while in sight of the house, she started the car and headed down the street. Savannah turned into the first parking lot she reached, found a vacant spot and shut off the engine.

Her forehead was halfway to the steering wheel when her phone rang, startling her. Convinced Siggy was calling to level more threats at her, Savannah was tempted not to answer. But she was a mother before anything and knew she at least had to check to see who was trying to get hold of her.

To her surprise, it was Corrine Scott, the agent she'd signed with late the previous afternoon. Corrine's offer of representation was the second one she'd received, and after spending half an hour with her, Savannah knew Corrine understood her priorities as a single mom as well as her preferences for roles.

"Hi, Corrine." With the way her day was going, Savannah braced herself for bad news. "I didn't expect to hear from you so soon."

"I didn't expect to be calling you so soon either, but when we spoke yesterday you said you were interested in looking at some movie projects. I had dinner with a producer last night and pitched you to him. He just sent over a script for a part that sounds perfect for you."

"Wow," Savannah said with a startled laugh. "You work fast." Her head was spinning from the rapid seesawing of her fortune over the last hour.

"Sometimes the perfect match between client and project takes a while—other times the stars align. I know you're flying back to Vegas, but do you have time to swing by and pick up the script to start reading?"

Savannah hadn't built in enough time for all the detours she'd encountered this morning. She closed her eyes and let her head fall back.

"I'll be by in half an hour. Would you possibly have a little time to talk about something of a personal nature? I could use an impartial point of view."

If Corrine was surprised that her new client was reaching out for some personal help, she didn't show it. "Sure. I'm happy to help any way I can."

Next, Savannah called the airline and changed her flight to later in the day, and then contacted Melody to give her the new schedule. As much as Savannah wanted to hug her baby boy, she had a legal issue and needed professional help.

Her phone rang again as she drove to Corrine's office. This time it was Trent.

"Melody said you were delayed in LA because of a project."

"I'm heading to my agent's office right now."

"Sounds like things are moving for you already."

"I'm surprised that they are. I never imagined she'd be able to find me something so fast. Of course, it's only an audition." Nevertheless, Savannah was consumed by optimism.

"What time is your flight? I'll pick you up at the airport."

"You don't need to do that."

"I have a surprise for you that won't keep."

"That sounds like trouble."

Savannah couldn't imagine what he could be up to and caught herself smiling as she ended the call. However, her delight didn't last long once her gaze fell upon the envelope containing the summons that she'd tossed onto the dashboard.

She had a tricky legal problem to deal with and if Trent learned the truth, he'd never forgive her for keeping such a huge secret from him. Which brought her thoughts back to the scene at Siggy's house. Had she really told him she'd hired Fred? And threatened to turn Gerry over to the police?

Trent was going to be unhappy with her for stomping

all over his clever plan, whatever it was. He'd been cagey when she'd quizzed him about his plot to save the label. Well, if he'd wanted her to stay on script, he should have given her more information.

It was too late to worry about that now. She had a lawsuit to fight and her future to secure. On the way back to Las Vegas she would figure out what sort of explanation she should give to Trent.

Airline passengers streamed past Trent as he scanned the arrivals display to find out which carousel would contain the baggage from Savannah's flight. His timing was perfect. Her plane had touched down five minutes before. He positioned Dylan's stroller where it wouldn't be missed when Savannah came to claim their luggage.

Savannah had only been gone three days, but it felt like a lot longer. They'd spoken frequently, their exchanges revolving around Dylan and her agent while Trent's mind formed the words that would convey how much he missed her. He hadn't said any of them. His reaction to her absence disturbed him. When she'd married his brother, he'd resolved to be done with her. And for the last sixteen months, he'd believed that was the case. What a shock to discover he had been lying to himself the whole time.

The way his heart leaped when he spotted her demonstrated that he was in deeper than ever. All too aware his emotions were on display, he crouched beside the stroller and focused on unbuckling his nephew.

"Dylan, there's your mommy. Let's get you out of here so you can give her a big hug."

"Oh, I've missed you," Savannah cried, snatching Dylan into her arms and plastering noisy kisses on his cheeks. "Goodness, you've grown."

"You've only been gone three days," Trent pointed out. His arms ached to enfold her in a passionate embrace, but he shoved his hands into his pockets and welcomed her with a smile instead. "I'm sure it's impossible for him to have gotten measurably bigger in such a short period of time."

"I know." Savannah began walking in the direction of the baggage carousels. "It's just my guilt tricking me because I left him."

"He did just fine." Trent meant the words to be reassuring, but when Savannah winced, he realized he was in a no-win situation. "Even though he missed you. But Melody and I did our best to keep him entertained."

"There's no one I'd rather he spend time with than you two."

Trent decided to switch to a less emotionally charged topic. "So your trip to LA was successful. Not only did you get an agent, but also an audition for a movie role. That's great."

"It was an eventful trip. I never expected things to go so well."

"Tell me about the movie."

"It's a bigger part than I expected it to be. I skimmed through the script on the flight here. It's a romantic comedy. If I get it, I'll be the lead's best friend."

"Where is it shooting?"

The carousel began to move and the first bags appeared moments later.

"It sounds like they'll be shooting in LA." Savannah split her attention between her son and the luggage circling past them and missed Trent's frown. "I'm going back next Wednesday for the audition."

"And if you get it? Does that mean you're going back to LA?" What he wanted to know was if she was moving back permanently. Before this trip, he'd gotten the impression she wanted to make Las Vegas her home base.

"While I'm filming." She pointed to a red Tumi suit-case. "That one's mine."

Trent lifted it off the carousel while Savannah put Dylan back in his stroller. The three of them left the terminal and headed for short-term parking.

"Feels like the heat broke," Savannah commented as Trent loaded her suitcase and Dylan's stroller into the trunk of his car.

For the flight, she'd donned a sleeveless cream fit-and-flare dress with chunky gold jewelry and black-and-cream-striped pumps. The look was elegant and professional, but as she settled into the passenger seat she kicked off her high heels, unfastened her sleek updo and peeled off her jewelry. With her wavy blond hair cascading over her shoulders in luxurious disarray and her clear blue eyes sparkling as she peered at her son in the backseat, she was once again the sensual, tantalizing woman who'd haunted his dreams these last few days.

"So, I promised you a surprise," Trent said, cursing the husky rasp in his voice. He started the car's engine and turned on the stereo. The CD was ready to go—all he had to do was hit Play. "I took Dylan to the studio while Melody was recording."

Savannah's smile turned eager. "Am I finally going to hear a bit of her album?"

"It's Melody's music," he said as he backed the car out of the parking spot and headed for the exit. "But I don't think this is going to be part of her new album."

"I've been dying of curiosity for the past six hours. Are you going to play me the song or what?"

"Here goes."

He keyed the CD and waited for her reaction. Her eyes rounded with delight and she clapped her hands over her mouth. Trent found himself unable to stop grinning as the song played.

"Is that Dylan singing?"

Singing was not quite what the infant was doing, but there was no question that he was babbling all the correct notes as Melody accompanied him on the piano and sang the verses. It was one of the tunes she'd written when she was a kid, and obviously it still appealed to the under-ten-year-old set.

"Apparently they've been working on this duet since she arrived."

"It's fantastic. What a wonderful surprise. Thank you."

The song ended and Trent was about to hit the rewind button to play it again when a new song began. Nate had burned the CD for Trent. Apparently he'd decided to add a second track.

Savannah cocked her head and listened to the first strains of the new song. "I know this, don't I?"

Trent knew it all too well—it was the intro to "She's the One." He'd sung it yesterday. He had only seconds to act before it got to the part he'd recorded. "Why don't we listen to Dylan's song again."

"Wait." Savannah placed her hand over his. "That's 'She's the One.' Is Melody going to put that on her new album?"

The tension in her tone caught his attention. Glancing over, Trent noticed that Savannah's expression had grown bleak. As his sister sang the first verse, Trent wondered what about the song had caused Savannah's shift into melancholy. He was equally curious how she would react when she heard him jump in at the chorus.

"I sure hope not," he said just as his voice filled the speakers.

Hearing himself made him wince. It wasn't as if he sounded off-key or out of practice, but singing for himself and singing in the studio with his sister were meant to be private performances. Now he felt exposed. He'd been thinking about Savannah while they recorded the song, and to his sensitive ears it sounded like it.

"I had no idea." Savannah brushed back her hair with a trembling hand. She didn't finish her thought. "You guys sound great together. Melody should put it on her album."

"She needs to do a duet with someone well-known."

"You don't think anyone would remember the lead singer of Chrome Pulse?"

Trent laughed. "I sure hope not."

After a couple seconds Savannah joined him in laughing. "I can't believe Melody talked you into singing with her."

"I can't believe Nate put the song onto this CD." Trent would definitely have some choice words for his business partner. "It wasn't meant for public consumption."

"I'm glad he did. And thank you for Dylan's song. It was really a fantastic surprise."

For a while they rode in silence, each occupied by their own thoughts. Trent wrestled with the urge to reach out and take her hand in his. Every shift in her body and subtle change in her expression caught his attention. He yearned to demonstrate how much he'd missed her. But her posture warned him that something was bothering her.

"You haven't told me much about your meeting with Fred. How did it go?"

"He's really great. I think he'd do a fantastic job running the company." She quit speaking before she ran out of air and seemed to hold the remaining breath in her lungs. It gave her statement an unfinished feel, as if she wanted to say more but decided against it.

"But?" he prompted as the silence stretched.

"I had a run-in with your father." From the way she was gripping her purse, it hadn't gone well. "I think your attempt to provoke him worked better than you thought it would."

"If he did anything to upset you…"

She blew out a shaky breath. "I might've tipped our hand about Gerry."

So that's what was bothering her.

"Why don't you start at the beginning and tell me what happened."

She took a few moments to collect her thoughts and Trent grew concerned at her reluctance.

"As I was leaving the hotel this morning, I was served with papers. Siggy is suing me for Dylan's shares in the company."

"On what grounds?"

Another long pause. "He's claiming Dylan isn't Rafe's son."

Trent tamped down irritation at his father's ridiculous tactics. "Obviously we have my father on the run, and I am glad to see that, but I'm sorry that you're the one on the receiving end of his despicable tactics. We'll get a lawyer and fight it."

"I already spoke to one today. I thought I'd better get ahead of this thing."

"Is this why you told my father that Fred would be taking over the company?"

"When I got the papers, I wasn't thinking very clearly. I stormed over to his house to confront him. I let my temper get the better of me."

Trent found this last bit rather funny. "Since when do you have a temper?"

All the times he'd stepped in and rescued her, she'd never shown any signs of being willing to fight for herself. Now that she had someone of her own to protect, she'd become more lion than mouse.

"Apparently I've grown a spine since giving birth to Dylan." The corners of her mouth lifted in a sad, ironic smile.

"You always had a spine," Trent told her, thinking about how many times she'd braved his temper after his father had gone off on him. Her only motivation had been to see if he was okay. And more often than not, he'd directed his misplaced anger at her. It had taken him years before he understood and appreciated her kindness and bravery. "You just didn't let anyone see it."

"Anyway," she said, her shoulders lifting and falling in a dismissive little shrug, "I told Siggy that I had hired Fred and intended to turn Gerry over to the police for embezzlement."

"You hired Fred?"

"I didn't. Or I hadn't at that point, anyway. But I called him later and explained the situation. He's willing to go into hostile territory and do what needs to be done. I told him it might be an interim position. Until the lawsuit is settled, everything is up in the air."

Trent blew out a breath. "You were busy."

Given all she'd accomplished, he didn't know if she needed him anymore. That bothered him more than it should. Their former dynamic gave him a mission he was comfortable with. She got into trouble. He helped her out. What role did he play in her life going forward?

"I just hope I didn't create a bigger mess."

"Whatever happens, we'll tackle it together."

Ten

Savannah considered Trent's statement in silence. When she'd explained how Siggy's lawsuit claimed Dylan wasn't Rafe's son, she'd expected Trent to grill her for answers. Instead, he perceived the legal action as a simple matter of his father playing dirty. Not for a moment had he doubted her. Savannah felt sick. Lying to Trent was eating at her. But telling him Dylan was his son would be so much worse. He'd never forgive her for deceiving him.

"I'm beginning to wonder if you shouldn't let me finish this up alone."

Trent's eyebrows went up. "You want me out just as things are getting interesting?"

"Who knows what crazy thing your father will come up with next? I don't want you hurt because of me."

"My father lost the ability to hurt me a long time ago."

Although that might be true, it didn't mean the damage had ever healed. Trent remained wary of becoming emotionally invested. And Savannah couldn't love him enough to fix what he refused to be made whole.

"That doesn't mean he won't try, and you know how he likes to play dirty."

"Trust me, when it comes to my father, I'm bullet-proof."

Savannah nodded. "I should also tell you that before I spoke to a lawyer, I offered to settle with Siggy. I offered him the shares back for the million in debt I owe." When Trent shook his head, she rushed on. "I know it was fool-ish, but I'm sick to death of the whole thing and just want to be done."

"What did he say?"

"He told me he's going to take back the shares and not pay me a cent."

Trent nodded. "He's a pretty good poker player, and he knows you pretty well. He probably expected a bluff like that would scare you. Was this before or after you told him about Fred and Gerry?"

"Before." She didn't want to admit that she'd been scared. "His arrogance made me so mad. And after what he pulled the day I closed on my house, I don't see him as an all-powerful threat anymore."

She didn't care about the shares and she didn't care about the money. Once she was working again, she could pay off the debt she owed. The only danger she faced was if the lawsuit made public the truth about Dylan's biologi-cal father.

"Don't get between a mama and her baby."

"Darn right."

Trent laughed. The sound made Savannah smile. She was enjoying being on the same team. Being estranged from him this last year and a half had plunged her into a bleak, gray world. They might not ever be together as a family the way she wanted, but being able to laugh with him and watch him with Dylan was pretty great, too.

When the trio entered the house, Melody was in the kitchen fixing dinner while Murphy sat at her feet, his huge brown eyes luminous as he begged for handouts. Trent had given Rhoda the night off. After having her offer of help rejected, Savannah took her suitcase to the guesthouse and unpacked while Dylan sat on the bed and checked out the new puzzle she'd bought him.

Half an hour later, the four of them sat on the terrace and ate hamburgers loaded with jalapeño, guacamole and fresh tomatoes. It was a familiar family gathering. While Melody and Savannah had lived in New York City, they'd made an effort to eat together at least twice a month—more often when Trent visited.

"I really liked the duet you and Trent sang," Savannah said as talk turned to Melody's new album.

"He played that for you?" Melody shot a surprised look at her brother.

"I don't think he meant to. It was on the same CD with the song you and Dylan sang. Which was amazing, by the way." Savannah saw Trent drop a bit of hamburger to the waiting Murphy and frowned at him.

"Wasn't he great?" Melody said. "I think if the album doesn't work out I might do one for kids."

"Your album's going to be great," Trent said. "But you might think about recording your other songs, as well. I can hear kids singing about noses, roses and toeses all around the world."

"I second that," Savannah said. "So when do I get to hear more of the album?"

"She's not including the duet on her album," Trent insisted. "As a matter of fact, I'm going to get Nate to destroy the master."

"So I'll have the only copy?" Savannah rather liked the idea.

She recalled the first time she'd heard the song. Melody had written it during their days in New York. It had been a collaboration of sorts: Savannah's life put to Melody's music. Trent had never caught on that the song was about him. Originally the song had been titled "He's the One," but that had hit a little too close to home. Once Melody had changed the gender, Savannah could pretend that the lyrics were about anyone.

"Can we talk about something besides my album?" Melody said.

"Sure," Trent said, sliding a look his sister's way. "Kyle's coming into town next week. He, Nate and I are going to talk about a new business venture."

Noticing that Melody hadn't commented on Kyle's imminent arrival and was instead fussing with her nephew, Savannah picked up the conversation. "Another club?"

"Kyle wants to open one in LA. Something he can manage on a day-to-day basis." From Trent's manner, he was trying to engage his sister. Obviously Melody hadn't divulged any details about what was going on between her and Kyle. "He's been scouting properties and has narrowed it down to three."

"I'm not surprised you're looking to expand, given how well Club T's is doing."

"Of course, LA is a different market. But one that Kyle knows pretty well. He said he's been out a lot lately. I suppose it's because he's been missing you while you're on tour." This last was directed at his sister.

"It has nothing to do with me," Melody said. "Kyle's never been one to sit around for long. He likes being busy. I'm surprised it's taken this long for him to take this step. I know whenever you need him to fill in for you at Club T's he really enjoys it."

"I know he does. That's why I've asked him to stick around for the next month. I have some business in LA that's going to require me to be gone from the club quite a bit."

"He's going to stay here?" Melody didn't sound happy. "Can he do that? Take time off from his other investments, I mean."

A line formed between Trent's brows. "I thought you'd be happy to have him around while you're working on your album."

"I'll be too busy to spend time with him."

"I'm sure you can make time to be together." Trent cocked his head. "Is there something going on?"

Melody pushed back abruptly from the table, her wrought-iron chair screeching against the patio tile. "Everything is fine," she snapped, picking up her plate and heading for the kitchen.

"What the hell is going on with her?" Trent looked to Savannah for explanation. "Are she and Kyle having problems?"

"I think the tour was hard on their relationship." Savannah didn't feel bad about sharing that bit of information. It only made sense that not everyone could handle a long-distance romance. "I think it will be good for them to spend some time together here." On neutral territory.

"And it will give you and me a chance to spend some time together in LA."

"You and I? Together?" Savannah's breath caught. What was he suggesting?

"I've been thinking about it since you left. I don't feel comfortable with you and Dylan in LA by yourselves."

"If you're worried about Siggy trying to take Dylan away from me, I think his attitude on that score has changed."

"I'm not worried about my father." Trent reached over and took her hand. "I missed you these last couple days."

Savannah's throat tightened. She lowered her gaze so he wouldn't see the tears that brightened her eyes. He'd never said anything to her like that before, and the joy she felt left her paralyzed.

"I missed you, too," she whispered, the strain on her vocal cords almost painful. "It would be nice to have you with us in LA."

"Then it's settled. Let's get this cleaned up and then I want to hear all about the movie you're going to audition for."

When they carried the dinner dishes into the kitchen, Melody chased them out before they could offer to help. "The kitchen isn't big enough for all of us."

Which wasn't at all true, but Savannah could tell Melody needed time to herself. She and Trent took Dylan to the comfortable couches in the outdoor movie theater. With the screen retracted, they enjoyed watching the sunset decorate the mountains in shades of orange and gold.

"It's beautiful here." Savannah let her head drop onto Trent's shoulder as they watched Dylan running around the open gas fireplace, currently unlit.

"Staring at that view, it's hard to believe that less than five miles away there are millions of lights and people."

"Do you ever get tired of just how crazy it is on the Strip and in the hotels? That was what drove me crazy about New York. It was always people, people and more people. I think that's why Tennessee appealed to me. Wide-open spaces where days could go by without seeing anyone."

"That's why I bought this place. To get away from it all."

"You do have your own little vacation spot here."

"Do you really want to go back to LA? The traffic? Everyone on top of one another?"

"If I want to get jobs, I'm pretty sure that's where I need to be."

"Scarlett makes it work, going back and forth."

"She has two careers and a husband who lives here." Savannah hadn't meant to imply anything by this last remark. Nevertheless, she felt Trent stiffen. Containing a weary sigh, Savannah patted him on his knee and got to her feet. "It's past Dylan's bedtime."

She expected Trent to be happy to escape after the direction the conversation had gone, but he surprised her by dogging her steps to the guesthouse. When she gave him a questioning look, he shrugged.

"I've been reading Dylan a bedtime story. I know it's something you do for him every night, so I thought he'd expect it."

Once again Trent had taken her by surprise. "That's nice, but I've got this."

"Sounds like you're trying to get rid of me."

"Not at all." But suddenly she understood a bit of what Melody was feeling. Keeping disappointment or upset hidden wasn't easy. But the last thing she wanted to do was talk about how she was feeling and have it end in an argument. "I just thought maybe you'd be tired of babysitting."

Savannah entered Dylan's room and began pulling out what she needed to get him ready for bed. Trent demonstrated just how much time he'd been spending with Dylan as he made himself useful, gathering diapers and baby wipes.

"We still haven't talked about the movie," he said, spreading a changing pad on the bed.

Savannah laid Dylan down and began stripping off his clothes. "We can talk about it tomorrow."

"You are trying to get rid of me."

She didn't answer right away but kept her hands busy and her attention focused on her son. But their nighttime routine of tickling and giggling couldn't distract her from the tall man standing beside her, observing their antics. At last all the snaps on his pajamas were closed and her son was ready for bed.

"Who's ready for bed?" she crooned, making her son smile. His upper teeth were starting to come in, and she was struck by how fast he was growing up. Overcome by a rush of sentimentality, she lifted him into her arms and snuggled him against her chest, but to her shock, he reached out to Trent.

"I think he wants me to read him a story."

Flabbergasted, Savannah turned her son over to Trent. He settled with Dylan in the chair and pulled out a board book. While Savannah watched her two favorite men, Trent read one book after another until he had gone through Dylan's library.

"That's enough reading for one night," Savannah said, her tone firm.

She picked up her sleepy son and settled him in his crib with his favorite toy. She turned on the lamp that threw dancing shadows on the ceiling and then headed to the door. With one last glance at the crib, she turned off the overhead light.

"Are you okay?" Trent asked as they made their way into the living room.

"Fine. Why wouldn't I be?"

"You and Dylan have been alone for a long time. With so many of us taking care of him now, I thought you might miss having him all to yourself."

He'd captured a little of what she was feeling. "Not at all. I'm thrilled that he has so many people in his life who love him."

What bothered her was how attached Trent had become to Dylan. It made her all the more conflicted about not telling him that Dylan was his son. While she'd watched Trent reading the silly stories Dylan loved so much, she'd been consumed by guilt. All the time she'd kept the two of them apart, never imagining Trent had any interest in children.

Trent took her hand and guided it to his cheek. Her other hand he pulled around his waist. Held close, she inhaled the comforting masculine scent of him and her pulse danced. She could get used to coming home to Trent. When he'd visited her in New York, she'd rushed back to her apartment and fallen into his arms after a long day of shooting.

But those moments, wonderful though they were, had been short-lived. Trent might enjoy a week or two of domestic bliss, but he grew restless soon after. Having her and Dylan stay with him was a novelty. Soon enough they'd be in his way. She wanted to be gone before that happened.

"On the way back from LA, I did some thinking."

"Tell me later."

Before she could protest, his mouth found hers and she was lost in the sweeping power of his kiss. What good was it to fight the magic between them? In the future, she would have months and years to ache for him. Today, she intended to take whatever he would give her.

Trent didn't know why this particular Friday night at the club was driving him crazy. It wasn't as if more things than usual were going wrong. At the moment he was staring at his most experienced waitress. She'd messed up the tab for one of their biggest VIPs. Trent had to decide whether to eat the twenty-thousand-dollar mistake and keep the client happy or risk pissing off someone who had been known to drop upward of three hundred grand in the club when he was in town.

"Give this to Jason and tell him not to bother Khalid." Trent signed off on the report she brought to him about the discrepancy and handed it over.

"I'm really sorry, Trent."

"Figure out what happened and get it fixed."

Gina nodded and raced away. Trent watched her go with more than a trace of impatience. Normally he wouldn't be this short with his staff even over a mistake of this size, but Savannah had been in LA for four days and this time she'd taken Dylan with her. Dammit, he missed her. He missed both of them.

"So this is where you're hiding." Kyle Tailor entered Trent's office, his long legs carrying him across the room in four strides. "I've been looking all over the club for you. The place is packed."

"When did you get in?"

"Half an hour ago. I came here straight from the airport."

Trent was wondering why his best friend had chosen to visit Club T's over reuniting with the woman he loved first. "Are you meeting Melody here?"

"No, it's late. I'll see her tomorrow."

"I'm sure she'd like to see you tonight."

"I really don't want to bother her."

"Bother her?" Trent stared at his friend in dismay. "I was right. There is trouble between you two. Is it because she was on tour for so long?"

"What has she said?"

"Nothing. And that's what's weird. Normally she talks about you all the time. It's kind of annoying."

"Well, maybe that's because she's not in love with me anymore."

"Has she said that?"

"Not in so many words."

"Then what are you basing it on?" Trent waited for his friend's reply. When Kyle kept his lips pressed together, a belligerent scowl pulling down his brows, Trent said, "I know my sister. If she wasn't in love with you, she'd let you know." Still, Kyle said nothing. "Did you do something?"

"What makes you think it's my fault?"

Disgusted, Trent shook his head. "Because she's down in the dumps and you sound defensive."

"Can we not talk about your sister? I'm here to have some fun. Let's grab some drinks and find some women who want to have a good time."

Trent couldn't believe what his best friend was saying. They'd just been talking about the problems he and Melody were having and Kyle wanted to chase women? But when he took a harder look at Kyle, Trent recognized the desperate edge in his friend's expression. As if he intended to have fun even if he didn't feel like it. Deciding Kyle wasn't as indifferent to his problems with Melody as he was trying to appear, Trent swallowed the harsh lecture he'd been about to deliver.

"I can't right now," Trent said. "It's been a crazy night, with one thing after another going wrong." Almost as if on cue, Trent's phone buzzed, delivering another text message. Now they were running out of a particular vodka that one of their VIPs preferred. He exhaled and got to his feet. "To top it off, our DJ got sick at the last minute, so I've got Nate up on stage."

"I saw. The crowd seems to be enjoying him a lot."

"You know, for an introvert, he's a pretty decent showman."

They both laughed. Few people would characterize the front man for Free Fall as an introvert, but in truth, as much as he enjoyed making music, Nate needed a lot of downtime during his tours.

"Come on," Trent said, heading for the door. "Why don't you come with me while I put out a couple fires, and then I'll show you some of the upgrades we've done to the outside since you were last here."

Kyle grumbled about coming to Vegas to play, not work, but he accompanied Trent on his rounds. To Trent's surprise, his friend stuck with him the whole night, even though he had several offers to hang out with some very beautiful women. They parted ways at three. Kyle was heading off to try his luck at the tables and Trent still had work to do.

At five he debated the feasibility of heading home for a couple hours. He had a meeting with a new liquor distributor at eight. If he stayed on his couch, he could catch an extra hour of sleep. But as he lay staring at the shadowy ceiling, his overactive mind kept him awake.

He was back to thinking about Kyle and Melody. Although Trent had been opposed to their relationship when he'd originally learned of it, he'd come around after seeing how happy his sister was with Kyle. Now, however, he was worried that Melody was going to get hurt, and he knew she would be furious with him if he interfered.

A few hours later, the meeting with his potential distributor went well. Trent had managed to catch enough sleep to give the guy a fair hearing. The addition of some unique, high-end product would enhance the appeal of Club T's in an already cutthroat market. The club's closest competitor might be seven million a year behind them in sales, but that could change if Club T's had a couple bad months.

Eager to catch a few more hours of sleep, Trent headed home. The smell of coffee hit him as he entered his open-concept living space from the garage. He sucked in a big breath and felt revitalized. All thoughts of heading off to bed vanished as he spied Savannah and Dylan out on the terrace. She was sitting on the concrete while Dylan put a ball through a miniature basketball hoop.

Leaving his tie and suit coat draped over the banister, Trent poured himself a cup of coffee and headed out to enjoy the cool morning.

Savannah glanced his way as he approached. "Are you just getting home?"

"It was a late night and I had a meeting at eight this morning." He sat in the chair nearest the pair and sipped from his mug. Murphy came over to greet him, and Trent lifted the Frenchie onto his lap and gave him a thorough scratching. The dog snorted with pleasure. "I grabbed a couple hours' sleep on the couch in the office."

She acknowledged his statement with a nod and arced the ball through the hoop. Given the size of the target and her distance of five feet, it was an impressive toss.

"Score," she called, raising her arms, and Dylan mimicked her.

Despite her obvious pleasure in watching her son, Savannah seemed quieter than normal. Trent noticed that although her lips curved in a smile, her eyes never lit up. Given her friendship with Melody and the fact that Kyle's car wasn't parked in the driveway, Trent suspected she was worried about his sister.

"Is something wrong?" Trent asked, not wanting to come straight out with his own concerns until he knew which way the wind blew.

"My lawyer called a little bit ago and told me your father's backing down on the lawsuit." Savannah's gaze tracked Dylan as he chased his ball along the terrace. "Not only that, but he's offering to pay me one point five million for Dylan's shares."

Given her somber mood, this wasn't at all what he'd been expecting. "That's not even close to what those shares are worth."

"I know, but it's enough to pay off Rafe's debts and give me a nest egg."

"You should counter."

Savannah looked horrified at his suggestion. "I'm just relieved to have it all done."

So why didn't she look as if things were going her way?

More than anything Trent wanted her to be happy. His father had caused her enough harm. And should have to pay.

"Do you have any idea what caused him to change his mind?" Trent asked.

"No, and my lawyer also questioned his abrupt turnaround, as well. He did a little investigating and discovered someone wants to buy West Coast Records."

"So there's a chance for you to make even more money."

"And a chance for Siggy to ruin the whole thing."

"So you've made up your mind." He set the dog back on the ground and watched him run over to Dylan.

"I've already given the go-ahead to sell the shares back to Siggy."

"Then why aren't you celebrating?"

"I should be. It's stupid that I'm not."

Trent was starting to understand. "You wish you'd been able to fight him to get what the shares were worth."

"No, I'm happy with our deal the way it stands. I didn't marry Rafe for his money. I married him to give Dylan a traditional family. Now that Rafe is dead, I have accepted that Dylan and I will be fine on our own."

It wasn't the first time Trent was filled with admiration for her. The girl he'd grown up with, the woman he'd known in New York, hadn't been confident and strong. Savannah might still need help from time to time, but she didn't need rescuing. She'd stood up to his father and participated in Trent's scheme to provoke his father into acting. She might not have anticipated what Siggy would do, but she'd taken charge when he threatened her with a lawsuit.

"So what is really going on?"

Her big blue eyes turned sorrowful. "There's something I should've let you know a long time ago."

Anxiety twisted his gut at the pained expression on her face. "Like what?"

"It has to do with your father's lawsuit. He claimed Dylan isn't Rafe's son." She clenched her fists and leaned forward. "It's true."

Trent's thoughts froze. Once again his perception of her changed. "So that's why you chose not to fight him? Because you knew you'd lose?"

"No. I meant what I said about the money. I only wanted what's fair."

"Did Rafe know Dylan wasn't his son?" For the first time since he'd found out that Rafe and Savannah were getting married, Trent felt sorry for his brother. "Or did you lie to him, too?"

Hurt flickered in her eyes, but she didn't let her chin droop. "Rafe knew before he proposed to me. At the time I didn't understand why he would want to raise a son who wasn't biologically his. I didn't realize it at the time, but the cancer treatments had made him sterile. Your father had drilled the concept of dynasty into Rafe's head for so long that even as he was dying, he was determined to make Siggy happy."

"So you both lied to my father."

"Yes. At the time I was in a vulnerable place—pregnant and terrified of raising Dylan alone." She didn't need to add that Rafe had been there to pick up the pieces after she and Trent had broken up.

"That first night in my office, when you told me Dylan was Rafe's son." Trent wasn't sure he recognized the woman standing before him. "You were lying."

She shook her head. "As far as Rafe was concerned, Dylan was his son. But he wasn't his biological child."

Never before had he perceived Savannah as being duplicitous. But she'd lied to him and to his family. Could she also be lying about Rafe knowing that Dylan wasn't his?

"Is lack of money for a long, drawn-out legal case the

reason you're no longer fighting Siggy for Dylan's right to the stock? Or are you suffering a guilty conscience?"

"Will you condemn me if I tell you it's a little of both?"

Trent held perfectly still and stared at her. A question was burning a hole in his heart. Who was Dylan's father? He thought he knew Savannah inside and out. Had she had a fling or a one-night stand? The thought disturbed him.

"I never in a million years thought you'd do something like this." His voice sounded flat and wooden.

"Like what?"

"Pass a stranger's child off as Rafe's."

"I didn't. Don't you understand?" Savannah released a long-suffering sigh at his head shake. "He has your smile."

"Who does?" Trent had no idea what she was getting at.

"Dylan."

What was she trying to say? Trent stared at her, his mind blank.

Savannah looked miserable. She'd obviously been expecting a different reaction. "Trent, Dylan is your son."

Eleven

Funny how easily the confession slipped free. She'd been dreading this moment since the pregnancy test had come back positive. But in the end it wasn't as traumatic as she thought it was going to be. She'd already lost her self-respect and her uncomplicated future to the lie. Trent's confession that he'd not wanted their relationship to end had cut deep. What if instead of being afraid to be rejected she'd gone to him when she first found out she was pregnant? Her life might have turned out very differently.

"That's impossible," Trent said. "We were always very careful."

"This is going to sound crazy." Savannah braced to defend herself, suspecting Trent would be skeptical of her convoluted explanation. "When I came to visit you in Vegas that last time, I did so on Rafe's recommendation."

"Rafe told you to come see me?"

"As I was getting settled in LA, he and I began to spend time together. He said he'd been in love with me a long time and wanted us to be together. I liked Rafe, but he knew I loved you."

"If he wanted you, wouldn't it make more sense for him to keep you away from me?"

"Yes, if he'd actually loved me. But as I found out after we got married, he was merely using me." She studied Trent's face and saw only confusion and doubt. "And using you."

"Using us how?"

"He needed an heir. He wanted one who looked like a Caldwell." She raised her eyebrows and stared at him, waiting for him to understand what she was saying.

"But we were careful," he repeated.

"That last time we were together…the condoms we used… Rafe gave me those condoms and told me to get you out of my system."

"Seriously?" Trent looked completely shell-shocked. And angry. "You didn't think that was strange?"

"Maybe." She thought back to how desperate and miserable she'd been at the time. "I thought he was trying to be helpful. I never imagined he'd do something as crazy as sabotage the condoms."

"He *wanted* you to get pregnant? To what end?"

"So that there'd be a Caldwell to eventually take over at West Coast Records."

"Do you hear how insane that sounds?"

"I've been living with this for the last year and a half." Savannah's strength was draining. She crumpled into a nearby chair and put her hands in her lap. "I was the one he duped. How do you think I feel?"

"You don't think we're both victims in this?"

Trent paced away toward the terrace and stood with his back to her. He remained as still as a statue for a long time until he finally asked, "Were you ever planning on informing me Dylan is my son?"

She should have been better prepared for this question. As it was, she'd spent all her time worrying about what the fallout for her and Dylan would be if—when—Trent learned the truth.

"To what end?" Her response might have been harsh, but Trent had made his opinion clear. "You never wanted to be part of a family. Rafe did."

"You had no right making that decision for me." Trent turned to face her. His expression was bleak.

Remembering how that final conversation with him had gone, Savannah hardened her heart. "That last morning we were together, you told me you had no time or energy for anything but the club."

"And at that particular moment I didn't. We'd been open barely six months and every day there was something new going wrong. We'd made a huge investment and in order to make it pay off, I had to give it a hundred and ten percent."

"I heard that loud and clear. You didn't have time for me. Why would I think you would have time for me and our child?"

"You should have told me," he insisted.

Savannah refused to regret the decision she'd made. Loving Trent had led to heartache. Marrying Rafe had seemed a safe and sensible alternative.

"You know now," she said, her strength returning as she settled on a course of action. Savannah got to her feet and headed toward him. "You have a son, Trent. What do you intend to do about it?"

She'd never challenged him directly before. Her question was born of frustration and longing. More than anything she needed him to step up and demand to be in Dylan's life. To be part of her life.

"Honestly, I don't know." He raked his hand through his hair. "I need some time to think."

She barely registered the disappointment that washed

through her. His answer didn't surprise her at all. "You know, nothing about your life needs to change the least bit," she told him. "Something's going to break for me in LA. In fact, I just found out I have to head back there tomorrow."

"Already?"

"My agent is excited about my acting prospects. She was able to line up another audition. It looks like my future is there."

Maybe she'd look for a rental. It hurt to give up her plans for buying a house in Las Vegas and living near Trent, but he didn't appear as if he was going to step up and be Dylan's father.

"Your future?" he echoed. "You're not going to stay in Las Vegas?"

The question gave her the opening she needed to ask what was burning in her heart. "Do you want us to stay? Dylan needs a father. I…" She sucked in a breath for strength before putting it all out there. "I need you. I always have."

Trent's features turned to stone. "You can't expect—"

"No." Between one heartbeat and the next, Savannah embraced Courtney Day. The character gave her the dignity to speak mildly and conceal her anguish. "I don't expect. And that's why I'm leaving. Moving to LA is practical. I'll be closer for auditions and meetings." When Trent didn't say anything, Savannah rushed on. "I need to pack. I'll be by later to say goodbye."

And before she was overwhelmed by the sobs tearing at her throat, she left him.

Outrage consumed Trent as he watched Savannah pick Dylan up and walk away with her head held at a defiant angle. He couldn't get past how many times she had looked him in the eye and let him believe Dylan was Rafe's son.

And then today she'd acted as if by keeping the truth hidden she'd done him some sort of favor.

Realizing his hands were clenched into fists, Trent shook his arms to release the tension. But nothing could unravel the knot in his chest. He headed for his room and grabbed a quick shower. There was no way he was going to be able to sleep, so he headed back to the club.

In the months following his breakup with Savannah, Trent had thrown himself into making Club T's into the go-to spot on the Strip. Besides having a killer lineup of DJs, he was constantly looking at ways to improve service and ambience. He had a list of things he wanted to upgrade, including the lighting and sound.

When he got to his office, he was surprised to find Kyle there.

"Where have you been?" Trent asked. If he asked a little more forcefully than he needed to, it was due to his concern for Melody. "I expected to see you at the house. Tell me you didn't hook up with somebody."

"Nothing like that." Kyle didn't overreact to Trent's aggressive tone or nosiness. "I took a suite here at the hotel."

"Why aren't you staying at the house? Have you called Melody? What the hell is going on with you two?" Trent knew he wasn't giving his friend a chance to answer, but his own troublesome morning had put him on edge.

"Look, I didn't say anything last night, but we've had a rough patch."

"How rough?"

Kyle's expression darkened. "I'm here, aren't I? In Vegas, I mean. And at Cobalt. I don't know what's going on at the moment."

He looked utterly miserable, so Trent decided to cut him some slack.

"So what brings you here this morning?"

"You got your start in the LA club scene. I know they

make a tenth of what we bring in at Club T's. Do you think it makes sense for us to open something in LA?"

"I'm looking at some other business opportunities in LA," Trent said, thinking about Savannah and the rebirth of her acting career. Of course, when he'd started considering ventures that would take him to LA and into her orbit, he hadn't known she'd been keeping his son from him for a year. "I thought I would explore expanding into LA."

"Great. I talked with Nate for a while last night and he's on board, as well." Kyle crossed the office to the window that overlooked the club. "He told me that you have Savannah staying with you. Are you sure that's a good idea?"

"I'm just helping her out for old times' sake. She and Siggy have been at odds over the label and he's been playing dirty."

Kyle gave a rough laugh. "Just like old times, then."

"Just like."

"I found out something just now." Trent had no idea he was going to share Savannah's revelation until the words came out of his mouth. "Savannah told me Dylan is my son."

"She cheated on Rafe with you?"

Trent had no idea why Kyle had leaped to that conclusion. "No, she married him after finding out she was pregnant with Dylan."

"She never told you she was pregnant?" Kyle looked appalled. "That's messed up."

Hearing his own opinion echoed by his best friend, Trent began to feel a little vindicated. "She should've come to me."

"Absolutely. Your poor brother."

"Rafe knew. Apparently his cancer had made him infertile. He was glad to be a father and have a son to pass the business along to."

Trent felt at that moment that he understood what his

brother had been up against. Maybe setting up Savannah to get pregnant had been a crazy act, but with the cancer eating away at his mind, no doubt he hadn't been thinking rationally.

"What would you have done if she'd told you before marrying Rafe?"

This was a question Trent should have asked himself already, but he'd been so consumed with anger at being lied to. "I don't know. Obviously I would have taken care of her and the baby." Taken care of her financially was what he meant to say.

"But would you have married her? I know how you feel about getting tied down, but you've been crazy about Savannah for a long time."

"Maybe." *Probably not.* "We'll never know." Funny how twenty-four hours earlier he'd been thinking how great things were between them and how much he was enjoying having Dylan around.

"So that's it then? You guys are done?"

Were they done? Of course they were. A bone-deep chill struck Trent.

"She's planning on restarting her acting career." He sounded calm and detached. Numb. "That means she's going to be spending time in LA."

"How much time?"

He had to think about their last conversation. "Probably full time."

And just like that it hit him. Savannah wasn't going to be back and forth between Las Vegas and LA like she'd first talked about doing.

She was leaving and taking Dylan. His son. Trent was still reeling from the knowledge that he was a father. Now it occurred to him that he and Dylan were going to be very far apart.

"How are you going to see Dylan if they're living there?

I mean, if it was my kid, I'd never want to be away from him."

Kyle had made a good point. Did Savannah expect that Trent would just give up his son? "I haven't really thought the whole thing through."

"You should talk to her about sharing custody."

"I don't know if she'd be open to that."

"You could demand it."

Trent recoiled from Kyle's suggestion. He was sick of being at odds with Savannah. Until recently he hadn't been able to admit how his world had been disrupted when he'd lost her.

"I'll think about it."

"I don't envy you," Kyle said. "When the kids come into the picture, it messes everything up."

With that said, Trent changed the subject. The two men talked business for a couple hours before grabbing lunch. Then they went to Nate's studio and brought him up to speed. By the time Trent returned to his house at three, he was fighting the drag of exhaustion from his sleepless nights.

Unfortunately any hope of a catnap before he headed back to the club was shattered when he opened up the door between the garage and the house and discovered his houseguests in high spirits. Their excited voices reached his ears and raked across his raw nerves before he stepped across the threshold. On the edge since he left the house earlier that day, Trent felt a snarl form on his lips.

"What's going on?" he demanded, eyeing the open bottle of sparkling grape juice on his breakfast bar and the almost-empty flutes.

"We're celebrating," Melody said. "Savannah just found out she got the movie."

Trent should've been happy for her, but he hadn't gotten over what he'd learned that morning. "You must be thrilled."

If she noticed that he was less than enthusiastic, she didn't react. "I'm more nervous than anything else."

"You don't have to be," he said, mood softening as he noticed her uncertainty. "You're going to be great." He remembered watching her on the set of *Loving New York*. She'd been confident and professional. Before that, he'd been accustomed to thinking of her as a naive girl. The transformation to accomplished actress had forced him to reevaluate who she was. "When do you start filming?"

"Next month, but they want me next week for wardrobe." She looked dazed by all the sudden changes.

He understood how she was feeling. He was off balance, as well.

"How long is shooting supposed to take?" Melody asked.

"I was told to expect ten to twelve weeks."

"You're going to need a place to stay," Melody said. "I have a friend who might be able to help you with that."

"Actually, I've already found a small house to rent for the next six months."

"Sounds like everything's working out." Trent tasted bitter disappointment at how fast everything had been arranged. He wasn't prepared for her to leave him and take Dylan away. His gut twisted and sweat beaded on his skin.

The conversation with Kyle rose in his thoughts. Should he demand partial custody? But was that really what he wanted? For his son to be shuttled back and forth between Las Vegas and LA?

Savannah didn't look at him as she said, "Dylan and I have imposed on you long enough. We'll be out of your hair tomorrow."

"That's not how I feel about having you here." But the words lacked sincerity.

She'd lied to him, and he couldn't get past that. Even so, her expectant expression tore at him. She was waiting for him to say something heartfelt and romantic. Maybe that he wanted them to stay. That he couldn't live without her or their son.

But so much was wrong between them and anger was a familiar, uncomplicated emotion. He held on to it even as concern over losing her and Dylan gnawed at him.

"Nevertheless, it's time we start the next chapter of our life." Savannah glanced at her son as he yawned. "Looks like someone's ready for his nap. I'd better go put him down."

Savannah had barely stepped out onto the terrace when Melody rounded on Trent.

"You're not really going to let her move to LA, are you?"

"She has a part in a movie that's filming there. I don't know why you think I'd stop her."

"I'm probably the last person to be giving romantic advice, but you two belong together. I've known it since those days in New York. I know it upset you when she married Rafe." Melody held up her hand to forestall the denial that leaped to his lips. "Don't even try to deny it. I saw you at the wedding."

"Sometimes it doesn't work between people."

"Sometimes people are unwilling to work at it."

"Are we talking about Savannah and me? Or you and Kyle?"

"All four of us, I think."

"So what are you going to do about it?"

"This isn't about me. This is about you. You are about to let go of the only woman you've ever loved. And why?"

"She lied to me. She's been lying to all of us. Dylan is my son."

"Yikes." Melody grimaced but didn't look surprised. "She finally told you."

"You knew?"

"Since the day before she married Rafe. She was having serious doubts about going through with the wedding. I told her to follow her heart. I thought that meant she would tell you about the baby."

"But she didn't." Trent remembered how he'd expected her to call off the wedding right up until the moment she actually said, "I do." He'd left right after the ceremony and never congratulated her or his brother. "Obviously she found what she needed in Rafe."

"In some ways, I think she did. You should've seen her that morning. She was a wreck. Pacing. Hyperventilating. I thought for sure she was going to call it off. And then Rafe came in." Melody's eyes took on a faraway look. "He sat her down and knelt before her. He took her hand in his and very calmly convinced her that he would make sure everything was going to be all right." Melody blinked back tears. "None of us knew that he wouldn't be around to fulfill that promise."

A complicated mix of emotions churned in Trent's gut. He'd loved his brother and resented him in equal measure. He'd learned that Rafe had betrayed him, but he also had to acknowledge that by marrying Savannah, Rafe had tried to take care of her the way Trent had refused to.

He didn't want to think about Rafe being a good guy. It was easier to dwell on all the things he'd done wrong. And yet without Rafe, there would be no Dylan and Trent might never have had a second chance with Savannah.

A second chance that had ended as badly as the first one.

"I wonder," Melody continued, "after all this time, Savannah changed her mind about telling you the truth."

"Siggy was suing her for the shares in the company Rafe left Dylan. He was claiming Dylan wasn't Rafe's son. I think she expected the truth to come out. So she let me know."

"Are you sure that's why? Maybe she hoped once you knew Dylan was your son that you might ask her to stay. She still loves you. I just know it."

"That's not the way it seems to me."

Savannah had given up her dream of a blissful, traditional family with him. She'd decided being Dylan's mom was enough. And for some strange reason that angered Trent more than all the rest put together.

"Is this really what you want?" Melody demanded, irritation snapping in her voice.

For the last twelve hours, Trent had been too preoccupied by how he'd been wronged by the people who should have his back to give much thought to what he wanted.

"What do you mean?"

"Do you really want to live here alone while your son and the woman you love live in a different state?"

"The woman I love?" He gave a bitter laugh, wishing he'd kept his distance from Savannah the way he had for the last year and a half. "What I want is to take back the last two weeks."

"You don't mean that."

"I do. I wish Savannah had never come to Vegas to ask me for help. Because if she hadn't, I'd never have learned the truth."

On the terrace edge, out of sight of the living room's occupants, Savannah heard Trent's declaration and felt neither shock nor hurt. In fact, she was a little relieved. Now she didn't have to wonder if returning to LA was the right decision. Trent didn't want her or Dylan in his life. She could stop looking back and move forward.

Savannah entered the guesthouse and closed the sliding glass doors to the patio. With her bags packed and her flight several hours away, she kept herself busy cleaning the bathroom and little-used kitchen until Dylan woke.

Feeling restless and needing to get away from the house, Savannah took Dylan to the nearby mall and window-shopped for a couple hours. She kept melancholy at bay by thinking about what homey touches would warm up the cute mission-style house she'd rented. By the time she returned to Trent's house, it was close to six and she knew he would have left for the club.

Melody's car was gone as well and Savannah was able to relax knowing she wouldn't run into either of them. She set about heating up the leftover chicken she'd fixed for dinner the night before. Dylan was a good eater. He scarfed down the chunks of carrots and potato as well as the bits of thigh meat Savannah arranged on the high-chair tray.

Later, Savannah sat with Dylan on the couch and read to him, losing herself in the rhythm of the words and her son's delight. When she ran out of books, she turned to her phone and the playlist that contained all his favorite songs. He laughed and clapped his hands while she sang. For a while longer she was able to escape her sadness. And then she heard the first few notes of the song Dylan and Melody had recorded. Days earlier, she'd uploaded the song, and now she played it for him often. His ability to mimic the tune amazed her. Before she could hit the repeat button, the other song from the CD began to play.

Savannah's finger hovered over the stop button. Dwelling on her foolish dreams wasn't conducive to moving forward. But the magic of Melody's lyrics being sung in Trent's deep voice was hard to resist. She didn't realize she was crying until she noticed that Dylan was watching her with solemn eyes. He put his palms on her wet cheeks. With a shaky laugh, she kissed his damp fingers and dashed the remaining moisture from her skin.

"Mommy's being silly, isn't she?" The last strains of

"She's the One" faded and the room grew silent. Needing a distraction, Savannah got to her feet. With Halloween a week away, she'd bought Dylan a costume but hadn't yet tried it on him. "You're going to be the cutest dragon LA has ever seen," she promised as she slipped his chubby thighs into the blue-and-green suit with orange wings and spikes down the tail.

Once she had the zipper up and the hood lifted into place, she started working on his roar. He was slowly learning his animal sounds and mastered the dragon's growl after a few minutes. Laughing at the cuteness overload, she spun with Dylan in her arms and he shrieked with delight.

Why had she once worried so much about being a part of a traditional family with Trent when what she should have wished for was a perfect family? Because somehow that's the exact sort of family she'd become with Dylan. Perfect.

Twelve

Club T's throbbed with ear-blasting electronic music and pulsed with a dazzling light display. Trent sat in his favorite spot and watched the crowd drink and dance, laugh and flirt. A stunning blonde sat to his right. He'd forgotten her name as soon as they'd been introduced. She was a friend of the redhead Kyle had plucked out of the crowd waiting behind the velvet ropes.

Trent's cell phone buzzed with an incoming text from Nate.

You don't look like you're having fun.

He glared over to where Nate sat on the far end of the curved couch, his lips twisted in a sardonic smile. The club was too noisy for conversation to carry over that distance, so Trent texted back.

I'm working.

Nate checked the incoming message and responded without looking up.

Kyle and I have this. Maybe you should get out of town for a few days.

Where the hell was he supposed to go? He rejected the first idea that popped into his head. Going to LA to check out the potential club properties Kyle had scouted would put him too near Savannah and Dylan. He wasn't ready to deal with that situation yet. His emotions were too raw.

Amid the loud music in the club, Trent reflected on the playful growls and unrestrained laughter that had drifted across his quiet backyard the other night. He'd been standing on his terrace, overlooking his pool when the sounds had first caught his attention. Drawn by the joyful noise, he'd crossed half the distance to the guesthouse before reality had caught up with him. Unfortunately, although he'd stopped himself from joining them, it had taken him ten minutes to turn away. The memory of how he'd ached standing there alone in the dark compressed his lungs.

He would head to New York City and put the entire country between him and Savannah. Visiting his mother would take his mind off his troubles. She was directing her first off-Broadway musical and had been pestering him for months to fly out and see it. He texted Nate back.

Sounds good.

Figuring he might as well get started immediately, Trent left the couch, shaking off the blonde woman who'd clutched at his jacket sleeve. He hadn't consumed more than a single scotch, but as he made his way out of the club, he felt disconnected from his environment, as if he'd overindulged.

Six hours later he checked into his hotel in Times Square and ordered breakfast from room service. By the time he ate and showered, it was late enough that he could call his mother without waking her.

"You're in New York City?" At eight in the morning, she sounded wide-awake and delighted to hear he was in town.

"I came in a few hours ago. Kyle and Nate are both in Las Vegas, so I thought I'd take some time off and come visit you."

"I'm so glad. I have to be at the theater at ten. We're making some minor changes to one of the scenes." The play had opened a week before to mixed but mostly positive reviews. His mother was a perfectionist, always taking her craft up a notch. "You can take me to lunch and tell me all of what's going on in your life."

"I'll be there."

Trent hung up and headed for the lobby. His favorite thing to do when he came to New York was to walk the streets and absorb the energy. The city's pace was just as hectic as Las Vegas's, but here people moved with purpose, the vibe oriented toward both business and artistic pursuits.

At five minutes before ten, he met his mother on the sidewalk in front of the theater. She wore a long gray sweater belted over black leggings and a slouchy black trench coat. Bright red lipstick emphasized her broad smile. These days she was always happy. It hadn't been that way when he was young. Sometimes when Siggy hadn't been home she would sing with Trent and Melody, but even then her eyes had carried shadows.

"How wonderful to see you." His mother trapped his face between her hands and brought his head down so she could kiss his cheek. Then she peered at him. "You look tired."

"I flew the red-eye and didn't sleep."

"With all the crazy hours you work at that club of yours, I would think you'd be used to it." She linked her arm through his and drew him into the theater. "I hear Melody's back in the studio. Is she ever going to finish her album?"

"Nate has given her a deadline and threatened to pick the songs himself if she doesn't start making some decisions."

"Is she happy?"

Trent gave his mother's question serious consideration. It wouldn't do to fire off a hasty answer. "Yes and no."

"Why, yes?"

"I think she's glad to be done with the tour. The traveling and performing are not her cup of tea. And she's having fun playing in the studio. It's what she loves. It wouldn't surprise me if one day she stopped singing and went into production full-time."

"It's too bad Siggy can't appreciate musical genius. She would've been a great asset to West Coast Records." His mother slipped off her coat and draped it over her arm. "So would you."

Trent shrugged. He'd given up on pleasing his father before he'd become a teenager. "Siggy didn't want me within a mile of his company, and he only sees Melody as a little girl."

Naomi shook her head. "So why is my daughter unhappy?"

"I don't know for sure, because neither of them is confiding in me, but I think Melody and Kyle are having problems. Right now they are both in Las Vegas, but from what I can tell they haven't seen each other yet."

"That's the feeling I get, as well," his mother said, her sigh speaking volumes. "She stopped talking about him three months ago. I think something happened when she broke from the tour to visit him in LA."

"They'll figure it out."

His mother regarded Trent with surprise. "That's very optimistic of you."

"You don't think I'm right?"

"No, I think you're right." Her eyes narrowed and she seemed to be searching for something in his expression. "I'm just surprised that your opinion is so upbeat."

"I don't understand what you mean."

"You aren't exactly a believer when it comes to romance and relationships. Do you remember saying that your brother's marriage wouldn't last a year?"

And it hadn't. Just not for the reason Trent had thought.

"I didn't think Rafe and Savannah were meant for each other."

"Because she was your girlfriend first?"

Two years ago he'd never imagined he would lose her. By the time he figured out that he didn't want to live without her, she'd been engaged to his brother.

"I had my chance."

And he'd blown it. But he couldn't say the words out loud. His regrets were private.

"I understand she's been staying with you in Las Vegas."

"Siggy threatened her, saying he was going to fight for custody of Dylan. I offered her my guesthouse until things could be sorted out."

"Why would Siggy try to take away Dylan?"

"He lost Rafe and saw Dylan as his replacement."

"And he wanted control over the shares of the company that Rafe left his son."

"And he didn't want to pay for them. Rafe left Savannah a lot of debt, and she was trying to sell the label's shares back to Siggy so she could get out from under it."

His mother rolled her eyes. "Tell me you haven't left her to deal with Siggy alone."

"Everything has been sorted out. Another record company offered to buy West Coast Records, so Siggy bought Rafe's shares back and Savannah should be able to pay off her debts. She's moved back to LA and has taken a part in a movie."

Trent decided this was the perfect opportunity to tell his mother about Dylan being his son, but as he opened his mouth, they were approached by an obviously frazzled man. After his mother introduced her assistant director, they headed off. Trent chose a seat in the dim theater and watched his mother work, enjoying the competent way she directed the actors. It was obvious she had a vision in her head regarding the changes, but it took her an hour and twenty minutes to achieve the results. At long last she clapped her hands and sent everyone on their way.

Collecting her coat and purse, Naomi came up the center aisle toward Trent. "Shall we go to La Masseria for lunch?"

Located in the theater district, the Italian restaurant was one of her favorites. During one of his many trips to visit Savannah, they'd met his mother and her current husband there before a Broadway show. The entire evening had been a great success. His mother had talked about Savannah for months afterward, prodding him about his future plans. Trent had given her noncommittal replies, and as time went on she'd stopped asking questions.

After they were seated, Trent gave the menu a quick glance. He wasn't really hungry. Being in this restaurant brought up happy memories of his time with Savannah, of his mother's hopes for his future and the satisfaction she'd found with a man who supported and loved her.

"Earlier I mentioned that Siggy threatened to seek custody of Dylan, but what I didn't say is that he gave up after discovering that he isn't Rafe's son."

"It sounds just like Siggy." His mother waved to someone, apparently unconcerned at the bombshell regarding her grandson's legitimacy. "He's obsessed with his legacy."

"Doesn't it bother you about Dylan?"

Naomi met her son's gaze. "Why should it? I love Dylan. Whether or not he's Rafe's biological child doesn't change the fact that he's my grandson." She studied Trent for a long moment. "Does it bother you?"

"It bothers me that Savannah lied."

Why had he thought his mother would be outraged that Savannah had lied, too? Melody hadn't been bothered. Rafe had created the situation in the first place. At this point, the only other member of his family who seemed at all upset was Siggy.

"I don't see why. As you said earlier, you had your chance with her and things didn't work out. It seems as if this is her business and Rafe's. He married her, after all." His mother turned her attention to the waiter who'd approached the table, leaving Trent to stew over her matter-of-fact assessment.

As soon as they'd placed a drink order, Trent spoke again. "It bothers me because Dylan is my son."

"I see." His mother had been perusing a menu she no doubt knew by heart. Now she set it down and gave him her full attention. "Can I assume since you haven't mentioned this before that you just found out?"

"Savannah told me a few days ago."

Naomi laced her fingers together and set her clasped hands on the table. "Does this change things between you?"

"By change things, do you mean am I going to marry her?" Trent heard his aggrieved tone and saw his mother's eyebrows lift.

"You love her, don't you?"

For some reason the question threw salt on his already raw wounds. "She and I were together a long time. I didn't want to end things, but I couldn't give her the normal family life she craved."

"So marriage is off the table. Do you intend to have a relationship with your son? Or are you going to be like your father?"

If she had stood up and shrieked at him, he would've been less shocked. That she would place him in the same category as his father in anything cut deep. Trent slammed the door on his emotions. Ice filled his veins.

"I haven't decided what I'm going to do."

"Oh, don't be like that." His mother picked up her menu and once more began to peruse the entrées. "Your father used to shut down the exact same way."

"Stop comparing me to him."

"I will when you stop behaving like him. Siggy has no heart and very little soul. He is bullheaded and unforgiving."

"But you married him and had three children. Why do that if he's so terrible?"

"I was young, idealistic and ambitious. He told me I was talented, and I thought with him backing me I would have an amazing career as a singer." Trent's mother sighed. "And in the beginning he charmed the pants right off me."

"What changed?"

"He thought I had an affair."

The waiter brought their drinks, giving Trent a moment to assimilate what his mother had said.

"Did you?"

Naomi didn't look surprised or annoyed by his question. "I didn't sleep with Marco, but I did fall in love with him. He was an incredibly talented musician I met shortly after he signed with West Coast Records."

"Marco? I don't recall anyone by that name at the label."

"That's because your father destroyed his career. He never made an album and eventually gave up music." Naomi got a faraway look in her eye. "It was a year after Rafe was born. Siggy promised that I could record my second album. I'd been working on songs while pregnant with Rafe. One of those was a duet. Marco and I recorded it together. He had the most amazing voice. If he'd signed with any other record company, he probably would've been huge."

Trent couldn't figure out why she was telling him all of this. "Does Siggy think this Marco is my father?" It would explain why he could do no right in his father's eyes. Trent hadn't realize how much he'd needed his father's favoritism to have a basis in logic.

"No. He ran a paternity test on all three of you." Her smile had an acid bite. "That was the moment I stopped trying to make my marriage work. The day I discovered he would never trust me."

"Then why does he hate me?" It was the cry of a small child who didn't understand what he'd done wrong. And it was a question he'd never asked his mother before.

"Because you were my beautiful, musical boy and I doted on you. Rafe didn't inherit my talent or my joie de vivre. He was a serious baby with the most solemn eyes. It was almost as if from birth he was weighed down by his father's expectations." Trent's mother gave her head a sad shake. "You, on the other hand, and your sister after you, were exuberant and artistic. For all his early success with West Coast Records, Siggy was a businessman, not a visionary. He related better to Rafe."

Trent pondered what he'd learned and realized he'd never stopped being angry with his father. In fact, he'd gone a step farther and used his contentious relationship with his father as an excuse to keep people at bay.

"I don't want to be like my father."

"You're not like him at all."

"So you think I have a heart and a soul?"

His mother smiled. "I never doubted it for a second."

* * *

Savannah poured candy into a large bowl and set it on the small table just inside her front door. It was five o'clock on Halloween, but she didn't expect trick-or-treaters to show up for another hour. She and Dylan had been living in LA for a week. The mission-style house she'd rented was about the same size as Trent's guesthouse and beautifully furnished, but Savannah was having a hard time settling in.

She'd had several meetings with the director, her fellow actors and the wardrobe department, and was anxious to start filming. As she'd done after starting the soap opera, she'd hired an acting coach to help her prepare for her new role. But her down time offered abundant opportunity to worry, and lately she'd been revisiting the multitude of ways she could have handled things better since leaving New York two years earlier.

Her doorbell rang. Trick-or-treaters already? Savannah glanced to where her son sat in the middle of the living room, wearing his adorable dragon costume. Seeing that he was occupied with Murphy, also dressed like a dragon, she picked up the bowl of candy and opened her front door.

Instead of an adorable child dressed as a princess or a superhero, a tall, leafy plant with legs stood before her.

"Hello?"

The day before, she'd received a lovely fruit basket from the movie's executive producers, welcoming her on board. She couldn't imagine whom the plant was from.

To her utter shock, the face that emerged from behind the foliage was Trent's.

"I hope it's okay that I dropped by."

Savannah made no move to invite him in. "What are you doing here?"

"I went to New York to visit my mother. She wanted to send you something congratulating you on your new role. I offered to deliver it myself."

"Why would you bother?"

He ignored her blunt question. "Can I come in?"

Reluctantly she stepped back and made a sweeping gesture with her arm. Once Trent and his enormous plant were inside, she put the bowl back on the entry table and closed her front door. Trent looked around the snug living room for a place to set down his burden.

"You don't have a lot of room."

Stunned by his criticism, she crossed her arms over her chest. "It's only Dylan and me. We don't need a lot of space." That said, she stared at him.

"How about if I put it here for now." He set it on the breakfast bar, well out of reach of Dylan's grasp. "I like his dragon costume."

"He's dressed up for Halloween."

"Are you taking him trick-or-treating?"

"We went to the mall yesterday for a Halloween event. Tonight I thought we'd stay home and hand out candy."

"Sounds like fun. Do you want some company?"

She couldn't believe he was standing in her living room, acting as if he didn't wish she'd never come back into his life. Should she confront him on what she had overheard? Her grandmother had often said that those who eavesdrop shouldn't expect to hear good things said about themselves.

"While I appreciate whatever this is you're attempting to do," she began in a severe tone, her broken heart jabbing at her ribs with each breath, "I can't have you popping into and out of our lives anytime you want. I grew up being shuffled between my father and grandmother, and that's not what I want for Dylan. He deserves stability and consistency."

"Is that your way of saying that you don't want me to be part of his life?"

His audacity left her dumbfounded. "Last week you wished you'd never learned the truth."

"I never told you that."

"I overheard you talking to Melody." Savannah's voice broke. "You don't want to be a father. I get it. Why do you think I didn't tell you in the first place?"

"I was upset. I should never have said that."

"But it's what you felt." And as much as the truth had hurt, she preferred it to the lies Rafe had told her.

"Only for a brief moment. You caught me off guard. All I could think was that you'd kept a huge secret from me, and I couldn't accept that you had your reasons for doing so."

"I'm sorry I didn't tell you right away. I never should have listened to Rafe."

"He told you to keep the truth about Dylan from me?"

"He explained to me about that girl in college." When Trent stared at her blankly, Savannah continued, "The one who got pregnant. You helped her take care of it?"

At last comprehension dawned. "Lisa Wheeler. What does that have to do with our situation?"

"You didn't want to be a father then any more than you do now."

"Wait." Trent raised his hands in a stop gesture. "I didn't get Lisa pregnant. I just helped her. She was a friend. She helped me get a B in a poetry class. We never even dated. She'd been raped and was severely traumatized. I tried to get her to go to the police, but she was from a conservative family and didn't want them to know."

"But why would Rafe..." Savannah's stomach turned over. "He lied to me." And why not. Rafe had deceived her several times before that.

"I had no idea your opinion of me was so low." Trent's lips twitched into a sardonic line.

Perhaps in this instance she'd judged him a little too

harshly. "To be fair, you were pretty vocal about your view regarding the whole marriage and kids thing. You didn't want anything to tie you down."

"You were right to listen to Rafe. I gave you no reason to think otherwise. At some point I let my father's negative opinions define me. I figured if I was going to be labeled selfish and no good, I might as well act that way."

"So, what did you hope to gain by coming here?" She didn't understand what he wanted from her. "If you're interested in being part of Dylan's life, I welcome that. I would never keep him from you."

Her son recognized his name and got to his feet. He toddled over to Trent and lifted his arms, asking to be picked up. Savannah's throat tightened as Trent scooped up Dylan and checked out the costume.

"This is really cute. I especially like his horns." Trent's crooked smile had a detrimental effect on Savannah's equilibrium.

She cautioned herself not to read too much into his visit. Just because he'd made an effort to stop by didn't mean his opinions had changed.

Her son was an excellent diversion from her tumultuous emotions. "Dylan, what does the dragon say?"

To her delight Dylan growled, first at her and then his father. Trent laughed.

"I heard you two doing this the night before you left. You were having so much fun. I didn't know how to handle how I was feeling." He lifted Dylan into the air, making him giggle. Trent stared at his son for a long moment, his smile fading. At last he returned his attention to Savannah. "Since then I've had time to think. I want to be part of your life."

"I think that would be great for Dylan." And she meant it.

"What about for you?"

What about her? Having him around all the time would be bittersweet. In her life, but never truly hers.

"I've really missed you." She thought that was safe to admit. But to keep him from getting the wrong idea, she continued, "We were friends for a long time before anything happened between us in New York. It'll be great to be on good terms once again."

"Do you want to go back to being just friends?"

She opened her mouth to say no, but the word couldn't make it past the lump in her throat. The last thing Savannah wanted was to be just friends with Trent, but she couldn't go down that road to heartache again.

He began before speaking again without waiting for her answer. "At one point you thought you'd be okay living in Vegas. Do you still think that's a possibility?"

"We could talk about it. Now that I'm working, my financial situation isn't so dire and I can afford more house there than here."

"And you're okay about traveling back and forth?"

Now that his father was no longer entertaining him, Dylan decided he wanted to be put down and squirmed until Trent set the boy on the floor once more.

"Scarlett has made it work. I don't see why I can't, as well." Savannah watched Dylan head to the bin where she kept his musical train. Plastic clattered as he pulled the pieces out. "My son's happiness is important to me. If living in Las Vegas means you and Dylan get to spend as much time together as possible, then that's what I'll do."

"What about your happiness?"

Since leaving Trent behind and moving to LA she'd discovered peace, but not joy. "I've learned I can be content anywhere as long as I have my family."

"I've learned something, too." He took her hands in his. "The only time I'm happy is when I'm with you."

Savannah stared at Trent while blood pounded in her

ears. Had she heard him right? Or was she imagining the words she longed to hear?

"But you said…"

"Forget what I said. I was an idiot. I've been an idiot for a long time. Nothing else explains why I ever let you go." Trent tugged her up against him. "I love you."

A stunned Savannah was marveling at her abrupt turn of fortune even as Trent's lips closed over hers. His kiss reflected all the hunger and longing that filled her. She held on for dear life as her future shifted onto a new track. When at long last he broke the kiss, she was breathless and gloriously happy.

"I love you." His deep voice gave weight to the phrase. "I made the mistake of letting you go once. I can't let that happen again."

Savannah's chest ached at the pain and loss she glimpsed in his gaze. "I'm not going anywhere." She glanced at Dylan, who could not have been less interested in what was going on between his parents. "We are not going anywhere."

"Promise?"

"I promise."

Trent pushed her to arm's length and narrowed his eyes. "I think I need something more concrete than your verbal acceptance."

She laughed. "Do you want it in writing?"

"Absolutely. I demand a legally binding agreement." He reached into his pocket and pulled out a box. He popped the lid and showed her a gorgeous diamond ring. "Will you marry me?"

The engagement ring blurred as tears filled Savannah's eyes. Unable to shake her uncertainty, she whispered, "Are you sure about this?" Her breath stopped as he plucked the ring free of the box and slid it onto her finger.

"I've never been more sure of anything in my life."

"Then, yes." Giddy beyond anything she could imagine, Savannah threw her arms around his neck and hugged him tight. Crushed in his return embrace, she couldn't stop smiling. "I love you so much."

"You and Dylan are my everything. I never want us to be apart ever again."

That brought up a logistical problem. "It's going to be a while until that happens, with me here doing the movie and you in Las Vegas running Club T's."

"I've already got that covered. Both Kyle and Nate are in Vegas for the foreseeable future. Nate plans to get back in the studio, and Kyle has his relationship with my sister to save." He put his arm around her. "I'm going to stay in LA and take care of Dylan while you're working."

That he'd obviously thought this through and was delighted with the prospect lightened her heart. Yet, she remained cautious.

"That's all well and good," Savannah said, appreciating Trent's willingness to throw himself into being Dylan's father, but unsure whether the new role would be enough to satisfy him. "But won't you be bored without some business venture to challenge you?"

"No, because in addition to looking for space for a location for a new club here in LA, I have recently become part owner of a record label in desperate need of help."

"You have?" Something about his self-satisfied expression stirred her suspicions. "You don't mean..."

"Siggy sold the label to Ugly Trout Records. Nate and I now own West Coast Records." Trent's smug grin was difficult to resist, and Savannah found her lips curving in response.

"How?"

"Nate made Siggy an offer he couldn't refuse."

"But you and Nate are business partners in the club. Didn't Siggy realize that?"

"We're also partners in Ugly Trout Records. I helped him with the start-up five years ago."

"Aren't you worried he'll find out you're behind this?"

"Siggy is a bastard. He was so determined to keep me away from West Coast Records that he was willing to dump the company to keep it out of my hands." Trent gave a dismissive shrug. "And anyway, it's too late for him to pull out. The papers are signed."

Savannah smiled as she imagined what her father-in-law's reaction would be when he found out. "He's going to have a fit."

"Too bad. He should have done his research."

"And now you own the company that should have been yours all along." Savannah lifted on tiptoe and brought Trent's lips back to hers for a passionate kiss that left them both breathing hard. "You are clever, talented, and I love you."

Trent's, his smile faded. "I never thought you'd look at me like that ever again."

"Like what?"

"Like I was someone you believed in." He grazed his fingertips across her cheeks and cupped her face. "Ever since I can remember, my father has told me I'm selfish and flawed. He said I would ruin people's lives the way I had ruined his. While I couldn't figure out what I'd done wrong, I accepted that he was right. In the end it became my excuse for the way I'd let you down." He pressed his lips to her forehead. "Every time I saw how I'd disappointed you, I ached for the pain I caused."

"I've always believed in you." Savannah had long known that Siggy was to blame for Trent's commitment issues. "It was believing in us where I lost faith."

An intense glow lit his eyes, transfixing her. "I promise to do everything in my power to make sure that never happens again."

And as he sealed his vow with a slow, reverent kiss, Savannah knew wherever she lived in the future, as long as she was with Dylan and Trent, she would be home.

* * * * *

ONE SECRET NIGHT, ONE SECRET BABY

CHARLENE SANDS

Special thanks to my wonderful son-in-law, Zac Prange, who helped me with the on-set moviemaking details of this story. Your support and expertise really meant a great deal, keeping the story honest and authentic. With love to you, Nikki our fabulous daughter, and of course your two sweet princesses who brighten our lives every day, Everley and Lila.

One

She wasn't a one-night stand sort of girl.

Emma Rae Bloom was predictable, hardworking, ambitious and least of all, adventurous. *Boring*. She never did anything out of the ordinary. She was measured and sure and patient. *Double boring*. The one time she'd crushed that mold, breaking it to bits, was at her neighbor Eddie's blowout bash at Havens on Sunset Boulevard in celebration of his thirtieth birthday last month. She'd partied hard, lost her inhibitions as well as her mind during the now infamous Los Angeles blackout and wound up in bed with her best friend's brother, Hollywood heartthrob in the flesh, Dylan McKay.

She'd had secret dibs on Brooke's brother since the age of twelve. He was the older boy with sea-blue eyes and stubble on his face who'd treated her kindly and given her a measuring stick to compare all men against.

There was no going back to reclaim their night together, although her memory of her time with Dylan was almost nonexistent. Just her luck, she had her first ever one-night stand with the hottest guy on earth and her mind had gone as foggy as a London winter day. Too many mango mojitos could do that, she'd been told.

She stood at the port-side railing of Dylan's yacht now. As he approached her, his head wrapped with gauze bandages, a haunted look on his face spoke of sadness and grief. It was a somber day, but beaming rays of sunshine and stunning marshmallow fluff clouds didn't seem to know that. She pushed her sunglasses farther up her nose, grateful to hide her true emotions.

Roy Benjamin was gone, killed in the freakish stunt accident on the set of Dylan's Navy SEAL movie. The tragedy had rocked Hollywood insiders and made a big splash on the news, even eclipsing the story of how the lights went out in the city just the day before. It wasn't just Roy's death that had rocked the entertainment world and hit the headlines with a bang, but Dylan's amnesia resulting from the same blast that had killed his friend.

"Here, have a soda." Brooke walked up beside her brother and offered Emma a glass. "You look like you could use one."

"Thanks." She accepted the benign drink. No more alcohol for her, thank you very much. "It's a hard day for everyone." She sipped her cola.

Standing between her and Brooke, Dylan wrapped his arms around them. "I'm glad you both are here with me today."

Emma's nerves squeezed tight. She hadn't seen Dylan since the night of the blackout. The supportive arm around her shoulders shouldn't elicit any of the sensations she was having. It shouldn't. She sighed. His hand caressed her upper arm lightly, sending shock waves through her system. As the yacht backed out of its slip, his body lurched, two hundred pounds of solid granite shoulder to shoulder with her. She stopped breathing for a second and gripped the railing.

"Of course we'd be here," Brooke said. "Roy was a friend of ours, too. Right, Emma?"

She gave Dylan a quick smile. It was such a tragedy that a man so vital and strong as Roy had died at such a young age. He was a Dylan look-alike, his stunt double and a close friend to the McKays. Emma only knew Roy through them and he'd always been nice to her.

Dylan's lips curled up a little, the subdued smile of a man in mourning. "I miss him already."

He tightened his hold, bringing their bodies close. He was the consummate movie star, sunglasses shading his face, blond hair blowing in the breeze and a body carved from hard gym workouts and daily runs. He was Hollywood royalty, a man who'd managed to steer clear of lasting relationships his entire adult life. Darkly tanned, as talented and smart as he was good-looking, he had it all.

Emma should be concentrating on Roy's death instead of her dilemma. Yet as she'd dressed this morning readying for Roy's memorial, she'd rehearsed what she would say if Dylan remembered anything that happened between them during the blackout.

I wasn't myself that night. The blackout freaked me out. I've been afraid of the dark since I was a kid and I begged you to stay with me. Can we just go on being friends?

Now it looked as if she could dodge that confession. Soul-melting blue eyes, dimmed now from grief, settled upon her as they always had. He saw her as his sister Brooke's friend, nothing more. He had no memory of their night together. The doctors termed it dissociative amnesia. He was blocked and might never remember the hours or days leading up to the blast that took his friend's life and sent a hunk of shrapnel tunneling into his head. He'd been knocked unconscious and had woken up hours later, in the hospital.

He let her go to sip his soda and she began breathing normally again. Cautiously she took a step away from him. Having his hand on her played too much havoc with her brain. She had escaped telling him the truth today, and the devil on her shoulder whispered in her ear, *Why rock the boat?* Clever little fiend. *This can be your little secret.*

Could she really get away with not having to tell him?

She battled with the notion as the yacht made its way out of Marina del Rey, traveling past the docks at a snail's pace. Pungent sea scents filled her nostrils, seagulls squawked overhead and one white-winged bird landed on a buoy and quietly watched the yacht head into open seas.

"I guess it's time," Dylan said, minutes later, once they were far enough out to sea. Dylan wanted to do this alone, with just his family. Later today, a memorial would be held at his Moonlight Beach home open to Roy's friends and fellow crew and cast members, the only family he'd ever known. That's when Emma and Brooke would go to work, hosting an informal buffet dinner in Roy's honor. It definitely wasn't a Parties-To-Go kind of event, but Dylan had turned to them for help. "Roy always joked, if he missed the net from a ten-story fall, to make sure I tossed his ashes from the *Classy Lady*. He loved this boat, but I never thought I'd ever have to do this."

Brooke's doe eyes softened on her brother and Emma hurt inside for both of them. Brooke and Dylan were miles apart in most things, but when push came to shove, they were always there for each other. Emma envied that. She had no siblings. She had no real family, except for foster parents, two people who'd taken her in and then neglected her as a child. She hadn't hit the jackpot in the parent department, that was for sure. Not like Brooke. Brooke was Dylan's younger foster sister whom his parents had eventually adopted. They were totally amazing. They'd been better parents to Emma than the two who'd collected monthly checks on her behalf.

Dylan made swift work of saying heartfelt words about his friend, his voice tightening up to get it all out, right before he opened the urn, lifted it up and let the wind carry Roy's ashes out to sea. When he turned around, tears filled his eyes and his mouth quivered in heartbreak. She'd never seen this vulnerable side of Dylan and she gripped the railing tight to keep from going to him. It wasn't her place.

Brooke went to him and cradled him in her arms the way a mother would a child, whispering soft words of sympathy in his ear. Dylan nodded his head as he listened to his baby sister. After a few minutes he wiped the tears from his eyes and the solemn expression from his face. He gave Brooke a sweet smile.

Dylan McKay was back.

It was the first time Emma had ever seen him let his guard down.

It touched her soul.

Secret dibs.

Dylan's kitchen could swallow up her little apartment in one large gulp. Every kind of new age appliance ever conceived was set on the shiny onyx granite counter and in the textured white cabinets. It was a culinary dream kitchen and his housekeeper, Maisey, made great use of it. She'd cooked up a storm for the fifty-plus people who'd come to pay their respects to Roy Benjamin. Aside from Maisey's home cooking, the caterers Emma had commissioned delivered trays of finger foods, specialty breads and appetizers. Everyone from grips to the president of Stage One Studios was here. Emma and Brooke, dressed in appropriate black dresses with little ornamentation, set out the food and offered drinks to the guests. They weren't acting as Parties-To-Go planners today as much as they were Dylan's hostesses for this sad event.

"Did you see what Callista is wearing?" Brooke muttered under her breath.

Emma set out a plate of sweet-cream-and-berry tarts on the dessert table, shooting a quick glance to the living room, where many of the guests were gathered. Callista Lee Allen, daughter to the Stage One Studio mogul, was on Dylan's arm, hanging on his every word. She wore Versace, and the only reason Emma knew that was because she'd overheard the blonde gloating about it. It was a silver glimmer dress with detailed layering and jewels dripping off her throat and arms. "I see."

"It's not as if the Fashion Police are trolling. Roy deserves better. This day isn't about her."

Emma grinned. "Tell me how you really feel, Brooke. At least she talks to you. I'm invisible to her." Being a friend of Dylan's sister didn't rank high enough on Callista's status scale to award Emma an iota of her attention.

"Be grateful. Be very grateful."

Emma stood back from the arrangement, giving the presentation scrutiny. They'd draped the dessert table with tablecloths in varying colors and edged each platter with flowering vines. This is what they did. And they did it well.

"It's none of my business, but Dylan's on-again, off-again relationship with her isn't good for him," Brooke said.

Emma shot them another glance. Callista's eyes flashed on Dylan's bandage, one hand possessively on his arm as she reached up with the other to touch the injury. Emma watched the scene play out. Dylan was deep in conversation with Callista's father and didn't seem to notice her unabashed attention.

Sucking oxygen in, Emma glanced away and tamped down pangs of jealousy swimming through her body. She'd be ten times a fool to think she'd ever have a chance with Dylan. He was her friend. Period. "He's a big boy, Brooke."

"I never thought I'd say this, but thank God my brother doesn't commit. She's all wrong in so many ways." Brooke lifted her hands in a stopping motion that was her signature move. "But like I said, none of my beeswax."

Emma smiled at her friend and put the finishing touches on the dessert table. Maisey had made coffee and there was hot water and a sampler box of teas available.

Dylan approached, gorgeous in a tailored dark suit and tie. He'd changed his clothes from the jeans and black silk shirt he'd worn this morning on the yacht. "Do you two have a minute?" he asked quietly. His brows were gathered in question. Brooke and Emma nodded and he guided them to the far side of the kitchen, out of earshot of anyone. It was all so curious.

"You girls have done wonderful today. Thank you," he began and then shook his head. "I'm figuring you'd give it to me straight. Callista and I…are we a thing again?"

Emma held her breath. She wouldn't comment on her thoughts about the bottle blonde. Dylan didn't exactly confide in her about his love life, but his earnest question made her stomach ripple in guilt. She had a truth to tell him, too, and maybe it would help spark his memory, but it could also make things weird between them, which was the last thing she wanted.

Brooke seemed eager to answer, but shook her head as if formulating her thoughts. "You don't remember?"

"No. But she's acting like we're ready for the altar. From what I remember, that wasn't the case. Am I wrong?"

"No, you're certainly not wrong," Brooke shot back. "Not even close. Before…before your accident, you told me you were going to break it off with her for good."

"I did? I don't remember." Poor Dylan was struggling. His gaze lifted to the wide windows that opened out onto the sea, as if he were searching for answers there. He seemed lost right now, not his usual self-confident, always-one-step-ahead-of-everyone, charming self.

"If she says it's more, Dylan, I'd be careful," Brooke offered. "She's banking on your amnesia to worm her way back into your…"

Dylan turned to his sister, his brows lifting and a crooked smile emerging. "My what?"

"Your good graces," Emma finished for her.

Dylan slid her a knowing look. "Always the diplomat, Em. But somehow, I don't think that's what Brooke was going to say." He began nodding. "Okay, I get the picture." He glanced at Callista, who was now surrounded by a few other actors in the film. She was deep in conversation yet constantly casting him furtive glances at every opportunity, sizing him up and staking her claim.

Brooke was right—Callista was all wrong for Dylan. How difficult it must be for him not to remember some things, not to have a grasp on his feelings. "You're the only ones I can trust," he said. He rubbed his brow, just under his bandage. "I can't tell you how bizarre this feels. I see some things clearly. Other things are fuzzy at best. And then there's a whole chunk that I don't remember."

Emma plunked three ice cubes into a glass and poured him a root beer, his favorite from childhood. "Here, drink up."

"Thanks," he said, "though I could use something stronger."

"The doctor says not yet. You're still on pain meds." Brooke's internal mother came out. It really was sweet seeing how close the two had become since the move from Ohio to Los Angeles years ago.

"One drink won't kill me."

"Let's not find out, okay? I was worried enough when you were sent to the hospital. And Mom just went home two days ago. If I have to call her again to tell her you're back in Saint Joseph's, she'll have a heart attack."

Dylan rolled his eyes. "You see how good she is, Emma? She knows exactly how to lay on the guilt."

A chuckle rumbled from Emma's throat. "I know all about Brooke's tactics. I work with her."

"Hey!" Brooke said. "You're supposed to be on my side."

"Like I said, Emma's a diplomat. Thanks for the drink." He lifted his glass in mock toast and then pivoted around and walked away.

"He'll be okay," Brooke said, watching him head back to his guests. "We just have to do whatever it takes to help him along."

Dread formed a tight knot in Emma's stomach. She hated keeping secrets from Brooke. They usually shared everything. But how exactly could she come out and say, *I begged your brother to sleep with me the night of the blackout and all I remember is his body on mine, heated breaths and sexy words whispered in my ear.* She didn't remember how she got in bed or when he left her that night. She couldn't recall how they'd ended things. Were there parting words recognizing the big mistake? Or had he promised to call her? He had no knowledge of what they'd done, but geesh, she didn't recall much of that night, either.

"Oh, brother," she mumbled.

"What?" Brooke asked.

"Nothing. Nothing at all."

"Brooke, you did a wonderful job today," Callista said, leaning her arms over the granite island, spilling her cleavage and smiling her billion-dollar smile. The sun was setting and all but one guest had left the memorial service. "You helped make the day easier for your brother."

"It wasn't just me, Callie," Brooke said. "Emma did her

fair share of the work and we'd both do anything to help Dylan get through this day."

Callista's gaze darted Emma's way as if she'd just noticed her standing there. *Hello, I'm not invisible.* "Of course, you, too, Emma." She spoke to her as if she were a child. What was it with rich powerful women that made them feel superior, just by right of wealth? Emma could probably run circles around her SAT scores. "You did a marvelous job."

"Dylan's a special guy and I'm happy to help."

Callista gave her a cursory nod, eyeing her for just a second as if measuring the competition, and then turned away, writing her off.

"Brooke, do you know where Dylan is? I want to say goodbye to him and tell him his eulogy was touching."

"Yeah, I do. He said to say goodbye to you for him. The day tired him out. He went to sleep."

"He's in bed already?" Callista straightened and her gaze moved toward the hallway staircase. She knew exactly where Dylan's bedroom was. "Maybe I should go up and wish him good-night."

"He, uh, needs uninterrupted rest. Doctor's orders." Brooke's accomplished smile brought Emma a stream of silent chuckles. Leave it to Brooke. She was in defense mode now.

"Yes, of course, you're right." She nibbled on her lip, shooting another longing glance at the staircase. Then her expression changed. "He does need to rest up so he can be back on set as soon as possible."

The SEAL movie had been shut down for a month already and it was costing the studio big bucks, so Dylan's return to the set was essential. Even Callista recognized that fact. "Tell him I'll call him."

"Will do, Callie. I'll walk you out."

"Oh, that's not necessary," Callista said.

"I don't mind."

After the two left, Emma couldn't contain her laughter. She knew for certain Callista Lee Allen hated to be called Callie, yet she let Brooke get away with it because she was Dylan's sister.

What a day it had been. Selfishly, Emma was glad it was over. She didn't like walking around with a cloud of guilt over her head. She hoped "out of sight, out of mind" would work on her. As soon as she left Dylan's house, maybe her head would clear and she'd be free of this grating bug gnawing at her to tell Dylan what happened between them.

Finished with her duties, the house clean and back to normal, thanks to Maisey and her efforts, Emma took a seat on one of the many white leather sofas in the living room. A pastel pop of color fading on the horizon grabbed her attention as she looked out the window. The sunset was beautiful on Moonlight Beach. She leaned back, closed her eyes and listened to the sound of the waves breaking on the shore.

"Mission accomplished," Brooke said, clapping her hands. "She's gone."

Emma snapped to attention as Brooke sat down beside her. "You're a regular Mama Bear. Who knew?"

"Normally, Dylan can take care of himself, but right now, he needs a little help. What else are meddling little sisters for anyway?"

"To keep conniving women away from him?"

"I try my best." Brooke propped her feet on a cocktail table and sighed. "I'm getting excited about the celebrity golf tournament coming up. This is one of the biggest events we've ever booked. And we got it all on our own. No intervention from Dylan. They don't even know he's my brother. Dylan doesn't play golf."

"I don't?" Dylan walked into the room looking adorably rumpled. It was the five-o'clock shadow, the mussedto-perfection hair and those deep blue bedroom eyes that did Emma in. He wore a pair of black sweats and a white T-shirt.

"No, you don't," Brooke said, eyeing him carefully.

He grinned. "Just joking. I know I don't play golf. At least I have memories of tanking every shot. Never did get the hang of it."

"Brat. What are you doing up?"

On a long sigh, he ran a hand down his face. "I can't sleep. I'm going for a walk. I'll see you guys later. Thanks again for everything."

Brooke's mouth opened, but he was out the back door before she could stop him. "Darn it. He's still having dizzy spells. Will you go with him, Emma? Tell him you're in the mood for a walk, too. He already thinks I baby him enough."

Emma balked. She was three minutes away from escaping to go home. "I, uh…"

"Please?" Brooke begged. "If you're with him, he won't get it into his head to start jogging. I know he misses it. He's been complaining about not doing his daily runs. It's almost dark on the beach. He could collapse and no one would know."

It was true. The doctor said he shouldn't overdo any physical activity. How could she deny Brooke the peace of mind? She'd been worried sick about her brother lately. "Okay, I'll go."

"That's why I love you." Brooke sounded relieved.

Emma bent to remove her heels and rose from the sofa. "You better," she said. "I don't chase handsome A-list movie stars for just anyone." With that, she walked out the back entrance of Dylan's mansion, climbed down the stairs, searched for signs of him and took off at a jog when she'd seen how far he'd already traveled.

"Dylan," she called, her toes squishing into wet sand as she trudged rapidly after him. "Wait up."

He turned around and slowed his pace.

"Would you like company?" Her breathing ragged, she fibbed, "I feel like a walk, too."

"Let me guess. Brooke sent you."

She shrugged. "Maybe I just felt like taking a walk?"

His mouth lifted in a dubious smile. "And maybe the moon is green."

"Everyone knows the moon is made of cheese, therefore it's yellow."

He shook his head, seeming to relinquish his skepticism. "Okay, let's walk. Actually, I would like your company."

He took her hand, his fingers lacing with hers.

How...unexpected. Her breath froze in her chest.

"It was a nice memorial, wasn't it?" he asked as he resumed walking.

There was a slight tug on her hand that woke her from her stupor and she fell in step with him. "It was heartwarming. You honored Roy with a wonderful tribute to his life."

"I'm the only family he had, aside from his crew. He was a great guy and it's just a ridiculous shame. Roy was obsessed with his stunts. He spent his whole life perfecting them. He was the most cautious man I've ever known. It just doesn't make sense."

"They're saying it was a freakish accident."

Dylan took a sharp breath. "That's what they say when they don't know what happened. It's the standard answer."

They walked on in silence for a while, the heat from where he held her hand warming her entire body. It was actually a perfect evening for a stroll on the beach. Breezes blew at the twist of hair at the back of her head. She reached up and pulled it out of its band, freeing the long waves that touched the middle of her back.

"So tell me what's going on in your life, Emma."

Her brows gathered at the oddity of the request. Dylan knew just about everything about her. She was Brooke's friend and business partner. She lived in a tiny apartment twenty minutes away from Moonlight Beach. She loved her work and didn't go out much.

Oh, no! Did he remember something? Blood drained from her face as her mind worked overtime for signs that he'd remembered that blackout night. But as she dared to gaze at his profile, his eyes didn't probe her but stayed straight ahead, his neutral expression unchanged. She let out a relieved sigh. Maybe he needed to break the silence. Maybe he was just making conversation. And maybe her guilty conscience was wringing her dry.

"The same old, same old," she answered. "Work, work, work."

"Still hoping to make your first million before thirty?"

Her laugh came out a little too high-pitched. Brooke must've told him of her long-term goal. How embarrassing. Ever since she was a child, money had been scarce. Her foster parents didn't have much and were stingy in sharing. She didn't know that until she'd grown into a teen, of course, and witnessed how they'd splurge what they did have on each other. Never her. She grew up mostly wearing thrift store clothes. From the age of thirteen, Emma knew she'd have to find her own way in the world. She'd worked her ass off, achieving a full scholarship to college, and vowed she'd become financially independent one day. The promise she made herself was that by the age of thirty, she would make her first million. She had several years to go, but her hopes were high of expanding Parties-To-Go into a million-dollar franchise.

"Your sister, my best friend, needs to button her mouth."

"Don't blame Brooke," he said softly. "I think it's commendable to have goals."

"Lofty goals."

"Attainable goals and you work hard, Emma."

"Without your investment, we wouldn't even have a business."

"I just helped you get started, and in the two years since you've been working at it, you've come a long way."

"We owe you, Dylan. You've been amazing. We want to make you proud."

Dylan stopped, his Nikes digging into the sand, and when she turned to him, a genuine smile graced his handsome face. Gone was the sadness from before. A glint of appreciation twinkled in his eyes. "You don't owe me anything. And I am proud. You're a hard worker, and you're paying me back faster than I expected or wanted. But, Em, I have to tell you, as much as you believe Brooke has helped you through the growing-up years, you've helped her, too. She came to California hoping to become an actress. God, it's a tough business. I've been lucky…more fortunate than I could've hoped, but it's not the same for Brooke. She's much happier now, being in business with her best friend and earning a legitimate living doing what she loves. I owe that to you. So thank you for being…*you.*"

Dylan leaned in, his face coming within inches of hers. Her heart rate escalated as she stared at his mouth. She understood now why his female fans swooned. He was breathtaking and yummy. There was no other way to describe it. "You're the amazing one, Emma," he whispered.

Her mind going fuzzy, she whispered back, "I am?"

As he inched closer, taking her into his arms, angling for her cheek, her entire body relaxed. Of course, he'd give her a sisterly kiss on the cheek. She closed her eyes.

His warm lips came down softly.

On her mouth.

Oh, she'd died and gone to heaven. His lips were warm and giving and soothing. She wrapped her arms around his neck and brazenly returned the kiss. Wow. It was all so new. And exciting. Dylan McKay was kissing her on Moonlight Beach at sunset and she was fully in the moment this time. There were no gaps of memory from a fuzzy brain. There wasn't anything but right now, this speck of time, and she relished the taste of him, the amazing texture of his firm lips caressing hers, the strength and power of his body close to hers.

But something still seemed slightly off with his kiss. She couldn't quite put her finger on it. Was it just that she was fully aware, fully attuned to him right now?

Dylan broke off the kiss first, and instead of backing away, he grasped Emma to his chest tightly like a little boy needing the comfort of his favorite stuffed toy. Elmo or Teddy or Winnie the Pooh.

She stood in his embrace for long moments. He sighed and continued to hold her. Then his mouth touched her right earlobe and he whispered, "Thank you. I needed your company tonight, Emma."

What could she say? Was she foolish enough to think he remembered their night of passion and wanted more? No, that wasn't it. Dylan needed comforting. Maybe what she considered to be a heart-melting kiss, only counted as a friendly measure of comfort for a man whose life was full of adoration. At least, she could give him that.

Her secret was safe.

"You're welcome, Dylan."

Glad to be of service.

Two

Dylan wasn't himself. That had to explain why he'd kissed Emma as though he meant it. Actually, he *had* meant it in that instant. She was familiar to him. He knew the score with her, his sister Brooke's best friend. Someone he could trust. Someone he could rely on. The meds he was taking lessened his headaches and he was recovering, feeling better every day. But having a chunk of his memory gone affected his decision making and confidence, made him vulnerable and uncertain.

But one thing he was certain about: kissing Emma had made him feel better. It was the best kiss he'd had in a long time. It packed a wallop. He knew that without question. Those big green eyes that sparkled like emeralds wouldn't steer him wrong. He'd needed the connection to feel whole again. To feel like himself.

Had he gotten all that from one mildly passionate kiss? Yeah. Because it was with Emma and he knew his limitations with her. She was untouchable and sweet with a side of sassy. So he'd kissed her and let the sugar in her fill him up and take away the pain in his heart.

"You're quiet," he said to her as they walked back toward his house. "Was the kiss out of line?"

"No. Not at all. You needed someone."

He covered her hand with his again and squeezed gently. "Not just anyone, Emma. I needed someone I could trust. You. Sorry if I came on too strong."

"You…didn't."

But she didn't sound so sure.

"It was just a kiss, Dylan. It's not as if you haven't kissed me before."

"Birthday kisses don't count."

She was quiet for a second. "I didn't have a lot of affection when I was younger. Those birthday kisses meant a lot to me."

He gave her another quick squeeze of the hand. "I know. Hey, remember the face-plant kiss?"

"Oh, God. Don't bring that up, Dylan. I'm still mortified. Your parents went to a lot of trouble to make that cake for me."

He chuckled at the image popping into his head. "Damn, that was funny."

"It was your fault!"

Dylan's smirk stayed plastered on his face. He couldn't wipe it clean. At least his long-term memory was intact. "How was it my fault?"

"Rusty was your dog, wasn't he? He tangled under my feet and in that moment I figured it was better to fall into the cake than snuff out your dog. I would've crushed that little Chihuahua if my full weight landed on him."

"What were you, twelve at the time?"

"Yes! It said so on the birthday cake I demolished."

Dylan snorted a laugh. "At least you got to taste it. It

was all over your face. The rest of us just got to watch. But it was worth it."

"You should've given me my birthday kiss before your mom kindly wiped my face clean. Then maybe you wouldn't have felt so deprived. The cake was good, you know. Chocolate marble."

"Oh, don't worry, Em. I wasn't deprived."

She stopped abruptly, taking a stand in the sand, pulling her hand free of his and folding her arms across her middle. "What's that supposed to mean? You enjoyed seeing me fall?"

The phony pout on her face brought him a lightness that he hadn't felt in more than a week, since before the accident.

"Oh, come on, Miss Drama Queen. It was many moons ago." And yes, he knew stuntmen, Roy included, who couldn't have done a better pratfall. It had been hilarious.

"Me? Drama queen? I don't think so. I'm standing here, looking at a true-life drama king. Mr. Winner of two Academy Awards and God only knows how many Golden Globes."

"Three." He grinned.

She rolled her eyes. "Three," she repeated.

He walked back to where she'd made her stand and grabbed up her hand again, tugging her along. He liked Emma Rae Bloom. She'd had a tough life, raised by neglectful foster parents. Just by the grace of all good things, she'd become his sister's best friend, and thus, a member of the McKay clan.

They were almost back to his house. It was sundown, a time when the beach was quiet but for the waves washing upon the shore. Moonlight illuminated the water and reflected off the sand where he stopped to face Emma. "Well, you've succeeded where many have failed this week, Em. You've put a smile on my face."

Her pert little chin lifted to him, and he balked at the urge to take her into his arms again. To kiss that mouth and feel the lushness of her long hair against his palms. She was petite in size and stature, especially without shoes on, and so different than the tall lean models and actresses he'd dated.

He wouldn't kiss her again. But it surprised him how badly he wanted to.

He pursed his lips and went with his gut. "Hey, you know, I've got this charity gig coming up. If the doctors say I'm good to go, I'd love for you to join me for the meet and greet at Children's West Hospital."

Emma turned away from him now, to gaze out to sea. "You want me to go with you?"

"Yep."

"Don't you have agents and personal assistants to do that sort of thing?"

"Em?"

"What?"

Tucking his hands in his pockets, he shrugged. "It's okay if you don't want to go."

She whipped her head around, her eyes a spark of brightness against the dim skies. "Why do you want *me* to go?"

"The truth? I'm a little mixed-up right now. Having a friend come along will make me feel a little safer. I haven't been out in public since the accident. Besides, I know the kids will love you. I was going to ask Brooke, too."

"Oh." She ducked her head, looking sheepish. "These kids, are they all ill?"

"Mostly, yes. But many are in recovery, thank goodness. I'm slated to do a promo spot in a few days with some of the kids to raise funds and awareness about the good the hospital does. I've donated a little to the new wing of the hospital and I guess that's why they've asked me."

"You donated 1.3 million dollars to the new wing, Dylan. I read that online. It's going to be amazing. The new wing will have a screening room with interactive games for the kids."

He smiled. "So what do you say?"

"Yes, of course I'll go."

"Thanks, Em. Now, let's get back inside before Brooke sends out a search party for us."

Emma's laughter filled his ears and made him smile again.

Late Wednesday afternoon, Emma hung up the phone with Mrs. Alma Montalvo, rested her arms on her office desk and hung her head. The client was delirious about details and had sapped Emma's energy for two long hours. Yes, they'd found a local band to play fifties tunes. Yes, they'd rented a '57 Chevy and it would be parked strategically at the top of their multitiered lawn for added effect. Yes, they'd have a photo booth decked out with leather jackets, poodle skirts and car club insignia for the guests to wear as they had their photos snapped. Yes, yes, yes.

Thank goodness the party was this Saturday night. After it was over, she and Brooke could take their big fat check from Mrs. Montalvo and say, *Hasta la vista, baby. Parties-To-Go has come and gone.*

The chime above the door rang out Leslie Gore's classic song "It's My Party" and Emma glanced up.

"Hey, I thought you were going home early today," Brooke said, entering their Santa Monica office.

"I thought I was, too, but Mrs. Montalvo had other ideas."

Brooke rolled her eyes. "We'll impress the hell out of her, Emma. The party is going to be top-notch."

"It better be. I've put in extra hours on this one."

Brooke grinned and set down shopping bags on the

desk adjacent to Emma's. The office furnishings were an eclectic mix, all colorful and light to convey a party atmosphere for clients. The desks were clear Plexiglas, the walls were painted bright pastels and the chairs were relics that had been upholstered in floral materials. Photos of their parties and events adorned the walls from hoedowns on local ranch properties to rich, elaborate weddings with a few celebrity endorsements mixed in, thanks to Dylan.

They had two part-time employees who came in after school and on weekends to answer phones, do online research and work the parties whenever needed.

"Take a look at this," Brooke said, pulling a mocha cocktail dress from a box in one of the bags. "Isn't it... perfect? I got it at the little shop on Broadway."

"Wow, it's gorgeous. And not black. I bet it's for the San Diego golf dinner, right?"

Brooke was shaking her head. "Nope, not at all. You'll never guess."

Emma's thoughts ran through a list of upcoming events and couldn't come up with anything. "Don't make me, then. Tell me!"

Brooke put the dress up to her chin, hugged it to her waist and twirled around, just like when they used to play dress-up and pretend to be princesses ready to meet their special prince.

"I have a date." Brooke sang out the words and stomped her feet.

It shouldn't be that monumental, but Brooke seldom dated. After graduating from college, they'd both been focused on the business. And Brooke was picky when it came to men. So this was a big deal, judging by the megawatt, light-up-Sunset-Boulevard smile on her face. "The best part is, he doesn't know who I am."

Or rather, who her brother was. Most people, men and women alike, showed interest in Brooke once they found out that Dylan was her big brother. It sucked big-time and made Brooke wary of any friendliness coming her way. She was never sure if there was an ulterior motive.

"I mean, of course he knows my name is Brooke. We met at Adele's Café. We were both waiting for our take-out lunch orders and it took forever. But once we got to talking, neither of us minded the long wait."

"When was this?"

"Yesterday."

"And you didn't tell me!" Wasn't that like breaking the BFF rule?

"I didn't know if he'd call." She hugged the dress one last time, before carefully stowing it back in the box. "But he did this morning and asked me out for the following weekend. And get this, he wanted to see me sooner but I told him about the event this weekend and he seemed really disappointed. We don't have anything next weekend. Tell me we don't. The golf tournament is in three weeks, right?"

Emma punched it up on her computer and glanced at their calendar. "Right, but you're so excited, even if we had an event, I'd relieve you of your duties. I've never seen you so gaga. What's his name?"

"Royce Brisbane. He's in financial planning."

Emma dug her teeth into her bottom lip to keep from chuckling. "You, with a suit?"

"Yes, but he looks dreamy in it."

"Wow, Brooke. You really like this guy. You shopped." Brooke was not a shopper. She had one color in her wardrobe arsenal, basic black, and she wore it like armor every day.

"I think I do like him. A lot. It was so easy talking to him. We have a lot in common."

"Tell me more."

After getting the full details on Royce Brisbane, Emma's thoughts went to Brooke's upcoming date on the drive home.

Emma had to admit, the guy sounded good on paper. If he made Brooke happy, then she was all for it. She hadn't seen Brooke smile so much in months. That could be a good thing, or a bad thing. A very bad thing. The more you care about someone, the more they could potentially hurt you. But Emma wouldn't poke a hole in Brooke's happy balloon; her friend deserved to have a good time.

Emma parked in her apartment structure and climbed out of her car. Her legs were two strands of thin spaghetti tonight. It was an effort to walk across the courtyard to her front door. She shoved the sticky door open with her body and glimpsed her comfy sofa with cushy pillows and a quilt she could curl up in. She dropped her purse unceremoniously onto the coffee table, sank down onto the sofa and let out a relieved sigh.

A hundred details ran through her head. The upcoming golf event was first and foremost in her mind. It wasn't for a few weeks yet, but it was a big opportunity for the business. She did yet another mental check, making sure all bases were covered, before she could really relax. Somewhat confident she hadn't forgotten anything, she lay her head down and stretched her legs out, allowing the cushions to envelop her weary body.

If only she could go mindless for a while. Sometimes she envied people who could close everything off and go blank. Just…be. She tended to overthink everything, which made her excellent at her job, but a sad prospect for a carefree lifestyle.

The night of the memorial for Roy Benjamin played in her head and she immediately zoomed in on Dylan McKay. The way he had held her on the beach, the way she had felt when his hand covered hers possessively, the way his mouth had moved over hers and claimed her in a kiss. It wasn't a birthday kiss. It wasn't a friend's kiss, either, though Dylan seemed to think so. It was much more for her. And the memory floated through her body and filled in all the lonely gaps.

Secret dibs.

She smiled. It was never going to happen, yet part of her fantasy had come true. Dylan had made glorious love to her. Okay, so she wasn't sure about the glorious part. She'd been too out of it to know if he was a good lover or not. But in her fantasy world, Dylan was the best. *Appeal* magazine had said so, too. He'd been voted Most Sexy Single this year. And there had been endorsements by his former girlfriends. So it had to be true.

Her eyes grew heavy. It was a battle to keep them open with the cushions supporting her fatigued body and the quilt covering her. All tucked in, she gave up the fight and surrendered to slumber.

Ruff, ruff...ruff, ruff.

Emma bolted upright, her eyes snapping to attention. She found herself on the sofa, half covered with her favorite quilt. How long had she been out? Squinting, she glanced at the wall clock. It was eight thirty. Wow, she'd been asleep for ninety minutes. She'd never taken a night-time nap before.

Ruff, ruff...ruff, ruff.

Her phone rang again. She grappled for it inside her purse and put it to her ear. "Hello."

"Hello."

It was Dylan. There was no mistaking that deep baritone voice that had half the female movie-viewing population panting to hear more. "Oh, hi."

She hinged her body up, planted her feet on the ground and shook her head to clear away the grogginess.

"I didn't wake you, did I?"

Did she sound as if she'd been sleeping? She tried her best to pretend she was wide-awake. "Not at all. I'm up."

"Busy?"

"No. Just sitting here…going over a few details in my head." A yawn crept out and she cupped her hand over her mouth to hide the sound. "What are you doing?"

"Nothing much. I spoke with Darren on the phone and my manager stopped by to check on me tonight. To be honest, I'm going a little stir-crazy."

"You're used to being busy."

"I can't wait to get back to work. But then, I'm dreading it at the same time."

"I get it. It's because of Roy. It'll be strange for you to go about your daily routine knowing that he's gone and you're going on with your life."

"How come you're so smart, Em?"

"I got lucky in the brains department I guess." She chewed on her lip. She still wasn't comfortable speaking to Dylan with this big black cloud hanging over her head. It made her feel guilty and disingenuous. And why was he suddenly her best friend? Did that knock to his head change his perspective? They'd always been cordial, but since his rise to celebrity status, she hadn't exactly been on his radar. All of a sudden, he was behaving as if they were best buds.

He was disoriented. Fuzzy in the brain. And in need of someone he could trust. But as soon as he was comfortable in his own skin again, things would change. She had no doubt. Dylan was a busy, busy man, sought after by the masses and the media, with who knew how many opportunities for work.

She scrunched up her face. *Don't get used to his attention, Emma.*

"Well, I won't keep you," he said. "I'm calling to confirm our date."

Date? A bad choice of words. "You mean the hospital thing?"

"Yes, it's this Friday morning. How about I swing by your place around nine to pick you up?"

"That's fine. I'm still not sure of my part in all this, but I'm happy to help out."

"You are helping out. You're helping *me*."

The way he said it, with such deep sincerity, tugged her heart in ten different ways. And it dawned on her that it wasn't just returning to work he was partially dreading, but going out in public for the first time with everyone expecting to see Dylan McKay back in true form. That was clearly worrying him. He didn't know if he was ready for that. He needed the support of his sister and friend.

"And you're going to make a difference in a lot of children's lives."

"I hope to. See you around nine, Em. Sleep tight."

"You, too."

Emma ended the call and sat there for a few minutes taking it all in again. She had to stop dwelling on Dylan McKay. Food usually kept her mind occupied. But oddly, she wasn't hungry. In fact, the thought of eating right now turned her stomach, so she nixed that plan and picked up the TV remote. She hit the on button and her small flat-screen lit up the dark room. The channel, tuned to the local network, was airing a movie. She settled back, propping up her feet, and stared ahead.

Dylan McKay's handsome face popped up, filling most of the screen, his bone-melting blue eyes gazing into the pretty face of Hollywood's latest darling, Sophie Adams. The cowboy and his girl were about to ride into the sunset. The camera zoomed in for the movie-ending kiss, and just like that, something cold and painful snared Emma's heart as Dylan's mouth locked onto Sophie's.

Hitting the off button did little to calm her. Why couldn't she get away from Dylan?

Falling for the unattainable was romantic suicide. She wasn't that stupid.

She'd just have to get over her secret dibs.

End of story.

She was ready at precisely nine o'clock. When the doorbell rang, she took a quick glance in the mirror, checking her upswept hairstyle, snowy-white pants and the sherbet-pink blazer she wore over a dotted swiss top. A tiny locket nestled at the base of her throat; that, silver stud earrings and a fashionable chunky watch were all the jewelry she'd opted for. She was going for a professional look without appearing unapproachable to the children. A little thrill ran through her body. Seeing Dylan aside, she was looking forward to meeting the kids, knowing firsthand how hard it was for a youngster to be outside the mainstream. She'd been one of those kids. Lucky for her, she had been healthy, but she'd been different, unloved and unwanted, and she'd never really felt as if she belonged.

Today was all about the kids.

She opened the door and was immediately yanked out of her noble thoughts as she took one look at Dylan standing on her doorstep. She'd expected his driver. But there Dylan was, in the flesh, his bandage gone now, the scar on the side of his head that would eventually heal only making him appear more manly, more dangerous, more gorgeous. Dressed in new jeans and a tan jacket over a white shirt, he smiled at her. "Morning. You look great."

She didn't feel great. She had woken up pale as a ghost and feeling boneless from tossing and turning all night. But his compliments could get to her, if she put stock in them. He was smooth. He was the consummate lady-killer. He knew which buttons to push to make females fall at his feet. And with her, she was sure, he wasn't even trying.

"Thank you. Is Brooke with you?"

He shook his head. "Brooke cracked a tooth this morning. She called me in a panic and said she had to get it fixed right away. I guess it's because of your event tomorrow, but she bailed. She's got a hot date with the dentist in twenty minutes."

Or rather a hot date with Royce next week and she couldn't go toothless. "Oh. Poor Brooke."

"She didn't call you?"

Emma lifted her phone out of her purse and glanced at the screen. "Oh, yeah, she did," she said. "Looks like a voice mail this morning. I was probably in the shower."

Dylan's eyes flickered and roamed over her body. Gosh, he was Flirt Central without even knowing it.

"I'm ready. Or would you like to come in?" Oh, boy, had she really invited him in? The last time he'd been here, they'd…

He glanced behind her and scanned her apartment as if seeing it for the first time. It was clear he didn't remember coming here.

She put those thoughts out of her mind and wondered what he would think of her two-bedroom apartment tucked into an older residential area of Santa Monica. There were no views of the ocean, no trendy, glamorous furnishings or updated kitchen. But it was all hers. And she loved having…stuff of her own.

"Maybe some other time," he said politely. "We should probably hit the road."

After she locked up her apartment, Dylan took her arm and guided her through the courtyard to the limousine parked by the sidewalk. "Here you go," he said as the driver opened the door. She slid in and Dylan followed. "I haven't gotten clearance to drive yet," he explained as he settled into the seat across from her by the window.

But it wasn't as if being carted around in a limo was foreign to him.

"Thanks again for coming with me today."

Again, she was struck by his sincerity. "You're welcome. Actually, I'm looking forward to it."

He stared at her, waiting for more.

She shrugged. "It's just that my own childhood wasn't ideal. If I can do something for these kids, even just as a bystander, I'm all for it. But how are you doing? This is your first venture out in public since the…"

"Accident?" His lips tightened and he sighed. "Let's just say, I'm glad you're here."

"Even though you'll have your team waiting for you there?"

"My agent and PA are great, don't get me wrong. But they see me one way. I don't think they get how hard this has been for me. Losing those days of my life, and losing Roy, has put me at a disadvantage I'm not used to. There are missing pages in my life."

And she could fill in some of those blanks if she had the courage.

He reached for her hand and laid their entwined fingers on the middle seat between them. "Brooke had good reason to jump ship today. I'm just glad you didn't bail."

"I wouldn't."

"I know. That's why I asked you to join me. I can count on you."

They reached Children's West Hospital, a beautiful building with white marble walls and modern lines. The limo slowed to a stop right in the circular drive that led to the entrance.

"Ready for the show?"

Several news crews were waiting like vultures, snapping pictures even before the driver got out of the limo. Dylan made headlines everywhere he went, and his first time out in public since the accident was big news. She recognized Darren, his agent, and Rochelle, his prim assistant, also waiting along the lineup. "Ready." Emma gave off much more confidence than she was feeling.

Dylan waited two beats, sighed as if grasping for strength and then nodded to his driver, who had one hand on the door handle. The door opened and photos were snapped immediately. Dylan got out, waved to the crowd and then reached inside to take her hand. She exited the limo and was dragged into the fray by Dylan, who seemed to tighten his hold on her. A hospital official came forward to greet them and introductions were made as security guards ensured that none of the news media followed them into the hospital lobby. His agent and PA also followed behind, eyeing everyone. Still, Emma saw cameras pressed up against the windows, the paparazzi snapping photos of Dylan and his entourage as they moved along the corridors with Richard Jacoby, the hospital administrator, and a few other ranking hospital officials.

Mr. Jacoby stopped at a double-wide door and turned to their small group. "The children are excited to meet you, Dylan. We've gathered our recovering patients here, in the doctor's lounge. And later, we'll go up to see the other children who are still in treatment."

Emma assumed that he was talking about the kids who couldn't make it out of bed. Her heart lurched and she braced herself for what was to come.

"Afterward, we'll shoot your promo spot with Beth and Pauly."

"Sounds good to me," Dylan said.

"We had a little movie premiere of *His Rookie Year* last night for everyone to get acquainted with who you are. Most of them already knew of you. Eddie Renquist was quite a character."

The rated-G movie hadn't won Dylan any awards, but he'd garnered a whole new audience of youngsters with that role. It was on Emma's Top Ten Favorite list.

"After you," Mr. Jacoby said, and they entered a large room filled with kids of all ages, sitting on grown-up chairs, their eyes as big as the smiles on their faces. They began waving at Dylan. With Emma at his side, he made his way over and spoke to each child. The younger boys called him Eddie and asked him all about baseball, as if he really was a star athlete like his character in the film. Dylan was quite knowledgeable actually and always reminded them he was only acting out a role. Some of them got it, others weren't quite sure. The girls were all over the map, the teens telling him he was hot and they loved him, while the younger ones wanted to shake his hand or give him a hug.

Dylan wasn't stingy with his hugs. He gave them freely and laughed with the kids, shook hands and recited lines from his movies when asked. Some of the kids with shaved heads had peach fuzz growing. They were the lucky ones, the ones who would eventually go home to live normal lives. Some wore back braces or leg casts; others were in wheelchairs. But all in all, every one of them reacted positively to Dylan. He was good with them and managed to bring Emma into the conversation often.

"This is my friend Emma. She plans parties and knows a lot about everything," he said.

"Have you ever planned a Cinderella party?" one of the younger girls asked.

"Well, of course. Cinderella and Belle and Ariel are friends of mine," she said.

A cluster of little girls surrounded her and asked her dozens of questions.

Dylan caught her eye and nodded as he continued to make his way around the room. Once Dylan had greeted every single child, he came to stand at the front of the room and asked if they would like to sing a few songs. "Emma has a great voice and knows lots of songs."

It wasn't exactly out of her wheelhouse to entertain children, but this had come out of the blue. "Oh, of course. We can do that." She jumped right in.

She led them in Taylor Swift and Katy Perry songs as well as a song from *Frozen*, for the little ones, and then Mr. Jacoby signaled to her that their time was up. Dylan walked over to his personal assistant and she handed him a packet of cards.

"Thanks for giving me a chance to meet you all," he said to the kids. "I'm going to come around the room again one more time and hand out movie passes for you and your families."

And afterward, they were whisked away, riding up in the elevator to the third floor where the really ill children lay in beds. What really struck Emma was how happy all the children seemed to be, despite the bald heads, wires and tubes going through them, limbs in casts and machines humming. Experiencing their unqualified acceptance and genuine gladness to see them was as heartwarming as it was heartbreaking. Emma sent up silent prayers for all of them, wishing that affliction wouldn't strike ones so young. But their spirit was amazing and many adults, including her, could learn from their sense of joy and gratefulness.

Dylan treated these kids in the same way he had the others. No pity shone in his eyes; instead, there was a sense of camaraderie and friendship. He was one with them, talking movies and baseball and family with these wonderfully unaffected children.

"It's a lot to take in," Dylan said once they were alone in the hallway.

"They're sweet kids."

"They shouldn't have to deal with this crap. They should be allowed to be kids."

This wasn't just a photo op for Dylan. "You're a softy. Who knew?"

She knew. She'd seen it firsthand and she'd learned something about Dylan today. His compassion for the less fortunate was astounding.

"Shh. You don't want to wreck my image, do you?" He grinned.

"Heavens, not me."

His agent and PA called him away, and he excused himself. When he returned, he was frowning. "The little boy Pauly who was to do the shoot with us had a setback. He's not healthy enough to do the promo spot right now. They're giving me the option to do it with only Beth or to pick another child, or I can wait for Pauly. The camera crew is all here, everything's set up, but here's the thing. Pauly was really looking forward to this. They tell me it's all he's talked about all week." Dylan ran a hand down his face. "What do you think?"

He was asking her advice? She didn't know about the technical nature of this business or the cost involved, but she had only one answer for Dylan. "I'd wait for Pauly. It might make the difference in his recovery, if he has this to look forward to."

Dylan smiled wide, his eyes locking to hers in relief. "That's what I was thinking, too." He leaned over and kissed her cheek. "Thanks."

He turned away before he could take in her shocked expression. He'd kissed her again.

It had to be the surroundings, the children, the good that he'd done today to brighten lives here at Children's West Hospital, and that's all Emma would read into it.

When they walked out of the hospital a short time later, the press vultures were waiting, snapping pictures and shooting questions at him from behind a roped-off line. She stood in the background with Darren and Rochelle, noting how perfectly Dylan handled the situation, stopping them with a hand up. "I'll make a brief statement. As you can see, I'm doing well and recovering. I'll be back to work very soon, but today is not about me. It's about the wonderful work this hospital is doing for the children. The doctors and staff here are dedicated and so willing to give of themselves. We're hoping to shine a light on Children's West Hospital today. Visit their website to see how you can help these brave children. Thank you."

With that, Dylan ushered Emma into the limo and it sped off before she could get her seat belt on.

"Whoa," he said, and for the first time today, she glimpsed beads of sweat on his brow.

"Dylan, are you okay?"

He sank down, shrugged into his seat belt and tossed his head against the headrest. "I've been better."

"Dizzy spell?" She clamped her own seat belt on.

"Nope, it's just a little bit…crazy, isn't it? I'm not feeling myself just yet."

"That's understandable, Dylan. You've been through a lot. But you handled them like a pro."

He turned to her, shaking his head. "Maybe I should've kept you out of it. Your picture might just make the front page of some of those rags."

"I did hear several questions shouted about the redhead." A giggle sounding more like a hiccup escaped her mouth. She'd lived in Los Angeles long enough to know how desperate the paparazzi could be. "I noticed you ignored those."

"Think they'd believe me if I said you were a friend of the family? Not on your life. Let 'em guess."

"Yeah, let them guess." Bet they'd never guess she'd been the one-night stand Dylan McKay had no memory of. Now, that was a story for the tabloids.

"Thank you for coming with me today. It made a difference having you here."

She was his surrogate sister. She didn't mind. Not today.

"You know, I'm glad I came, too, and if I helped you in the process, that's a bonus."

"You did." Dylan leaned over, gave her a sweet kiss that seemed to linger on her lips, then retreated to his seat and closed his eyes. "Thanks."

She was pretty sure surrogate sisters didn't get kisses like that.

In fact, she didn't remember much about his kisses at all.

And that stumped her. A man like Dylan…well, a girl shouldn't forget something like that, drunk on mojitos and in a blackout or not.

The Montalvo party went off without a hitch, except for one boisterous guest who'd gotten smashed on martinis and fallen off the top tier of the multilevel grounds. Luckily for him, it was only a five-foot drop and he'd fallen on a shelf of border boxwoods that pinched like the dickens but broke his fall and prevented major damage. After causing a momentary ruckus, the man sobered up real fast, skulked off like a pup with his tail between his legs, and the party picked up again from there.

Emma was proud of the display they'd put on for the fifties party and their company was hired on the spot by a theatre producer in attendance to host a similar event. It had been a win-win night.

She'd worked her butt off these past few weeks. Brooke had her head in the clouds after her date with Royce and they'd seen each other three times since. Emma didn't mind picking up the slack, except that she'd been extremely tired and with her resistance down she managed to catch Brooke's cold. Now both of them weren't feeling well. But while Brooke had only sniffles and sneezes, Emma had an upset stomach, as well. She couldn't look at food for days and even now the thought of eating anything but a piece of fruit made her tummy grumble. And the big golf tournament event was in just four days.

"Emma, get your ducks in a row," she muttered. She lay on her bed praying for strength. A commercial for a big sloppy hamburger came on the television screen and she didn't turn her head away in time. "Oh, God." Her stomach soured instantly and her legs tangled in the sheets as she fumbled from bed and raced to the bathroom. She landed on her knees and made it to the toilet just as her stomach contracted.

Wonderful…just wonderful. After she flushed the toilet she sat back on her knees. The little energy she'd had this morning had seeped out of her. But the flu bug would not get her down. She wouldn't miss their big charity event coming up. She grasped the bathroom counter for support and lifted herself up. Her head spun for a second, until finally her eyes focused and she mustered every ounce of strength to stay upright.

"Okay, Emma," she whispered. "You can do this."

Carefully, she stepped away from the sink. The merry-go-round in her head was gone. *Thank you, Flu Gods.* But just a second later gripping pain attacked her stomach. "Oh." She held her belly and flew toward the toilet again. Sinking down onto the floor, she emptied everything into the porcelain bowl, until there was nothing left.

An hour later, after managing to climb her way back into bed, her body shaking, her bones weak, she clutched her cell and pushed Brooke's number. "Hi," she whispered.

"What's wrong?"

Brooke knew her so well.

"I'm down, Brooke. Can't make it out of bed right now. The flu."

"Oh, Em. I'm so sorry. I got you sick and now you're getting the brunt of it. You sound terrible."

"My stomach's finally eased off, but it wasn't pretty an

hour ago. I'm so…tired. I'm gonna try to make it into the office later today."

"No, you're not. You need to stay in bed all day and rest. I've got things handled here. You know we've been right on schedule with this charity event. I just have a few last-minute things to take care of. You rest up and get better so you can make it on Friday."

"Okay, I think you're right."

"Sleep. It's the best thing for you."

"Thanks, and, Brooke, no way am I missing this weekend."

"I'll come over later and bring you some soup."

"Ugh, no. Just the thought of food right now turns my stomach."

"All right. I'll call you later."

When the call ended, Emma turned her head into her pillow, closed her eyes and slept the entire day. She woke up bathed in a stream of dim light coming from the night-light on the opposite wall. She blinked herself awake. Outside, darkness had descended, but she was safe, protected. Since the night of the blackout, she kept night-lights on day and night in her apartment to keep from ever being alone in total darkness. She also now had an entire bedroom shelf devoted to pillar candles, scented and unscented. It didn't matter, as long as they did the trick. She took them with her when she traveled, too, just in case, and had also started carrying a mini flashlight in her purse. Not that she couldn't use her cell phone—someone had turned her onto a flashlight app, which came in handy—but cell phone batteries died on occasion and she couldn't chance it.

A look at her cell phone now revealed that it was seven twenty-five. Wow, she'd slept for nine hours. Funny, but she didn't feel rested at all. Or hungry. Just the thought of food made her queasy all over again.

Brooke called and they spoke for half an hour, going

over the final details of the golf event, the dinner, dancing, silent auction and raffle. At two thousand dollars a head and with an expected one hundred fifty guests in attendance, there were lots of fine points to check on.

"I'll see you tomorrow, Brooke," Emma said, feeling optimistic as she hung up the phone. Her stomach had eased back to normal and she figured she'd been through the worst of it.

By the morning of the next day, she knew that she'd figured wrong. She emptied her stomach twice before it settled down. She managed to go into the office, but once Brooke took a look at her pasty face, she ordered her back to bed. Emma didn't have the strength to argue.

By Thursday morning, nothing had changed. She spent the morning in the bathroom next to her new best friend. Suspicions were running rampant in her head. What if she didn't have the flu? What if there was something else wrong with her? Something permanent? Something rest and hot soup wouldn't cure?

Eyes wide-open now, she fought the invading rumblings in her belly, quickly dressed and dashed to the local drugstore. Once she got back home, she peed on a stick at three different intervals of the day, only to get the same result each time. Opening her laptop, she keyed it up and researched a subject she thought would be years down the road for her.

She was as sure now as she would ever be; she had all the symptoms.

She was pregnant.

And Dylan McKay was her blackout baby's father.

Three

"You're trying to hide a smile, Brooke. You don't fool me."

"I'm not trying to fool you, Emma. I think it's kinda cool that you and my brother…"

"No, it wasn't like that, really." Oh, boy.

Having Brooke stop everything at the office and come over right away might have been a mistake. But this was big and she couldn't hide her pregnancy from her best friend. Especially not when Brooke had a stake in this, too; she was Dylan's sister after all. Emma needed her right now. She had no one else to turn to and time was running out. She had morning sickness, big-time. Immediate decisions had to be made and she'd have to deal with Dylan at some point.

"We're not romantically involved," she said to Brooke.

Her friend sat on the sofa next to her, her mouth twitching, the smile she couldn't conceal spreading wider across her face. This was no laughing matter. Obviously, Brooke thought differently.

She'd given Brooke the bare facts about what had happened that night between her and Dylan, explaining how she'd panicked when all the lights had gone out in that nightclub. The entire city had gone dark from what she could tell and she hadn't been in any shape to drive home. At least she got that part right. No drunk driving for her.

But instead of Brooke coming to pick her up as she'd hoped, Dylan had come to her rescue, as any good guy would. Emma tried to make clear to Brooke that she'd been the one to initiate the lovemaking. Emma remembered that much; she'd begged him to stay with her. She had no recollection of exactly how it all went down, those hours fuzzy in her head, but it was all on her. She'd been scared out of her wits and inebriated. And Dylan was there. She'd lived out her fantasy with him that night, but she didn't tell Brooke that. Some things were better left unsaid.

"Brooke, I'll say it again, and this is hard to admit, but I probably climbed all over him that night. I swear, he didn't take advantage of me." The worst would be that Brooke would hold anything about that night against Dylan.

Brooke covered her ears. "Emma, pleeeze! No details. I can't think of Dylan that way." And then she lowered her hands. "But it's sweet that you're trying to protect him. You don't want me to think badly of my brother. I get that, Em. And I don't. No one's to blame."

"Okay, no details." Not that she could remember any. "Dylan doesn't know any of this happened."

"Are you sure of that?"

"I'm sure. I'd know it, if he remembered. I'd see something in his eyes. And he's never mentioned my phone call that night, or the fact that he came to pick me up from the nightclub. When he came to my apartment the day we went to the children's hospital, he didn't seem to recognize anything as familiar. I'm certain that night was erased from his memory."

"I think so, too. Just making sure there were no signs."

"Nope, not a one."

Brooke nodded and then gazed warmly into Emma's eyes for several ticks of a minute. "You're going to be the mother of my niece or nephew," she said as softly as Emma had ever heard her speak. The tone was rich and thick as honey. "And my brother is going to be a father."

The way Brooke put it was sort of beautiful. Emma could get lost in all the wonder of motherhood, of nurturing a new life and having a man like Dylan father her child. But the wonder didn't come close to erasing the plain facts. That she and Dylan didn't plan this child. That he didn't even have a clue what was happening, yet his life was about to change forever.

"Oh, Brooke. I'm just wrapping my head around it. The baby part has me feeling…I don't know, protective already and scared." Emma shivered. "Very scared."

"You'll be fine. You have me. And Dylan. He'd never turn his back on you."

"Gosh, it's all so new. Part of me feels guilty not telling him about that night. It might've triggered some of his memories."

"You'll have to tell him now, Em. He has a right to know."

It was inevitable that she tell Dylan. But she wasn't looking forward to that conversation. Gosh, he'd been like a big brother to her and now nothing between them would ever be the same.

"I know. I will."

"Good. You're in no shape to do the golf event, Em. You're exhausted and still having morning sickness."

Emma chewed on her bottom lip. She didn't want to miss this weekend. All those hours, all that planning. Brooke needed her, but how could she function when she was running to the bathroom all morning long? "Yes, but it's getting better. Maybe I could come along and help out in the afternoon and evening."

Brooke was shaking her head. When had she turned into a mama bear? "I've got it covered, Emma. You can't come. You'd be miserable. I've got Rocky and Wendy on standby."

The part-timers?

"I've been briefing them and they're up for the task. I don't want you to worry about a thing. You should concentrate on the baby and feeling better. We'll do fine."

"Are you saying you don't need me?"

"I'm saying, we'll make do without you, but of course, we'll miss you. Thanks to your unending efficiency, we've got all the bases covered. You should take this weekend to adjust to all of this. That's what I want for you. It's what you need."

Emma sighed and gave her friend a reluctant nod. Brooke was right. She couldn't very well carry out her duties in San Diego with her stomach on the blink every hour and her body feeling as though it had been hit by an eighteen-wheeler. "Okay, I'll be a good girl."

"It's too late for that," Brooke replied with a grin.

"Don't I know it."

Brooke's eyes melted in apology. "You're not letting anyone down, Emma. Just the opposite. I know the situation isn't ideal right now, but you're having a baby with Dylan. My best friend and my brother...how can I not think it's just a little bit wonderful?"

Brooke's arms came around her and the hug warmed all the frigid ice flowing through her veins. She was wrapped up in comfort and support and friendship. "How come you always know the right thing to say?"

"Since when?"

"Since...now."

"Oh, Emma. Do you want me to be there when you tell Dylan?"

"No!" Emma pulled away from her friend. The thought of having that conversation gave her hives, but having Dylan's baby sister there? There was no number on the Awkward Scale high enough to describe such a scene. "It'd be too weird. I can't even picture any of this in my head right now, but I suspect this is one time I need to be alone with Dylan."

The tight lines on Brooke's face crumbled and her expression resumed some semblance of normalcy. "Whew, thanks. I have to agree. I love my bro and I love you, but…"

"But I made my bed, now I have to toss off the tangled sheets and come clean."

"Yeah," Brooke said, giving her that same melting look. "Something like that, sweetie."

"Promise you won't worry about me this weekend?"

"If you promise me the same. Don't give a thought to the golf event."

They stared at each other, knowing unequivocally that would be impossible.

"Sure," Emma said.

"Gotcha," Brooke added, her smile falsely quick. Then Brooke kissed her goodbye on the cheek and brought her mouth near her ear to whisper, "The sooner you tell Dylan, the better."

"I know," she said, nodding. "I will."

Problem number one: she didn't have a clue *how* or *when* she could bring herself to do that.

"A little bit of fresh air will do wonders for you, Emma," Dylan said as he strolled into her apartment wearing jeans and a vintage T-shirt, the Stones logo stretching wide across his chest. The shirt hugged him tight and hinted at a ripped torso underneath. Before she got caught ogling, she shifted her attention to his face and was struck by the scruffy, tousled look that appealed to her on so many levels, it was ridiculous. "Brooke is worried sick about you."

Emma had had about half an hour advance warning from Dylan that he was coming to visit her, his text announcing he was on the way, leaving her no option. He was on a mission, commandeered by Brooke, no doubt, and Emma had raced around her apartment destroying evidence of just how sick she'd been. She'd picked up blankets tossed across the sofa and folded them, sprayed the room with cinnamon spice air freshener—the place now smelled like Christmas—slipped off her smelly sweats, taken a shower and put on a sleeveless denim dress and a pair of tan boots.

Evenings were her best time of day lately, so she was pretty sure that she could pull off seeing him without doing a sprint to the bathroom. "I'm feeling much better, Dylan. There's no need for you to be here. Gosh, you must have better things to do on a Friday night."

He smiled her way, that megawatt lady-killer smile that either slowed breathing or caused it to race. Right now, her breath caught in her throat and she reminded herself to breathe. He was just a man.

And the father of your baby.

"Nope, no plans. And since I'm already here, I was hoping not to eat alone tonight. Come back to the house with me. Maisey's made an amazing meal. We can eat on the patio. It's a gorgeous night."

God, getting some fresh Moonlight Beach air did sound appealing. She'd been stuck in her house for eons, it seemed.

Her hesitation wasn't lost on him. He eyed her carefully, taking a quick toll of her state of health. She didn't want to seem ungrateful for the gesture although she knew he was here solely at Brooke's bidding.

"Brooke says you haven't been eating. You need a good meal, Em."

She did, and her traitorous stomach growled quietly, but he didn't appear to notice, thank goodness. "I don't know."

"You want to. Come for an hour or two."

It was hard to refuse, with the look in those beautifully clear sky-blue eyes. When aimed at her, she usually succumbed. It had always been that way. What could she say? She, like a zillion other adoring fans, had it bad for Dylan McKay. And she knew darn well, he wouldn't be here if it weren't for Brooke's nagging. She wouldn't get off his case if he didn't succeed in making sure Emma was well cared for tonight.

Why had Brooke put her in this position? As sweet as it was, she wasn't anyone's charity case. She hadn't been for a long time, and she wasn't ever going back there. She'd learned to fend for herself since her foster care days and didn't want to be thought of as an obligation in order to ease anyone's conscience. She had a mind to refuse him flat, but those bone-melting eyes kept a vigil on her and a look of hope spread across his face.

"Well, maybe just for a little while, but only to get you off the hook with Brooke."

Gesturing in his own defense, he turned his palms up. "I don't know what you mean. This was my idea."

She snorted. "And the sun doesn't shine in LA."

Glancing out the window at the dimming skies, he grinned. "It isn't at the moment."

Okay, she could share a meal with him. She didn't have to tell him the truth. Not yet. She wasn't ready for that, and this way, he'd report back to Brooke that all was well and she'd have the rest of the weekend in peace. "I'll get my jacket, then."

He nodded, looking ridiculously satisfied.

A few minutes later, they were barreling down Pacific

Coast Highway in his licorice-black SUV, the windows down and warm spring breezes lifting her hair. Dylan, recently cleared to drive again, was concentrating on the road, and she took a second to gaze at his profile. He had classic good looks: a solid jawline, a strong chin, a nose that was just sharp enough to suit his face and eyes the color of Hawaiian waters, deep blue with a hint of turquoise. His hair was streaked by the sun, a little long right now so that it swept over his ears. Most times he wore it combed back away from his face, but there were these locks that always loosened from the pack to dip onto his forehead that drove her crazy.

Would their child have his hair? His eyes?

Or would the baby look more like her? Green-eyed with dark cranberry tresses?

Her stomach squeezed tight thinking of the secret life inside her, growing and thriving despite her frequent bouts of nausea. She really did need a nourishing meal and Maisey's cooking was too good to turn down.

"Here we are." Dylan pulled into the gated circular driveway of his beach home. There were times she couldn't believe this was all his. He'd grown up in a normal American household, the son of a high school principal and a civil engineer. Dylan's dad had died one year before he was due to retire, but Markus McKay had lived a full and happy life. The love he'd had for his wife and family, the life they'd led filled with generosity and kindness, had restored Emma's faith in mankind.

Once he parked in the multicar garage on the property, Dylan made an attempt to wind around the car to open the door for her, but she was too quick. She stepped out on her own, ignoring how his smile faded as she strode past him toward the service door that led into his house. "Hey, Sparky, wait up," he said, coming to stand beside her.

He unlocked the door and opened it for her. She took

a step to enter, just as his arm shot out, blocking her way in. Suddenly, surprisingly, she was trapped between his body and the door. Trapped by the compelling scent of him. Several beats ticked away and then she lifted her lids and locked onto his gaze.

"Do me a favor," he said softly, the fingers of his free hand coming to rest under her chin. His innocent touch kicked her senses into high gear. He didn't wait for her answer, but continued, "Don't pretend you're completely recovered just to prove a point. I see how tired you are. Your face is pale, and you've obviously lost weight."

He'd hit the nail on the head. The shudder that erupted inside probably wasn't visible on the outside, but boy, oh boy, how it rattled her all the way down to her toes. His noticing her body was shock enough, but noticing how bad she looked brought new meaning to her humiliation. What next? Would he point out her warts and moles, too?

"I've been around the theatre long enough to know an act when I see one. All I'm asking is for you to relax tonight, eat a delicious dinner and have a good time. You don't have to pretend with me. Just be yourself."

As he lowered his arm allowing her to pass, Emma blurted, "Yes, Dr. Dylan. Will do." All she needed now to accompany the nod she gave him was a military salute.

His eyebrows lifted at her sarcasm. "Your mouth… sometimes I want to—" And then he leaned in before she could grasp his intention and brushed a soft kiss to her lips.

She gasped, raking in air, but quickly recovered. "Shut me up?"

He shook his head, chuckling. "That's one way to put it. But I was thinking of it more as a way to sweeten the sass blistering your tongue."

Well, he'd shut her up *and* sweetened her mouth with one tiny kiss. Dylan could get away with things like that. He'd been gifted with an accommodating good nature that charmed any woman in his path. She'd seen it over and over again. His reputation with the ladies had been mulled over, talked about and dissected by the media. Magazine covers, television interviews and social media platforms had him figured out. He wasn't one to be tied down, but he'd gotten away with it with the press, because he never infringed. He'd been crowned a one-woman kind of man, and the woman he was currently dating received all of his attention. A smart move on his behalf, it kept him out of trouble.

And all it had taken was a power outage burdening most of the city one night to shake his very well-protected reputation. Only, he didn't know that yet.

Oh, boy, when Emma did things, she did them all the way.

The minute they entered his luxurious home, Dylan went about opening the massive beveled glass French doors in the living room. Balmy breezes immediately rushed in bringing scents of salty sea air and powdery sands. Emma followed him into the kitchen, where he opened the doors leading to the Italian-stone-and-marble patio deck. Succulents and vines grew vertically up one wall in a landscaping masterpiece Dylan had recently commissioned, adding just the right touch of greenery to the outdoor landing. Patio tables and a cozy set of lounge furniture were strategically placed around a stone fire pit to allow the best views of the Pacific.

"Want to have a seat out here?" he asked. "I'll heat up the food Maisey left for us and you can soak up some fresh air."

She'd rather do something with her hands than sit outside. Alone. In the dark. "No, thanks, I'll help you."

"Suit yourself. But I can handle it. I give Maisey the weekends off usually."

"You mean you cook for yourself?"

He smiled as he walked over to the double-door cabinet refrigerator and grabbed a covered dish. "Unless Maisey takes pity on me and leaves me something wonderful like this chicken piccata, I've been known to throw a meal together." He set the dish down and opened the oven door.

"Impressive," she said.

"I can also wash a dish and toss dirty clothes in the washing machine, too."

He gestured and she grabbed a casserole dish of rice pilaf from the fridge and handed it to him. Into the oven it went, right next to the chicken. A basket of bread, something garlicky with bits of sun-dried tomatoes, was nestled on the onyx counter next to a tray of homemade chocolate chip cookies. All the combined scents should make her queasy, but she found them actually whetting her appetite. She was hungrier than she'd been in a week. "Such skills. I'm impressed."

Once the meal was set to reheating, Dylan leaned against the granite island, folding his arms across his torso, and pinned her down with those baby blues. "You're forgetting how I grew up. Mom and Dad expected us to do everyday chores, just as they did. I washed cars, cooked meals, did laundry, made beds, and good God, I even scrubbed toilets."

"I bet you don't anymore."

He shrugged and slid her a crooked grin. "Not if I can help it."

Thinking about her recent toilet incidents, she didn't blame him. "Your mom and dad were wonderful people. They taught you well."

"Yeah, but at the time I didn't think so. I did more work than any of my friends. Before I could go out and play ball, I had a list of chores to get through. Weekends were especially gruesome."

"They were building character."

"Yeah, now I play characters on the screen."

"And you still wash dishes and make your own meals. The last conversation I had with your mom, she told me how proud she was of you."

"She is now, but when I left college in my sophomore year to pursue an acting career, my folks were both pretty bummed. Especially my dad. He had high hopes of me going to medical school. He lost his chance at being a doctor and tossed all of his hopes and guilt onto me. He wanted to be a pediatrician." He made a noisy sigh and scrubbed at the dark blond stubble on his chin. "I guess I really disappointed him when I ran away with Renee."

Renee had been no good for Dylan. Emma had heard that a zillion times from Brooke and Dylan's folks. Emma hadn't been too happy with her, either. At the tender age of fourteen, Emma's heart had been crushed when Dylan had fallen in love with a cheerleading beauty who'd convinced him he could make it big in the movies. She had connections. She could get him in to see all the right people.

"Maybe it wasn't in the cards for you to be a doctor. Your dad lived long enough to see your success. He had to know you made the right decision for yourself."

"Dad didn't think I knew what I was doing. And maybe I didn't. Renee was my first girlfriend and I was crazy about her." He pumped his shoulders a couple of times, hopelessly, and something faint and hidden entered his eyes. "But enough about ancient history. How about a soda?" He opened the fridge again. "Lemonade? Wine or beer? Anything else? Maisey keeps the fridge pretty stocked."

"Water sounds good." It was safe. She couldn't trust her stomach right now, and even before she'd found out about the baby, she'd given up alcohol.

He handed her one of those cobalt blue water bottles

that cost more than a glass of fine wine and then plucked out an Indian Brown Ale for himself. His throat moved as he tipped the bottle to his lips and took a swig. She looked away instantly. She was never one to hide her emotions and the last thing she needed was to have Dylan catch her eyeing him.

They'd had their one night. Unfortunately neither of them remembered it.

Dylan's cell phone rang out the theme song to his latest action flick. How many people actually had their very own ringtone? He grabbed it off the counter and frowned at the screen. "Sorry, Emma. I have to get this. I'll make it quick. It's the head of the studio."

"Go right ahead. I'm fine right here." She gestured for him to take the call.

He nodded, his eyes sparkling with gratitude as he walked out of the room, the cell to his ear. Emma grabbed the salad from the refrigerator, set it on the granite island and then scrounged through drawers to find tongs. Coming up with a pair, she leaned against the counter as Dylan's voice drifted to her ears.

"It's Callista's thirtieth birthday? Yeah, I think she'd love a party. Up at your house?"

And then after a long pause, "I'll do my best to be there, Maury. Yes, yes, I'm recovering nicely, thank you. I'm back at work on Monday. Thanks for the call. See you soon."

He walked back into the kitchen, frowning and running a hand down his face. "Sorry," he said. "Business crap."

"Sounds like Callista's having a party." She tilted her head. "Sorry, I overheard."

"Yeah, she's turning thirty. Maury likes to remind me he's not getting any younger. He expects me to be there." Dylan sighed.

Maury Allen had power and influence. That much, Emma knew. According to Brooke, he'd been pushing for

Dylan to make a commitment to his daughter, but so far, Dylan had resisted. Their relationship had been on and off for three years. "And you don't want to go?"

Dylan leaned back against the counter, picking up his beer. "Maury's been good to me. Gave me my first break. I sort of owe him my loyalty. If he wants me at his daughter's birthday celebration, I'll go."

Dylan McKay and Callista Lee Allen made a gorgeous couple. Whenever they were together, there were headlines. To all the world they probably seemed like a perfect match.

Which made Emma's predicament suddenly jump to the forefront of her thoughts and curdle her stomach. She was feeling a little weak-kneed anyway and needed to sit down.

Dylan's hand came to her elbow and his eyes locked onto hers. "Emma, are you okay? You're looking pale. I need to get food into you. Come, sit down."

Why was he always touching her? She had enough to deal with right now, without getting all fan crazy over Dylan's slightest brotherly touch. "Okay, maybe I should sit."

He guided her to the outside patio table closest to the kitchen. "Wait here. I'll get some plates and bring out the food."

She sat, dumbfounded by her fatigue, and stared straight out to sea. The waves gently rolled onto the shore, and stars above lit the sky as low-lying fixtures surrounding the deck gave off soothing light. Fresh scents from the vertical garden on her right drifted to her nose and the whole effect made her feel somewhat better.

Emma wasn't a wilting flower. Nothing much rattled her, well, except being alone in complete darkness. Overall, considering her lousy childhood, she'd fended well in the world, but this whole Dylan thing—secretly carrying his child, losing her cookies every morning and not holding up her end with Parties-To-Go—overwhelmed her. The walls were closing in from all directions and right now her body wasn't up for the fight.

Dylan came back loaded down with food and went about serving her as if she was the Queen of England. Then he offered her the tan suede jacket she'd brought from home. "It's getting a little cool out here," he said.

She nodded and he helped her put her arms through the sleeves. "There you go. Better?"

She nodded. The jacket fit her snugly. She wondered how much longer she could wear it and then, just like that, tears welled in her eyes. Her mouth began to quiver.

It had to be hormones.

Dylan didn't seem to notice. He was too busy making sure she had everything she needed at the table. "Eat up, Emma."

He finally sat and they both picked up their forks. The food was delicious and she managed to eat half of everything on her plate. An accomplishment, considering she hadn't eaten this much in days.

"You're not worried about your girlish figure, are you?" he asked, eyeing her plate. His grin and the twinkle in his eyes were right on par for Dylan.

"Should I be?"

His lids lowered as he slowly raked his gaze over her body. "Not from where I'm sitting."

She had no comeback. He'd once touched every inch of her and seemed to have no complaints that she could remember.

She managed a smile, though suddenly her energy waned. "The food was amazing. I feel full and satisfied," she fibbed. Actually, she wasn't feeling so great. "Please be sure to thank Maisey for me."

"I will."

"Dylan?"

"Hmm?"

"I'm really exhausted. Would you mind taking me home?"

He hesitated and something that resembled regret flickered in his eyes. "Sure…if that's what you want."

"It is." She rose and pushed back her chair. Before she could take a step, heat washed up and over her, spinning circles inside her head. Her legs buckled and soon she was falling, falling.

And then Dylan's arms were around her, easing her to the ground. "Emma!"

A sharp pat to the face snapped her eyes open. She'd been slapped.

"Emma, thank God. You fainted."

Her head felt light and she saw two Dylans leaning over her on bent knee. "I did?"

"Yeah, you were out for a few seconds. I'm going to get you inside and call 911."

"No, no!" His words were enough to rouse her and refocus her eyes. "I don't need the paramedics."

"You do, honey. You've been sick for days now. You should see a doctor." The resolve in his voice frightened her. This was going sideways fast.

"No, no. I'm not sick."

"Something's wrong with you, Emma. I have to get you help."

"Dylan, no." She gazed into his worried face. "I know what's wrong. I'm not sick."

"You're not?"

She shook her head. "No, I'm not. I'm…pregnant."

Four

"Pregnant?" Had he heard Emma right? He didn't know she'd been seeing anyone. He softened his voice, attempting to keep his surprise concealed. "You're pregnant, Em?"

She nodded, chewing on her lower lip, her eyes down.

Where was the guy? Did he bail on her? And why did he feel sharp pangs in his gut consisting of an emotion he refused to name? "Are you sure?"

"Yes," she whispered, still averting her eyes.

It seemed that she hadn't come to grips with it yet. Softly, he brushed fallen locks off her forehead, the tendrils flowing through his fingers like silk, which brought her pretty green eyes up to his. "Well, damn."

She swallowed.

"Is it okay for me to lift you up now?"

He was holding the top half of her body off the ground. Another few inches and she would've landed hard on stone.

"I think so. I'm not dizzy anymore."

He knew something about getting dizzy. Luckily, that

hadn't happened to him for days now. "Okay, slowly," he said.

He brought his face close to hers, breathing in a sweet scent that reminded him of lavender. God, he liked her. There was something sweet and real about Emma Bloom. She'd spent a lot of time in the McKay household while growing up and he'd always looked upon her as a second little sister. But now he wasn't altogether sure why he felt so close to her. Or why, whenever given a chance, he chose to kiss her. It was almost second nature with him lately, holding Emma and kissing her.

Gathering her in his arms, he guided her up, keeping her body pressed close to his. Her breasts crushed his chest and he tried not to think about how soft and supple they felt. Once they were upright, he kept his hold on her. "Do you think you can stand on your own?"

"Yes, I think so."

"I won't let go of you completely. I'll hold on to your waist, okay?"

She nodded. Color had come back to her face. It wasn't rosy, but she didn't look like a sheet, either, so that was a good thing.

She was unusually quiet and there was a stark look on her face. Stronger breezes had kicked up on the patio and it was getting chilly. "Let's go inside."

He stood beside her now, wrapping an arm around her slender waist. "I've got you." Shoulder to shoulder, they took small steps. They bypassed the kitchen and moved into the larger living room. Dylan stopped at his buttery leather couch, the most comfortable seat in the house, and helped her sit down. Her silence unnerved him. Was she embarrassed, scared, regretful? Hell, he didn't know what to say to her when she was like this.

"Thank you," she mumbled.

"You're sure you're okay?"

"I'm feeling better, Dylan.

"You really should see a doctor."

She looked down at the hands she'd folded in her lap. So unlike Emma. "I plan to."

"Does Brooke know?"

She nodded. "I told her just recently."

"I don't mean to pry, but what about the baby's father? Does he know?"

She shook her head. "Not yet."

Dylan didn't want to stick his nose into her business, but Emma hadn't led a charmed life. The kid didn't deserve to go through this alone. Dylan wasn't good with stuff like this, but she was here and had fainted in front of him. With Brooke gone for a few more days, Dylan had to step in. "I'm not taking you home until I'm sure you're feeling better."

"Dr. Dylan," she said, her lips quirking up. Signs of the real Emma Rae Bloom were emerging.

"Your friend Dylan."

She looked away.

"Let me get you some water. Hang on."

He left the room, and when he returned with a glass, Emma's eyes were closed, but there was no peace on her face. He sat down beside her quietly and put the glass in her hand.

She turned to him then and whispered, "Dylan...I need to talk to you."

"Sure. Okay. I'm listening."

Her chest heaved as she filled her lungs, as if readying for a marathon. And then she began. "You know how I was raised. My foster parents weren't very attentive, but they gave me a home. They fed me and I had clothes on my back."

They were reckless and selfish bastards. Heavy drinkers. But Dylan wouldn't say that.

She sipped water, probably needing fortification, then went on. "I was about ten when Doris and Burt went out to the local English pub one night. You might remember the one on Birch Street."

He nodded. "Darts and hard ales. I remember."

She gave him a quick smile. They had the same roots. Only, hers were laden with weeds instead of the pretty poppies little girls deserved.

"They'd put me to bed early that night and told me to stay there," she continued. "I knew they probably wouldn't come home until very late. What I didn't know was that the electricity had been turned off that day. They hadn't paid their electric bill, so when a bad storm hit that night I trembled every time there was thunder. And the erratic lightning really freaked me out. None of the lights in my room were working. I remember how black it was. And there were noises. Crazy, scary noises, shutters flapping against the house, wind howling, shrubs brushing against the outer walls sounding like devilish whispers. I ran downstairs, clicking as many light switches as I could find. Nothing worked. And then I remembered Burt kept a flashlight in a little storage closet under the stairs. S-somehow… s-somehow…as I climbed into that space, a gust of wind or something…slammed the door shut behind me. I was locked in that tiny dark space all night."

"Oh, man, Emma," Dylan said, taking her hand and giving it a squeeze. Her face was stone cold, as if reliving this memory had frozen her up inside. He could only imagine her terror that night. He had no clue what this had to do with her pregnancy, but he listened. Maybe she needed to get this off her chest. She could use him to unburden herself if that's what it took.

"It was the longest night of my life. I sobbed and sobbed most of the night, quietly, though, in case those devilish sounds materialized into something evil. My folks finally came home. It was almost dawn when they found me cowering in that closet. They told me everything was all right and that I'd be okay. Only, I wasn't okay. From then on, being in dark places has always screwed with my head."

"It's understandable that you get frightened. Those memories must be horrible for you."

Her lips tightened as she bobbed her head up and down.

He waited for more. A moment later, her sad eyes lifted to his. "Flash forward about sixteen years. It was the night of the blackout…my neighbor Eddie was having a big birthday bash on the Sunset Strip. It was one round of drinks after another. For the first time in my life, I indulged. In a big way. My friends kept my glass refilled until I was feeling no pain. My fuzzy head went on the blink, and unfortunately so did the lights. Before I knew what was happening, the entire club went black. I couldn't see a thing out the windows, either. Then I heard the rain. It wasn't a downpour, but it didn't have to be, just the steady pounding on the roof was enough. I freaked and began trembling uncontrollably. Luckily, I had Brooke on autodial, or I wouldn't have had the coordination to make the call. I couldn't reach her… She didn't answer."

Dylan leaned in, nodding his head. "Go on, Em. Then what did you do?"

Her eyes squeezed shut. This was hard on Emma but it was probably good for her to purge this memory. "When I couldn't reach your sister, I panicked and gave my phone to someone sitting on the floor next to me." She shook her head and took a deep breath. "My friend punched in your number."

"My number?" he repeated, and his forehead wrinkled as he scoured his memory for an inkling of recollection. Nothing came to mind.

"Yes… I…I thought Brooke might be with you."

His mind was a blank wall when it came to those days. "I don't remember."

Her eyes watered and she gave him half a smile, one of those unhappy smiles that tussled with his heart. "I was so scared."

"I'm sorry."

"Don't be. You came to rescue me. I just remember thinking *Dylan will come.* If he says he will come, he will come. He'll get me out of here. I couldn't wait to get out of that place."

He could've caught flies when his mouth dropped open and stayed that way. "What happened next?" And why didn't she tell him this before? She knew he was trying to piece together those lost hours before the blast.

"It's fuzzy, but I remember you finding me in the dark and carrying me out of there. You drove me home and... and..."

She gazed into his eyes then, and it hit him with dazzling clarity. He blinked rapidly several times. "You're not saying..."

She hadn't said anything yet. But a knot formed in the pit of his stomach. And he knew what she was going to say, not because he remembered it, but because she'd given him the full picture of her life leading up to that moment. And he was cast in the starring role.

"I wouldn't let you leave, Dylan." Her head down, she began shaking it. "I begged you to stay with me. I was scared out of my wits. The whole city was pitch-black and you knew I would freak out if you left me, so you agreed, and then...we, uh..."

"We made love?" He couldn't believe he was asking Emma, his little sister's friend, this question. Emma, the efficient one. The one always in control, the one who never took risks, never strayed from the straight-and-narrow path. Emma Rae Bloom. He'd bedded her?

Her eyes were filling with unshed tears. "It was my fault."

He winced. The entire script was now playing in his head. Emma had been intoxicated and scared and he'd come to her rescue and then seduced her. Crap.

He rubbed a finger over his eye. "I'm sure it wasn't."

"I wouldn't let you leave. I pleaded with you to stay with me. You kept saying something like *You've got it all wrong*, or *This is wrong*, but because of my fear and the alcohol I wouldn't listen. I just needed...you."

"I don't remember a thing, honey. I don't. So, you're sure..." Hell, what a creep he was, about to ask her if she was sure the baby was his. If it was anyone but Emma, he would ask that question. And demand proof. But Emma wouldn't lie. She wouldn't try to pull a fast one on him. Her story made sense. He wouldn't have left her to fend for herself that night. If she was in trouble, he would've gone to get her himself. But he thought he would've drawn the line at taking advantage of a frightened friend, tempting as she might have been. Damn it all.

Maybe his subconscious had known all along he'd been with Emma. Maybe that explained the reason behind his recent attraction to her. He'd always thought of her as off-limits, but after the accident, things between them seemed to change.

He kept his voice soft. "You're sure that you're pregnant?"

"I mean, I haven't seen a doctor yet, but the tests were all positive."

"How many did you take?"

She glanced away. "Seven."

"Ah, just to be sure."

"Yeah."

Dylan heaved a sigh. He realized his first words to her would have great impact, so he treaded carefully. But hell, he was stunned. And clueless about that night. He ran a hand through his hair and then mustered a smile. "Okay."

"Okay?"

"Yeah. I don't have any answers now, Emma. But you're not alone in this. I'm here. And we'll figure it out together."

He knew damn well he'd have to marry her. No child of his was going to grow up without a father and mother. He'd seen too much neglect and abuse over the years. Before Brooke came along and was adopted by his folks, they'd brought many frightened, insecure children into their family, cared for them and nurtured them until they could find a loving home. His child would have his name and all the privileges and love he could give. But now wasn't the time to propose marriage to Emma.

They were both in shock.

Dylan was trying to be charming, trying to be patient, but Emma could tell by the worry lines creasing his forehead he was at a loss. She was, too. But already, she was in love with her baby, Dylan's child, and would move heaven and earth to make things right.

She rose, steady on her feet, and Dylan bounced up from the sofa, his concerned gaze never wavering. "I need to use the restroom," she said.

"I'll walk you."

"No, I'm okay. I'm not dizzy anymore and I know where it is." Dylan's lips were pursed tight but he didn't argue as she walked away with steady measured steps and entered the bathroom.

She splashed water on her face, the cool, crisp feel of it perking her up. As her head came up from the sink, her reflection stared back at her in the mirror. The color had returned to her face. And her legs didn't feel like jelly anymore. Revealing a secret as big as this one was therapeutic, as if a light had been turned on and she could see again. She felt free, relieved and unburdened.

But that feeling lasted only a few seconds. As she exited the bathroom, Dylan was there, leaning against the wall with arms folded, his face barely masking his concern. He approached her and took her hand. "How are you feeling, Em?"

The slightest touch of his large hand on hers was enough to wake her sleeping endorphins. As they tried to spread cheer, all she could think about was pulling away from him. Pulling away from the caring way he said her name. Away from what she feared almost as much as being alone in the dark. Falling for him. Really, in the flesh, head-over-heels falling for him, leaving her broken and shattered.

She'd been unloved all of her life.

But to be unloved by Dylan would be the hardest of all.

"I'm fine. Much better actually."

"I want you to stay here tonight."

"Why?" She stared into the deep sea of his eyes. They weren't commanding exactly, but filled with expectation. Like the rest of him.

"You shouldn't be alone tonight."

"Isn't that how I got pregnant in the first place?"

It was a bad joke. Not a joke really, the truth, but Dylan didn't seem to take offense. His lips quirked a bit. "Oh, how I wish I knew."

"To be perfectly honest, I don't remember, either. My brain wasn't firing on all cylinders. I just have flashes here and there of how it was."

He nodded, staring at her as if he still couldn't believe they'd made love. As if the thought was foreign to him. He didn't say the words, but there was an apology on his expression. "Just for the record, and I do appreciate you *not* asking, but I'm sure it's your baby, Dylan. I haven't been sexually active in quite a while."

His tanned face became infused with color that wasn't there before. Dylan McKay blushing was a rare sight.

"I figured."

Her brows lifted at the quickness of his response. Had he just insulted her?

"I mean, you wouldn't lie to me, Emma," he explained. "I know you're telling the truth."

Better.

"I'm not staying here tonight, Dylan."

He'd walked her into the kitchen, where he handed her a glass of water. "You've been sick for days and you fainted just a few minutes ago. You need someone with you."

She sipped and took a moment to gather her thoughts. "You're not going to watch over me all night, Dylan."

"I didn't intend to. But there's nothing wrong with a friend checking in on a friend, is there?"

"That's what text messages are for."

He snorted, and it was sexy. How much trouble was she in?

"You're gonna cause me a sleepless night."

"Look, you can drop me off at home and then text me when you get back here. I promise to text you first thing in the morning."

"Whatever happened to phone calls?"

"Fine, I'll call you when I wake up."

"And what if you're sick again?"

"You'll come to my rescue. I have no doubt."

He rubbed his hand back and forth across the expanse of his jaw as he contemplated her words. "I wish you weren't so stubborn about this."

"I'm not stubborn, just practical. I think we need space right now…to think."

"That's my line, honey. And notice I didn't say it? Because right now, it's more important to make sure you get your health back."

"I've been taking care of myself for almost twenty-six years. I can manage, trust me."

He nodded slowly, giving her a stern fatherly look. God, she'd always hated when Dylan did that. He wasn't her guardian or big brother. "Fine, then. I'll drive you home."

Half an hour later, they pulled up to her building. Dylan insisted on coming into her apartment, his take on seeing her safely home. Her emotional well was dry and she didn't have it in her to argue the point.

"So this is where we, uh…conceived the baby?" His eyes dipped down to her belly and a searing heat cut through the denim of her dress as if she'd been physically touched. A tiny tremble rumbled through her system.

"Yes. This is it." She wouldn't say it was the scene of the crime. She couldn't label the new life growing inside as anything but wonderful. Whether or not Dylan or anyone else agreed. "In the bedroom, of course."

He shot another piercing look her way. "Right."

Dylan helped take her jacket off and then guided her to a seat on the sofa. She sat down without argument. He didn't sit, though. Instead, he walked around the room, scanning the picture frames on her bookshelf, looking at trinkets, the furniture and all the surroundings with a new and insightful eye. Then he turned to her. "Mind if I peek into your bedroom? See if it jars my memory?"

Oh, boy. This was awkward. But she understood the necessity. Things for Dylan would be so much easier if he could get those lost hours back. She nodded. "Just don't look in my lingerie drawers."

He laughed, his somber eyes finally twinkling.

He was gone only a minute before returning to her.

"Anything?" she asked.

He shook his head sadly. "No."

She understood his disappointment. All that she remembered from that night was a muscled body covering hers and the tender comfort his presence had given her. Afterward, she'd slipped into the tight cocoon of his arms and fallen into a drugged sleep. When she had woken up with the mother of all hangovers, Dylan was gone.

That next day, the power outage was old news in most parts of the city. The lights had come back on and everything had returned to normal. For most people. And the shocking death of Roy Benjamin on the set of beloved actor Dylan McKay's new film had usurped all the day's headlines.

Right now, she and Dylan were on even footing. Both were unsure of how that night had gone down. There was a chance Dylan would never get that time back. And her memory was fogged over and blurry at best. "I'm sorry."

"Don't be. It was a long shot."

His smile didn't budge the rest of his face. He turned his wrist and glanced at his watch, a gorgeous black-faced gold Movado. "It's ten thirty. What time do you go to bed?"

"Eleven."

He nodded and sat on the couch beside her.

"Let me guess. You're not leaving until I go to bed?"

"I'd like to stay."

Crapola. How many women would kill to have that offer from Dylan McKay?

"I'm just going to do some reading in bed before I turn in. You can leave now."

Dylan ran a hand down his face. "You're trying to get rid of me."

"Only because I don't need you to babysit me. I'm fine."

"Then I'll go," he said, standing up, leaving her gaze to follow the long length of his body as he straightened. "I'll text you at eleven and see how you're doing."

"My kind of guy," she teased.

His lips curved up. "You're not going to prevent me from checking on you."

She rose, too, and amazed herself at her own stability, considering she'd fainted just a few hours ago. "I'll call you in the morning. It's a promise."

"Thanks," he said, and she followed him to the door. When he turned to her, they were only a breath apart, him towering above her by six inches. The scent of raw power and lime emanated from his throat and lingered in her nostrils. His golden hair gleamed under the foyer light and his eyes, deadly and devastatingly blue, found hers. "Make an appointment with a doctor for next week. I'd like to go with you," he said.

It shouldn't have come as a surprise that he'd want to go with her, but Dylan escorting her to an obstetrician's office would be big news if word got out. And there would be repercussions. "Are you sure?"

"Absolutely," he said immediately. "I'll let you know my schedule."

He laced his hands with hers then and gave a little tug, bringing her closer. His beautiful mouth was only inches away. "I want you to move into my house, Emma. Think about it and we'll talk again tomorrow."

Without hesitation his head came forward and his lips met with hers. The kiss was brief, but amazing and glorious. A glimpse of what could be. A tease. A temptation.

And when she opened her eyes, he'd already turned away and was gone.

Yes, yes, yes would've been her answer. If only he'd asked for the right reasons.

But Dylan didn't want her. He wanted her baby.

And she wasn't about to live her life unloved.

Ever again.

Emma didn't pick up a book to read. Instead, she grabbed the phone and speed-dialed Brooke's number. She picked up on the first ring.

"Hi, Brooke. It's me, checking in."

"Emma, it's late. Are you okay?"

"Right now, I'm feeling fine. Did I wake you?"

"Gosh no. I'm dead on my feet, but wide-awake. I'm done prepping for tomorrow. Rocky and Wendy are doing their share and we're managing."

"That's great news. I've been thinking about you all day. How was the silent auction?"

"It went well. We had lots of bids and I'm guessing the charity made lots of money. I haven't tallied it up yet. That comes later tonight."

"Do it in the morning, Brooke. You sound beat."

"I am, but in a good way."

Emma's pangs of guilt resurfaced. Poor Brooke. The business side of things wasn't her forte. She had a creative streak a mile long and Pinterest could learn a few things from her when it came to party planning. But anything with numbers, and Brooke was at a complete loss.

"So, no snags for tomorrow?" Tomorrow was the celebrity golf tournament, the golf widow's luncheon and the formal Give a Dollar or a Thousand Dinner and raffle. All the celebrities golfing would attend the dinner. Their appearance made for heftier donations, but they came with a high price for their time. They were accustomed to and expected fabulous cuisine and service, so this task was even more daunting.

"Nope, not a one."

Emma breathed a sigh of relief. "Good."

"How are things with you?" Brooke questioned her in a softer tone that left no room for doubt what she was really getting at.

"You guilted Dylan into checking on me."

"Yeah, I did. I'm sorry, honey, but I'm worried about you. So, you spent time with him tonight?"

"Yes, and I…well…he knows my situation now."

"You told him!"

Her face scrunched up at her friend's enthusiasm. "Don't sound so happy. He's in as much shock as I am."

"But at least he knows the truth."

"Yeah, but nothing jarred his memory."

"That's not really the point. You can't worry about the past. At least you'll move forward toward the future."

Normally, she told Brooke everything, but tonight wasn't the night to tell her about Dylan's offer. She wasn't about to move into his mansion. And if Brooke knew, she'd probably side with her brother on this. Two McKays would be too hard to fight. "Yeah, I guess." She waited a beat. "I'm glad things went well tonight. And I know tomorrow will be amazing. You should hit the sack. That's what I'm going to do. Love you, Brooke."

"Love you, too. Sleep well."

Emma hung up the phone and undressed, slipping out of her street clothes and into her pajamas. She climbed into bed, shut off the table lamp and snuggled her face deep into her cushy pillow. Her body sank into the mattress and she sighed out loud. Nothing was better than a comfy bed after a rough day. But just as she closed her eyes, Dylan's image popped into her head.

She owed him a text.

Stretching her arm out, she fumbled for her phone on the nightstand, punched in his number and typed out her text.

I'm tucked in and feeling well. Good night.

Short and sweet. It'd been a long time since she'd had to answer to anyone. Derek Purdy, the man she now thought of as The Jerk, had cured her of that in her sophomore year of college. She hated even thinking of him anymore. He didn't deserve another second of her time.

But Dylan, on the other hand, would be in her life forever now.

He was no jerk, and from now on they would have to answer to each other.

For the baby's sake.

Five

"Rolling," the first assistant director called out as Dylan stood on his mark on the Stage One Studios back lot. The cast and crew of *Resurrection SEALs* became quiet. They were on the same dirt road where Roy had died and where Dylan had been hit with shrapnel. If being here didn't jog his memory, nothing would. Dylan tried to focus. He was a professional, and the crew had worked long hours this morning prepping this scene. The director called, "Action," and Dylan went into performance mode, delivering his lines. He stumbled once, mixing up the words, and looked to the script supervisor for his line.

Marcy offered it. "Whether or not you give me those papers, Joe, the colonel is going to hear about this."

They reshot the scene several times and Dylan went through the paces for coverage and tights on his face before his work was done. The director, Gabe Novotny, walked over and put a hand on his shoulder. "That first scene had to be hard on you. But you're through it now. How does it feel?"

"I can't lie. It's a little weird, Gabe. Mostly, it's knowing that Roy died right here, and now, here I am, doing my job, back to the status quo and moving forward without him."

"We're all feeling it, Dylan. But you managed the scene. And the next one will be a little easier, and then the next."

Dylan didn't have much choice. He was under contract, but a part of him wanted to bail on this project now, even though he'd done intense training, including daily ten-mile beach runs and weight lifting to become Josh O'Malley, Navy SEAL. "I'm hoping you're right. Still is strange to be here, though." He knew enough about survivor guilt to understand that the ache in the pit of his stomach wasn't going away anytime soon. He missed Roy, and if he'd been the one to get into the car that day as planned, instead of Roy, he'd be the one floating atop the high seas now with his ashes scattered all over the Pacific. "If we're done for now, I think I'll head back to my trailer."

"Actually, an officer from the LAPD is due in the production office any minute now. He's asked to speak to you and me, Marcy and the execs. Maury Allen was asked to be there, too, so it's something big if the police want the head of the studio there. You might remember the officer. He consulted with us early on in the film about two months ago."

"Oh, yeah. Detective Brice. He's a big Clippers fan. We talked basketball for a while."

"That's him. It's about Roy's death, Dylan." Gabe took his eyeglasses off and rubbed them clean on the tail of his shirt. "So I'm betting it's not a social call."

"All right."

Gabe glanced past the chaos of the crew taking down the rigging and spotted Marcy speaking with the girls from Hair and Makeup. "You about through, Marce?"

She slammed a folder closed, stood on her tiptoes and waved at him. "I'm coming."

Instead of golf-carting it, they walked to the offices together. When they entered the building, they were reintroduced to the detective, who was dressed in an austere gray suit. They all took a seat at a long table as if they were going to do a cold reading. But it wasn't play acting. Judging by Detective Brice's sullen expression, he didn't have good news.

"I'm here to ask a few more questions regarding the death of Roy Benjamin. After investigating the accident, it's been determined that the car in question had been tampered with before the stunt ever took place. We've already spoken with the stunt team supervisor and he's confirmed that they'd given the stunt the all clear. They went through a series of tests before Mr. Benjamin ever got in that car. There's a timeline factor that we're working with here. From the time the stunt team finished rigging the car until the actual shoot, there are thirty minutes unaccounted for."

"What are you saying exactly?" Maury asked, his brows gathered.

"Mr. Benjamin was to roll out of the car right before it blew up. But we believe someone sabotaged the rigging so that the car would blow up ahead of schedule."

"With Roy in it?" Dylan asked, barely recognizing the high pitch of his own voice.

Detective Brice nodded, his voice gruff. "That's right."

"So you think Roy was murdered?"

"That's what I'm here to investigate. Mr. McKay, do you have any recollection about that day, at all?"

He squeezed his eyes shut hating that he couldn't remember a damn thing. "No, none."

"Okay, well, if you do remember anything, give me a call." Detective Brice handed Dylan a business card that read Homicide Division. He stared at it, finding this whole thing bizarre, like something out of one of his movies. Who would want to murder Roy?

The officer proceeded to question Dylan about his relationship with Roy. How long had they been friends? How long had he worked as his stunt double? Any girlfriends? What was he like? Did he have any enemies? Dylan answered as honestly as he could, and when the detective moved on to the others, Dylan's mind wandered to some of the better times he'd had with Roy. They had a lot in common. Both liked to work out, both loved women, both enjoyed good whiskey.

By the time Maury, Gabe, Marcy and the other execs were through being questioned, they all began shaking their heads. They were as stunned as Dylan was. Then Gabe remembered one important thing. "Dylan was originally supposed to do that scene," he told the detective. "We changed the script a bit and decided the stunt was too risky for Dylan to handle."

Brice turned toward Dylan. "Is that so?"

"I don't remember, but that's what Gabe told me."

"I don't think it was changed on the call sheet for that day," Gabe offered.

"I'd like a copy of that, please," the detective said, and Gabe nodded.

Detective Brice was quiet for a while, writing things down in a notebook. "Okay. Well, until we get to the bottom of this, I'd suggest that all of you be wary of anything unusual around the studio and report any suspicious behavior. And, Mr. McKay, if that script change wasn't common knowledge, then there's a possibility that you could've been the target instead of Mr. Benjamin. Do you have any enemies?"

Dylan's head snapped up. He gazed into Detective Brice's serious eyes. "I get all kinds of fan mail. I have an assistant go through it. But she hasn't said anything about threats."

"Maybe you should ask her for details and start going through your mail for anything unusual. You might recognize something she doesn't."

"You don't really believe Dylan was the target?" Maury asked.

The detective shrugged. "It's better to take into account all the possibilities."

After the questioning, Dylan returned to finish his next scene, struggling with what he'd just learned. He couldn't believe someone was out to get him. He might have a few unhappy ex-girlfriends, but he was actually on good terms with most of them. He dug around his memory for anything else, anyone who might want to do him harm, and came up empty.

He left the studio unnerved and on the drive home made a call to his security team to beef up patrols around his house. Usually if he went out on studio appearances or interviews, he traveled with a bodyguard, so he was good there. And once he'd taken care of that business, he called Emma. She answered the call on the first ring. "Hello."

"Hi, it's me."

"Hi, Dylan."

"How're you feeling today?"

"Better. I went into the office today and did some work. It feels good to be back among the productive."

He smiled. "That's good. What if I told you I had a bad day and needed a friend? Would you have dinner with me tonight?"

Her silence at the other end of the phone made his heart race. It blew his mind how much he wanted her to agree.

"Would that be the honest truth?" she asked.

"It would."

Her relenting sigh carried to his ears. She wasn't happy

about the pressure he put on her and he was taking advantage of her good nature, but he really did need a friend tonight. He couldn't tell her about Detective Brice's visit on the set today, and even if he could, he wouldn't want to trouble her. Just seeing her tonight, knowing that she was carrying his child and something good had come out of that time he'd lost, would boost his spirits. "Then sure, I guess I could do that."

"Thanks." He released a pent-up breath. "I'll be there in half an hour to pick you up."

Emma faced Dylan across the tufted white leather booth at Roma's Restaurant in the city. Silly her, after he'd called, she'd waded through her closet and come up with the prettiest dress she could find: a soft sapphire-blue brushed cotton with lots of feminine folds and a draping halter neckline. She'd dressed for him and had been rewarded with hot, appreciative glances on the drive here.

Looking around the place, she noted that Roma's tables weren't covered with red-and-white-checked tablecloths, there were no plastic flower centerpieces and not a hint of sawdust was sprinkled on the creamy marble floors. Dylan was used to the best, and he'd come to think of these high-end places as the norm. But Emma wasn't used to eating pizza off expensive Italian dinnerware or having a violinist make the rounds from table to table, offering up a musical selection to soothe the soul.

"They make a mean eggplant parm here," Dylan said. "And the pizza is old-school, like back home."

"Eggplant sounds good," she said, folding the menu. "I'd like that."

Dylan nodded to the waiter. "Make that two, then, Tony, and two glasses of sparkling water."

After the waiter left, she picked up a wafer-like piece of

rosemary-and-garlic bread, almost hating to break up the fancy-schmancy geometric design in the basket.

"Feel free to order wine or whatever you want, Dylan. You don't have to drink water because of me."

God, tonight he looked as if he could really use a drink. He was a good actor, the best actually, but tonight he wasn't acting. His guard was down and she saw it in the pallor on his face, his sullen eyes and the twist of his otherwise beautiful mouth.

"Thanks," he said, giving her a nod. "Maybe I will order a glass of wine later."

"That bad a day?"

He glanced down at the pearly-white tablecloth. "Yeah, I guess. We had to resume shooting the scene in the location where Roy died. It was a hard day for everyone."

"For you especially, I would think."

He nodded. "It was just weird and sad."

"I'm sorry."

"Thanks. I guess there's nothing to be done about it. The show must go on," he said with a strained chuckle that barely moved his mouth.

A part of her wanted to reach out to him, to hold his hand or maybe fold him into an embrace. He looked a little lost right now. She knew the feeling and she was suddenly glad she'd accepted his dinner invitation.

"Enough about me," Dylan said. "How are you feeling?"

"I'm sitting here about ready to eat eggplant smothered in sauce and cheese and the thought of it doesn't turn my stomach, so I think I'm fine."

"No more morning sickness?"

"I didn't say that. I still get queasy, but it passes quickly and only seems to happen in the morning. Still, I'm not counting my chickens yet."

"Did you call the doctor?"

"Yes, the appointment is next Thursday at ten o'clock."

"Okay, good." He seemed pleased. He'd told her he wasn't filming on Thursday and she had been lucky enough to get an appointment with her ob-gyn that day.

"If you run into a bind or something, it won't be a problem. I can get myself there." She wanted to throw that out to him. She had other means, if he couldn't go that day. She was suddenly transported back in time to when she was a charity case, an unloved little young burden to those around her. She'd been a child then, scared of the future, but she wasn't now. Now she clung to her independence and needed it as much as she needed air to breathe. Single motherhood wasn't rare these days, lots of women did it and managed just fine. She wasn't looking to Dylan to be her savior.

"I won't run into a bind." His jaw was set as he spoke those firm words. He meant it. Dylan was a big enough star that schedules could be woven around his needs, and not the other way around. But still, she wasn't going to crumble if she did the mother thing alone.

"Brooke wants to go with me on an appointment later on," she said. "She wants to be a part of it, too."

"I'd like that. She'll be an amazing aunt."

Emma smiled. They both agreed on that. "She's been very supportive."

Dylan nodded. "What do you think of this Royce guy she's been dating? Is he the real deal?"

Ah, finally the conversation was moving away from her. She was glad for the distraction. "I haven't met him yet, but there's a bouquet of red roses on her desk at work that says he's an okay guy. She's seeing him tonight, as a matter of fact. She missed him like crazy while she was away."

Dylan made a grunting sound before he sipped the sparkling water the waiter had just delivered. "That always scares me."

"Why?"

He shrugged. "I want to see her happy. She's been disappointed before."

"Haven't we all," Emma blurted. And then squeezed her eyes shut but not before witnessing Dylan's brows lift inquisitively.

"I know."

She gave him a look that must have revealed her astonishment because his baby blues softened immediately. "Brooke told me about a guy in college you were seeing."

"When did she tell you that?" The witchy tone in her voice made her mentally cringe. She didn't mean to sound so darn defensive.

"A while back. I'm not prying into your life, Emma. I wouldn't put Brooke in that position, and if I want to know something about you, I'll ask you up front. But actually, my sister mentioned it a few years ago and I never forgot it because I thought you deserved better than a jerk who would verbally abuse you. I guess it always stuck with me. I sorta wanted to punch his lights out."

Emma pictured Dylan knocking Derek Purdy to the ground and grinned. "You've always been protective."

"There's nothing wrong with a friend looking out for a friend."

"I've always appreciated that." That was the truth. Dylan had never failed to be her champion when he was around. He had a thing for the underdog. It was quite commendable actually, but right now with her baby situation, she didn't want to be considered the underdog, or lacking in any way. "But it's old news now, Dylan. I've forgotten about him."

The meal was served and that part of the conversation ended. Emma dug in with tepid gusto, keeping in mind the capacity of her shrunken stomach and the queasiness that might rear its ugly head at any given moment, despite what she'd told Dylan. She didn't trust her gut not to act up. She was just getting used to the idea of eating a full meal and not paying the price afterward.

"It's delicious," she said. Steam rose up from the sizzling cheese and the garlicky scents made her mouth water.

"It's not too ostentatious for you?"

"The eggplant?"

His eyes twinkled with that you-know-what-I-mean look.

"The place."

"Let's see. I'm eating off handmade Intrada dinner plates while being serenaded by a sole violinist. The Waterford cut crystal and white rose centerpiece is a nice touch. Adds class to the joint. Nope, I'd say it's right on par with Vitellos back home."

He wiped his mouth with the cloth napkin. The gleam in his eyes became even brighter at her sarcasm. "How do you know all this stuff?"

"You're forgetting what I do for a living. It's my job to know about dinnerware and crystal and high-end table dressing."

"Right. I didn't put it together. You're good at your job. But you're not comfortable with all this, are you?"

"It's fine, Dylan. I have no complaints. If this is what it takes to cheer you up, then I'm all for it."

Dylan's smile faded a bit as he reached for her hand. "*You* are what's cheering me up. I enjoy being with you, Em. And I brought you here not to impress you, but because I knew you'd enjoy the food."

Her heartbeat sounded in her ears. She had no humorous comeback. "Oh."

She got a little more lost in his eyes. It was hard not to; those eyes could drown a lesser woman and she was certainly not immune. The clarity in them astounded her. Dylan knew what he was about, amnesia or not. There was no limit to his confidence, yet he wasn't arrogant or prissy. He was kinda perfect.

And that scared her more than anything.

"Maybe…uh, maybe you should have some wine now." She would if she could.

He shook his head, not breaking eye contact. "Not necessary."

"You're cured?"

He chuckled, the smile cracking his face wide-open. "For the moment, anyway." He squeezed her hand a little and a shot of adrenaline arrowed up her arm and spread like wildfire throughout her system. What was he doing to her? She'd come here to boost his spirits, not fall under his spell.

He glanced at her half-eaten plate of food. "Finish your meal, sweetheart." And he released her hand just like that, leaving a rich hum of delight in the wake of his touch. She filled up with deliriously happy hormones. "We'll talk about dessert when you're through," he added.

Dessert? She felt as though she'd already had a decadent helping of chocolate-espresso gelato with cherries on top.

The Dylan McKay Special.

And nothing was sweeter.

When they got back to her apartment, she made a feeble attempt to get inside with some semblance of grace and dignity. "Really, Dylan, you didn't have to walk me to my door," she said, her back to the front door and her hand on the knob.

His brows lifted and a lock of straight sun-streaked hair fell across his forehead. She was tempted to touch it, to ease it back into place and run her fingers through the rest.

"I never drop a lady off at the curb, Emma. I certainly wouldn't do that to you. You know that."

She did. But she couldn't invite Dylan in. She didn't

have willpower to spare right now. Yet she knew that's exactly what he wanted. "Well, now you've earned another gold star."

"I have many."

She imagined a black-and-white composition book filled with pages of gold stars. But she had to be kind in her not-too-subtle brush-off. "Thanks again for dinner. You must be tired after the day you've had. You should go home and turn in."

"I will soon enough. But you're not safely inside yet." His hand glided over hers to snare the key from her fingers. "Here, let me."

She nearly jumped from the contact and her hand opened. When he took the key, she moved away from the door and allowed him to insert it into the lock. With a twist, the door clicked open.

"Thanks again," she said breathlessly, again pressing her back to the door.

He leaned in so close she caught the slight scent of musky aftershave, a heady mixture that stirred all of her erotic senses. Oh, boy, she was in trouble.

She pressed her head against the door, backing away from him and staring at his lips that were coming way too close. "What are you doing?"

"I'm giving you a proper thank-you, sweetheart."

"The eggplant was thanks—"

And then his mouth came down on hers. Not roughly or aggressively, but not with tender persuasion, either. It was perfectly balanced, a kiss that could mean a dozen things that were not necessarily sexual. Yet as she raised her hands to push at his chest, he deepened the kiss, giving it more texture and taste, and the balance she relied on was starting to disappear. Her arms fell to her sides; there would be no shove-off-buddy move on her part. How could she think of ending something so amazing?

His hand came up beside her head, his palm flat against the door, and the darn thing moved, making her clumsily back up a step, then two. He followed her, of course, his lips still locked with hers, and the next thing she knew they were inside her dark apartment and breathing heavily. Dylan broke the kiss momentarily to guide her backward some more and then kick the door shut with his foot.

"Imagine that," he whispered. "We're inside your apartment."

"Uh-huh" was her brilliant comeback. She was too enthralled with his mouth, his tongue and the wonderful way he used them on her to think straight.

And then she felt his hand on her belly. Only someone who knew her intimately would notice the slight bulge above her waist. His fingers splayed out, encircling the whole of her stomach, and a throaty sound emanated from deep within his chest. "I've wanted to touch you here, Em. It's okay, isn't it?"

She nodded, not trusting her voice.

"I know it's not ideal, but, Emma, if there was ever a woman to carry my child, of all the women I know, all that I've been with, I'm glad it's you."

There was a compliment in there somewhere. Emma understood what he meant, but there were still issues, lots and lots of issues. She pulled away from him. "I'll turn on a light."

Before she was out of his reach, he was gripping her wrist and tugging her back to him. She landed smack against his chest and gazed up at his face, which was steeped in shadows. "Don't, Emma. You're safe with me. Don't be afraid."

She *was* afraid. Of where this was leading. "What do you want, Dylan?" she asked softly and heard the defeat in her voice. It was as if she couldn't compete, couldn't deny him, couldn't defend against him.

"Honestly, I don't know. You're good for me, Em. I like who I am when I'm with you. And I don't want to leave, not just yet."

Something almost desperate in his voice kept her rooted to the spot. Then he touched her, a light brush of his fingers feathering her face, a caress she had always dreamed about. And he kissed her again, tenderly and slowly, like a man treasuring a sacred prize. The prize, she knew, wasn't her, but the baby. She got that. She already felt the same way about the life growing inside her. She didn't blame the child for her bouts of sickness or regret the mere fact that the baby existed at all. Yet something was off. His kisses were new to her. His touch exciting and not familiar in the way she'd thought they'd be. They'd done this before, kissing and intimately touching when they conceived the baby, but she didn't remember...*him*.

"Dylan," she said softly, "we're friends."

"We could be more."

He nibbled on her lower lip. A blast of heat spiraled down to her belly and she closed her eyes, absorbing the pleasant torment while trying to contain the burning inferno that was building, building. Dylan's heat became her heat and she hardly noticed as they moved farther into her room, until Dylan was sitting on her sofa and she was being yanked down onto his lap.

His tongue danced with hers as he pressed her against the sofa cushions. His lips found her forehead, her cheeks, her chin, and then moved leisurely back to her waiting mouth. She ached for him and it was almost useless to try to fight the feeling. In her teenage imaginings, before his fame and fortune, Dylan had always been hers. She caved to those feelings now and moaned when his hand slipped under her dress and climbed her thigh, inching toward the part of her body that ached for him the most.

But Dylan bypassed that spot and moved his hand farther up to lay claim once again to her belly. He stroked her there gently and she caught a glimpse of the top of his head as he bestowed a loving kiss right above her navel over the spot where their baby resided.

She melted in that moment. Her eyes filled with tears. She bit her lower lip to keep from making a silly, revealing sound. But her heart was involved, now more than ever before. And it pained her in ways that she'd never dreamed possible.

"Dylan," she whispered.

He lifted his head and their gazes locked in the shadows. An unwavering gleam in his eyes spoke of the love he already had for his baby. He smiled. Dread pierced her stomach. She didn't have ammunition to fight Dylan when he was like this.

The next thing she knew, his hand was on her thigh again, moving up and down, rubbing away her apprehension and bringing on a new kind of tension. "You're soft, Emma. Everywhere."

Oh, God, but he wasn't. It was evident from the press of his groin to her hip. They were treading dangerous ground and she was too enthralled to put a stop to it.

He brought his mouth to hers again and again, his hand working magic over her throat, her shoulders, the steep slope of her breasts. His fingertips grazed her nipples and she jumped, sensitive and achy.

A groan rumbled from the depths of his chest and he moved more steadily over her, cupping her breast through the material of her dress, trailing hot moist kisses along her collarbones. Everything was on fire, burning, burning. The heat was combustible and then…and then…

The phone rang.

Her house line was ringing. It was used for emergencies, and only a handful of people had the number. The answering machine picked up and Brooke's voice was on the other end.

"It's me, Em. I'm looking for Dylan. Neither one of you are picking up your cell and it's sort of important. Is he there by any chance?"

Dylan immediately sat upright.

Emma gave him a nod and bounded up, adjusting her lopsided halter as she dashed to turn on a light and pick up the phone on the kitchen wall. "Hi," she said, breathless.

"Hi," Brooke said, drawing out the word. "Am I disturbing something?"

"No, no. We were just coming in from dinner. Dylan dropped me off. He's still here. Let me get him," she said. But there was no need. He was already behind her, his hands on her waist, planting a kiss on her shoulder as though they were a real couple, before he took the phone. "Hi, sis."

Emma walked out of the room to give him privacy, but her apartment had few walls and she could still see him and hear his voice. Her curiosity wouldn't allow her to turn away. "Renee?" He sighed heavily and after a few seconds said, "Okay, I'll take care of it." Then he ended the call.

Dylan squeezed his eyes shut and rubbed the back of his neck before turning to Emma. Their gazes locked and he moved toward her and grasped her hands. "I have to go. But I want you to promise you'll think about moving in with me. We could have a lot more nights like tonight. I want you with me, honey."

It was too much, too soon, and her head was still reeling from how close they'd come to making love. Inhaling a shaky breath, she shook her head. "I can't promise you that, Dylan. I'm not ready to make that kind of move."

He nodded and worry lines formed around his eyes. "Okay, but I'd like to see you again. Soon."

"Like a date?"

"Yeah," he said, his face brightening as if he was really warming to the idea. "I think we'll take one step at a time. Dating first. Can you manage that?"

She nodded. "I think so."

"Exclusively?"

Exclusive with Dylan McKay! She liked the sound of that. Not that she'd ever had a situation where she was dating two men at the same time. "Exclusively."

Seeming satisfied, he gave her a quick, chaste kiss goodbye and hurried away.

Leaving Emma to wonder about his ex Renee and what that phone call was all about.

Was *she* the exception to Dylan's rules of exclusivity?

Six

Dylan sat down at his desk as morning breezes blew in through the window, the fresh ocean air a jolt stronger than caffeine to rouse him out of his sleep haze. Each morning he'd scan his mind, hoping to get a glimpse of the time he'd lost, hoping his memory would be restored. It wasn't happening today.

He opened the drawer, pulled out his checkbook and wrote out a check for a larger sum of money than he'd normally sent Renee over this past year. The monthly checks weren't a fortune, but enough to help her get by and make sure her two children were fed, housed and clothed. She was in worse shape than a single mother. She had a lousy ex-husband who threatened to take her kids away from her on a regular basis and Renee needed to supplement her meager earnings as a waitress in order to provide for her family.

She seemed to be in a constant state of crisis.

Dylan had long ago forgiven Renee for breaking his

heart. But the fault wasn't just Renee's. He'd allowed himself to be persuaded to run away with her. He'd been crazy in love, young and impulsive, and so willing to do whatever Renee wanted to keep her happy. They'd been in a theatre production together in high school and had lofty notions of success. Later, at the age of nineteen, she'd convinced him to move to Los Angeles to pursue an acting career. He'd gone with her with eyes wide-open, understanding the risk, but when his success didn't come fast enough for her and Renee's so-called contacts in LA had dried up, her disappointment was hard to live with.

Then one day, he'd found her in the arms of another man, a director of a small theatre, an older man with a colossal ego who'd convinced her they were one step away from fame. That hadn't happened and she'd made one bad decision after another. While Dylan's career had finally launched through patience and perseverance, she'd given up on her dreams, becoming cynical and bitter, and wound up marrying someone who worked in the industry. Dylan had lost touch with her completely until last year when she'd reached out to his sister and asked if she could put her in touch with Dylan.

It was a pained conversation when they'd spoken, but Renee had touched something deep and tender in Dylan's heart as he remembered the young, vivacious girl she'd once been. She'd pleaded with him for forgiveness and he gave it willingly. She'd never once asked him for a handout, but after learning about her situation with an alcoholic, abusive ex-husband and hating the thought of her kids suffering, he'd started sending her checks.

"Knock, knock."

His head snapped up and he found Brooke dressed in a stretchy blue workout outfit standing at the threshold of his half-opened door. He gave her an immediate smile. "Hey, kiddo. Come in."

Once a week, he and Brooke exercised together in his gym on the second floor that overlooked the Pacific Ocean.

"Morning, bro. Ready for a workout?"

"Just about." He placed the check in an envelope and wrote out Renee's name on the front before sealing it. "You don't have to do this, Brooke. I can mail it."

"It's not a problem, Dylan. I know where Renee lives."

"It's half an hour out of town."

"Listen, I'm no fan of Renee's, but if she needs this pronto for her kids, then it's no big deal for me to put the check in her mailbox. This way, she'll have it earlier."

Dylan ran his hand along his chin. "Her daughter needs corrective eye surgery. She's in a panic about it."

"It's a good thing you're doing," Brooke said.

He didn't do it for accolades and no one besides his sister knew about this. Renee was part of his past, a one-time friend and lover. She needed help. Wouldn't he be a hypocrite to volunteer to help other charities and not help someone he knew personally who was in need? Why not give her a hand up?

"You have a big heart," his sister said.

"I can afford to."

"Yes, but she hurt you badly and I don't forgive as easily as you do."

"I didn't forgive her for a long time."

"But eventually you did. And she scarred you, Dylan. It was a betrayal of the worst kind."

"I'm hardly crying over it anymore."

But he'd lost his faith, and trust didn't come easily for him. He'd once believed in love, but not so much anymore. He hadn't come close to feeling anything like it since his last happy day with Renee. And then a thought rushed in and Emma's face appeared in his mind. He'd always liked Emma, and she was, after all, the mother of his child. Dating her was a means to an end. He was going to marry her and give the baby his name. At least he trusted her. As a friend.

Brooke took the check and plopped it into her wide canvas tote. "Let's go burn some calories."

An hour later, Brooke sipped water from a cold bottle, a workout towel hanging around her neck. "Inspiring as always," she said, glancing out the floor-to-ceiling windows at the low-lying clouds beginning to lift. It was going to be a blue-sky day.

Dylan set down his weights and sopped his face with his towel. "It's not half bad."

"You ready to talk to me about Emma?"

"Emma?" He sat down on a workout bench, stretched his legs out fully and downed half a bottle of water in one gulp. "What about Emma?"

She snapped her towel against his forearm. The painless rap and smirk on her lips had him grinning.

"Duh…" Brooke sat down next to him. "What's going on between you two?"

"Nosy, aren't you?"

"Concerned. I love you both."

Dylan flashed to the last night he'd been with Emma and the surprising, explosive way she'd responded to him. He'd taken liberties, but none that she hadn't wanted, and the feel of her skin, so soft and creamy smooth, the taste of her lips and plush fullness of her body against his, had him thinking of her many times since then. "I've asked her to move in with me, Brooke. She said no."

"You can't blame her for that," Brooke said. "She's struggling with all this, too. And you know her history. She's—"

"Stubborn?"

"*Independent* is a better word. And just because you're a celebrity doesn't mean every woman on the planet wants to live with you."

"I'm not asking every woman on the planet, Brooke. I'm asking the woman who's carrying my child."

"I know," she said more softly. "Give Emma some time, bro."

"I'm not pressuring her."

"Aren't you?"

"We're dating."

Brooke laughed. "Really? Like, in flowers and candy and malt shop hookups?"

His sister could be a pain in the ass sometimes. "Malt shop? I hadn't thought of that. Besides, little sis, isn't that what you're doing with Royce?"

Brooke's smile christened her flushed face. "Royce and I are much more sophisticated than that. We do art shows and book festivals and—"

"Intellectual stuff, huh?"

"Yeah, so far. We're still in the getting-to-know-each-other stage."

"Good, take it slow."

"Says the man who just asked a woman he'd never dated to move in with him."

"You're forgetting…that we—"

"Made a baby? Well, seeing as neither one of you recall much of that night, I say it's good you're starting out by dating. *S…L…O…W* and steady wins the race."

Dylan wasn't going to take it slow with Emma. No way. But Brooke didn't need to know that. She got defensive about Emma, and normally he loved that about his sister. She was loyal to her friends, but this one time, there was just too much at stake for Dylan to back off. He wouldn't give Emma a chance to run scared or go all independent feminist on him. He didn't want his child being raised in a disjointed home.

He had the means to provide a good life for both Emma and the baby. And the sooner she realized that, the better.

* * *

Emma tossed a kernel of popcorn into her mouth and leaned back in her maroon leather recliner seat, one of twenty in Dylan's private screening room. "I must admit, when you said you were taking me to the movies, I wondered how you would pull that off. I mean, it's not as if you can simply walk into a movie theater and not get noticed."

"Comes with the territory I'm afraid. Life has changed for me, but I'm not one of those people who complain about their fame. I knew what I was getting into when I started in this business. If I was lucky enough to succeed, then I wasn't going to cry about not having anonymity. I have a recognizable face, so I've had to alter a few things in my life."

"Like not being able to pop into a grocery store or travel unnoticed or window-shop?"

"Or take my date to a movie," Dylan added.

Emma laughed. "But you adapt very nicely."

"I'm glad you think so. So, what movie would you like to see? Chiller, thriller, Western, comedy, romance?"

"I'm at your mercy. You decide. You're the movie connoisseur."

Dylan picked an Oscar-nominated film about a boy's journey growing up and took the seat next to her. Wrapped chocolates, sour gummies and cashews were set out on a side table and a blue bottle of zillion-dollar water sat in the cupholder beside her chair.

"All set?"

She nodded. "Ready when you are."

Dylan hit a button on a remote control and the overhead lights dimmed as the screen lit up. Emma relaxed in her lounger and focused on the movie. They shared a bag of popcorn, and by the time they got to the bottom of the bag, her eyes had become a teary mess, a few escapees trickling down her cheeks from the poignancy of the film, its depiction of the heartfelt joy of family life, the struggles and cheerful moments and all the rest.

Picking up on her emotion, Dylan placed a tissue in her hand. She gave him a nod of thanks, wiped her watery eyes and focused back on the screen. It wasn't hormones that wrecked her heart this time. Whenever she witnessed a real family in action, the ups and downs and the way they all came together out of love and loyalty, she realized how very much she'd missed out on as a child. Though she was proud of the fact she hadn't let her childhood hinder her in any way. It had only made her more determined to seek a better life for herself, and now for her child.

Dylan reached over the lounger and took her hand. She glanced at their entwined fingers, his hand tanned and so very strong, hers smaller, more delicate, and she welcomed the comfort, the ease with which they could sit there together and watch a movie, holding hands.

The movie ended on a satisfying note and Dylan squeezed her hand, but didn't let her go. They remained in darkness but for the yellow floor lamps lighting a pathway around the room.

"Did you enjoy it?" he whispered.

"Very much."

"I didn't realize you're such a soft touch." His thumb rubbed over the skin of her hand in round, lazy sweeping circles.

"Only when it comes to movies."

"I find that hard to believe. You're soft…"

Her breath caught as she gazed into his heart-melting eyes.

"Everywhere."

Oh, boy.

He turned his body and leaned in, his mouth inches from hers. "I've been thinking about the other night. If we hadn't been interrupted, what would have happened?"

It wasn't really a question he expected her to answer. She thought of that night, too, so often. Wondering what if?

And then his lips were on hers, his mouth so exquisite as he patiently waited for her to respond, waited for her to give in. "Dylan."

"It's just a kiss, Em."

He made it seem so simple. "Not just a kiss," she insisted, yet she couldn't deny the temptation to kiss him back, to taste him and breathe in his delicious scent.

"This is what people do when they're dating," he whispered over her mouth.

"Is it?" Kissing Dylan wasn't anything ordinary. Not to her. It was the stuff of dreams.

"Yeah, it is," he said. "I want us to be more than friends, Em."

She wanted to ask why. Was it all about the baby, or had he somehow, after all these years, miraculously found her appealing and desirable? It was on the tip of her tongue to ask, but she chickened out. She didn't dare, because in her heart she already knew the truth.

He swept his hand around her neck and caressed the tender spot behind her ear. She closed her eyes to the pleasure and breathed deeply, soaking it in. His gentle touch and the power of his persuasion weren't anything to mess with. She could stay like this for hours, unhurried, just enjoying being the sole focus of his attention.

"I think we already are, Dylan. I'm having your baby. That puts us on a little higher level than friends."

"Maybe it's not enough," he rasped, and with a little tug, he inched her closer until their mouths were a breath apart. "Maybe we need to be more." And then he kissed her.

"What if that's not possible?"

He swept into her mouth again and deepened the kiss, his tongue working magic until her entire body grew warm and tingly. Her nipples pebbled and she gasped for sustaining breath.

"It's possible," he urged, rising from his seat and reaching for her hands. He seemed attuned to the exact moment when her body betrayed her. With both her hands in his, he gave a gentle yank and she came to her feet to face him in the soft glow of the floor lamps. "Let me show you."

Dylan was an expert at seduction; what he was doing to her now was solid proof. He took her face in his palms, looked deep into her eyes and then kissed her for long-drawn-out moments. Until her heart sped like a race car. Until her knees went weak. Until the junction of her thighs physically ached. It was too much and not enough. She was dizzy when he was through kissing her. Dizzy and wanting more.

"It's your choice, sweet Emma," he said, planting tiny kisses over her lips, his hands roaming over her body, taking liberties that she freely offered. She moaned a little when he touched her breasts and then gasped when he cupped her butt and pressed her firmly against his rigid, hard body so there was no doubt what he was about. He whispered softly into her ear, "We can take a walk on the beach to cool off, or walk into my bedroom upstairs and heat things up. You know what I want, but I'll abide by your decision, whatever it is."

She was out of breath. Her fuzzy mind told her to stall for time. As ardent as his kisses were, she couldn't wrap her head around him wanting to make love to her. It had once been her wildest dream. And yes, they'd done the deed already, but that wasn't really logged into her memory bank. Or his, either. "Is this what usually happens on your first dates?"

He laughed and took her into his arms, squeezing her tight as if she was a child asking an adorable question. "You know me. You know it's not what I do, Em."

Well, no. She'd never really quizzed him on his methods of seduction. How would she know how easily or often he took his dates to bed? He'd been in enough tabloids to wallpaper his entire mansion with the stories they'd concocted. And his sister defended him on every front. He'd even sued a few papers that had stepped over the line and had won his cases.

So, if she was to believe him now, then he was truly attracted to her. "I don't think I've ever seen your bedroom, Dylan."

He smiled then and nodded, and the next thing she knew, Dylan was lifting her in his strong arms and carrying her out of the screening room.

And up the stairs.

She roped one arm around his neck and laid her head against his broad shoulder as he marched to the double-door entry of his master suite. She felt featherlight in his arms, tucked safely into his embrace. He gave the door a nudge and pushed through, entering a massive room with an equally large bed. It faced wide windows that angled out with a magnificent view of the Pacific. Right now, only stars and a half-moon lit the night sky, but she heard the roar of the waves and smelled the brine of the sea coming through an opened terrace slider.

She wasn't sure about any of this, but lust and curiosity won over any rational sense inhabiting her brain at the moment. She'd done this before with Dylan, but now both were aware, both would remember. It was key. Monumental. Dylan would be in her life one way or another and she wanted this memory. Sane and rational or not, she simply didn't have the will to deny them both this night.

She did, after all, have secret dibs on him.

He lowered her down, her body flush against his until her feet hit the floor beside his bed. He let her go then, taking a step back to lock eyes with her and lifting his black polo shirt over his head. A rush of breath pushed from her lungs. His upper body was ripped and bronzed, his shoulders wide, the muscles in his arms bulging. He'd been working out hard for this Navy SEAL role and he had her vote. Hands down.

"We'll take this slow," he said.

Slow? She was on her first official date with him and about to get naked.

He reached for her and placed the palm of her hand flat against his concrete chest. His breath hitched and she lifted her lids to find the gleam in his eyes bright and hungry. Slowly, she moved her hand along the solid ridges that made up his six-pack and tiny coarse chest hairs tickled her fingers. He was amazing to touch, almost unreal. She'd never been with a man like Dylan before. It scared her, how absolutely perfect he was.

What was his flaw? Everyone had one, but she couldn't find it here, now.

He took her other hand, put it on him and encouraged her to explore. She did, running her hands over his shoulders, to his back and then returning to his torso. In her exploration, her fingers grazed his nipples and they grew taut from her touch. It was a turn-on, just seeing how she affected him.

He stood there, allowing her to know him, to feel his skin, absorb his heat and become familiar. She took her time, meeting his eyes once in a while, but mostly keeping a vigil on the beauty of his body.

He kissed her then, suckling her lips in a heady way that said he was ready to move forward. To take the next step.

"Should I undress the rest of the way?" he breathed over her mouth. "Or is it your turn?"

Fair is fair. She turned around and offered him he He didn't hesitate to unzip the long gold zipper little black dress she wore. The zipper hissed as it traveled all the way down to the small of her back. A shot of cooler air hit her as he pressed his hands to her shoulders and helped her shimmy out of her dress. Free of the fabric that pooled at her feet, he bestowed tiny kisses along her neck. Slowly, he turned her around and his eyes met hers once again, before drifting down her body over the slope of her ample breasts encased in her black lace bra, to her tummy that bulged slightly and the matching thong she wore. He rode his hands along her naked thighs and a tiny moan squeaked from her mouth.

"You are soft everywhere, sweetheart," he said, slipping his hand over her hip and edging up to her stomach. His palm against her growing belly, he stopped his exploration and bent on one knee to bestow a kiss there.

Her eyes slammed shut as Dylan worshipped their baby. It was a beautiful moment, so tender, so gentle, wiping away her fears. She couldn't fault him for anything. This situation was out of their control now. Maybe she'd been too hard on him, too rigid in her stance. He had a right to love their baby and want to share in the joy. She could give him that. She could try this dating thing, go in with an open mind and heart to see where it led.

He rose up then and stared directly into her eyes. "Our child will be beautiful like you, Emma. Inside and out."

Laying her hand flat against his cheek, scruff facial hair rough against her fingers, she whispered, "You're going to make a wonderful father, Dylan. I have no doubt."

Longing filled his eyes and he smiled. There was a moment that seemed to change everything; a newer intimacy and understanding passed between them in that moment.

And then Dylan reached for her again, pressing her fully against his hot, delicious body. Skin to skin, he kissed her for all she was worth. The next thing she knew, she was naked and they were on his bed and tangling in his sheets. Going slow was a thing of the past, and easily forgotten.

While one hand sifted through her long hair, his mouth created a dampened trail from her chin, along the base of her throat and farther down past her shoulders, until her breasts fairly ached for his touch. He came over her then and didn't disappoint, giving attention to one, then the other. Her back arched, the rosy nipples pointing up, hardened and sensitive, while white-hot heat scurried down past her belly, reaching her female core. A shudder ran through her, a beautiful sensual tremor as Dylan continued. She squirmed beneath him, the pleasure almost unbearable.

His mouth was masterful, his hands ingenious. When he moved, she moved and they were in sync, their bodies humming along together at a pace that suited her. She was in heaven, a bliss that she'd never encountered before. And it only got hotter when his hand slipped down past her navel, his fingertips teasing and taunting, edging closer to that one spot that would send her soaring.

She was damp and ready, and when he finally dipped into her soft folds, a tiny plea, a cry of pleasure, escaped her lips and she did, in fact, soar. The pressure, the light stroking growing firmer and more rhythmic worked her into a frenzied state. Dylan knew how to please. His kisses muffled her soft whimpers, his mouth devoured hers and his body radiated enough warmth to heat all of Moonlight Beach.

She reached a climax quickly. "Dylan, Dylan," she breathed, grasping his shoulders, clinging on, her heart pounding against her chest. He didn't let up until she shattered completely and was fully, wonderfully spent.

With glazed eyes, she watched him get up and remove his pants and briefs. Through the faint light streaming into the room she focused on the entire man, stark naked, virile and majorly turned on, and could only think, "Wow."

Before he climbed back onto the bed, he grabbed a golden packet from the nightstand, ripped it open and offered it to her as he lay down next to her. "For your protection."

There'd been someone before her. Probably Callista. And she was grateful for his concern, even though she was already pregnant with his child. She took it in her hands as he waited for her to slip it on him. The act was intimate, perhaps even more so than what had occurred just seconds ago.

She swallowed hard. When she was finished putting on the condom, Dylan wasted no time taking her back into his arms. "This all feels so new, sweet Emma."

"For me, too," she whispered, but there was no more room for small talk. Dylan was towering over her, using his thighs to move her legs apart. She was ready, watching him, his gorgeous face so determined, his body so in tune with hers, moving ever so slowly, nudging her core and finally, finally pushing forward, staking his claim.

She wound her arms around his neck and welcomed him. It was a glorious greeting, one that she'd always remember. Yet he took it slow, cautiously moving, giving of himself and making sure she was okay throughout.

He felt good inside her. As if she was home and where she belonged. As if she'd waited all of her life for this one moment. Safe. Secure. Happy.

But not loved.

She shoved those thoughts from her mind and concentrated on the amazing man making love to her. His blond hair was wild now, spiking up in sexy disarray. His chest heaving, his labored breaths fully accentuated his power and grace as he moved inside her. Muscles rippled and bunched. Skin sizzled and sensations ran rampant. Then those intent blue eyes locked on hers as he uttered her name and carried them both up, higher and higher.

Until the last thrust touched the deepest part of her.

She fell apart at the exact moment he did. In unison, they cried each other's names. He held on, allowing her to draw out the pleasure. And then he collapsed upon her, bracing his hands on each side of the bed to accept the brunt of his weight.

Looking at him now, she whispered, "Wow."

He grinned. The sexy man who'd just fulfilled her truest fantasy appeared to be quite satisfied. "Yeah, wow."

Rolling away from her, he landed on his back beside her. He took her hand and interlocked their fingers, staring out the window at the starry sky, listening to the pounding surf. She sensed him straining his mind, trying to recall that one night they'd shared before. "Anything?" she asked.

He gave her a quick noncommittal smile. "Everything."

She was taken by his sweet answer and the way he rolled over and kissed her. But he didn't remember anything from the blackout night. Nothing they did up until this point had triggered a memory.

"It doesn't matter if I remember or not. We've got this night and many more to come. We'll start out new, from here."

"I agree. It's a good plan." It was. She shouldn't dwell on the past any more than he should.

He laid his hand over her belly in a protective way. "New is good, Emma. Trust me."

She would have to trust him.

From now on.

"So everything looks good, Dr. Galindo?" Dylan asked, his face marked with concern. They were sitting in the office of Emma's ob-gyn.

"Yes, Mr. McKay, the baby is healthy and Emma's exam was right on point," the doctor said. She glanced at Emma and smiled. "All looks good. Be sure to continue to take your prenatal vitamins, and see me again in one month."

"Okay," Emma agreed. "I will."

"Do either of you have any further questions?"

"Just that," Emma began, "this isn't public knowledge, and we both expect our privacy to be respected."

Dr. Galindo gave Dylan a knowing look. "Of course. We honor every patient's privacy."

"Thank you. Where Dylan goes, news seems to follow."

The thirtysomething doctor smiled. Her eyes had repeatedly traveled to Dylan during the course of the consultation. Emma couldn't fault her. Dylan was A-list. He was hot and sought after and just about every woman from age ten to one hundred and ten ogled him. "Rest assured, your privacy will not be an issue with my office."

"I appreciate that." Dylan rose from his seat and shook the doctor's hand. "Thanks."

Emma noticed that his taut face had relaxed some as he led her out of the building and into his car. She, too, breathed a sigh of relief. "That went well."

"Yeah," he said. "The baby will be here in less than seven months. Hard to believe."

"For me, too. I'm grateful the baby is healthy. It was pretty cool hearing the heartbeat."

"It was awesome."

"I'll be big as a house soon."

"You'll look beautiful, Em," he said and started the engine.

"You're really okay with all of this, then?" she asked. He'd taken the news well and never once balked or hesitated when she'd revealed her pregnancy to him. It had been full steam ahead—they were having a baby together. Emma didn't quite understand his immediate acceptance, though she'd been grateful for it.

"I...am. I've always wanted to be a father. Just never found the right—"

He caught himself, but Emma knew what he was going to say. He'd never found the right woman to carry his child. Well, that decision had been taken out of his hands. She wasn't the right woman, but he was stuck with her. And she supposed that he was making the best of it.

He'd been attentive and had taken her on a date every night since that first one. One night they'd gone for ice cream at a local creamery, a place that Dylan's friend owned. They'd snuck in the back way and had taken a corner table, Dylan disguised in a Dodgers ball cap and sunglasses. The next night they'd gone to a concert at the Hollywood Bowl, Dylan scoring front row seats, and they'd gone in through a VIP entrance. Each time they went out, Dylan's bodyguards weren't far behind. It was kind of eerie knowing their every move was being watched, but as Dylan explained, it came with the territory.

She enjoyed her evenings with Dylan. And each night after their date, they'd wind up in bed together—sometimes in his gorgeous master suite and sometimes at her tiny apartment. They were growing closer each day, and getting to know one another on a different level. Dylan was kind and tender and as sexy as a man had a right to be. There were times when they were making love that she'd actually have to gasp for breath and remind herself this was really happening.

She had fallen in love with him. Truly and madly, and it had probably happened the night of their movie date. She'd always been halfway in love with him as a teen, but this was different. This was based on actually knowing him and spending time with him. It probably hadn't hurt that her orgasms were off the charts when they made love. Or that he was the father of her baby. Or that they shared a hometown history together.

But every morning, when she'd wake in his arms, he

would plant a bug in her ear. "Move in with me, Em. We could have all our nights and mornings like this."

It was a tempting offer, one that she debated for long moments, but ultimately always refused because, like it or not, she wasn't ready to give up her independence. To give Dylan her one last means of defense against heartbreak. He wanted to keep his baby safe and close at hand. She understood that, and it was a noble gesture, but what did that say about her relationship with him? It was what Dylan was *not saying* to her that fueled her resolve to stay out of harm's way.

"I don't understand why you don't want to, Em," he'd say. And she'd shrug her shoulders and shake her head. This was new to him, this constant rejection. He wasn't conceited or arrogant, but he'd been used to having women fall at his feet, she supposed, and he didn't understand her reluctance.

"I just can't, Dylan," would be her answer.

After the doctor's appointment, they went to lunch at a little private beach eatery and sat outside on benches facing the ocean. She had chicken salad and he had halibut in drawn butter. Afterward, Dylan dropped her off at the office. "Don't work too hard," he said, giving her a kiss.

"Never," she said, and he tossed his head back and laughed. He knew she was a workhorse, never settling until things were perfect and under control. He would tease her about that all the time. "You, either," she shot back.

"I won't. I'll be learning my lines for tomorrow's shoot. Which reminds me, the next two days will run long. We're having night shoots. I won't be home until after your bedtime. I'll miss you."

She smiled. "Me, too."

His eyes dipped to her belly. "Take care of the little bambino."

"Always," she said, placing her hand there protectively.

Touching her stomach and greeting the little one, warming to him or her and the idea of a baby, had become a habit.

She climbed out of the car, waved goodbye, and then he was off. She wouldn't see him for the next few days. Maybe that was a good thing. She watched him drive into the traffic stream before stepping into the office.

"Hey, how did the appointment go?" Brooke asked, gazing up from her desk.

"Wonderful. Everything is good."

Brooke grinned. "Great. I can't wait to find out if it's a boy or girl. I'm making up a shopping list and already have three my-auntie-is-the-best outfits picked out. Now, just gotta know if I'm buying blue or pink."

Brooke was definitely going to spoil the baby. "It'll be fun finding out."

"Yeah, but for now, I'm just happy knowing the baby's healthy."

Brooke rose from her desk and approached her. "Things are working out with Dylan, aren't they?" she asked. "I mean, you sound happy. You look happy and well. I know you've been dating, hot and heavy."

"Hot and heavy?" Emma's laughter sounded a little too high-pitched even to her ears and Brooke caught on immediately.

"Wow, so it's true. You and my brother are hooking up."

Well, yeah, she supposed they were. He'd asked her to move in with him several times, but never with any true sense of commitment. Was that what she was waiting for? Some hope, some sign that he wanted her, and not just because she was going to give birth to his child? Maybe what she wanted from Dylan was impossible for him to give. "Brooke, I have no name for what's happening between Dylan and me."

"At least something is happening." Excitement sparkled in Brooke's eyes.

"Maybe you should concentrate on your relationship with Royce," Emma countered, giving her BFF a wry smile.

"Oh, believe me, I do." Brooke giggled. "We're heading to hot and heavy, too."

"Wow, you two are moving fast."

Brooke sighed. "I know. It's crazy, but we're in tune with each other on every level."

"I'm happy for you."

"Thanks. Now, on to work issues. We've got the Henderson anniversary party on Friday night and then we've got Clinton's seventh birthday party in Beverly Hills all day Saturday. Which one do you want to confirm?"

"I'll take Clinton's party. I've made special arrangements for the petting zoo and the cartoon characters to show up and I've got the cake and food already set. I'll double-check it's a go, and you can make your confirmations for the anniversary gig."

"Okay, sounds good. It's going to be a busy weekend. Are you sure you're up for it?"

"I'm sure." Emma had been operating at 90 percent and feeling better every day. Dylan had been keeping her plenty busy at night, too, exhausting her in a good way. She'd been sleeping soundly and waking feeling sated and refreshed, but the thought of not seeing him for the next few nights suddenly cast a shadow of loneliness on her perspective.

How odd. Usually she valued her downtime and enjoyed being on her own.

"Oh, yeah," Brooke said, making a face. "I almost forgot to tell you, Maury Allen called today. Seems his event planner for Callista's big birthday bash had a family emergency and he can't continue the work. He wants us to take over. It's in two weeks."

"You told him no, didn't you?" Emma held her breath.

Brooke scrunched her face even more. "Well," she squeaked. "I couldn't do that. He used Dylan's name as a reference and made it seem like my brother recommended us to him. He's Dylan's boss and he said everything's pretty much done. All we have to do is show up and make things run smoothly."

"Brooke!"

"I know. But he took me by surprise and I didn't think I could worm out of it."

"Couldn't his planner get someone else from their company to step in?"

She shook her head. "They're all booked solid. And we're not. His secretary is overnighting the signed vendor contracts and the itinerary so we know what's planned."

Emma rolled her eyes. "That's just wonderful."

"Sorry." To Brooke's credit, she did seem genuinely apologetic. "You don't have to go. I'll get Wendy or Rocky to help out."

"Knowing Callista, it's going to be a giant production. You're going to need me."

Brooke ducked her head and looked sheepish. "I think you may be right."

Shoulders tight and arms crossed, Emma leaned against the wall and sent a disgruntled sigh out to the universe. "I guess I was destined to go to this thing."

"Destined? What do you mean?"

"Dylan asked me to go to Callista's party as his date. He said he wanted company in his misery, but I flat out refused. The woman barely gets my name right."

Brooke chuckled. "Just call her Callie, like I do. You know what they say about payback."

"I can't do that. She's our client now."

"Her father's our client."

"It's practically the same thing," Emma said. "She's got him wrapped around her diamond-ringed finger."

"True, but I wish I could be there when she…"

Brooke's expression was way too mischievous for Emma's curiosity. "What?"

"When she finds out you're carrying Dylan's child."

"Brooke! You're not going to say a thing. Promise me."

She glanced at Emma's belly bump and smiled. "I promise. But maybe I won't have to say anything. Maybe she'll find out on her own. Now, *that* would be worth the price of admission."

Emma couldn't suppress a smile. She grinned along with her friend. "You're wicked."

"Yes, and that's why you love me."

Seven

Emma dragged herself through the door on Saturday evening, her twenty-five-year-old bones aching. She was too tired to make it to her bedroom. She tossed her handbag onto the sofa, then plopped down next to it. The well-worn cushions welcomed her and she put her feet up on the coffee table. Stretching out, she closed her eyes.

Little Clinton's birthday party had done her in. It had gone fairly well for a seven-year-old's party, though there'd been a few potential disasters in the making. One of the goats in the petting zoo had escaped the pen and begun nibbling on the party decorations. The kids thought it hilarious, until the darn goat made a dash for the cupcake table and nearly downed the whole thing. Emma screamed for the zookeeper to do something, and he'd looked up oblivious to the goings-on from across the yard, giving her no choice but to navigate the stubborn animal back to the pen herself.

But that was an innocent mistake, unlike the guy dressed

in a furry purple character costume. Judging by the way he was walking, the guy must have been intoxicated. It was either that or balancing himself in the costume was too much for him. She'd kept her eyes peeled on him for the entire day and thankfully he didn't cause any trouble.

Then there was the incident at the taco bar. The kids took one bite of their tacos and their little mouths were set on fire from too much chipotle sauce added to the meat. Emma escorted those kids right over to the snow cone machine. Rainbow ice doused the flames and put smiles on their faces again. Disaster averted, but not before Emma scolded the cook. What had he been thinking?

Emma leaned forward and did slow head circles, first one way, then the other. The stretch and pull felt good, easing away a full day's worth of tension. Her cell phone rang and she had a mind not to answer it, but as she glanced at the screen name, she smiled and picked up. "Hi, Dylan."

"Hi," he said in that low, masculine tone that made her dizzy. "What are you doing?"

"Just putting my feet up. It's been a long day."

"Tired?"

"Yeah, pretty much. What are you doing?"

"Driving by your apartment."

"You are?" She bolted straight up, her heartbeat speeding.

"Yeah, I thought I'd take a chance and see if you were up to company. If you're too tired, I'll just keep on driving."

God, just the sound of his voice roused her out of exhaustion. It had been three days since she'd seen him. He'd been constantly on her mind. "I'm not too tired."

"You sure? You sound wiped out."

"I'm…not."

"I'll be right there."

A soft flow of warmth spread through her body. Her hormones were happy now. Beautifully, wonderfully happy.

Just minutes later, she opened the door and he walked

straight into her arms. He lifted her off the ground as he kissed her and moved her backward to the sofa, setting her down and taking a seat next to her. "I'm not staying. I just wanted to see you," he said, wrapping his arms around her shoulders.

"I'm glad. I, uh, I wanted to see you, too." It was always hard admitting how she was feeling toward Dylan. She wasn't playing hard to get. She was running scared, frightened that this big bubble of joy would pop at any moment.

"How was your day?"

"Chasing goats and kids and keeping parents happy, just a usual Saturday afternoon fun day."

Dylan smiled. "You love it."

"I do. I'm not complaining." It was what she was meant to do. She enjoyed every facet of event planning. Though it was a hassle at times and deadlines could be gruesome, the end result, a successful party, was her reward. She couldn't imagine having a nine-to-five job, although she thoroughly enjoyed keeping the books and managing the accounts, too.

Dylan grasped her hand and brought it to his knee. It was as natural as breathing for him to hold on to her this way. "I'm glad you're in business with my sister."

"Me, too. I think our talents complement each other. She's the creative one and I'm the practical one."

"You work hard. Don't take this the wrong way, but you look exhausted."

She sighed. "There's no fooling you."

"I'm quite perceptive." He smiled at her and his sea-blue eyes softened. "Turn around."

"What?"

"Turn your back to me and try to relax."

"Okay."

She angled away from him on the sofa and then his hand gently moved her hair off her shoulders. It fell in a tangle on her right side. Next, he placed both hands on her shoulder blades and began a firm but soothing massage. The tension was released immediately, and as he worked the kinks out and moved farther down her back, she closed her eyes. "Oh, that feels good," she cooed.

"That's the plan, sweetheart."

His hands on her body were a comforting, soothing presence lifting her spirits, a balm for her tired bones.

"Why don't we take this into the bedroom," he whispered, his breath tickling her ear. "Where you can stretch out and really relax."

She turned to face him.

"Just a massage, I promise. Deal?"

"Deal."

And then she was being lifted and carried toward her bedroom. Her independence had flown the coop the minute Dylan had shown up. But she loved his inner he-man and the way he took control of a situation. It was amazingly sexy.

She played with the curl of hair resting on his nape. "You don't have to make deals with me, Dylan."

"Don't tempt me. I know how tired you are and let's leave it at that."

She nodded.

A slender shaft of light from the courtyard illuminated her bedroom window. Dylan lowered her to a standing position by her bed and moved behind her. With one hand on either side of her back, he inched her blouse up and over her head, tossing it onto the nightstand. Then he helped to remove her slacks. Down to a white bra and panties, she kicked off her shoes and turned to face him.

There was a sharp rasp of breath as he looked at her. "This isn't going to be as easy as I thought," he muttered in a tortured tone. "Lie down. I'll be right back."

Emma pulled her sheets back and lowered down onto

her tummy, resting her head on her pillow. When Dylan returned, he held a bottle of raspberry vanilla essential oil. "This okay to use?"

She nodded and closed her eyes. She heard the sound of his hands slapping together as he warmed the oil and then felt the dip of the mattress as he sat beside her. "Ready?"

"Oh, yes."

He spread the oil onto her skin, his touch light and generous as he rubbed every inch of her back. The pleasing scents of raspberry and vanilla wafted to her nostrils in the most delicious way. Using his thumbs, Dylan pressed the small of her back in circular motions, his fingers resting on the slope of her behind. She tingled there and her breath caught noisily. This was quickly becoming more than a massage and almost more intimate than having sex with Dylan. He removed his fingers, using his thumbs to walk up her spine.

"Oh, so nice," she whispered.

"I'm glad you're enjoying this."

"Aren't you?"

"Too much."

She grinned and endorphins released merrily through her body.

He lifted his hands off her back and again she heard the smack of his hands as he warmed the oil. Next, he worked her legs, starting at her ankles, gliding his hands up and down, around and around, bringing new life to her tired limbs. First one calf, then the other, and then he was inching his hands up the backs of her thighs. He slowed his pace and stopped for a moment.

"Dylan?"

"I'm okay," he said, his voice quietly pained.

"This isn't supposed to make you tense."

"Too late for that, sweetheart. Just relax and enjoy."

But there was something too tempting, too genuine in

his voice for her to sit back and take this without giving
something back. She shifted her position, landing on her
back. One look at his gorgeous face, his gritted teeth and
set jaw had her gaze moving down below his waist. She
wasn't surprised to see the strain of material in his pants.

"I didn't come here for—"

"I know, and it makes it all the more sweet." She lifted
her arms and reached for him. "Come here, Dylan." she
said. "Let me do something for you."

"There's no need," he said, but it was too late. She
grabbed him around the neck and pulled him down on
top of her. He was careful where he landed and avoided
plopping on her belly.

"I'm not tired anymore. In fact, I'm feeling pretty loose,"
she said softly. "And you deserve a massage, too."

Emma stood over the sizzling range top, flipping pancakes on a griddle, a pleasing hum running through her
body. Last night's massages had turned into something
pretty spectacular and now she was famished. She'd crept
out of bed, leaving Dylan sleeping, to make him a nourishing breakfast. He'd sure earned it judging by the energy
he'd exerted making love to her last night.

When his arms wrapped around her waist, she nearly
jumped out of her skin. She hadn't heard him come up behind her. "Morning," he said, nibbling on her neck.

"I thought you were sleeping."

"I missed you."

God, he said all the right things. "Sweet."

"You're sweet to make us breakfast."

"Us?" She chuckled. "What makes you think this is
for you?"

He tightened his hold on her and then reached around
her body to turn the knob, shutting off the burner. "Dylan,
what are you—"

He turned her around and kissed her complaint away. Then he gave her a heart-melting smile and tugged her away from the stove. He'd already put his clothes from yesterday back on. They looked amazingly unwrinkled and fresh, while she was wearing gray sweats and a pink tank sporting the Parties-To-Go logo in purple glitter, her hair in a messy ponytail.

Holding her hand, he led her to the living area. Her heart was beating fast now. What was he up to? He turned to her and the expression on his face was dead serious. "I've been thinking, Em. About us."

She gulped. Us?

"You and I, we're going to be parents soon and I guess I'm an old-fashioned guy when it comes to kids and all. I see a bright future ahead for us, the *three* of us. We'll be a family, a real honest-to-goodness family, and I think the baby deserves the very best start in life. That means having a mother and father raise the child together. I care very much for you, Emma. You know that. We're good together, if last night isn't proof enough." His smile was a little wobbly now and Emma's heart pounded even harder. He was going to press her to move in with him.

"I'm not going to ask you to move in with me anymore, Em."

"You're not?" She blinked. This was new.

He shook his head. "No. That's not the solution."

He gazed deep into her eyes. "I want you to marry me."

Emma's mouth opened and a sharp gasp escaped. "Oh."

"I'm asking you to be my wife, Emma. I've given this a lot of thought and I can only see good things in store for the three of us."

She dropped her hand from his and shuffled her feet. Inside, everything was stirring, a mad mix of emotions and thoughts flying through her head. "This is...um, unexpected."

"Really, Em? It's not so far-fetched to think that two people conceiving a child together would get married, is it?"

He made it seem so simple. He cared for her. And Lord knew, she cared even more for him. She loved him. Could they make it work, even though he didn't say the words a woman being proposed to was meant to hear? There was no claim of undying love, nothing about how he couldn't live without her and how his life would be empty without her in it. Yet Dylan had spoken honestly, giving her genuine reasons why this was a good idea.

But doubts immediately crept in. He was Dylan McKay, eligible bachelor extraordinaire, a highly sought-after movie star, a man whose life was obviously filled with temptations at every turn. Could she place her trust in him not to break her heart and soul? Could she marry a man who didn't outright love her?

"Em, you don't have to give me your answer right now. Take some time," he said, his voice laced with tenderness and understanding. "Give it some thought. I'm not going anywhere. I'll be right here."

A huge part of her wanted to say yes, but she couldn't make this decision on the spur of the moment. She was being given the moon, but was it greedy of her to want the sun and the stars, too?

"Dylan," she began softly, "I can't give you an answer right now. Everything is happening so fast."

"I know. I get it, Em. I don't want to add to your stress. Believe me, I only want what's best for you. But I wanted to get my feelings out in the open. I think it's the right move, but I won't pressure you. I'll wait until you've made your decision."

"Thank you. I appreciate that. So, um…where do we go from here?"

Dylan grinned. "You finish making me breakfast. I'm

starving and those pancakes look pretty appetizing. And tomorrow night, we'll have a dinner date at my house. Sound good?"

She nodded. So they'd resume dating, *with the option of marriage.*

So that was it. He'd proposed and now they were back to the status quo. The ball was in her court, as they say. How on earth would she be able to make this decision? Her foster parents' marriage had been a train wreck. They'd fought constantly and Emma often felt she was to blame. She'd cower under a blanket in the far corner of her bedroom and cover her ears to block out their vulgar arguments. She never wanted a child of hers to go through that kind of pain and torment. Would Emma and Dylan end up hating each other and fighting constantly, just as her folks had?

Just as important, could she possibly say no to Dylan and refuse his marriage proposal? Or even more frightening, could she allow herself to say yes to him without having his love?

"Sounds perfect," she said with a manufactured smile.

Lying to Dylan and to…herself.

Monday morning Emma walked into her office, greeted Brooke, plopped into the chair behind her desk and began working. She was in the early planning stages of a Bar Mitzvah and had many calls to make. She worked diligently, struggling to keep her mind on business.

Later that morning, she met with vendors, a florist and photographer, and then returned to the office feeling somewhat accomplished. But all day long, she'd been distracted and had a difficult time focusing. She'd made a few mistakes along the way as well, giving the wrong dates to a vendor and then having to recalculate an estimate she'd given and call back a client with the bad news that she'd made an error. That never went over well and she'd wound up giving them a 10 percent discount to make up for it.

Brooke had cast furtive glances at her all day long and no matter how much she tried to behave like her normal self, Emma figured she hadn't fooled her friend. To add to her dismay, a gorgeous bouquet of pink Stargazer lilies had been delivered in a bubble crystal vase while she was gone. They sat on one corner of her desk now and flavored the air with a wonderful floral scent.

The note read: *Just Because. Dylan*

By late afternoon, Brooke approached, taking a seat on the edge of Emma's desk. "Hey, Em?"

Emma's lips twisted. She knew the drill, but refused to look up from her computer screen. "Hey, yourself."

"So what's wrong? You've been distracted all day."

"I can make an error once in a while, Brooke."

"I make errors all the time, but not you, Little Miss Organized. You don't make mistakes."

"Well, call me perfect, then."

"Emma?" Brooke put a motherly tone in her voice. "What's up? And don't tell me nothing. Did you and Dylan have a fight or something?"

Emma finally shifted her focus and looked into Brooke's concerned eyes. "No," she said emphatically. "We didn't fight. He asked me to marry him."

Brooke's face lit up. "Really?"

Emma ran both hands down her cheeks, pulling the skin taut. "Really."

"Oh, so you're bothered by his proposal?"

"It wasn't so much a proposal, but a sort of bargain, for the baby's sake. Not that I don't want what's best for the baby. I do, but I don't know. I'm...confused."

"Did he say he wanted to marry you?"

"Yes, of course he did."

"And did he say he wanted you, him and baby to be his family?"

"Yes. That's what he wants."

"He's very fond of you, Emma. He's always liked you."

"I know that."

"So how do you feel about him? And be honest."

Emma tugged on her long braid, twisting it around and around in her hand. Her mouth twitched and she blinked a few times. This was a hard thing for her to admit even to Brooke "I've fallen in love with him," she finally said.

Brooke didn't get excited about her admission and Emma was grateful for that. Instead, she took her hand and smiled. "I see the problem." Brooke knew her so well. "You're worried he may not return the feelings."

"Ever."

"Ever," Brooke repeated softly. "Well, all I can say is that Dylan is capable of great love. He accepted me from day one when I came to the McKay house to live. Here I was this little frightened girl with no family, and there was this older boy who seemed to have it all, a nice set of parents, and friends and a decent house to live in. I was afraid he'd hate me for imposing on his family, but he did just the opposite. He made me feel welcomed, and the first time he called me his little sister, I cried big sloppy tears and he hugged me hard and said something funny that made me laugh. From then on, I was okay with Dylan and he was okay with me.

"I can't tell you what to do, Emma. You're my friend and you deserve to be loved, but I know my brother will never intentionally hurt you. He's gonna love the baby you're carrying with all his heart. And I know you will, too. You'll have that in common and that's a bond that will carry you into the future. It's up to you, to figure out if that's enough." Brooke gave her hand a last squeeze, then stood up. "Are you okay?"

Emma nodded. "I'm much better. Thanks, Brooke. It helps."

A weight had been lifted from her shoulders. Brooke's rational, though slightly biased, opinion made sense to her. She had the moon in the palm of her hands, and maybe just maybe, the sun and the stars would come later on.

Late-afternoon runs always served to clear Dylan's mind, and today's jog along the shoreline did the trick. He wasn't running the ten miles he'd been doing before the accident, but he managed five miles today without too much problem.

As he climbed the steps that led to his house, he nodded to Dan, one of his bodyguards, who'd been on the beach running behind him and watching him diligently. That was another reason he hadn't resumed the longer runs. Dan wasn't up to it. Not too many people were. Dylan had been doing endurance runs for months during his training for this SEAL movie. His bodyguard was fit but hadn't been training as intensely as Dylan had.

He went inside and stopped in the kitchen, grabbed a bottle of water from the fridge and gulped it down in three big swallows. As he moved toward the staircase, he lifted his T-shirt over his head and used it to sop up beads of sweat raining down his chest. Emma was coming for dinner soon. He'd given Maisey time off today so that they'd have time alone. Yesterday, he'd jumped into the waters with both feet, spontaneously proposing to Emma, and he hoped he'd made an impression. He had a ring ready for her, one he'd been carrying around with him for days, but putting that ring on her finger would have to wait until she accepted his proposal.

When the doorbell rang, he blinked in surprise and strode to the front door. He'd given Emma the remote control to the garage door entryway and wondered why she didn't come through the back door as usual. Peeking through the peephole, his shoulders drooped when he saw Callista standing on the threshold. He made a mental note to change the code to his front gate.

Opening the door, he greeted her. "Hi, Callista, what are you doing here?" He put as much civility in his voice as he could muster.

"I came to check on you." She glanced at his bare chest and black running shorts, smiled and whizzed by him, entering his home. "Did I ever tell you how much I love this vertical garden? It's a masterpiece," she said, eyeing the lush wall of succulents spilling down from the tall ceiling in his foyer.

Dylan grimaced before facing her. She turned back around and waited for him to shut the door.

"No, I don't think you ever have." He closed the door.

"Well, I do. I love it."

He nodded and stood his ground.

"Aren't you going to ask me in?"

She was already in, but that was beside the point. He'd have to deal with her, explain that he wasn't interested in a relationship with her any longer and hope that they could still remain friends. She should've already gotten the hint, since he hadn't called her since the day of Roy's memorial service, but Callista wasn't easily put off. "Come in, please. After you." He gestured for her to lead the way.

She walked into the living room and leaned against one of the open double doors to the veranda. "It's a beautiful time of day, Dylan. I love the sea air. I've missed coming here."

He had nothing to say to that.

"It looks like you've been running."

"Yeah, I'm getting back into it. It feels good, clears my head."

"So, you're feeling better?"

"I'm doing well."

"That's good to hear. You look amazing."

"So do you, Callista. As always."

She was a beautiful woman, her honey-blond hair cut longer on one side than the other in a sleek style, her eyes a glistening blue, her body as slim as a supermodel's. She dressed impeccably, in the latest fashion, her clothes fitting her flamboyant personality. Unfortunately what she had on the outside didn't make up for her lack of humanity on the inside. She wasn't a bad person, just self-absorbed, and he couldn't lay all the blame at her feet. She'd been spoiled and indulged all of her life by her parents and her friends, and it had taken Dylan getting to know Emma as well as he did now to make the comparison and see which woman he wanted in his life.

"Are you okay, Dylan? I mean, really okay? Daddy told me about the possible threat to your life and I'm...I'm so worried about you."

"I'm fine. And they're not absolutely sure if it was an attempt on my life. But to put your mind at ease, I've added additional security around here and I travel with bodyguards all the time now. I'm sure your father told you to keep this private. There's an investigation going on."

"Yes, of course. On any given day there are hundreds of people at the studio, Dylan. How can they possibly find out who's responsible?"

"I don't know, Callista." At least he'd be finished shooting the movie in a few weeks and wouldn't have to go into the studio anymore. "All we can do is hope the investigation gives them some leads."

"Gosh, I hope so."

Dylan softened a little. Callista seemed genuinely concerned for him. He couldn't deny that they'd had a past relationship and that they still cared for each other's welfare. "Thanks. I appreciate it. I value your friendship."

She walked over to him, placed her palm on his cheek and locked her pretty doe eyes on his. "We're more than friends, Dylan. I'd hoped you'd remembered that." She brushed her lips to his and spoke softly over his mouth. "And it would make me very happy if you'd be my date for my birthday party."

Emma shut her mind off to all of her misgivings about Dylan and looked upon his proposal more openly now. Her conversation with Brooke had helped her see things in a new perspective. She was still debating about marrying him, but at least the roadblocks in her head were slowly being taken down. She'd realized this as she was baking him a chocolate marble cake today, just like the one she'd demolished on her birthday years ago. If they could have a good laugh over it, then the cake would serve its purpose. Smiling, she entered the gates of his home, noting a foreign sports car in his driveway she didn't recognize. Oh well, so much for having a quiet evening together. He had a visitor.

Emma parked her car in one of the empty garages on his property and carefully removed the cake holder, balancing it in one hand as she went up to the house and unlocked the back door with a hidden key. When she entered, she heard voices and debated about barging in, but as she moved into the kitchen, she recognized the seductive female voice.

Callista.

Emma set the cake down on the countertop and strode quietly toward the living room. She came to an abrupt stop when she saw Callista and Dylan tangled up in one another's arms at the far end of the room. She blinked several times, not believing what she was seeing. Her first thought was how wonderful they looked together, two stunning people living in the same high-profile world, a place where Emma didn't fit. They were the beautiful people, A-listers with friends who owned islands and airplanes and villas on the French Riviera. Seeing the two of them cuddled up good and tight, whispering to each other, brought it all to light. Emma didn't belong in Dylan's universe. Jealousy jabbed at her over the unfairness of it all.

But Dylan wasn't Callista's to ensnare. She wasn't the right woman for him.

Emma had had dibs on him since forever. Was she going to give him up without a fight? Shockingly, her answer was a flat-out no. She couldn't let Dylan get away. Jealousy aside, she wasn't going to hand her baby's father over to the wrong woman. Dylan had asked her, Emma Rae Bloom, to marry him, something he hadn't done since Renee had torn his heart to shreds. And now, Emma was beginning to see a life with him and their baby. So what was her problem? Why hadn't she jumped at his proposal last night? Why was she being so darn hardheaded?

To his credit, Dylan backed away from Callista instantly, wriggling out of her clutches before she could kiss him again. He didn't see Emma standing there, so there was no pretense for her sake. He really was rejecting the woman.

"I can't be your date, Callista," she heard him say.

Emma breathed a big sigh of relief.

"Why?" She approached him again, a question in her eyes. "I don't understand."

Emma gulped air loudly, deliberately. She'd heard enough. Both heads turned in her direction. Callista's mouth twisted in annoyance and Dylan, God love him, appeared truly relieved to see her. He put his arm out, reaching for Emma's hand, much to the other woman's horror, and Emma floated over to him and took it.

He smiled at her, and before he could say anything, Emma announced, "Dylan is my fiancé, Callista. I'm going to marry him."

Callista's mouth dropped open. Clearly stunned, she darted glances from Emma to Dylan and back again. And then her gaze shot like a laser beam down to Emma's slightly bulging belly. She was sharp, Emma had to give her that. "You're pregnant."

Dylan pulled her closer in, winding his arm around her waist in a show of support. "I'm sorry, Callista, but that's not an issue here. I was going to tell you about Emma and me."

"When, at my birthday party? The one she's supposed to plan and execute?"

Dylan's eyes never wavered. He was such a good actor. As far as she knew, Dylan had no knowledge of that latest development. "Under the circumstances, that's not going to happen now. I hope we can still be friendly, Callista. We've known each other a long time."

Callista ignored Emma once again, speaking to Dylan as if she wasn't standing there, in his embrace. "You can't be serious, Dylan. You're going to marry her?"

"Of course I'm serious. When have you known me not to be?"

"But...but..."

Emma stifled a giggle. She'd never seen Callista speechless before.

And finally, "You cheated on me with *her*!"

Dylan's brows gathered; his eyes grew dark and dangerous. "Don't go there, Callista. I never cheated on a woman in my life. We were on-again, off-again, and before my accident we were definitely off. Big-time off. And you know it."

Callista made a show of grabbing her purse and stomping away. Before exiting the room, she swiveled around and glared at Emma. "It'll never last. He's just doing this for the kid. Wait and see."

The front door slammed shut behind her.

Neither of them moved.

Seconds ticked by.

God, all of Emma's fears had come full circle in Callista's venomous declaration. Those three sentences revealed Emma's innermost doubts. A tremor ran through her. Could she do this? Could she really marry Dylan?

And then Dylan faced her, the darkness of his expression evaporating into something hopeful and sweet. His eyes gleamed and the way he held on to her as if she was precious to him, as if he was truly happy, convinced her to stay the course. She'd made up her mind and couldn't bear losing Dylan. If they had a chance at a future together, she was going to take it.

"You're really going to marry me? You weren't just saying that?" he asked.

"It wasn't the perfect way to tell you, but yes. I'm going to marry you."

His brilliant smile warmed all the cold places that threatened her happiness. "Good. Okay. Good. The sooner the better."

He kissed her then, and all of her doubts flittered away on the breeze. She would give herself up to him now. She wouldn't hold back. She was all in, and she would think only positive thoughts from now on.

After a long embrace, Dylan shook his head. "I'm sorry about that scene with Callista. I didn't know she was coming over."

"She was very upset, Dylan."

"She's dramatic and only upset because she didn't get her way. In her heart, she had to know we were over. But the truth is, I never cheated on her with you or anyone. It's important that you believe me."

"I do," she said. These past few weeks with Dylan had shown her what kind of a man he truly was. The tabloids liked to paint a less-than-rosy picture of celebrities, but

Emma didn't and wouldn't believe a word of it about Dylan McKay. She'd walked in on Dylan rebuffing Callista's advances and that alone was proof enough for her. She could place her faith in Dylan.

She had to.

He was going to be her husband.

Eight

Warm Pacific gusts lifted her wedding veil off her shoulders as she stood on the steps of Adam Chase's palatial oceanside home, waiting for her cue to walk down an aisle laden with red rose petals. They, too, blew in the breeze in sweeping patterns that colored the pathway in a natural special effect.

She looked out to the small cluster of friends and family in attendance, no more than thirty strong. Their secluded little wedding ceremony was about to begin. Dylan's mother was here, and Brooke, of course, was her maid of honor. She'd helped Emma into her ivory, Cinderella-style wedding dress. Wendy and Rocky were here, her part-timers who'd actually become dear friends. Dylan's agent and manager attended as well as his closest neighbors—Adam Chase, his wife, Mia, and their adorable baby, Rose, seated next to Jessica and her country superstar husband, Zane Williams.

It had been Adam's idea to hold the wedding here, the

reclusive architect offering a place for their secretive ceremony away from any paparazzi who might've gotten wind
of their engagement. To their surprise, Callista hadn't spread
any ugly gossip as yet and Dylan had insisted on marrying
quickly. Parties-To-Go had immediately been fired from
holding Callista's big birthday event, much to Brooke's glee.
Ironically, Dylan's hectic work schedule only allowed them
to get married on the very same day.

The music began, the traditional "Wedding March"
played by a string quartet bringing tears to Emma's eyes.
Her foster parents had declined the invitation to attend,
claiming illness—aka too much alcohol—so Emma began
her trek down the aisle on her own, the way she'd always
done things.

She didn't mind, though, because waiting for her at the
end of the white aisle, dressed in a stunning black tuxedo,
his blond hair spiky, his blue eyes twinkling, was the man
she'd always dreamed about marrying, Dylan McKay. As
she held her bouquet of delicate snowflake-white lilies and
baby red roses, beautiful emotions carried her toward him,
each step a commitment to making their marriage work,
to having the family she never thought she'd ever have.

The small group of guests stood as she flowed past them
toward Dylan, her eyes straight ahead. When she reached
him, he took her arm and led her to the minister and the
flowered, latticed canopy that would be their altar. There,
they spoke their vows of commitment and devotion.

For only a minute she was saddened that no words of
actual love were spoken. Wasn't it odd, a union taking
place where neither of the participants spoke of undying
love and devotion?

But once they were declared man and wife, Dylan
cupped her face and kissed her with enough passion to
wipe out any feelings of sadness. From this day forward...

she would look only to the future. She'd promised. And so had he.

"Family and friends," the minister said, "I give you Mr. and Mrs. Dylan McKay."

As they turned to face their guests, applause broke out.

"Hello, Mrs. McKay," Dylan said, kissing her again.

"Dylan, I hardly believe this is real."

"It's real." It was the last thing he said to her before they were separated and the guests bombarded each of them with congratulations.

Brooke ran over to Emma and hugged her so tight, her veil tilted to one side of her head. Brooke stomped her feet up and down several times, her joy overflowing. "I can't believe you're my sister now! I mean we always were like sisters, but now you're truly family. This is the best. The very best. Oh, here, let me fix your veil. My duty as your maid of honor."

She refastened the veil just as Royce walked up. "Congratulations, Emma."

"Thank you, Royce. It's great to finally meet you."

"Same here. And on such a special day. I feel honored to be invited."

"I'm glad you're here. Brooke looks great, doesn't she?"

Royce glanced at his date. Brooke was wearing a red halter gown, tastefully decorated with sequins along the bodice. She'd promised she wouldn't wear black, and when they'd shopped and she'd tried this one on, both knew it was perfect for her. Her gorgeous long dark hair hung in tight curls down her back and complemented the dress. "Yes, she does."

"Have you met Dylan yet?"

"No," Royce said. "But I'm looking forward to it."

"He's scared," Brooke said, grinning. "Meeting my famous big brother isn't in his wheelhouse. Isn't that right, honey?"

"Well…uh…I must admit, he's such a big star, I'm a little intimidated."

"Don't be. Dylan's a good guy," Emma said. "He's harmless."

"That's good to hear."

"I keep telling him that, too," Brooke said. "But you, Emma, are the beautiful one. You look like the happiest bride in the world, and that dress…well, you destroy in it."

Emma laughed. "Thanks, I think."

"You do look very pretty, Emma," Royce said.

"And I agree." Dylan came from out of nowhere to take her hand. "You look gorgeous today, Em. My beautiful bride." He kissed her cheek and played with a curl hanging down from her upswept hair.

Brooke wasted no time introducing Dylan to her boyfriend. The two men talked for a few minutes and Brooke seemed immensely happy that they seemed to be getting along.

Just a few minutes later, Dylan's mother walked into their circle and took Emma aside. "I've always thought of you as my second daughter, Emma, you know that. You've been part of our family since the first day Brooke brought you over to our house, but I can't even begin to tell you how happy I am that you and Dylan are married." Katherine McKay hugged her tight, just as she had when Emma was a kid. Growing up, Emma was made to feel welcome and accepted, not by her own foster parents, but by the McKay family. "I know you're going to be a wonderful wife and mother to my first grandchild," Katherine continued, her gracious smile widening. "I am very excited about the baby, in case you can't tell. If you ever need help or advice, please promise you'll ask."

"I promise, Mrs. McKay."

"I'd be honored if you called me Mom."

Tears rushed into Emma eyes. The notion was so sweet and exactly what she needed to hear. "I will, from now on."

"That's good, honey." Katherine kissed her cheek and winked. "Now, I have to congratulate my son. He's made a wise choice."

After pictures were taken and the cocktail hour was observed, dinner was served on the veranda. A stone fireplace crackled and popped, adding ambience to an already elegant day. The wedding had been small, but with attention to detail. Leave it to Brooke to make all the last-minute arrangements. She was a dynamo, and Dylan spared no expense. It was a dream wedding as far as Emma was concerned.

As a disc jockey started setting up, Adam Chase, Dylan's best man, gave a toast. "To my neighbor and good friend Dylan," he said, holding up a flute of champagne. "May you enjoy the very same kind of happiness that I have found in Mia and my daughter, Rose. I'll admit it takes a very special young woman to get Dylan to the altar. He's avoided it for too many years, so to Emma, for making an honest man out of Dylan."

Laughter rippled through the crowd and cheers went up. Everyone but Emma sipped champagne. She opted for sparkling cider and enjoyed it down to the last drop. Dylan held her hand and nodded to Zane. To her surprise, the country crooner slid a chair over to the front of the veranda near the steps, took up his guitar and sat down. "If you all don't mind, I'd like to dedicate this song to my friend Dylan and his new bride, Emma. It's called 'This Stubborn Heart of Mine.' Dylan, feel free to dance this first dance with your wife. And no, this song wasn't written with you in mind, my friend, but if the shoe fits."

Another round of laughter hummed through the guests seated at their tables.

Dylan pulled Emma out onto the dance floor. "May I have this dance, sweetheart?"

And as Zane sang a sweet, soulful ballad, Dylan took her into his arms and twirled her around and around, his moves graceful and smooth. Emma was happier than she'd ever been, but still the notion of getting married to the most eligible bachelor on the planet at a beachfront mansion and having her own personal country superstar dedicate a song to her was surreal.

"You're quiet," Dylan said halfway through the dance.

"I'm…taking it all in. I'm not used to this much…"

"Attention?"

"Everything. It's…kind of perfect."

Dylan hugged her close as the song came to an end, whispering in her ear, "Kind of perfect? Just wait until tonight."

Emma snapped her head up, gazing into his incredibly seductive, amazingly clear blue eyes.

Maybe this marriage-to-Dylan thing would work out after all.

The light of a dozen candles twinkled all around Dylan's master bedroom, but nothing was brighter than the wedding ring he'd put on her finger today. The brilliance of the oval diamond surrounded by perfect smaller diamonds had stunned her into tears. The sweet scent of roses flavored the air, and her bouquet and flowers from the ceremony decorated the room as well, reminding her, as if she could forget, that Dylan was now her husband.

He'd succeeded in making her wedding day a fantasy come true. Now she faced him still wearing her wedding gown, feeling very much like Cinderella. Handsome in his tux, he gazed upon her, his mouth lifted in a smile. "Are you ready for the rest of our life?"

"Oh, yes."

He took her hands in his. "You were a beautiful bride

today, Emma, but now it's time to take this dress off and make you my wife."

Emma's body sang from his words and the anticipation of what the night would bring. "I'm ready."

She stood still as Dylan circled around her. He lifted the tiara from her head, the veil having long ago been removed. Cool air struck her back as he unfastened one tiny button after another. Her body warmed with each flick of his finger as he skimmed her skin. Once done, he spread the satiny material off her shoulders and kissed the back of her neck. A prickling feeling erupted there and followed the path of his hands as they moved the dress down her body. His gentle touch unleashed something wild in her, even as he took his time and took care with her dress. She stepped out of it and he gathered it up and set it over a chair. She stood before him in white lace panties, and as he approached her with fire in his eyes, he undid his bow tie, shed his white shirt and unbuckled his belt.

Pangs of impatient longing stormed her body. They'd gone the old-fashioned route and hadn't slept with each other since the day she'd agreed to become his wife. Now all that pent-up hunger was ready to explode and she couldn't remember ever feeling this way before. Not even on that first night, when she'd dragged Dylan on top of her during the blackout and they'd made reckless love. She knew the difference now. She understood why it seemed so different, answering a nagging question that had plagued her foggy memory. That time, she'd been desperate, eager to have a friend banish her fears. But this time, there was no desperation, only intense passion and true desire, and for her...love.

Dylan went down on his knees, caressed her rounded belly and placed a kiss there. His hands wound around to her butt. Holding her firm, he rested his head on her stomach, and after few reverent seconds, he rose and drew her close in his arms. "Welcome home, Emma," he whispered over her mouth. He lifted her up carefully and swung her around once. "This will have to take the place of carrying you over the threshold."

He laid her down on the bed.

"Thresholds are overrated," she whispered, reaching for him.

Dylan came to her then, climbing into the bed beside her. He leaned over and kissed her again and again until her head swam, her body ached and every nerve tingled. He cupped her breasts and made love to them with his mouth. Her hips swung up, her back bowing, the straining, pink peaks of her nipples sensitized and gloriously begging for more.

She wound her arms around his neck and caressed his shoulders, her palms flat against the breadth and strength of him, solid and sure and smooth. Her fingers played in the short blond spikes of hair, the military cut grown out some, and for the first time, she could say she possessed him as much as he possessed her.

"Ah," she cooed as his tongue licked at her and her entire body strained.

She had to touch more of him, to give as much as she was receiving.

She rolled him away and came up over him, kissing his lips and flattening her palms over his chest. His skin sizzled and she absorbed the heat, gloried in the rapid heartbeats nearly exploding from his chest. She kissed every part of it and a groan escaped his lips when she wandered down and hovered around his navel. His body pulsed, his breath caught. She wouldn't deny him what he wanted. She slipped her hand under his waistband and met with raw, powerful, hot silk.

"Emma," he rasped, almost in a plea.

She wound her hand around his full length and stroked

him, settling into a rhythm. Breath hissed from his mouth, as sensation after lusty sensation drove her on. She unzipped his trousers and he quickly removed his remaining garments. He lay naked before her. He was beautiful, broad where he should be broad, muscled in a jaw-dropping way and lean everywhere else. There wasn't bulk, but rugged, hard-won sculpture. She couldn't believe Dylan was her husband. How had she gotten so lucky?

She continued to caress his upper body as she dipped her head down and took him to a place that had both of them panting and hungry. Dylan's pleasured groans inspired her lusty assault. But then he grabbed her shoulders and backed her away. "Enough, sweetheart," he said. Yet his expression said anything but. His restraint was endearing and tender, even as both of them were nearly destroyed.

He rolled her under him and began the same kind of lusty assault, using his hand first and then his mouth. Pleas and moans slipped from her lips, over and over, until she reached the very edge of pleasure. Her release came fast and hard. It shattered her, split her in half and half again. It was powerful, explosive, the pinnacle of pleasure. When she came back to earth, Dylan's eyes were on her, watching her in awe. She couldn't pretend she wasn't immensely satisfied, nor would she want to. Dylan was an expert lover and she was attuned to him and his body.

She reached up to touch his face. He placed a kiss in the palm of her hand. She slipped her index finger into his mouth, and his hazy eyes widened, new energy erupting from him. No words had to be said. He growled and rose up over her. Within seconds, they were joined. She'd already gotten used to the feel of him inside her, the surge of power even as he took things slow, making sure she was comfortable. He couldn't possibly know how right this felt to her, how her body wrapped around his with possession and adoration. She had let go of her fears when she was in bed with him and gave of herself freely.

Dylan appreciated that—she witnessed it in his expression. She'd never tire of watching him make love to her, to see the complexities on his face, the hunger, the passion and raw desire. She watched him and he watched her and they moved in unison, his thrusts coming stronger now, filling her to the max, giving her another round of hot pleasure.

Dylan's guttural groan echoed in her ears. He reached as high as he could go. She, too, was there with him, arching up and taking that final earth-shattering climb. And then they exploded, sharing the precarious cliff and taking the fall together.

She gloried in the aftermath of his lovemaking and lay beside him, with no words, just feelings of total acceptance and tenderness and protection. If Dylan couldn't give her his love, at least she had that.

Dylan grasped her hand, lacing their fingers together. "My wife."

It was like a song to her ears. "My husband."

"After I finish this movie, I'd like to take you on a real honeymoon, Em. I have a place in Hawaii, or we can go to Europe. If the doctor says it's okay. If not, we can go somewhere locally. We'll find a hideout, maybe up north. A friend of mine has a cabin by a lake."

"Any of the above sounds wonderful."

"Really?"

"Really. I'm low maintenance, Dylan."

He turned onto his side to face her. Leaning on an elbow, he twirled a thick strand of her hair around his finger. "I love that about you, Em. You're easy."

"Hey!"

He laughed and the sound was beautiful and husky and

filled with joy. "I meant you're easy on the eyes, easy to get along with, easy…and fun."

"You think I'm fun?"

His eyes narrowed and his brows lifted in a villainous arch. "So fun," he said. He removed his hand from her hair and used his index finger to circle and tease the pink areola of her breast. Both nipples grew hard and pebbled. Gosh, she *was* so easy.

He bent and kissed both breasts and then sighed. "I should really let you get some sleep. You must be tired."

"Not all that much." Being in bed with him gave her energy and excited her as nothing else ever had. She ran her fingers through his mop of spiky, military-cut hair, grateful to have the freedom to do so—to touch him whenever she wanted. "Did you have something in mind?"

"You don't want to know what's on my mind." His mouth twitched, his smile wicked. But then he gathered her up in his arms and covered them both with the sheets. "Sleep, Emma. I'm not going to wear you out tonight."

"Darn."

He chuckled.

She rested her head on his chest and closed her eyes.

She'd have a lifetime of nights like this with Dylan.

She couldn't imagine anything better.

Cameras flashed like crazy as a dozen photographers on the red carpet of the premiere of Dylan's romantic comedy, *A New Light*, caught sight of him with Emma as they exited the limousine. Just one look at her and they started tossing out questions.

"Who's your date, Dylan?"

"You've been holding out on us!"

"Are you going to be a father? Is she your baby mama?"

Dylan hugged Emma closer, his arm tight around her waist. She looked gorgeous in an organza gown he'd had tailored just for her. Her belly bump couldn't be hidden any longer, but the Empire style of the dress and the floral colors showcased her skin tone and her pregnancy in a beautiful way. "Sorry, honey. This is my life."

"It's okay, Dylan," she said. "You warned me about this."

Selfishly, he'd wanted Emma by his side tonight. Hiding the news of his marriage and the upcoming birth of his baby was proving harder each day. He'd talked to his publicist and they'd both decided that tonight during the movie premiere would be the best time to introduce Emma as his new wife to the world. At least the media would get the scoop from him, and not have to speculate or make up lies to fill their pages.

So right there on the red carpet, with a crowd gathering and the media in his face, Dylan proudly announced, "I'd like to introduce my new bride, Emma McKay. We were married last week in a small ceremony on the beach. Emma and I have known each other since my days in Ohio. I'm happy to say we'll be parents by early next spring. She's an amazing woman and we're both thrilled to have a baby on the way."

"Is it a boy or a girl?" someone shouted.

"We don't know that yet."

"When did you get married?"

"Last Saturday."

"What is Emma's maiden name?"

"Bloom," Emma answered, and Dylan slid her an appreciative glance. She wasn't going to let him take all the heat. She'd have to learn to deal with the media and it might as well start now.

The reporters angled their microphones her way now. "How do you feel marrying the world's most eligible bachelor, Mrs. McKay?"

"I've never really thought of him that way. He's just

Dylan to me. His sister and I have been best friends since grade school."

"Are you going to—"

"Please," Dylan said, putting up a hand. "My publicist will issue a statement in the morning that will answer all of your questions. The movie is about to begin and my wife and I would like to enjoy the premiere together. Thank you."

With bodyguards in front and behind him, Dylan moved through the crowd keeping Emma right by his side. It wouldn't be long now. He'd make headlines and their secret marriage would be a thing of the past. He felt the loss in the pit of his stomach. He loved the anonymity, the intimacy of having Emma all to himself these past few days. Now the news would be out and their lives would change, once again. Lack of privacy was a penalty of fame and he accepted it graciously for himself, but there was Emma to consider now. And their baby.

"You handled yourself pretty damn well, Em," he whispered in her ear.

"I winged it."

"I like a woman who can think on her feet."

He took her hand and entered the iconic movie theatre. It was one of the last few truly historic theatres in Los Angeles, with its plush red velvet seats, sculpted walls and miles and miles of curtains. "Well, what do you think?"

Her pretty green eyes took all of it in. He wanted so badly for Emma to experience the same sort of awe that he did. Moviemaking was in his blood. He was producing more and planned to continue to direct other projects in the future.

"I've never seen anything like this, Dylan. I can picture this theatre back in the day. All those classic movies flashing on that big screen. The actors, directors and producers who've taken their seats here. It's all so...grand."

He smiled. She got it. Emma *was* an amazing woman. He hadn't lied to the press today. He was falling for her and it didn't scare him, or make him nervous. Brooke had said Renee had scarred him for life, but maybe it had taken a woman like Emma to make him realize he was completely healed.

He kissed her cheek then, and she glanced up at him. "What was that for?"

"Can't a man kiss his wife just because?"

She smiled and his heart warmed. He took her hand again. "C'mon, Mrs. McKay, there are bigwigs who would love to meet you. I guess we should get this over with before we take our seats."

"I'm down with that," she said. And he cracked up.

So far, marriage to Emma had been anything but dull.

Nine

"Honey, I'm home," Dylan called out as he entered his house on Monday afternoon. He'd always wanted to say that, but now that he had, his wife was nowhere to be found. He was home fairly early from the set, though. He took a look at his phone and saw that she'd texted him.

I'll be home a little late. Behind on work today. See you at 6ish.

Dylan was disappointed. Each day, he looked forward to coming home to Emma. He'd find her doing pregnancy exercises or poring over a book of baby names or helping Maisey make a healthy dinner for the two of them. Each day also brought him closer to fatherhood, something he discovered he could hardly wait for now. He and Emma had plans to design the nursery. It would be just another few weeks before they found out the sex of their baby.

"Emma's not here, Dylan," Maisey said, greeting him

in the hallway off the kitchen. "I've got dinner ready. It's in the oven, keeping warm. If you don't need me, I'll be heading home."

"Thanks, Maisey. Sure, go on home. I might as well take a run. Emma's going to be a little late."

"Have a good evening, then," Maisey said.

He waved goodbye and dashed up the stairs to change his clothes.

A few minutes later he was on the beach, the shoreline nearly empty as he began to jog. He started out at a good warm-up pace and did at least half a mile before he kicked it into higher gear. It was cloudy and cool, making the run more enjoyable. What had started out as a chore—a fitness program for his role as a Navy SEAL—had become a ritual lately, one he enjoyed. His runs helped him think, helped him work out his upcoming movie scenes and gave him a way to reflect on his life. He'd asked his bodyguards to keep their distance. They had trouble keeping up anyway and he loved the idea of solitude on the beach.

Once he got going, his mind clicked a mile a minute and he made mental tallies of his thoughts as they rushed by, one after the other. And as he ran, he thought back on the night of the blackout. If only he could remember his last day with Roy...

And then images popped into his mind. He was sitting in his house, drinking with his buddy Roy. He was laughing and they were talking about the upcoming stunt and then his phone rang. It was Emma. She was freaking out and slurring her words. She was drunk. She'd said there was a blackout in the city. Dylan's lights were still on. The power outage hadn't reached the beach. He still had full power. Emma was looking for Brooke to come pick her up. Dylan immediately told her to stay put, and he'd come get her.

Dylan slowed his pace, thinking back, happy to have

the memory return. To see Roy in his mind, who looked so much like him they could've been brothers. To remember their laughter and then...then he remembered Roy getting pissed at him. "Dylan, you're in no shape to drive. You've worked your way halfway through that bottle of Scotch. Give me your keys. I'll go get Emma."

The scene played out in his head. He'd been stubborn with Roy, but when he'd tried to rise to go get Emma, the room began to spin and he'd sat back down.

Holy crap.

He came to an abrupt halt on the beach, his feet digging into the sand. His limbs wouldn't hold him; they were like rubber now. He dropped to his knees, his face in his hands. He saw himself handing Roy the keys to his car.

Dylan's face crumpled. Tears burned behind his eyes.

Images that he'd prayed would return now haunted him. He'd let Roy pick up Emma that night, because his friend had been right—Dylan was in no shape to get Emma. Roy picked Emma up that night. Roy...made love to Emma. It was Roy all along.

And the next day on the set, right before Roy got into that car, they'd argued. About Emma. Roy told him what happened and said he'd let things get carried away with her that night. Dylan had gotten hot under the collar, accusing him of taking advantage of Emma. And minutes later, the car exploded, with Roy inside. A fire cloud went up and Dylan was hit with shrapnel.

Dylan dug his fingers into the sand to keep from collapsing entirely. His head was down as he rehashed his thoughts, trying to contradict what he knew in his heart to be true. A woman walked over to him, the only other jogger on the beach beside his bodyguard. "Are you okay?"

Dylan nodded. "I'm...okay," he told the woman. "J-just need a little break."

He warned Dan off. The woman wasn't a threat, but he

might never be okay again. His whole future had been destroyed. The baby Emma carried wasn't his. He was married, but his wife had lied to him. Was it all a ruse? Had she deceived him on purpose? How could she not know what man she was screwing?

The woman walked off slowly and Dylan waited until she was out of sight before he tried to rise. His legs barely held his weight. His entire body was numb from neck to toes. His head, unfortunately, was clear for the first time in weeks, and the clarity was enough to squeeze his gut into tight knots and suck the life out of him.

He walked along the beach, feeling broken, each step leading to his house slower, less deliberate. He was more broken than when Renee had dumped him.

More broken than at any other time in his life.

Emma tossed her purse down on the living room sofa and went in search of Dylan. His car was in the garage; he must be home. She couldn't wait to see him. They'd talked about planning the nursery and she'd brought home paint samples of blues and pinks, greens and lavenders. The sex of the baby would determine the color themes, and they'd find that out pretty soon. At least they could narrow down their options, if Dylan wasn't too tired tonight to help her make some selections.

Unless he had other things on his mind, like taking her to bed early. Lately, they'd been doing a lot of going to bed early and *not* sleeping.

She smiled as she walked the downstairs hallway, popping her head inside rooms in search of him. A delicious aroma led her to the kitchen. She opened the oven door and peered at the meal Maisey had left for them. The garlicky scent of chicken cacciatore wafted in the air.

She closed the oven door when she heard Dylan enter from the beach. He was dressed in a tight nylon tank and black running shorts. Her heart skipped a beat, he was so gorgeous.

"Hi," she said. "How was your run?"

Dylan didn't answer right away. He headed to the bar in the living room. She followed behind him, noting the lack of pep in his step. His shoulders slumped and he was extremely quiet. "Dylan, are you all right?"

Silence again. She waited as he poured himself a drink of some sort of expensive whiskey and gulped it down in one shot. "Did you have a bad day?"

He looked at her then, his face ashen, his cloudy blue eyes dim and lifeless. There was something so bleak in the way he looked at her. "You could say that. I got my memory back."

"Oh? Isn't that a good thing, Dylan? It's what you've been hoping for."

"Sit down, Emma," he said, his voice ice-cold. He pointed to the sofa and she sat. He poured another shot of alcohol and took a seat opposite her, as if...as if he needed to keep his distance. Her heart pounded now as a sense of dread threatened to overwhelm her. Something was very wrong.

"I remember it all, Emma. The night of the blackout, the call you made to me."

She nodded and blinked her eyes several times. Dylan's teeth were gnashing. He had a grip on his temper, but just barely. "I didn't come for you that night," he said, looking down at his whiskey glass. "It wasn't me. It was Roy."

"What do you mean it was Roy? You came for me. I called you looking for Brooke and you...you—"

He was shaking his head adamantly. "I was drinking with Roy that night. Roy didn't think I was sober enough to drive. He took my keys out of my hand and picked you up."

"No, he didn't." Emma's voice registered a higher pitch.

"Yes, he did."

"But…but…that would mean—" Emma bounced up from the sofa. This wasn't right. This wasn't the truth. Dylan had it wrong. It was all wrong. "Dylan, that can't be true. It can't be."

Dylan rose, too, his blue eyes hard and dark as midnight. "It is true. Are you denying it? Are you going to tell me you don't remember sleeping with Roy?"

"That's exactly what I'm saying. I didn't sleep with Roy. I wouldn't do that."

Dylan stood firm, poured whiskey down his gullet and swallowed. "But that's exactly what you did. You slept with Roy, and after he died, you told me the baby was mine."

"I…uh, oh no! I didn't. I mean, if I did, I didn't know it was him. I wouldn't do that, Dylan. I didn't lo—"

"Which is it, Emma?" Dylan asked, in a voice she didn't recognize. He sounded harsh and bitter. "You knew you were screwing Roy, or you didn't?"

Tears welled in her eyes, the truth slapping her hard in the face, but it was Dylan's mean-spirited words that hurt the most. How could she come to terms with what Dylan was implying? She thought she was making love to Dylan that night. Even in her drunken state, even as scared as she was, she would've never knowingly slept with Roy.

Yet he looked enough like Dylan to fool his fans. And he'd come for her in Dylan's car. Because of the blackout and her blurry head, it could have been Roy after all. But she never once thought he wasn't Dylan coming to her rescue.

But Dylan didn't believe that. And he probably never would.

Her memory sharpened to that night and all the things the man she thought was Dylan had said to dissuade her. *You've got this wrong. It's a mistake.* Those pleas made sense now, because she wasn't imploring Dylan to stay with her, it had been Roy all along. Roy who had held her tight and comforted her, Roy who had finally given in when she pressed him to make love to her. No wonder there were differences in Dylan's lovemaking since that first night. She couldn't put her finger on it before and blamed it on her drunken state. But now she knew why it had felt different making love to blackout Dylan versus the real deal.

The truth pounded her head. The truth hammered her heart. The truth made her stomach ache.

"I'm carrying Roy's baby," she said, her voice flat, monotone, as if saying it out loud would make it sink in. She trembled visibly, her arms going limp, her legs weakening. She wanted so badly to sit back down and pretend this wasn't happening. But she couldn't. She mustered her strength, though she bled inside for the life she might have had with Dylan. The bright future she'd only just come to believe in had been snuffed out forever.

She should've known her happiness wouldn't last. When had she really been happy? Only lately, working with Brooke and starting their business. "I can hardly believe this."

When she lifted her eyes, wondering if there was a way around this, a way to make this right, a way to preserve the goodness that had come from marrying Dylan, she met his hard, glowering stare. He blamed her for all this. He didn't believe her. He thought she'd betrayed him.

Like Renee.

Nothing was further from the truth, but it didn't matter. She saw it in the firm set of his jaw. Ice flowed in his veins now. He was convinced she had deceived him.

She faced facts. She wouldn't be Dylan's wife much longer. She'd file for an annulment and wouldn't take a dime of the prenup Dylan's lawyer insisted she sign. She didn't want his money. She had only hoped one day to earn his love.

"I'll pack my things and be gone in the morning, Dylan. Have your attorney contact me. I don't want anything from you. I'm sorry about this. More than you could ever know."

"Emma?"

"Don't worry about me, Dylan," she said, biting her lip, holding back tears. This news crushed her, but she didn't want his pity. She'd never wanted anyone's pity. "I'll land on my feet, as usual. We both know you only married me because of the baby and now that we know the b-baby isn't y-yours…" She couldn't finish her thought. She'd been robbed of the joy of carrying Dylan's child. She'd love her baby, but now her child would never know its father and never have the love of both parents.

Dylan was quiet for a long time, staring at her. His anger seemed to have disappeared, replaced by something in his eyes looking very much like pain. This wasn't easy for him, either, but she had no sympathy for him right now. She was in shock, devastated beyond anything she could ever imagine.

"I'll make sure the baby wants for nothing," he said.

She shook her head stubbornly. "Please, Dylan…don't. I really don't need anything from you. I'll manage on my own. Goodbye." She turned away and kept her head high as she made for the door.

"Emma, wait!"

She stopped, her tears flooding her face. She didn't pivot around. "W-what?"

"I'm…sorry for the way things turned out."

"I know. I am, too."

Then she dashed out of the room.

Dylan sat in his dressing trailer, on the studio lot, feeling uncomfortable in his customized honey wagon, staring at his lines for this evening's scenes and repeating the words over and over in his mind. Nothing stuck. It was as if he was reading hieroglyphics. He hadn't been able to concentrate since Emma had packed her bags and left home two days ago. Brooke had told him that Emma had returned to her apartment. She still had time left on her lease. And his ears still burned from his sister's brutal tongue-lashing that had followed. Brooke had defended Emma and basically called him a jerk for letting her leave that way.

He'd been hard on her. But how on earth could a woman make love to a man and not know who he was? The idea seemed ludicrous to him and yet Brooke had believed her without question and insisted that a man worthy of Emma should have, too. Which told him maybe they weren't meant to be together. Maybe the marriage had been a mistake all along.

Keep telling yourself that, pal.

He'd tried to convince himself he'd done the right thing in letting her go. He didn't love Emma. She was a friend, a bed partner and his wife for a little while longer, but he couldn't deny the reason he'd married her. The only reason he'd married her. He thought she'd been carrying his child and he'd wanted to provide for both of them.

Now the loss seemed monumental. He'd fallen in love with the baby he presumed was his and the notion of fatherhood. He'd begun to see his life differently. Having a family had always been a dream, something he'd wanted sometime in the future.

Now that future was obscure. He was more confused than ever.

He missed Emma. And not just in his bed, though that was pretty spectacular. He missed coming home to her at night, seeing her pretty green eyes and smiles when he walked through the door. He missed the infectious joy on her face when they'd talked about the baby and fixing up the nursery.

All of that was lost to him now.

Someone pounded on the trailer door. He rose from his black leather lounger and peered out the window. It was Jeff, one of his bodyguards. Opening the door, he took a look at the guy's face and the hand he held over his stomach. "Hey, Jeff. What's up? You're not looking too good."

Which was an understatement. His skin had turned a lovely shade of avocado. "Must've been something I ate. I'm sorry, Mr. McKay. I've put in for my replacement. He'll be here in an hour."

"Don't worry about it, Jeff. Go home. Do you think you can drive?"

He nodded and the slight movement turned him grass green. "I'll wait for Dan to get here."

"No, you won't. You can barely stand up. You go home and take care of yourself. There's plenty of security around here. I'll be fine and the replacement will be here soon. You said so yourself."

"I shouldn't."

"Go. That's an order."

Jeff finally nodded. Gripping his stomach, he walked off and then made a mad dash for the studio bathroom. Poor guy.

Dylan grabbed his script and took a seat again. He had to learn his lines or they'd all be here until after midnight. Sharpening his focus, he blocked out everything plaguing his mind and concentrated on the scene, reciting the words over and over and finally getting a grasp of them. He closed his eyes, as he always did, to get a mental picture of how the scene would play out—where his marks were and what movements he would make throughout.

The caustic scent of smoke wafted to his nostrils and he was instantly reminded of the day Roy died. The memory of the blast and the smoke that followed had now fully returned. It was so strong that every time he came upon a group of people smoking on their coffee breaks, he'd relive that moment.

He shook it off, determined to run through his lines one more time before rehearsal was called. But his throat began to burn and he coughed and coughed. That's when he noticed a cloud of gray haze coming toward him from the back end of the trailer. Seconds later he saw flames darting up from his bedroom. Right before his eyes, the fire jumped to the bed and wardrobe racks. Within moments, his entire bedroom was engulfed in flames. He ran for the trailer door and turned the knob. The door moved half an inch, but something was blocking it from opening from the outside. He pushed against it with his full weight. It wouldn't budge. Peering out the window, he looked around and shouted for help.

Flames lit the entire back end of the trailer, the heat sweltering, the smoke choking his lungs. Dylan darted quick glances around the trailer, looking for something sharp to break the small kitchen window. He grabbed his wardrobe chair and shoved the legs against the window above the sink with all his might. Once, twice and finally the window shattered. He broke out as much glass as possible with the chair and then dived headfirst, tucking and rolling his body the way Roy had taught him.

"Ow!" He met with gravel, landing hard, and instantly sucked fresh air into his lungs. The flames were blazing now and he struggled to his feet. He had to get away before the whole thing blew.

Members of the movie crew had now seen the fire and came running over. Two of them grabbed his arms and dragged him away from the trailer. In the distance, he heard sirens blasting.

"Are you okay?" one of the crew members asked.

"Dylan, talk to me." He recognized the assistant director's voice. "Say something."

"I'm...okay."

"Mr. McKay," another voice said, "we're getting you to safety. Hold on."

Once they were fifty feet from the trailers, a blanket was tossed onto the ground and he was laid down. Blood oozed out from scrapes on his body and his clothes were torn from the leap out the window. The stench of smoke and ash permeated the area. Within seconds, the studio medic arrived and assessed him. An oxygen mask was put over his mouth and soon a fresh swell of air flowed into his throat and down his lungs.

"Take slow, normal breaths," the medic said. "You got out in time. Looks like you're going to be fine."

Dylan tried to sit up but he was gently laid back down. "Not yet. You're not burned, but you do have abrasions on your arms and legs. You banged up your face pretty good, too. An ambulance is on the way."

He groaned. "Someone tried to kill me," he said.

"We figured. Those honey wagons don't just light themselves on fire. And we noticed how your door was blocked with a solid beam of wood from the Props Department. The police are on their way."

"I can't believe you didn't call me last night," Brooke was saying softly near his hospital bed. Concern over him was the only thing keeping her from unleashing her wrath.

Accompanied by a police escort, he'd been taken here for observation and to clean up his wounds last night after the fire, and decided not to call his sister until dawn. She didn't need to worry about him and lose sleep over this, but he had to call her before the story hit the morning news.

"There's a freaking police guard outside your room, Dylan. I had to practically strip down to my panties to get in here to see you."

"I bet that was fun," he said, winking the eye that wasn't bruised.

"Ha-ha. Well, at least you haven't lost your sense of humor. But this is serious, brother," Brooke said, her eyes misting up. "You're all bandaged and look like a train wreck. God, I don't want to lose you."

Brooke had a blunt way of putting things, but he knew what was in her heart. He took her hand and squeezed. "I don't want to be lost. They'll find whoever did this, Brooke. It has to be someone with access to the studio lot."

Brooke frowned. "That narrows it down to about a thousand or so."

"I'll be fine, Brooke. I'm going home with a police escort this afternoon."

Dylan flopped back against his pillow. A part of him was disappointed that Emma hadn't shown up here. Had Brooke told her? He couldn't ask, because then his well-meaning sister would give him another lecture. Emma would find out soon enough, if she looked at a newspaper, logged onto the internet or turned on a television set.

He'd already spoken to his manager, his agent and his publicist. They were taking care of business for him. He was set to be released from the hospital later today. Not that he wasn't grateful to the staff, but if one more person told him how lucky he'd been last night, he would scream. Someone was out to kill him. A crazed fan? Some lunatic who wanted fifteen minutes of fame? Or was it someone he knew? A tremor passed through him at the thought. Who hated him enough to want him dead?

He'd been questioned extensively by the police last night and he'd told the detectives everything that had happened that day. They'd been thorough in their questioning, and unfortunately, Dylan was still at a loss as to who might want to murder him.

"I called Emma and told her what happened to you,"

Brooke said, her chin tilted at a defiant angle. "She's your wife, Dylan, and has a right to know. At least she won't hear about it first on the morning news. She's pretty messed up right now."

"I didn't mean to cause her pain, Brooke." Yet that's exactly what he'd done. She was pregnant and his wife, and even though the baby wasn't his, he should've treated her better than he had. The fact that he wanted to see her, wanted her to come just so he could look into her pretty face and be comforted, made him question everything. "Please tell her that I'm all right and that she can talk to me anytime, but honestly, Brooke, until they figure out who's doing this it's best that you and Emma stay away from me."

Brooke opened her mouth to protest just as the nurse walked in. God, he'd never been so happy to have a medical procedure in his life. "Time to get your vitals and check on your bandages, Mr. McKay," the woman said. "If you don't mind stepping out of the room, please?" she asked of Brooke.

"Of course. I'll see you a little later, Dylan," she said, blowing him a kiss. "Be safe."

By five in the afternoon, Dylan was home. Both of his bodyguards were on the premises, keeping an eye out for anything unusual. His first order of business was to go through the past few months of fan mail. He'd had Rochelle skim the letters back when suspicions had first been raised about the cause of Roy's accident, but now that he was certain someone was out to get him he sat behind his office desk and read through each one. His cell phone rang and he sighed when he saw the caller's name pop up on the screen.

"Hello, Renee."

"Dylan, thank God you're all right. I heard about the fire at the studio." Renee sounded breathless.

"I'm fine. I got out safely."

"Oh, Dylan, I hope I'm wrong about this, but I think I know who's out to get you."

Dylan bolted upright in his seat. "Go on."

"My ex-husband is a maniac. I mean, Craig's gone off the deep end lately. He's been trying to get custody of my kids for months now. A few weeks ago, he stormed into the house, screaming at me. He found out about the money you've been sending to help us. Money he thinks is keeping him from getting his hands on the kids. Dylan, I don't know for sure he's behind it. As you might know, he… he…has a background in film and stunt work. He might be working at the studio. And I know he hates you."

"Why does he hate me? Aside from the money?"

"I guess he's always been jealous of you. He knows about our history, Dylan. And, well, he got it in his head that I'm still in love with you. That I compared him to you and he always came up short. I don't know… I guess I did. I've always regretted the way things ended between us. But I never thought he'd go to such extremes. Like I said, I'm not sure…but my gut is telling me it's him."

"Okay, Renee. Sit tight. I'll call the police. They'll want to question you. And, Renee, thanks."

"Of course, Dylan. I couldn't stand it if anything happened to you. Be careful."

"I will."

After hanging up with Renee, he called Detective Brice and relayed the information about Craig Lincoln. He gave him Renee's address and phone number and Brice thought it was a good lead. If her ex was involved, he wouldn't be hard to track down if he worked on the studio lot. Even if he'd used an alias, crews would recognize his face.

Dylan's heart raced. He hoped Renee was right and that Lincoln would be caught. A man like that could be dangerous to her and her kids, too, if he would resort to murder.

Dylan ran a hand down his face.

He needed a drink. As he headed toward the bar, one of his bodyguards entered the house and approached him. "Here you go, Mr. McKay." Dan handed him today's mail.

Dylan wasn't allowed outside to pick up his own mail. He was trapped in his house, a prisoner to the whims of a killer. The studio had shut down all production until the investigation concluded.

"Thanks." He poured himself a whiskey as Dan headed back outside.

He took his mail over to the kitchen table and sat down. Thumbing through ads and bills, he came across an unmarked letter. There was no postal stamp or address on the envelope. It simply read "McKay."

His gut constricted. His breathing stopped for an instant. There was something about this that didn't pass the smell test. He should turn the letter over to Detective Brice, but that could take hours.

It could be nothing or…

His hands shaking, he peeled the envelope open carefully and unfolded the short note.

"You took my family, now I'll take yours."

Dylan froze, staring at the threatening words. Momentary fear held him hostage. His mind raced in a dozen directions and came to a grinding halt. Emma.

His wife.

She could be in danger.

And Brooke, too.

His sister.

He had to get to them. "Dan! Jeff! Get in here, now!"

Ten

Emma sat at her desk at Parties-To-Go working on the numbers for an upcoming wedding. It was after five in the evening, but she'd rather be here than in her lonely apartment. She went through the motions robotically with none of her usual enthusiasm. Debbie Downer had nothing on her. She'd sent Wendy and Rocky home early. She needed to dive into her work with no distractions. She'd been on the receiving end of their sympathetic glances and worried expressions all afternoon. No one knew about her breakup with Dylan yet, aside from Brooke, but her employees were astute and of course had heard about the murder attempt on her husband's life. She was worried sick about Dylan, and missed him so much. She'd spent a good part of the night at the hospital waiting on word of Dylan. Once she knew he was doing well and they expected a full recovery, she'd breathed a sigh of relief and left the waiting room. She didn't want to bring him any bad memories by showing up. He didn't need a confrontation and he'd made himself clear about how he felt about her and their situation.

Resting a hand on her tummy, she closed her eyes and then…the baby kicked! It was more like a flutter, a butterfly taking flight, than an actual kick, but oh, her heart pinged with joy. This was amazing and so absolutely miraculous. A miracle that should be shared and treasured, and her mind went back to Dylan and how happy he'd been thinking he was going to be a father.

She couldn't dwell on what wasn't to be anymore. She was on her own, and her focus had to stay finely tuned to the child she carried.

From now on, she wouldn't be totally alone.

The back door jingled. She stopped to listen. Someone was trying to get inside. Her heart raced and she rose from her desk. She did a mental tally: the part-timers had been sent home, Brooke was on a special date with Royce. She heard more jingling and a couple of loud bangs as if someone was pressing their body against the door, struggling to get in. She glanced around, picked up a kid's baseball bat left over from a party and strode to the door just as it burst open.

"Brooke! You scared me to death."

"Sorry," her friend said. "The dang lock keeps sticking. We've got to get that fixed."

"I wasn't expecting anyone. Aren't you supposed to be with Royce tonight?"

Brooke shut the door and glimpsed the baseball bat in Emma's hand. That's when Emma noticed the hollow look on her friend's face. "What is it?" Bile rose in her throat. "Is it Dylan? Is he okay? Did something else happen to him?"

"Dylan's fine, honey. I've talked to him three times earlier today. He's been released from the hospital and had a police escort home. There's no damage to his lungs and his bruises are superficial. He told me he wanted to rest. Translation—stop bugging him. And I got the hint."

"Oh, thank God. But he's all alone there now. Are the police watching him?"

"He's got two bodyguards round-the-clock and you know about the added security he has around his house. He told me not to worry."

"How can you not? Someone tried to kill him."

"I know. Freaks me out." Brooke took the bat out of her hand. "Must've freaked you out, too."

"Yeah, well…this whole thing is so scary."

Brooke took a shaky breath. Her eyes were rimmed with red. She moved into the office and sat down. Emma did the same. "So why are you here? Shouldn't you be with Royce tonight?" she asked carefully.

"Royce and I are over."

Emma's brows lifted. She didn't expect this. "What do you mean, you're over?"

"I walked out on him, Em."

"Why?"

Brooke sighed. "When Royce said he had something special he wanted to give me, I thought, oh my goodness. A key to his place maybe, or a piece of jewelry, maybe even a ring. I let my imagination run wild. I mean, come on, he knows what I've been through this month with Dylan. And he actually used that. He told me he knew I was worried about my brother and that he'd probably have time on his hands, now that the studio shut down production, so—"

"He didn't!"

"Oh, yes, he did. He gave me three scripts for Dylan to look at. Scripts that were his pride and joy. He said he'd been working on them for two years and he knew Dylan would love them and want to produce and star in the movies once he read them."

"Oh, Brooke, I'm so sorry. You must've been…"

"Pissed and hurt and most of all shocked. That's the part that gets me. I was shocked and I shouldn't have been. I really thought he was the one guy I could count on, who didn't want to get close to me because of my brother. He's in finance, a Wall Street type. I didn't think there was a creative bone in his body. And I loved that about him. I mean…I really thought… Oh, I shouldn't feel sorry for myself. Not in front of you."

"Are you saying I have bigger problems than you?" Emma leaned in to give Brooke a goofy smile. "Is that what you're telling me?"

"No. Yes. You know what I mean."

"I do know. So, we're both hurting right now."

Brooke nodded. "But I'm not going to let that idiot ruin my life. I'm not going to fall to pieces."

"Promise?"

"I…uh…well, maybe a little crumble." Her voice shook.

Emma took Brooke's hand and they sat there for a few minutes, holding on to each other and trying not to cry.

"You know what?" Brooke said. "We should get out of here. They're showing a special screening of *The Notebook* at the Curtis Cinema down the street. If we're going to cry, it might as well be over our favorite chick flick. Let's go and then have a late dinner. Just like old times."

"I like the sound of that. No more moping."

"Pinkie swear?"

They locked their pinkie fingers, just as they did when they were kids. "Pinkie swear."

"We'll shut down our cell phones and have a night free of worries."

"Shouldn't you check in on Dylan?" Emma asked.

"I will, as soon as the movie ends. Deal?"

"It's a deal," Emma said, her spirits lifting for the first time in two days.

* * *

"Damn this traffic." Dylan sat shotgun as Dan navigated the streets leading to Emma's apartment, cutting in and out of the lineup of cars on Pacific Coast Highway whenever he could. "It would have to be the busiest time of day."

After Dylan had called Detective Brice about the threatening letter, he was ordered to stay put at home. That had lasted only half an hour. His nerves had been bouncing out of his skin and there was only so much pacing he could do. How could he sit around and wait when Emma's and Brooke's lives could be in danger? Neither of them were answering their phones and their part-time employees confirmed they didn't have an event tonight. He'd left countless messages at their homes and at the office, which had gone straight to voice mail. His texts hadn't been answered, either.

He'd moved fast then, ordering Dan to drive, while Jeff followed behind, both in black SUVs. The first stop was Emma's place. She should've been home from work by now. Dusk had settled in, a gray cloud cover shutting out the lingering light.

His unanswered voice mails put fear in his heart. Emma was in danger, he was sure of it. That creep Lincoln couldn't get at him after two failed attempts and now he was going after his unsuspecting pregnant wife.

Emma.

As soon as he'd read that damning note, his first thoughts were of her and the child she carried. *She* was his family now, along with the baby. That child was his best friend's baby, an innocent in all this, and someone who deserved to be loved. Dylan was ashamed of himself for turning away from Roy's baby. He hadn't been thinking clearly. He'd felt the same sense of deceit and betrayal from Emma as he had from Renee. It had all been too much; his hopes and dreams had been paralyzed and he'd lashed out at the injustice, but none of it was Emma's doing. He believed that now. Deep down he'd always known Emma wouldn't resort to that kind of devastating deceit.

Good God, had his heart been so hardened that he couldn't recognize true love when it slammed him in the face? Had it taken a threat to her life to make him realize what she meant to him?

He was in love with her.

And the very thought of Emma and the baby being hurt was too hard to imagine.

"Hurry, Dan. I can't let anything happen to her."

Once they finally reached Emma's apartment building, Dan parked on the street and Dylan threw open the car door.

"Wait!" Dan ordered. "You can't go running in there. It might be a trap."

Jeff raced over, blocking him from getting out of the car.

"Then what are we going to do?"

"The smart thing is to wait for the cops to arrive," Jeff said.

Dylan shook his head. "Think of another option."

His cell phone rang and he immediately picked up. "Dylan, it's me."

"Brooke, thank God. I've been trying to reach you. Are you okay?"

"I'm fine."

He got out of the car now, listening to the sweet sound of his sister's voice. "Where are you and is Emma with you?"

"Yes, I'm with Emma. But first tell me, are you okay? I panicked when I saw a dozen missed calls from you. Your texts said Emma and I were in danger?"

"Yeah, you might be. The creep who tried to kill me sent a note saying he was going after my family. You're sure Emma's fine?"

"Uh, well, she will be. We were at the movies and she started feeling weak. When I looked at her face, she had gone completely white. I didn't let her argue with me. I drove her straight to the emergency room. We're at Saint Joseph's."

Dylan stopped breathing. God, if she lost the baby, he'd never forgive himself. He loved the both of them with all of his heart. "What's wrong with her, Brooke? It isn't the baby, is it?"

"The baby's fine. Emma's been under a lot of stress lately. She hasn't been eating and, well, she's been upset and crying lately. She's dehydrated. Could've been really dangerous, but we caught it in time. They're pumping her full of fluids now and the doctor said she's going to be okay."

Dylan ran his hand down his face. "Okay." He heard the relief in his own voice. "I'll be there in a few minutes. And I'm calling Detective Brice to put a guard on her door. Don't leave the hospital under any circumstances."

"That won't be necessary." At the gruff-sounding voice, Dylan turned and found Detective Brice approaching, a frown on his face that would scare the devil. "You don't listen very well, do you, McKay? You almost blew our cover coming here."

"Brooke," Dylan said into the phone. "I'll call you back in a sec. Just stay with Emma." He hung up the phone, surprised to see Brice. "What do you mean?"

"We had the apartment under surveillance since this morning. Your sister's place, too, just as a precaution. Sure enough, we found Lincoln tonight, lurking in the bushes in the courtyard. He's in our custody now and he's not going to be able to harm anyone ever again."

The courtyard gates opened and Dylan faced the man who'd murdered Roy. Blood ran hot in his veins. Here was the man who'd tried to kill him twice, who was lying in wait to harm his pregnant wife. Lincoln was in handcuffs, two officers flanking him and three others following behind. All Dylan wanted to do was meet him on equal turf and beat the stuffing out of him. He took a step toward him and Brice got in his way, his hand firm on Dylan's chest. "McKay, don't be an idiot."

Lincoln's eyes bugged out of his skull when he saw Dylan. "You sonofabitch! You home wrecker! You don't deserve to live!" Lincoln was out of his mind, wrestling with the officers restraining him. "You think you can take my kids, my wife. Ruin my life! You hotshot, you'll live to regret this!"

Two of the other officers grabbed Lincoln, restraining his arms and maneuvering him into the squad car that had pulled up behind Jeff's SUV.

Dylan shook his head. "He killed Roy."

"He'll pay for that," Brice said. "And all the other crimes he's committed."

Dylan nodded. "Yeah."

"He's deranged, but something set him off. You said over the phone his ex-wife called you."

"Yeah, she was the one who figured it out after she saw the headlines today about the attempt on my life. I don't know too many details about her life, just that we were close once and that more recently she was near poverty, trying to raise her kids and keep her ex away from them. I've been sending her money to keep food on the table for her children. That was my crime. That's why he hates me."

"He's going away for a long time." Brice patted Dylan on the back. "It's over now, McKay. You can go on being a superhero, *on film*," he said, giving him a teasing smirk.

"There's only one person I want to think of me that way."

And unfortunately, it was the one person he'd hurt the most.

"Are we through here?" he asked.

"I'm going to need your statement," Brice said.

"Can I give it to you later tonight? I just found out my wife's in the hospital and I want to see her as soon as I can."

"Sorry to hear that." Brice puffed out a breath. "Okay. Sure. Go check on your wife. You both had some close calls lately. I hope she's going to be okay."

Dylan hoped so, too. "Thanks." Dylan shook the detective's hand. "I appreciate what you've done for my family. Your team did excellent work."

"It's all in a day's work. Sometimes things go sideways, but this one turned out in the best way possible. No one got hurt today. I'm proud of these guys."

Dylan left the detective to speak with his bodyguards. He dismissed them for the night, thanking them for their help, explaining that he wanted to see Emma on his own. He needed time alone to think things through on the drive over and he didn't want to show up at the hospital with an entourage. He'd had plenty of experience sneaking in and out of places—fame did that to a man, made him hunt for ways to go undetected. He borrowed Jeff's ball cap and his oversize gray sweat jacket as a disguise.

Dylan called Brooke back on the way to the hospital and told her the entire story. His little sister nearly broke down on the phone and he couldn't blame her. What had transpired was like something out of a bad B movie. But they were all safe, he assured her, and he told her to hang tight. He would be there shortly.

As the SUV's tires hit gravel on the way to the hospital, one thought continually nagged at him. How in hell was he going to make this up to Emma? He had no doubt he was responsible for her unhealthy state. She hadn't been eating well and she'd been terribly upset lately. All because he'd misjudged her and had the foolish notion that he couldn't love completely again.

At the hospital, he found Brooke sitting in a waiting room. She took one look at him, bolted up and flew into his arms, tears streaming down her face. "Dylan, my God… to think what could have happened to you. To Emma. I'm a freaking basket case."

"I know. I know." He brought her into his embrace and held on tight. Her face was pressed to his chest, her quiet sobs soaking his terrible disguise. "We're all going to be fine now, Brooke. The police have the guy in custody. He's not going to hurt anyone anymore."

"He murdered Roy."

"Yeah, he did." Dylan would have to live with that guilt the rest of his life. "How's Emma? I need to see her, Brooke. I need to tell her… I just have to see her."

Brooke pulled out of his arms, sniffled and gave him a somber look. How quickly she'd transformed into a mother hen. "Dylan, she's sleeping now. They gave her a sedative and she'll stay here for the night. She needs to rest and she especially needs no further drama in her life. Doctor's orders."

"I got that covered, sis."

"Are you sure? Because you can't mess with her, Dylan. She's not as strong as she looks. She's had a rough life. And she—"

"Brooke, I know what my *wife* needs."

Brooke's lips lifted in a smile and the defiance in her stern eyes faded. "And you're going to make sure she gets everything she deserves?"

"Yes. I've been a fool and I plan on rectifying that now. But I'm going to need your help. Are you willing to help me win my wife back?"

"Is it going to cost me her friendship?"

"No, it may even earn you a spot as godmother to the baby."

"Well, shoot. I've already got that in the bag."

"But you'll help me anyway because you love me?"

"Yeah, big brother. I'll help you. Because I love you *and* Emma."

Emma sat at her office desk and laid a hand on her belly, thanking God that her baby was thriving and growing as it should. The scare she'd had the night she went to the movies with Brooke couldn't happen again. She couldn't let her emotions get the best of her like that anymore. She was eating well now, drinking gallons of water a day, or so it seemed, and taking daily walks. All in all, she felt strong. Facing the future didn't frighten her as much as it once had. Emma adapted well and she was learning how the new life growing inside her only encouraged her own private strength.

"Look what just arrived for you," Brooke said, walking over with a vase full of fresh, snowy-white gardenias. "I love the way they smell."

"Your brother has a good memory." Emma admired the flowers Brooke set down on her desk. "Either that, or he's a good guesser. It's my favorite flower. You didn't tell him, did you?"

Brooke shook her head. "No. He must've remembered how you'd always ask Mom if you could pick a gardenia off the bush to put it in your hair. You'd wear it until the leaves turned yellow."

A fond memory. Emma smiled. "That's when the scent is sweetest."

Every day since her hospital stay, Dylan had done something thoughtful for her. The day she was released from the hospital, he'd sent her a basket of oils and lotions to pamper herself along with a gift certificate good for a dozen pregnancy massages with a message that simply read "I'm sorry."

Yesterday, he'd sent her an array of fresh fruit done up in the shape of a stork. It was really quite ingenious, with wings made of pineapple slices and cherries as eyes. Again, there was a note, which read "Forgive me."

And today, the flowers. She lifted the note card from its holder, her hand shaking. She wasn't over Dylan, not by a long shot.

He'd wanted to see her. To apologize in person, but she wasn't up to that yet. She needed time and strength and to make sure the baby was thriving again. She feared seeing Dylan would break her heart all over again. Luckily, because Brooke warned him off visiting her, he hadn't pressed her about it.

Brooke had already walked back to her desk. It wasn't like her *not* to nose around and ask what was going on. But then, Brooke's heart had been broken, too. She didn't believe in love anymore. Together, they were the walking wounded.

"I miss you," the note read.

Tears pooled in her eyes. The gifts were getting a bit much. Why was he torturing her like this? Didn't he know that she needed a clean break from him? That he owned her heart and soul and she was fighting like mad to take them back.

The capture of his stalker had made headlines and Dylan hadn't been back to work yet, according to Brooke. The investigation had shut down production at the studio for a few days. His adoring fans had been outraged at the murder attempt and the police thought it best for him to keep a low profile. Dylan had his hands full with news helicopters circling his home, reporters at his front gate and paparazzi trying to get glimpses of him. He'd hunkered down at his mansion on Moonlight Beach and had his publicist offer a statement, thanking the police for their diligence, thanking his fans for their support and asking for the press to abide by his privacy during this difficult time.

Emma, too, had been the source of news, especially since she'd been a target as well, and as Dylan's newly estranged bride, well…her life had become very public, very quickly. Emma refused to comment to the press and Dylan assigned Jeff to escort her to and from work each day to basically stand guard over her. It was weird having her own personal bodyguard, but she appreciated the gesture. No one had gotten near her, thanks to Jeff. Today, an equally juicy scandalous news story had broken and she hoped that she and Dylan were off the hook, at least for the time being.

This afternoon, she was working on a retirement party for a man who'd started his own business in foldable cartons back in the early 1950s. The exuberant senior citizen was finally retiring at the ripe young age of ninety-four, giving up the helm to his grandson. The party would be full of guests of all ages and she and Brooke worked tirelessly to throw an event that would encompass every one of the three generations attending.

Brooke turned away from her computer screen for a second. "Are you still on board for our meeting with the manager of Zane's on the Beach tonight?"

"Yep, I'll be there."

"Okay, he'll make time for us at around eight and we can go over the details for the party. I'll meet you there, though. I have to run a few errands after work."

"Sure. Jeff and I will meet you." Emma lifted her lips in a smile.

Brooke rolled her eyes. "It's for your own sanity, you know. Dylan's used to having a swarm of reporters dogging him, but you're not."

"The reporters have backed off. Dylan's probably getting the brunt of it."

"He can handle it. The press loves him. Especially now. Since his murder attempt they're treading carefully and trying to give him the space he needs."

"For his sake, I hope so," Emma replied. She'd lived in his world for a short time. There was never a time when people weren't gawking at him, sneaking peeks or flat out trying to approach him.

"Me, too," Brooke said. "Love that guy. I'll be forever grateful he wasn't hurt by that creep. I only wish…"

"What do you wish?"

"Nothing," she said, dipping her head sheepishly. "I've got to go." Brooke tossed her handbag over her shoulder and then bent to give Emma a kiss on the cheek. "See you later, Em."

Emma closed up shop at precisely five o'clock, exited by the back door and found Jeff waiting for her by her car. He stood erect in his nondescript black suit, waiting. When he spotted her, she put her head down, stifling a frown. "I'm going home to have dinner. And then I've got an appointment."

"Okay. I'll follow you home. What time are you going out again?"

"Seven thirty. And I want you to eat something before you come back. Promise?"

He nodded and a silly smile erupted on his face. She was mother henning him to death, but in some weird way she thought he actually liked her fretting over him. If she was a better liar, she'd tell him she was calling it a night and going to bed early, but with her luck, she'd get caught in the lie and then feel bad about it for weeks. So, the truth had to be served.

Once she got home and Jeff was on his way, she created a healthy chicken salad with vegetable greens, cranberries and diced apples. She took her food over to the sofa, plopped her feet in front of the television screen and turned on the news until a report came on about Dylan's would-be killer. She hit the off button instantly, shaking her head. She knew all she wanted to know about Craig Lincoln, Renee's homicidal ex-husband, thank you very much. Her stomach lurched, but she fought the sensation and ate her salad like a good mother-to-be.

After dinner, she walked into her bedroom, took off her clothes and stepped into the shower. Until the warm spray hit her tired bones, she didn't realize how very weary she was. For the past few weeks, she felt as if her emotions were on a wacky elevator ride going up and down, never really knowing where she was going or when it would finally stop. She lathered up with raspberry vanilla shower gel and lost herself in thought, allowing the soothing waters to take effect.

After her shower, she threw her arms through the sleeves of a black-and-white dress that belted loosely above her waist. There was no hiding her pregnancy any longer; her baby was sprouting and making its presence known. A cropped white sweater and low cherry heels completed her semiprofessional look. Next, she applied light makeup, eyeliner, meadow-green shadow and a little rosy lip gloss. The last thing she cared about right now was how she looked, but this was an important meeting.

She stepped out of her apartment at precisely seven thirty and there was Jeff, waiting for her. How long had he been standing guard outside her apartment? Gosh, she didn't really want to know.

"Hi again," she said.

Jeff stood at attention, his gaze dipping to her dress, and a glimmer of approval entered his eyes. Something warmed inside of her that she thought had been frozen out. She told him where she was headed.

"I know the place" was all he said.

She arrived at the restaurant a little before eight. She

didn't see Brooke's car in the parking lot so she waited until eight sharp and there was still no sign of Brooke.

She got out of her car, and Jeff did the same. It was dark now, except for the full moon and the parking lot lights. The roar of the ocean reminded her of Dylan and the time she'd spent living as his wife and she sighed. Fleeting sadness dashed through her but she had no time for self-pity. She had a client to meet.

Jeff did a thorough scan of the grounds as he approached her. "I'm meeting my partner here," she said, "but since it's already eight, I'd better go inside to start the meeting."

"I'll walk you inside."

"Is that necessary?"

He smiled. "It'll make me feel better."

She smiled at his comment. He'd taken a page from her mother-hen book. "Okay."

When they reached the front door, he opened it for her. "After you."

"Thank you." She stepped inside the restaurant and her heart seized up at the sight before her eyes. Hundreds of lit votive candles illuminated the empty space. "Oh, no. We must've gotten the date wrong. Looks like someone is setting up for a party," she said to Jeff.

When he didn't answer, she turned around. Jeff was gone. Vanished into thin air.

Her heart pumped harder now and she was ready to scurry away, when a figure walked out of the darkness into the candlelight—a man wearing a dark tuxedo with lush blond hair and incredible melt-your-soul blue eyes.

"Hello, Emma. You look beautiful."

Her hand was up at her throat. She didn't know how it got there. "Dylan?"

He smiled, eyes twinkling, and walked over to her. She nibbled on her lip, trying to make sense of all this, and when he took her hand and held on to it, as if for dear life, she was beginning to see, beginning to hope that she knew what all this meant.

"I've been a fool," he said.

Oh, God, yes. Not the fool part, but that, too. He was here for her. "Why do you say that?"

"Come," he said, pivoting around and guiding her with their hands still clasped to a table set for two overlooking Moonlight Beach. Roses and gardenias at the center of the table released an amazing sweet aroma. A chilled bottle of sparkling water sat in a champagne bucket, along with two flutes. The crystal glassware and fine bone china reflected the candlelight, added sparkle and a heavenly aura to the room. Right now, that's exactly how she felt: out of this world.

"As you might've guessed, there is no appointment for you to keep tonight. Just dinner with me."

She blinked and blinked and blinked. "You arranged all this?"

He nodded, but his smile seemed shaky and unsure, not the usual confident Dylan smile. "I know the owner."

Zane Williams. Of course. He'd attended their fateful wedding. "And I wanted to do something for you that was as special as you are, Emma."

"I'm not that special," she whispered.

"To me, you are. To me, you're everything I've ever wanted and it's taken me nearly losing you to that maniac to figure it out. When I thought you were in danger, I panicked and my thick head finally cleared. I was willing to do anything to keep you safe."

"Jeff told me you were ready to risk your life for me."

"Jeff, huh? Well, it's true. The thought of you getting hurt made me realize that my life, all of my success, everything I have now, would mean nothing if you weren't right there beside me. You and the baby. God, I've been so selfish, Emma. I only thought of what I'd lost when I found out you were carrying Roy's baby. But I never stopped to realize what I'd be gaining. Until I almost lost you."

"I was never in any real danger."

"Not that night, no. But if Renee hadn't called to warn me, things might've turned out differently. He threatened your life. He probably wouldn't have stopped until... I can't think about it."

"Well, I'm thankful to Renee for putting the pieces together."

Dylan nodded. "I owe her for that. And the best way to repay her isn't by sending her money. A friend of mine has a job waiting for her, as a personal secretary. She's going back to work and she's happy about it. The job pays well and she'll be able to hold her head up high again and support her family."

"Dylan, that's wonderful. You're giving her a second chance."

He nodded. "I hope so."

"You're a good man, Dylan."

"Good enough for you to give me a second chance?"

"Maybe," she said softly. "After the attempt on your life, I came to the hospital and made Brooke promise not to tell you. I wanted to see you so badly, but I didn't want my being there to upset you, so I stayed outside your room until I found out you were going to be okay."

"I wanted to see you. I'd hoped you would come."

"I didn't think it would be wise."

"Emma. I'm sorry for how I've behaved. I'm sorry about everything. I should've stopped you from walking out on me. I let you leave my house pregnant and alone to face an unknown future. I hope you can forgive me for being obtuse and selfish."

"I think I already have, Dylan. I couldn't hold a grudge when your life was in danger. And I've made mistakes, too. I shouldn't have lost my head and gotten so drunk that night that I didn't realize what was happening. I told you the baby was yours. It was only natural for you to be disappointed to find out the truth. I'm sorry you were hurt. Truly."

"Apology accepted. Now it's time for us to put those mistakes in the past and look to the future." Dylan went down on one knee then, and her out-of-this-world experience got *real*, really quickly. "Emma, I want to do this right this time. I love you with all of my heart. I love the child you're carrying, my best friend's baby, and it's my hope that we raise the baby together and—"

"Wait!" She put up her hand and the hope on Dylan's face waned. It wasn't that she hadn't heard him the first time or that she wanted him to stop, but she'd waited a long time for those words. They were worth repeating. "Can you say that again?"

"The I-love-you-with-my-whole-heart part?"

"That's the one."

"I do, Emma, I love you," he declared. "I didn't think I'd ever let myself love again. After Renee, it was just easier to have casual relationships with women. No risk, no injury. I guess it was a way of protecting myself from ever feeling that kind of pain again. I'm not making excuses, but for me, falling in love wasn't an option, mentally and emotionally. I wanted no part of it. Everything changed, though, when you became part of my life. Suddenly, everything I've ever wanted was right in front of me. It took a blackout and a baby to make me see it. It was a strange journey to be on, but I can't imagine my life without you and the baby in it. You're my family, and I see a wonderful future ahead for us. So, sweetheart, will you please come back home…to me? Be my wife, mother of our child. I propose for us to stay married and love each other until the end of time. Could you do that?"

Tears of joy streamed down her face. Dylan's proposal

was everything she'd ever wanted. She loved him beyond belief. How could she look at that man, see the truth in his humble blue eyes and not love him? "I can. I will. I love you, Dylan. And I want a life with you. That's all I've ever wanted."

On bended knee, he caressed her growing belly and placed a sweet kiss there. The outpouring of his love was evident in the reverent way he spoke about the baby, spoke of his love for her. She believed in his love now, believed in their future.

Then he rose to his full height, his gaze clouded with tears. "I love you, Emma. And our child. The best I can do is promise to share my life with you and try to make every day happy for our family. Is that enough?"

"More than enough," she whispered.

She was drawn into the circle of his arms and he bent his head to claim her mouth in a deep, lingering kiss. By the time he was through, her mind was spinning and only one fulfilling, delicious thought entered her head.

She'd finally claimed *dibs* on Dylan McKay. And quite fantastically, he'd also claimed dibs on her.

And that would be no darn secret anymore.

* * * * *

HIS BEST FRIEND'S SISTER

SARAH M. ANDERSON

To the ladies of the YMCA water aerobics classes. Twice a week, you all listen to me babble about plot points and encourage me to keep moving, even on days when I hurt. Thanks for all your support and for laughing at my silly stories!

One

"I thought you hated the rodeo."

That voice—Oliver Lawrence knew that sweet voice. Except it was richer, deeper. It sparked memories—memories of smiling, laughing. Of having fun. When was the last time he'd had fun?

He couldn't remember.

"But here you are, surrounded by pictures of the rodeo," she went on. He could hear the smile as she spoke. She'd always smiled at him. Even when he hadn't deserved it.

Oliver jerked his head up from where it had been buried in his hands. It wasn't possible. *She* wasn't possible.

But there Renee Preston stood, just inside the door to his office as she studied the framed pictures of the All-Stars that Bailey had artfully arranged along one wall of the office.

Although her back was to him, he was stunned to realize that he recognized her anyway. The pale gold of her hair fell halfway down her back in artful waves, the curve of her backside outlined by a dark blue dress.

How long had it been? Years? He shouldn't even recognize her, much less have this visceral reaction to her. Seeing her now was a punch to the gut, one that left him dazed and breathless. And all he could think was, *I hope she's real.* Which made no sense. None at all. But given the headaches he'd had running Lawrence Energies—why were Mondays so awful?—he wouldn't be surprised if his sanity had taken a breather.

He stared but she didn't move. Bad sign. "Renee?" He blinked and then blinked again when she didn't turn around.

Okay, he was having a bad morning. Because the truth was he did hate the rodeo—the Lawrence Oil All-Around All-Stars Pro Rodeo. He'd hated it ever since his father had won the circuit in a poker game thirteen years ago. But there weren't many people who knew it. It was bad for business if the CEO of Lawrence Energies, parent company of Lawrence Oil—and, by default, the All-Stars—publicly announced how much he hated his products.

So how did Renee know?

His assistant, Bailey, came charging into the room, looking flustered. Finally Renee moved, tilting her head to look at him. "Mr. Lawrence—I'm sorry," Bailey said, breathing hard. He gave Renee an accusing look. "She's *quick.*"

Thank God Oliver wasn't hallucinating the arrival of the last person he'd expected to see today. Renee Preston was actually in his office in Dallas in the middle of a Monday morning.

"It's all—"

But just then, Renee turned the rest of the way around

and Oliver got a look at her in profile. Her little button nose, her sweetheart chin, her gently rounded stomach that curved out from the rest of her body...

Wait.

Was she *pregnant*?

Slowly, Oliver stood. "Renee, what's going on?"

Bailey hung his head. "Should I call security?"

Oliver waved away. "No, it's fine. Ms. Preston and I are old friends." That was not exactly the truth. Her brother, Clinton, was an old friend. Renee had always been an obnoxious little sister who, when she teamed up with Oliver's sister, Chloe, had been a real pain in the butt.

The full impact of her appearance hit him. She gave him a soft little smile that barely moved a muscle on her face. He didn't like that smile. It felt unnatural somehow.

He looked at her dress again. Maybe it wasn't dark blue. Maybe it was black. She looked like she'd decided to stop by his office—some fifteen hundred miles away from New York City—on her way to a funeral.

"No calls," Oliver said to Bailey. If Renee Preston was here, wearing a funereal dress while pregnant, something had gone wrong.

Suddenly, he remembered the email from Clint Preston. Had it been two months ago? Or three? Ever since Oliver's father, Milt, had uprooted the family from their Park Avenue address in New York City and relocated them to Dallas, Oliver and Clint hadn't exactly kept up a friendship. But he remembered now—that odd email that had been sent at four in the morning. *Look after Renee, will you?*

Oliver had never replied. He'd meant to, but...honestly, he'd been confused. Why did *he* have to look after Renee? She had a family. She was a grown woman. It hadn't seemed urgent, not at this time.

Clearly, it was urgent now.

Just when he thought things couldn't get any worse, they did. Served him right for thinking that in the first place.

"Actually," she said after Bailey had closed the door after him, "it's Renee Preston-Willoughby now."

Instead of pulling his hair out, he attempted to smile at Renee. "Congratulations. I hadn't heard." Although... hadn't Chloe said something about Renee getting hitched? It'd been a few years ago and Oliver had been in the middle of what was basically a corporate takeover of the business from his father.

That particular piece of information did nothing to shine a light on why she was in his office. He hadn't seen her since...

Five years ago at her brother's wedding? And Renee had still been in college. He remembered being curious because she hadn't been the same little girl in pigtails.

In fact, she'd been gorgeous, her smile lighting up the room even in the hot-pink bridesmaid's gown. But she'd had a boyfriend and Oliver wasn't going to poach another man's girl, so he'd appreciated the way she had grown into a lovely young woman from the safety of the bar, where he'd been getting sloshed with a bunch of Wall Street financiers who wanted to know if *everything* really was bigger in Texas.

Oliver dimly recalled his growing frustration that no one had believed him when he'd said he'd give anything to be back in New York City. To those idiots, Texas had sounded like a vacation. Barbecue, babes and bulls—as if that was all anyone did in Texas. All the cowgirls in the world hadn't made up for being stuck running the family businesses—and the family—then and it didn't make up for it now.

Besides, cowgirls tended to go for Flash, his younger brother. Not serious Oliver.

He almost hadn't come back to Dallas after that wedding. He'd woken up with a killer hangover and a new resolve to tell his father where he could shove the All-Around All-Stars Rodeo and his ten-gallon Stetsons and his stupid fake Texan accent. Oliver was going back to New York, where he belonged.

But he hadn't. He couldn't go back on his word to his mother. So he'd done the next-best thing—wrestled control of Lawrence Industries away from his father. The old man was still chairman of the board, but Oliver was CEO of the whole thing. Including the damned rodeo.

His attempts to relocate corporate headquarters to New York after the takeover had failed, though. Some days, he thought he'd never get out of this godforsaken state.

Had he and Renee spoken at the reception? Had she asked about his rodeo? Had he been drunk enough to tell the truth? Damn.

Even in that sad sack of a black dress, she was still the most stunning woman he'd ever seen. He wanted to sink his hands into her silky hair and pull her against his body and *feel* for himself that she was really here. Even her skin seemed to glow.

But as he looked closer, he saw other things, too. Beneath her tastefully understated makeup, he could see dark shadows under her eyes. Was she not sleeping? And even as she stood there, submitting to his inspection, her left hand beat out a steady rhythm on her leg, a *tap-tap-tap* of anxiety.

He was staring, he realized. He had no idea how long he had been staring at her. Seconds? Minutes? When had Bailey left?

He cleared his throat. "Well. This is unexpected. What brings you to Dallas?"

Her stiff little smile got stiffer. "Actually," she said, taking a deep breath, "I'm looking for Chloe." Her voice cracked on Chloe's name and she turned around quickly, but not quickly enough. Oliver just caught the way her face crumbled.

He took a step forward before he knew what he was doing. He had the oddest urge to put his arms around her shoulders, to take some of the weight from her. But he didn't. It wasn't like she'd come for him. And he couldn't imagine that she'd welcome what was essentially a stranger giving her a hug. So instead he pulled up short and said, "It's rodeo season."

She was silent for a moment, but she nodded. "And Chloe is the Princess of the Rodeo," she said in a wistful way.

Renee had been the tagalong little sister and then the bridesmaid. He knew nothing of her life. But she was clearly in distress and that bothered him.

His job was to solve problems. He'd promised his mother, Trixie, on her deathbed that he would keep the family from falling apart. That's why he was the CEO of Lawrence Energies instead of taking another job—one that didn't involve managing his father and his siblings. That was why he was still in Texas instead of going back to New York City. That's why he sucked it up and managed the damned rodeo.

Renee Preston-Willoughby was a problem and he had no idea how to solve her.

"She's in Lincoln, Nebraska, right now—and after that, it's Omaha. And after that..." He shrugged, although Renee couldn't see it. "It's rodeo season," he finished lamely. "I think she'll be back in Fort Worth in a month."

Chloe opened and closed every show in the All-Stars circuit. She had for years. She lived out of a suitcase for months on end, all because she liked to dress up in a sequined cowgirl top and ride her horse into the arena, carrying the American flag.

Oliver didn't know how his sister could stand it. He *hated* the rodeo. The swagger of the cowboys, the smell of the horses and cattle, the idiocy of people who voluntarily climbed on the back of wild horses and angry bulls—yeah, that included Flash. There was nothing he liked or even tolerated about the All-Stars.

Now more than ever—what with Chloe demanding that she should be given a chance to prove she could run the thing and his father digging in his heels and insisting that only Oliver could do it. Never mind that Oliver absolutely didn't want to do it or that Chloe would do a better job because she actually *liked* the damned rodeo.

"I should've guessed," Renee said, her voice a little shaky. He saw her shoulders rise and fall with a deep breath and then she turned around, her face curiously blank. "I'm sorry I barged in on you," she said, her voice placating. He liked that even less than the fake smile. "Thank you for not calling security on me. It's been good seeing you, Oliver."

This day just got weirder and weirder. She had her hand on the doorknob before he realized that she was waltzing out of his office just as quickly as she had waltzed in.

He moved, reaching the door just as it swung open. He slammed it shut with his hand, causing Renee to squeak. "Wait," he said and then winced as his voice came out in a growl.

He was too close to her. He could feel the warmth of her body radiating through her clothes, through his. He should step back, put some distance between them. She was pregnant, for God's sake. Who knew what else was going on?

Slowly, she turned. Close enough to kiss, he dimly realized as he stared down into her soft blue eyes. She gasped, her eyes darkening as she looked up at him through thick lashes. He was powerless to move away. "Renee," he said, and his voice came out deeper than normal. "Why are you here?"

He wasn't sure what he expected her to do. He wasn't all that surprised when her eyes got a wet look to them—it went with the dress. But then her mouth opened and instead of a sob, a giggle came out. "You don't know," she said, her eyes watering even as she laughed harder. "Oh, God—you really don't know?"

So he was out of the loop on the New York scene. "Know what?" A tear trickled down her cheek and he lifted his other hand to wipe it away. When it was gone, he didn't pull his hand away. He cupped her cheek and kept stroking her skin. It was almost like a hug, right? "What's happened?"

"Oh, nothing," she said, an edge of bitterness creeping into her voice. "It's just…" The giggle ended in a hiccup that sounded suspiciously like a sob. "It was all a lie, wasn't it? My entire life has been a lie."

He caught another tear before it could get far. "I don't understand."

"Don't you? I can't believe you haven't heard." She closed her eyes and he could feel the tension in her body. "They're calling it the Preston Pyramid. My family's investment company was nothing but a pyramid scheme and it's all come crashing down."

How could he *not* know? The collapse of Preston Investment Strategies wasn't just a New York scandal. Renee's father—with the help of her brother and her lying, cheating husband—had bilked hundreds of thousands of investors out of millions of dollars all across the country. She'd thought everyone knew about the Preston Pyramid.

But then again, wasn't that why she was in Dallas instead of New York? She just needed to get away. Away from the reporters camped out in front of her apartment building. Away from the gossip and the threats. She needed to go somewhere where people might not look at her like she was the Antichrist's daughter. And Clint had told her to trust the Lawrence family. He'd said Oliver would take care of her, but Renee was done with people telling her what to do.

Chloe had been her best friend, once upon a time. Chloe never took crap from anyone. Chloe would help her.

Except Chloe wasn't here. Oliver was. And Renee was out of options.

This was how far she'd fallen. Slipping past his executive assistant, barging into his office and doing her level best to keep it together.

Which was hard to do when he was touching her so tenderly. Not that those tender, sweet touches would last when he realized the true magnitude of what had happened. She stared at him as he processed the news. She saw her own emotions reflected in his face. Shock, disbelief—a lot of disbelief. "Your father ran a pyramid scheme? How?"

She shrugged. She should move away from him. He basically had her pinned against the door and was staring down into her face with his intense brown eyes. But he kept stroking her cheek and she couldn't break the contact. It took everything she had not to lean into the touch, not to ask for more.

It had been Clint's wedding, hadn't it? The last time

she'd seen Oliver Lawrence? She remembered Crissy Hagan, another one of the bridesmaids that Renee had thought was a friend until about six weeks ago. Crissy had gushed about how gorgeous Clint's old friend was, but... Renee had blown Crissy off. Oliver wasn't hot—he was irritating. He'd always looked down upon her. He'd been serious and grumpy, even as a kid. He'd never liked her and he'd made it difficult for anyone else to like him. Why he and Clint had got along, she'd never known.

When Renee had found herself next to him at the bar, she'd tried to strike up a conversation by asking about the rodeo. He'd promptly informed her he hated the damned thing in the meanest voice she'd ever heard.

Oliver Lawrence was not someone she could rely on. At least, he hadn't been.

She still didn't know if he was or not.

But Crissy had been right. Oliver had been hot then—and he was hotter now. He was one of those men who was just going to get better looking with age. How old was he? Twenty-eight? Twenty-nine? Clint had turned twenty-nine in jail, so Oliver was around there.

He was not the same boy she remembered. He had four inches on her and he seemed so much...*more* than she remembered from five years ago. Taller, broader. More intense.

Stupid hormones. She was not here to lust after Oliver Lawrence, of all people. She was here to hide.

"Apparently," she said, remembering he had asked a question, "very well. No one caught on for years. Decades. He generated just enough returns that people believed the lies he sold them. Reinvestment, they called it. He convinced everyone to reinvest the profits they made, sometimes investing even more than the original amount. Of course there were no real profits," she said, her emotions rising again. She struggled to keep them in check. "There were never any profits. Not for the investors. It all went to him." She swallowed, forcing herself to look away from Oliver's intensity. "To us. I didn't know anything about it, but there's no denying that I benefited from his schemes. I can't *believe* you haven't heard," she repeated.

Anger and shame burned through her. She was so damned mad at her family—and she hurt for all the people who'd been swindled. Her father had ruined lives so he could buy a fourth vacation home. It was evil, what he'd done.

But worse than that—how could she have gone twenty-six years without realizing that her father was nothing but a glorified con artist?

When Oliver didn't say anything, she glanced back up at him. His jaw was hard and there was something dangerous in his eyes. "Okay," he said. "Your father bilked investors out of a lot of money. I'm going to guess that your brother had something to do with it?"

"Of course." She sighed. "Clint and my husband were both involved."

Abruptly, Oliver stepped back. "I'm sorry I missed your wedding. How long have you been married?"

"I'm not anymore." She took another deep breath and squared her shoulders. She wouldn't let this fact hurt her. She wouldn't let Chet hurt her, not ever again. "Chet Willoughby is dead."

Oliver recoiled another step as if she'd slapped him and then turned and began to pace. "I understand that it is unforgettably rude to ask, but are you..." He waved toward her midsection.

She almost smiled. After the last two months, his apologetic question was the least rude thing she'd heard. "Four and a half months."

Oh, the press had had a field day with that. Preston Pyramid Princess Pregnant! had blared from every newspaper and website for days. *Weeks.* The media loved a good alliterative headline.

Oliver burrowed his fingers in his hair, causing his brown hair to stand up almost on end. "Right. Your family's fortune was stolen, and your husband, who worked for your criminal father, is dead, and he left you pregnant. Am I missing anything?"

The fact that there was no judgment in his voice, no sneering or laughter—that was when Renee realized she'd made the right choice. Even if Chloe wasn't here, getting out of New York was the best thing she could have done. She could breathe in Texas. That's all she wanted. Just enough space to breathe again. "Those are the basics. Oh, my mother took what was left of the money and ran away to Paris. That might be an important detail."

It was an *extremely* important detail to the authorities.

"Yes, I can see how that might be significant." He launched a wobbly smile at her, as if he couldn't tell if he should laugh or not. When she couldn't so much as manage a chuckle, he leaned against his desk and pinched the bridge of his nose.

If she'd had any other options, she wouldn't be here. He'd looked like he was already having a terrible day and that was before she unloaded her tale of woe upon him. Her life wasn't his responsibility.

But she had no place else to go. Getting permission to come to Texas had used all of her remaining political capital.

"Did you know about the scheme?"

She shook her head. "I am fully cooperating with the

investigation. The authorities know where I am and I may be summoned back to New York at any time. I am not allowed to leave the country under any circumstance." That had been the deal. She didn't have much testimony to offer because her parents had maintained that Renee's entire job was to make the family look good. Her appearance was the only thing of value about her. At the time, it had bothered her deeply. How could her own father look at her and see nothing but a pretty face? How could he ignore her and leave her to her mother?

But now? Now she was glad that her father had kept her separate from his business dealings. It was literally the only thing keeping her out of prison.

Her main value to the authorities at this point was convincing her brother to testify against their father. And Clint was in no hurry to do that. He was holding out for a better deal.

Oliver studied her closely, his arms crossed and his hair wild. He stared for so long that she was afraid he was going to kick her out, tell her to go back to New York and deal with this mess by herself. And she couldn't. She just couldn't. If Oliver wouldn't help her, she'd…

She'd go find Chloe. Not for the first time, she wished that her so-called friends in New York hadn't turned on her. Because really, what kind of friends were they? The kind who went running to the gossip websites, eager to spill anything that would make the Preston family look worse than they already did. Not a single one had stood by her. She'd been neatly cut out of her social circle, an object of derision and scorn.

So if Oliver called security, it really wouldn't be that different. She wouldn't blame him at all. She was nothing to him, except maybe a distant childhood memory.

"You need to hide?" he asked just as she had given up hope.

"Yes," she said, her heart beginning to pound faster.

He shook his head and muttered something she didn't catch, something about Clint, maybe? Then he looked at her and said, "I'm sorry about your husband."

One should not speak ill of the dead. It was one of the last things her mother had said to Renee before she'd disappeared with three million dollars of other people's money. But Renee couldn't help the bitter laugh that escaped her. "I'm not."

He thought on that for a moment, his gaze lingering on her stomach. Her skin flushed warm under his gaze. Stupid hormones. Oliver Lawrence was not interested in her. No one in their right mind would give her a second glance.

In fact, it was definitely a mistake that she'd come. She was toxic to everyone and everything surrounding her. Here he was, a good man, and she'd all but thrown herself at his feet.

She was desperate. But she hoped the taint of Preston scandals didn't smear him.

Please don't lie to me, she found herself praying. Even if the truth were brutal—like he was going to throw her out—all she wanted from him was the truth. She couldn't handle another person looking her in the eye and telling a bald-faced lie.

"All right," he said, pushing off the desk and crossing to her. He put his hands on her shoulders, but he didn't draw her in. He just looked at her and even though it was a risk to him for her to be here, she still knew she'd made the right choice—especially when he said, "Let's get you hidden."

Two

He did not have time for this. He was skipping out on important meetings that were guaranteed to draw his father out from his hunting lodge and stick his nose back into Lawrence Energies's business—and for what?

To rescue a damsel in distress. There was no other way to describe Renee. She had one piece of luggage: a carry-on suitcase. That was it. If she was going to be here longer than a week, he was going to need to arrange for her to get some more clothes.

"Is it very far away?" she asked, sounding drained.

He was not a gambling man, but he was willing to bet that Renee was going to be here for much more than a week. "We're going to Red Oak Hill," he told her as they drove away from the Lawrence Energies corporate headquarters on McKinney Avenue and in the opposite direction of his condo on Turtle Creek. "It's my private ranch. The traffic's not too bad this time of day, so we should be there in less than an hour and a half." By Dallas standards, that was practically right next door.

"Oh," she said, slumping down in her seat.

"The way I see it," he said, trying to be pragmatic, "you have two choices. You can either rest on the drive out or you can explain in a little more detail what's going on." Because he thought he had a decent grasp on the basics. Corrupt family, financial ruin, dead husband, four and a half months pregnant.

But a lot of details were missing. He'd told Bailey on his way out to pull up what he could find on the Preston fraud case and send him the links. He'd read them when he got to the ranch. He couldn't help Renee unless he knew what the extenuating circumstances were.

She made an unladylike groaning noise that worried him. "I still can't believe you haven't caught at least some of this on the news."

Worrying about her was pointless. He was doing the best he could, given the situation. Bailey had canceled his meetings for the rest of the day and had been given instructions in case anyone came sniffing around—and that included Milt Lawrence, Oliver's father. No one was to know about Miss Preston or Mrs. Willoughby or Ms. Preston-Willoughby.

"We're acquiring a pump manufacturer, the rodeo season just kicked off and my father is out of his ever-loving mind," Oliver said, trying to keep the conversation lighthearted. "I've been busy."

Besides, none of the Lawrence Energies family fortune was invested in Preston Investment Strategies—or their damned pyramid scheme. And he would know, since he had wrestled financial control of Lawrence Energies away from his father four years ago.

"Is he really?"

Oliver shrugged. "There are days I wonder." His father was only sixty years old—by no means a doddering old man. But the midlife crisis that had been touched off by the death of Trixie Lawrence had never really resolved itself.

He could've explained all about that, but she wasn't here to listen to him complain about his family. She was here because she was in trouble.

Look after Renee, will you?

He should have replied with questions to Clint's email then. If he had, he might have answers now.

He waited. Out of the corner of his eyes, he could see her rubbing her thumbnail with her index finger, the constant circle of motion. Otherwise, she seemed calm.

Too calm.

Oliver did not consider himself the family expert on women. That honor went to Chloe, who was actually a woman—although Flash, their younger brother, gave Chloe a run for her money.

Nevertheless, he had grown up with Chloe and a healthy interest in women. He was not comfortable with the idea of Renee crying, but he was prepared for the worst.

She surprised him with a chuckle. "A lot of it is in the news."

Knowing Bailey, Oliver would have several hours of reading material waiting for him, so there was no point in making her relate something he could just as easily read—with a healthy sense of detachment, instead of listening to her shaky voice and fighting this strange urge to protect her.

"Tell me the part that's not in the news."

"The part that's not in the news," she said softly, still rubbing her thumbnail anxiously. "You know, I don't think my husband was ever faithful to me."

O…kay. "Then why did you marry him?"

"My parents said we looked good together. He worked for my father and my mother thought we'd have gorgeous babies, as if that was the only thing that mattered. He was suave and sophisticated and hot. We were featured on the *Vanity Fair* weddings page online. 'A Storybook Dream' was the name of our photo essay." She laughed, but it definitely wasn't a happy sound. "I wanted a small ceremony, but no. I had to have ten bridesmaids and the craziest party favors ever." He lifted an eyebrow at her without taking his eyes off the road. "Oh, yes. Everyone got a custom engraved pair of Waterford crystal champagne glasses, a bottle of Dom Pérignon with a custom label and a Tiffany & Co. silver ice bucket engraved with our names and wedding date, as if people cared." She sighed heavily.

It wasn't that the elite in Dallas couldn't be just as ostentatious in their displays of wealth—they could. Hell, his condo was worth a few million alone and the ranch was easily worth twice that. Dallas was not a two-bit town by any stretch of the imagination.

But it was different here. As cutthroat as Dallas high society could be, there was just more heart in Texas.

He must have been having one hell of an off day if he was mentally defending this state. He hoped his father never found out that there were things Oliver actually liked about the Lone Star State. "It sounds a tad over-the-top."

"Oh, it was—but it was a beautiful wedding. Just beautiful," she murmured and he remembered what she'd said.

It was a lie. Her husband had never loved her, never been faithful.

"I am *such* an idiot," she said miserably, and that bothered him. Strange how it did. He hadn't thought of her in so long but now that she was here, he found he needed to do something.

"Hardly. You were always smart enough to get the drop on me and Clint, weren't you? I'm thinking of a specific incident involving water balloons off a balcony. Remember?"

That got him a shadow of a smile. "That was Chloe's idea—but I did have pretty good aim."

That shadow of a smile made him feel good. The world was bleak—but he could still make her feel better.

He drove his Porsche Spyder faster, whipping in and out of traffic. The best—and only—thing he could do for her was get her safely out to Red Oak Hill. There, she could have some peace and quiet and, most important, privacy. Once he had her settled, he could get back to town and try to deal with his schedule and his family.

"I don't know if this part is in the news yet or not," she went on, sounding resigned. "I'm sure people have been doing the math ever since I began to show—and I began to show very early, to the disgust of my mother. But do you know?" She paused for a second and Oliver tried to get his head around the fact that her mother was disgusted by her pregnancy. She looked stunning, showing or not.

But that was the sort of thing that he couldn't just blurt out. This was a rescue, sort of. He wasn't whisking her away for a weekend of seduction or anything. Definitely not a seduction. So instead, he just said, "What?"

"He woke me up early that morning and we…" She cleared her throat. "And afterward, he told me he loved me. I normally said it to him—he rarely said the words. Usually he just said, 'Me, too,' as if he also loved himself. But he was different that morning and he surprised me, and I didn't say it back."

This was far more than Oliver wanted to know. He kept his mouth shut like his life depended on it.

"And then he went to work, screwed his secretary, gave her the rest of the day off and blew his brains out, coward that he was. By my count, there were at least three—possibly five—women at the funeral who could have been current or former mistresses."

"That seems like a lot." One would've been too many, but to think that man had had that many women on the side in a year and a half of marriage?

Chet Willoughby was clearly a bastard of the highest order. Or he had been anyway.

"And the thing was I didn't even know I was pregnant for another two and a half months. When I missed my period, I thought it was due to the stress. Isn't that hilarious?"

She turned to him and he glanced over to see a huge, fake smile on her face. "Not really."

Her smile froze. "Some people think it is. Some people think it's the funniest thing they've ever heard. That I'm getting exactly what I deserve. There's also a lot of speculation that I was cheating on him and drove him to his death." Her voice cracked.

His heart damn near broke for her. "Those people are heartless cowards." It was a good thing that Chet Willoughby and his suave face were already dead because otherwise, Oliver would've strangled the man himself. What kind of asshole did this to his wife?

"He knew the pyramid was going to fall and he was going to go with it. My mother tried to paint this as a noble thing. He wouldn't turn on my father. Wasn't that thoughtful of him? Not like Clint's going to, maybe. And the baby?" She shook her head. "She said the baby would be a living reminder of Chet. As if I want to remember him or his betrayal," she finished bitterly.

She was crying, he realized. Softly, quietly—but tears were trickling down her cheeks.

He didn't want to know how everyone she'd ever trusted had betrayed her. Even Clint, who Oliver had thought was a good guy. It was physically painful to know that she was hurting and, worse, to not be able to do much of anything about it.

"I don't think your child would be a reminder of betrayal," he said, feeling his way as he went. "I'd think that the baby would be a testament to your strength, your courage. Others may have cut and run, but you stood strong, Renee. That's what's going to make you an amazing mother."

She gasped and he could tell she was staring at him with huge eyes. He kept his gaze firmly locked on the road in front of him. "Do you really think so?"

He nodded like he was certain, instead of shooting compliments like arrows and praying to hit the mark. "You're welcome to stay at Red Oak Hill as long as you want," he went on. Because, aside from a lucky compliment or two, shelter was the only thing he could offer her. "I'm usually only there on the weekends. I do have a housekeeper, but I can give her some time off if you'd rather be alone."

She nodded, surreptitiously swiping at the tears on her cheeks. "Will anyone else in your family be there?"

Oliver laughed. "Absolutely not. Red Oak Hill is mine. No one will know you're there."

"Thank you," she whispered and there was so much pain in her voice that, without thinking, he reached over and wrapped his hand around hers. She clung to him fiercely. "You won't even know I'm there, I promise."

Somehow, as his fingers tangled with hers, Oliver doubted that.

It would be impossible to be around Renee and not be aware of her every movement.

As soon as he got her settled, he was driving right back to Dallas. He didn't have time to comfort Renee Preston-Willoughby.

No matter how much he might want to.

Three

Renee had not expected this. Red Oak Hill wasn't a long, low-slung ranch house in the middle of dusty cow pastures. In fact, she didn't see any cows anywhere as Oliver pulled up in front of what was undeniably a grand mansion at the top of a small hill. Towering trees she assumed were red oaks cast long shadows against the sweltering Texas sun.

The house looked like something out of a magazine. And she knew quite a bit about that. Something white caught her attention on the small lake on the other side of the driveway. "Are those…swans?"

"Fred and Wilma? Yes. They came with the house."

Renee had had a terrible day. Well, given the last five months of her life, that wasn't saying much. But somehow, the idea that Oliver had inherited a pair of swans made her giggle. "Did you name them after the Flintstones or did they come with those names?"

He quirked an eyebrow at her. "Don't know if you can

really name swans, per se. They don't come when called. But…" He shrugged again, a mischievous glimmer in his eyes. "They seemed like Fred and Wilma to me. They have cygnets this year. Pebbles and Bamm-Bamm."

She didn't remember Oliver having a sense of humor. Had he always been this funny? She remembered him being uptight and grumpy. A stick-in-the-mud, she and Chloe had decided once. That was Oliver Lawrence.

But was he, really? She thought back now to the water balloon fight he'd mentioned. She and Chloe had got the drop on them from the balcony—that'd been Chloe's idea. But Oliver and Clint had retaliated with a garden hose. And Oliver had been aiming the hose.

"Renee? You all right?"

She blinked and realized that he was standing at the passenger door of his sporty red convertible, hand out and waiting for her.

His lips curved into a small smile when she realized she was staring at him. Oh, heavens—she was probably making a fool of herself. Then again, that was nothing new. "I don't know." It was the most honest thing she'd said in so long…but somehow, she knew she didn't have to put on a brave face for him.

"Here." Taking both of her hands in his, he helped her from the low-slung car. But instead of letting go of her or stepping back, he stayed where he was. Close enough to touch. "I got an email from your brother a couple of months ago," he said, staring down into her eyes. "All it said was to look after you. Renee, I'm sorry I didn't follow up. If I had realized…"

She didn't know whether to laugh or cry. Oliver Lawrence was *apologizing*. To her! She didn't need his apologies, but all the same, she felt something in her chest loosen. Everyone else had abandoned her. But this man—

an old acquaintance, a childhood friend at best—was sorry that he hadn't got to her sooner.

Or was this one of those things people said to smooth over the unpleasant truths? Was he saying this because he meant it or because it was a cover?

God, she hoped it was real. She blinked hard and wondered at this strange urge to throw her arms around his neck and lean into his touch. Would he hug her back? Would he wrap his arms around her and press her against his chest? Would the heat of his body reach her through her clothes and the ironclad armor she hid behind?

Or would he stand there stiffly for a moment and then disentangle himself as politely as possible to protect her feelings? She didn't know.

Just then, one of the swans—Wilma, she decided—made a weird whooping noise that broke the moment. "Let me show you around," he said, releasing her hands and getting her luggage out of the car.

She turned to look back at the mansion. There was no other word for it. Three and a half stories of warm red brick welcomed her to Red Oak Hill. On this side, a huge wraparound porch of pristine white wood faced the lake. Trellises of yellow roses ran up the side of the wraparound porch, their sweet fragrance filling the air with every breeze.

The Preston real estate, like everything of value the family had owned, now belonged to the feds. She supposed, once all the trials were over and the sentences had been handed down, the properties and jewels and art would all be sold at auction and the money returned to the investors her family had scammed. It wouldn't be enough, but she certainly didn't have a spare billion or so lying around.

She hadn't even kept her wedding ring. They'd offered to let her hold on to the three-carat diamond in a princess setting—for now anyway—but Renee had been happy to hand it over. It had never stood for love and honor. All it'd been was another lie. Hopefully, however much they could get for that ring would help make things right.

The entrance hall of the mansion gleamed with warm polished wood—red, of course. The sweeping staircase led up to the second floor. The doorway on the right led to what appeared to be Oliver's office, with a massive desk in the center of the room and rich brown leather sofas arranged around the Persian rug.

He gave her a brief tour and started up the stairs but then he stopped and waited for her. "Doing all right?"

In that moment, Renee wished she hadn't come. Yes, Oliver was being a perfect gentleman—and a surprisingly compassionate friend. Yes, this mansion by a pond with a pair of swans was the perfect place to hide.

But she couldn't shake the feeling that she'd put Oliver at risk by coming here. She'd done nothing wrong, but her name was ruined and everything she did—everything she touched—was tainted by the sins of her family and her husband.

She didn't want to do anything that might hurt Oliver or Chloe. She didn't want to hurt anyone anymore.

"Renee?" He came back down the stairs and stood before her. When he lifted his hand and cupped her cheek, she knew she should pull away. It wasn't right to let him care for her.

It wasn't right to care for him.

"I'm sorry," she said. Sorry for all of it.

"It's been a long day," he said, misunderstanding. And, fool that she was, she wasn't strong enough to correct him. "Let me show you to your room. You need to rest."

And even though she knew she shouldn't, she leaned into his touch and asked, "Will you be here when I wake up?"

His thumb caressed her cheek so tenderly that she had to close her eyes. When was the last time someone had touched her like they cared? Chet Willoughby had not been capable of tenderness unless it benefited him directly. Nothing about her presence here benefited Oliver, directly or indirectly. She was nothing but a risk. And yet he was still being kind to her.

She almost exhaled in relief when his hand fell away, breaking that connection. But then he set down her suitcase and the next thing she knew, she was cradled in his arms. "I've got you," he said as he carried her up the stairs. "It's all right. I've got you."

All she could do was rest her head against his shoulder. It wasn't all right. It might never be okay ever again.

But right now, he had her.

And that was good enough.

Somehow, Oliver got Renee's heels off her feet and her legs swung up onto the bed without thinking about her bare skin against his palms too much. He couldn't get her under the covers, so he laid her on the bed, where she promptly curled on her side and shut her eyes.

Blankets. He hurried into the next room and grabbed the coverlet off the bed. By the time he made it back, she was breathing deeply and her face had relaxed.

He tucked the blanket around her shoulders, pausing only when she sighed in her sleep. But she didn't stir.

He could feel his phone vibrating in his pocket—he left the sound off because the chimes interrupted his thinking. Bailey was undoubtedly forwarding him news articles. Oliver should get some work done. He'd need to smooth ruffled feathers from canceling his meetings this afternoon.

Especially the one with Herb Ritter. Ritter had been in business with Lawrence Energies for close to thirty years. He was mean and crotchety and, unfortunately, a damned good oilman. And he'd been Milt Lawrence's best friend ever since the Lawrence family had relocated to Texas, which only made things worse. It was bad enough he had to manage his father, but also dealing with Ritter felt like a punishment. And the hell of it was Oliver had no idea what he'd done to deserve it.

He'd kept his promise to his mother. He ran the family business and kept his father from going completely off the deep end and Chloe as much in the loop as he could and Flash—well, no one could tell Flash a damned thing. Oliver managed the damned rodeo instead of doing something for himself. Even if he wasn't sure what that *something* might be anymore.

He did his job and kept his word. Wasn't that enough? Would it ever be enough?

But even this urgency wasn't enough to pull Oliver away from Renee's bedside.

God, she was beautiful. Tired and worried and pregnant, but beautiful all the same. He wished he could go back to Clint's wedding all those years ago. If only he'd struck up a conversation. If he had reconnected with her then, maybe he would've been able to spare her some of this heartbreak.

He brushed a strand of hair away from her forehead.

His phone vibrated again. Crap. He leaned forward and brushed the lightest of kisses against her cheek before he forced himself to walk away.

He had eighteen emails waiting for him by the time he got rid of his tie, grabbed a beer and sat down at his desk. The cold, heartless truth was that he did not have the time to take care of Renee Preston-Willoughby. He was running a major oil company, overseeing expansions into solar, wind and hydropower—expansions that he had fought his father for and finally won. And the damned All-Stars had just kicked off.

Business that required his full attention.

Will you be here when I wake up?

That heartfelt plea was the only reason why he was sitting in his office at the ranch instead of heading right back to his office in downtown Dallas.

She had asked.

This was only until she was settled in, he reasoned. She hadn't even seen the kitchen yet. He wasn't comfortable leaving her, not until he was sure she would be all right. He couldn't abandon her.

So he would stay.

Two hours later, Oliver had a much better grasp on the Renee situation.

It was a hell of a mess. Preston Investment Strategies was accused of bilking investors out of over forty-five billion dollars over the course of twenty years. Renee's father, Darin Preston, had been in jail for the last two months, unable to make bail since his wife had run off with the remaining money. Clinton Preston was also in jail, although it appeared that negotiations for his testimony and a lighter sentence were ongoing. Chet Willoughby, Preston's son-in-law, had committed suicide four and a half months ago. It didn't appear that the public had made the connection between that suicide and the pyramid scheme until Clint and his father had been arrested, along with most of the other people who worked at Preston Investment Strategies.

Bailey was thorough in his research. In addition to articles from the *Wall Street Journal*, *Business Insider* and *CNNMoney*, he also forwarded articles from the *New York Post* and even the *Daily News*. Those articles were filled with sly quotes from friends and acquaintances, all taking swipes at Renee and her mother. It only got worse after Renee's mother disappeared. It seemed there was an open debate as to whether or not Renee knew that her family was corrupt or if she'd been too dim to figure it out. Either way, the pieces were not flattering. Neither were the pictures posted with them. Awful paparazzi shots, catching her with red eyes, making her look far more pregnant and jiggly than she was in real life.

Disgusted, he stopped reading the articles because they were only pissing him off. How the hell had this happened? How had Darin Preston managed to get away with this pyramid scheme for this long? How had Clint— a guy Oliver knew was a good guy—allowed himself to be sucked down to these levels? It didn't make sense. None of it did.

His phone buzzed insistently. He picked it up—hell. His father was calling.

"Yeah, Dad?" Oliver said, closing the windows on all of the information Bailey had sent him.

"You done pissed off Herb Ritter, boy," his father drawled in a thick Texas accent. "I thought you knew better than to do that."

Oliver rolled his eyes. His father had been born and raised in New York City, although his family did come from Texas. Oliver's grandfather Mitchell had abandoned Texas when Lawrence Oil Industries—the forerunner to Lawrence Energies—had made him a multimillionaire.

Milt had lived in New York full-time until he was in his forties. Before thirteen years ago, he spent no more than a few weeks in the fall in Texas every year. The Lawrence family had maintained a house here for tax purposes and because this was where Lawrence Energies was based—but his father was *not* a Texan.

He sure liked to pretend he was, though. "I've made my apologies to Ritter," Oliver said, keeping his voice level. "We've already rescheduled the meeting."

"That's not going to be good enough."

Oliver gritted his teeth and decided to change the subject before this call devolved into a shouting match. "Dad, have you heard about Darin Preston?"

Milt was silent for a moment. "That con man? I never did trust his get-rich-quick schemes." He paused, making a low humming noise in the back of his throat. He always did that when he was thinking. "Wasn't he in the news recently?"

"He was." Oliver didn't want to tell Milt that Renee was asleep upstairs. He had promised her privacy, after all.

It was the only thing he could promise her.

"Why do you ask?"

Oliver decided to hedge the truth. "I had a strange message from Clint. It seemed he was helping his father scam people."

"Now, that's too danged bad," Milt said. "Clint was good people. And his sister—what was her name?"

"Renee."

"Yeah, Renee. She and Chloe got along real well. Trixie…" He paused and cleared his throat. Oliver knew that his father's eyes were watering, not that he would ever admit to it. Even after all these years, the mention of his beloved wife choked Milt up. "She thought the sun rose and set on Renee. She used to take the girls shopping. Always made sure to include that girl whenever she could. Hell, she always included Clint when she could. But she had a soft spot for Renee." He hummed again. "Your mother, God rest her soul, didn't think too highly of Rebecca and Darin Preston. And you know she was an excellent judge of character."

Oliver considered this. He honestly had no memories of his mother doting on Renee. But then again, it did seem like the little girl had always been underfoot, hanging out with Chloe and plotting how next to irritate Oliver and Clint.

The Preston kids had eaten a lot of meals at the Lawrence table—and Oliver didn't remember going over to Clint's house very much. Hardly at all, actually. There'd been a few times he and Clint had sneaked into Clint's house to get some trading cards or the latest video games...but they always sneaked right back out and high-tailed it to Oliver's house.

It hadn't struck him as odd then. But what if it'd been more than that? Clint had told him they had to be quiet— no, not quiet, but *silent*. He hadn't wanted his mother to know they were in the house. No noise and no touching anything.

Looking back now, Oliver had to wonder—had Clint been afraid of his mother?

"I read that Mrs. Preston ran off to Europe with the rest of the money."

"Hell. What a family, eh? The Preston kids were good kids, but there's only so much a kid can do when they're raised in a pit of vipers. It's a shame that they got caught up in this. At least you had your mother and me. For a while anyway." He cleared his throat again.

It was a damned shame. "I did. We all did." Most days, dealing with his Tex-ified father left Oliver frustrated and bitter. But it was true. Before Trixie Lawrence's death,

Oliver had loved his parents. Both of them. For fifteen years, the Lawrence family had been happy and healthy and stable. Not everyone had that.

He'd promised his mother that he'd take care of his family. They may not be as happy or as stable—thank God they were all healthy—but at least they hadn't all been arrested and indicted. That had to count for something.

But it wasn't enough for his father. It never was. When Milt spoke again, Oliver could hear the forced cheer.

"Have you finished negotiations with ESPN about running the All-Stars?"

"I had to reschedule that meeting today. Something came up." And unlike Herb Ritter, Oliver was in no hurry to get back to this one. "You should let Chloe take the meeting. She'd do a great job."

"She's the Princess of the Rodeo and she's doing that clothing line," Milt reminded him, as if Oliver could ever forget. "I don't want that Pete Wellington anywhere near her."

Oliver rolled his eyes. He didn't like Pete Wellington any more than his father did but the man was too much a born-and-bred cowboy to ever lay a hand on a woman. As evidenced by the fact that he hadn't killed any members of the Lawrence family yet. And he'd had plenty of opportunity. "He wouldn't hurt her."

Not for the first time, Oliver considered signing a minority stake in the rodeo back over to the Wellington family. It'd been their damn rodeo before Pete's father, Davy, had lost it in that poker game. Pete had never forgiven either his father or Milt. Which meant he bore one hell of a grudge against anyone with the Lawrence last name. Oliver would be more than happy to cede a little control of the All-Stars back to Pete. Hell, if Oliver thought it would help, he'd just outright hire Pete to run the damn thing.

The only problem was Pete's pride wouldn't settle for merely working for the All-Stars. He maintained Milt Lawrence had stolen the All-Stars and he wanted it back. All or nothing.

Which meant he got nothing. Funny how winning here felt a lot like losing. "Chloe would be great in the meeting." She'd have the marketing team eating out of her hand and they both knew it.

As usual, though, Milt ignored Oliver. "She's already doing her part. You make sure you do yours." With the final *hmph*, Milt hung up.

The rodeo was good for the business, Oliver repeated silently, just like he did every single time he had to deal with the damn thing. The All-Around All-Stars Rodeo was 60 percent of their marketing and had been consistently in the black for the last six years.

That didn't mean Oliver had to like it.

He pushed the All-Stars out of his mind and focused on the problem at hand. He didn't have to like anything about the Renee situation. He wasn't enjoying this trip down memory lane, where he couldn't remember if his mother had taken Renee under her wing or not. Hell, for that matter, he still hadn't recalled how Renee knew he hated the rodeo.

He *hated* not knowing. Starting from a place of ignorance—about his childhood memories of the Preston kids, about the Preston Pyramid scam, about the woman currently upstairs in bed—that was how bad decisions got made. No matter how the saying went, ignorance was not bliss. It was disaster. And he was tired of this day feeling like a runaway train about to crash into the station.

He couldn't get off this train and continue to let it barrel down on Renee like everyone else had. Her brother and father? They hadn't so much abandoned her as they'd been taken into federal custody. But her husband, her mother—hell, even her friends—all had. No one had stood by her.

He couldn't add himself to that long, long list. Not when he thought back to the way he'd coaxed a small smile out of her when he'd told her the names of his swans. Not when she'd looked at him, trying so hard to be strong, and asked if he'd still be here when she woke up.

Not when his own father remembered Renee as a little girl who'd needed a friend.

Something had to give. He hit the number for Chloe. "What?" she said, sounding breathless.

"And good afternoon to you, too. Listen," Oliver said, bracing himself for the lie. He was not naturally good at deception. "You get to deal with ESPN. The contract negotiations are yours."

There was a pause on the other end of the line. "Is this a joke? Because it's not funny, Oliver," she snapped. "You know Dad would never let me do anything beyond carry the flag."

"No joke," he assured her. "Consider it a…" His mind scrambled for a reasonable explanation that wasn't simply *I don't have time for this.* "A test run. You do a good job on this, and we'll give you more responsibilities. Because I think the rodeo should be yours." That, at least, wasn't a lie.

"And Dad agreed to this?" she asked, doubt heavy in her voice.

That was the problem with Chloe. She was too perceptive for her own good. "He wants the deal done." He hedged. "He wants to see how you handle this and the clothing line."

It'd been Chloe's idea to capitalize on her popularity as the Princess of the Rodeo by launching an eponymous clothing line. She'd been overseeing the development of jeans, tailored T-shirts and sequined tops with the intent of launching with this year's rodeo season. So far, so good.

But could she keep up that success and handle high-level negotiations? God, Oliver hoped so.

She was quiet and Oliver wondered if she'd say no. If she did, Oliver was screwed. "You're sure this isn't a joke?"

He was surprised at how young she sounded. "Chloe, you know I don't have a sense of humor."

"Ha. Ha. Fine." She blew out a long breath. "I can do this, you know."

"I know. I'll forward you the information and let the ESPN people know you're handling the account from here on out. And Chloe?"

"Yeah?"

He almost told her Renee was upstairs and maybe Chloe could come home for girlfriend time so he could get back to work? But at the last second, Renee's face floated before him again, a single tear tracing down her cheek. He remembered the way her skin had felt under his hands as he'd wiped that tear away.

Renee needed him. Chloe needed to prove herself with the rodeo. And maybe it was wrong or selfish, but Oliver would rather help Renee than negotiate a TV distribution deal. Besides, all he needed to do for Renee was get her settled and see what he could do to help her out. How hard could that be?

He'd keep Renee's presence here a secret just a little bit longer. He told Chloe, "Keep an eye out for Pete Wellington. Dad's concerned he's going to pull something."

"Oh, wonderful. There's nothing I love more than unspecified threats from disgruntled cowboys." Oliver heard something in her tone beyond annoyance. But before he could figure out what that was, Chloe went on, "Fine. Anything else?"

"And keep Flash out of trouble," he added, because that was what he always asked her to do. Not that it ever worked. No one could keep that man on the straight and narrow.

"You're up to something," she said, but he could hear the smile in her voice. "And when I find out what it is, you're gonna pay." With that parting shot, she hung up.

He looked at the clock on the wall. It was already three thirty. He had no idea how long Renee was going to rest but there was no shot in hell of him making it back to the office during the workday at this point.

She needs a friend. Oddly, the little voice that whispered this in his mind wasn't his own or even Chloe's—it was his mother's.

Renee was not family. She wasn't grandfathered under the long-ago deathbed promise Oliver had made. He didn't *have* to take care of her.

And yet...

She needs a friend.

Had Trixie Lawrence said that once upon a time, perhaps when Oliver had complained about how much Renee and Chloe were bugging him and Clint?

He didn't know. But one thing was clear. If he didn't do his level best to help Renee out of this situation, his mother would be disappointed in him. Or she would've been anyway.

He stared at nothing in particular and then made up his mind. If he was going to get to the truth of the matter, he had to go straight to the source. He hit his lawyer's number. "Miles? It's Oliver. I need—"

"No, no—let me guess. Did you finally strangle your father? Or your brother? I've got twenty bucks riding on the answer," Miles Hall replied with a laugh.

"Neither." Oliver shouldn't be doing this, shouldn't be doing any of this. Funny how that wasn't stopping him. "I need to talk to Clinton Preston. He's in jail in New York City on fraud charges for—"

"The Preston Pyramid guy?"

He scowled. Did everyone know about the scam but him? Sheesh. He'd have to have Bailey add "major scandals involving people I used to know" to his morning news briefs. "Yeah. Well, the son anyway. I need to talk to him on the phone. Can you make it happen?"

Miles was quiet for a moment. "Give me thirty."

"Thanks."

Clint had a hell of a lot to answer for. Starting with why he'd helped his father steal that much money and ending with why he'd asked Oliver to look after Renee.

Then, once Oliver had his answers and made sure Renee was comfortable and safe, he could get back to work.

But the thought of making Renee comfortable, of carrying her back to bed and this time, staying with her…

Hell. He definitely had to get back to Dallas tonight.

Four

Renee came awake slowly. It was so quiet here. New York was never quiet. There was always someone shouting, horns honking, sirens blaring. A person could barely think in New York City.

She couldn't remember the last time she'd slept so deeply. Usually, it was because terrible nightmares woke her up every few hours, panting and crying. Right now, she felt surprisingly calm. She wouldn't go so far as to say peaceful, but she was thrilled with calm.

A *thunk* from somewhere below her finally got her eyes open. She started when she focused her eyes on the clock. Was it four thirty already? She had been asleep for hours. She needed to get up and…do something. What, she had no idea.

But it wasn't like her to laze the day away. Even back when she'd been little more than a trophy wife, she'd still kept busy. She'd been on the boards of several charities, including her favorite, One Child, One World. She liked helping kids but…since the Preston Pyramid collapsed, she'd resigned from all those boards rather than taint their good works with her family's scandals.

Which left her at loose ends. But it was fine. No one was missing her in New York, that was for sure. This was part of her plan to hide in Texas. If she wanted to nap, she would nap, by God.

She tossed back a blanket and forced herself from bed. It was tempting to go right back to sleep, but…

Oliver had said he would wait for her to wake up.

She was hungry and she had to pee. She stretched, trying to get the kinks out of her shoulders. Over a dresser there was a large mirror and she recoiled in horror when she caught sight of her reflection. Her hair was lopsided and her makeup had not survived the nap. Plus, her dress was wrinkled horribly, and besides, it really wasn't very comfortable.

But her lawyer had recommended that, if she went out in public, she maintain a somber, mourning appearance. It wouldn't do anyone any favors if she were seen looking frivolous or, God forbid, *happy*. Not that there was a lot of risk of that, but Renee understood the point.

Her entire life had been about keeping up appearances. The bereft widow, the horrified daughter—they were all just another role to slip into.

She tore the dress off and kicked it under the bed. She couldn't wear it for another moment, couldn't maintain the fiction that she mourned her husband.

She looked around the room. Had she fainted? She didn't remember coming into this room. She only remembered… Oliver's arms around her, holding her close. His deep voice rumbling in her ear, although she couldn't remember the words. A light touch on her forehead, then her cheek. The smell of his cologne.

She remembered feeling safe and cared for. That was all she needed.

But this was a nice room. There was a small sitting area with a low coffee table—her bag was on it. The love seat ran along one wall and a fancy desk that looked like it belonged in the parlor instead of a guest room was on the other side. The walls were a pale green and the bedding was pristine white. It was calm and peaceful and reminded her of a garden in the early-morning sun.

She took a deep breath and let it out slowly. She could breathe here.

She dug into her bag. Along with her wedding ring, she had left most of her couture and designer clothing for the feds. Her wardrobe had been worth hundreds of thousands of dollars—but it had been just another prop in her never-ending role as the adoring wife, the picture-perfect daughter. She was tired of living that lie.

She dug out leggings and a slouchy tunic. This was her normal outfit for yoga classes—but it was forgiving enough that she could still wear it comfortably. She might even get several more months out of the top. She'd love to take her bra off because the damned thing barely fitted anymore and sleeping in it had not been a good idea. But the thin, creamy cotton of her shirt wouldn't hide anything from anyone. Especially Oliver.

A chill raced over her and her nipples tightened, which was exactly why she had to keep the bra on. She really hoped Oliver wasn't involved with someone else. But the moment that thought crossed her mind, she scowled at herself in the mirror. Okay, he was amazingly hot. And yes, he was being really sweet to her. That didn't mean there was any mutual attraction here and even if there was, what was she going to do? Seduce him? Please. She was the hottest of hot messes and almost five months pregnant.

Fine. It was settled. No seduction. At least…not on her end anyway.

Purposefully *not* thinking of what Oliver might do if she paraded around braless, she used the en suite bathroom and fixed her hair and face, opting for a simple ponytail and just enough under-eye concealer to hide the worst of the dark circles. When she was done, she took stock again.

She looked not-quite-so-pregnant in her loungewear and the nap had helped a lot. She didn't look like the woman she'd been six months ago. The salon-perfect hair was gone, as was the expertly contoured foundation. And she could see the pregnancy weight rounding out her face and her arms. Her mother had called her fat right before she'd run to Paris.

No, Renee was not the same woman she'd been six months ago. Was that such a bad thing? She'd been a mannequin then. Someone to be seen and coveted but not heard. The problem was, she wasn't quite sure who she was now.

She wouldn't allow her voice to be silenced again. As she stroked her stomach, she made a promise to herself and her child—she would do better. Better than her mother. Better than Renee herself had been. She'd be… someone like Oliver's mother. Renee would be the fun mom who made cookies with her child and friends or took them for ice cream in the park. Whether she had a boy who liked fashion or a girl who played soccer, it didn't matter. Just so long as Renee was a better mom. A better woman.

She dabbed at her eyes. Stupid hormones. If there was one thing she'd learned growing up, it was how to keep her emotions on lockdown to avoid getting into trouble. But suddenly she was pregnant and hiding and she couldn't keep her stupid eyes from watering stupidly. Gah.

Besides, there was no need to get teary now. She had a long way to go before tea parties and sports. She had to start being this new, improved woman before the baby got here and it wasn't likely to happen in the bathroom. She needed something to eat and… Well, food first. Plans second.

Quietly, she made her way downstairs, listening hard for the sounds of people. A low hum seemed to be coming out of Oliver's study. He was talking to someone, she realized—probably on the phone. A wave of relief swept over her. He'd made a promise to her and he'd kept it— even if it was an inconsequential promise to hang around for a few hours. He'd still kept it.

Guilt wasn't far behind. She'd pulled him away from a workday. He was probably trying to get caught up. She shouldn't interrupt him. He'd said the kitchen was in the back of the house, right? She should go.

But then, in a voice that was more of a shout than a whisper, Oliver clearly said, "You are, without a doubt, the most vile, abhorrent, morally bankrupt *idiot* I have ever had the misfortune to know and that's saying something. You know that, right? I mean, what the hell were you thinking, Clint?"

Renee stumbled to a stop. Eavesdropping was not exactly on the moral up-and-up, but was he talking to her *brother*? How the hell had he pulled that off?

She moved to stand just on the other side of the door to his study. There were some pictures here, so she pretended to look at them. But really, her entire attention was focused on one half of the phone conversation happening in the next room.

"Yeah, she's here. What the hell, man? You send me a one-line email with no other explanation, no other context—no, I didn't know your entire family had crashed and burned. I'm busy!" This time, he was shouting. "I have my own family to manage, my own business to run—a business that does not steal money from investors! So you'll excuse me if I haven't kept up with all the ways you've destroyed your life!"

A wave of nausea roiled her stomach and she didn't think it was morning sickness.

"No, I know." He said this in a weary voice, and Renee honestly couldn't tell if it was better or worse than him shouting. "Yeah, she told me. How could you let her marry someone like that?"

Renee bristled. Her brother was not her keeper. She was a grown woman capable of making her own decisions and her own mistakes, thank you very much.

That, however, hadn't stopped her from wondering the exact same thing a hundred times over the last few months. Clint had known who Chet was. They'd both worked for her father for several years before the wedding. And yet her own brother had done nothing to warn her that she was marrying a serial cheater and a con artist.

It was hard not to be bitter when there was so much to be bitter about. Growing up, she and Clint had stuck together. So much of her childhood had been the kids against the parents. Even when they'd fought—and they *had* fought—they'd still protected each other from the icy punishment of their mother and the casual neglect of their father.

But when she'd really needed her brother, he hadn't been there for her.

Instead, it was Oliver who was mad on her behalf. Oliver who was defending her.

"That's a shitty excuse and you know it," Oliver snapped. "She trusted you. Your investors trusted you. Hell, I trusted you. And you did nothing to earn it... No,

I'm not going to take it out on her. I'm not a monster, unlike some people I know… Yes," he said, sounding defeated. "She did? I thought you two were going to go the distance. But I guess she couldn't live being married to a snake oil salesman." Another pause. "Renee really didn't know, did she?… I didn't think so. Look, I said I'd take care of her and I meant it. Enjoy your time in jail, buddy."

Renee sagged against the door frame as relief pushed back against the nausea. Oliver believed she hadn't been a part of the scheme. He understood, at least on some level, how badly the betrayal by her family had hurt her.

She shouldn't have come here. She shouldn't have listened to the phone call, either. She didn't want to put Oliver at risk for being a decent human being to an old friend and she didn't want to put either of them in a position where he felt like he had to lie to her.

But she was so glad she was here.

"Renee? Will you come in here?"

She jumped, her heart racing. Had he known she was listening the entire time? Oh, heavens. *Busted.*

She swallowed and felt her face go pleasantly blank, felt her shoulders square up and her chin lift. The reactions were hard-wired at this point and she was helpless to stop them.

With one final deep breath for courage, she stepped into the study.

And stumbled to a stop.

Oliver was leaning against his desk, his ankles crossed and his arms folded in front of his chest. He looked very much like he had earlier—had it only been this morning?

But the differences. Oh, the differences! He'd lost his suit jacket and his tie. His white button-up shirt was now open at the neck and he had cuffed the sleeves, revealing strong forearms. And strangely enough, he was barefoot.

Oh, dear God. He'd made business professional look good but he was making casual look positively sinful. Her mouth went dry and for a moment, she forgot how to speak.

Then everything got worse and better at the same time because he notched an eyebrow at her at the same time the corner of his mouth curved up into a smile, revealing a dimple she didn't remember being there before. Had she ever really seen him smile like that? He was so impossibly gorgeous that her mouth disconnected from her brain, and she blurted out, "I wasn't listening," like an idiot because obviously she had been.

That got his other eyebrow in on the action. But instead of calling her on her juvenile defense, his gaze swept over her. Her skin flushed as he took in her shirt, her leggings, her own bare feet. When he lifted his eyes, Renee could tell that, even from across the room, they were darker, more intense.

Was it hot in here or was it just her?

"I see the nap did wonders for you," he said, his voice low and serious and nothing like how he had sounded on the phone with Clint.

It was broiling in here. She was starting to sweat. "I hope you don't mind that I changed into something more comfortable. Since I have no plans on going back out into public today. Or tomorrow," she finished lamely.

"Or even the day after that?" he teased, pushing off the desk and coming to stand in front of her.

Renee knew not to show fear. Showing guilt was even worse. She had trained herself to keep her head up and her eyes open, no matter what cutting comments or terrifying punishments her mother had decreed.

But this was Oliver. Serious, grumpy, stick-in-the-mud Oliver. And he was smiling down at her, warmth and humor in his face and maybe just a little concern as he said, "My house is yours for as long as you need it. I want you to be comfortable here. I want you to be yourself," as he settled his hands on her shoulders.

Wonderful. Her eyes were watering *and* she was sweating. Maybe she should've stayed in bed a little longer. "Do you know—" and she was horrified to hear her voice waver "—that no one has ever wanted me to just be myself?"

His smile faded. But then his thumbs began to rub little circles on her shoulders and she didn't know if she was getting closer to him or if he was getting closer to her. Maybe they were both moving, drawn together by strange circumstances and an even stranger attraction.

Whatever it was, she found herself in his arms, her breasts pressed against his chest, her chin tucked in the crook of his neck—and her bare toes brushing his. The contact felt shockingly intimate, and for a moment, she forgot how to breathe.

It wasn't right, how much she sank into his touch. It certainly wasn't proper, the way she wrapped her arms around his waist and held on as if her life depended on it.

"I'm sorry I eavesdropped," she muttered against the collar of his shirt. "And I'm sorry I lied about it. I'm… still getting used to honesty." It didn't sound any less lame, but at least it was the truth.

"It's all right," he said softly, and one hand began to rub her lower back in small, delicious circles of relief that made her sigh.

"How did you know I was listening?" She'd thought she'd been quiet. But not quite enough, apparently.

"I heard you get up. I'm sorry you heard me call your brother a vile idiot."

"Even if he deserved it?"

Oliver chuckled, a rich sound that rumbled out of his chest. "Especially if he deserved it." He leaned back and Renee looked up at him. This close, she could see the flecks of gold in his brown eyes like hidden treasure. Something in her chest tightened as he stroked the finger over her cheek and down her chin. "Renee…"

She held her breath. God, she needed…something. She needed to hear the truth.

But then again, what was the truth here? She was naive and gullible at best? Complicit? An idiot, vile or otherwise?

She'd work on facing the truth soon. Tomorrow. Right now, she desperately changed the subject. "Thank you for being here when I woke up."

"I gave you my word. I keep my promises."

She shouldn't, but she couldn't help herself. She buried her face against his shoulder and automatically, his arms tightened around her. "That's…that's good to know," she mumbled against the collar of his shirt. "Not everyone does that."

"I'm not everyone."

Thank God. But she didn't say it out loud. Instead, she said, "Now what?"

"Hmm." She could hear the steady thrum of his heart-beat. That was what made him safe.

But what made him dangerous was the way his body began to rock almost imperceptibly, pulling her along into a rhythm. What made her weak was the way his hand splayed out against the small of her back, pushing her into his solid chest.

Her nipples went painfully hard and given how very little separated him from her, she was sure he could feel those hard points against his chest. Her cheeks flushed and she shivered at unbidden images of her in Oliver's arms, but with far less clothing and far more moving.

Oliver was everything and nothing she needed right now. She absolutely was not thinking about sex, especially not with him. She still hadn't determined if he was involved with anyone else, for crying out loud! She wasn't interested and she wasn't looking to get lucky. End of story.

Good lord, it was hot in here.

And he still hadn't answered her question. That *hmm* didn't count, especially not when she was breathing in the scent of his cologne—something light and spicy and warm that smelled perfect on him.

Then, so slowly she almost missed it, he began to pull away. His arms loosened around her chest and he leaned back to look down at her again. But even then, he kept letting go of her, one moment at a time. "I need to get back tonight," he said, his voice low and serious and perfectly Oliver. She didn't know if that was supposed to be a good thing or not. Was he happy he was getting out of here before she lost her composure again? Or was she only imagining that there was a hint of regret in his tone?

"That's…" She cleared her throat and broke the contact between them. "That's fine. I'm sure you have someone waiting on you to get home." She had to turn away when she said it.

It was for the best if he left. She'd come here for the peace and quiet, right? And she definitely didn't feel peaceful when Oliver was around. Far from it.

He snorted. "Renee."

She put her face back together. She could do this. She didn't want to worry him and besides, she was probably just hungry. And pregnant. It wasn't a great combination. "Yes?"

He'd retreated back to his desk. She could feel the distance between them and, irrational as it was, she hated it. "I won't leave until you're settled."

She bit back the laugh. She might never be settled again. But instead, she said, "I appreciate it."

"I won't be able to get back out here for a few days," he went on, sounding nothing like the man who'd been holding her moments ago. "But if you need anything—clothes, medicines, weird foods—just let me know. I'll plan on spending at least part of the weekend out here."

Was he coming to see her or to babysit her? "All right."

He looked at something on his computer and then put his phone in his pocket. "And to answer your other question," he said, walking back toward her, "no, there's no one waiting on me at home. But I do have to work tomorrow. It's…"

"Rodeo season," she finished, trying hard not to smile. It shouldn't matter that he was available and that she was—well, maybe not available. But certainly unattached.

But it did.

"Dinner?" he said, a friendly smile on his face. His dimple didn't show.

Right. He was being friendly because they were friends and nothing more.

"Dinner," she agreed.

At the very least, it was good to have a friend.

Even if he was Oliver Lawrence.

The whole drive back to Dallas, Oliver tried to solve the problem that was Renee Preston-Willoughby.

He failed.

Instead of running through viable solutions to keep Renee safe and secure for the short and medium term—possibly up to and including the birth of her child—he was thinking of how she'd looked when she'd stepped into his study this afternoon. Gone were the hideous black dress, the dark hose and the understated black pumps. And in their place…

Oliver did not know a great deal about women's fashion, but he recognized the kind of clothes Renee had been wearing. Chloe loved to knock around in the same kind of leggings and loose tops.

It was safe to say that he had a vastly different reaction to Renee in leggings than he did his sister.

The top had come to just below her hips, leaving every curve of her legs outlined in tight black fabric. It'd taken everything in his power not to picture those legs wrapped around his waist at the time. The last thing anyone needed was for him to get a raging hard-on at the exact moment she'd needed to be comforted by a platonic friend.

Now? He adjusted his pants. He had a long drive ahead of him.

Damn, this was ridiculous. He had a million things he needed to do and none of them involved replaying the way Renee's body had fitted against his over in his mind. What he should be doing was talking to Bailey and getting caught up on everything Oliver had missed while he was out of the office today. Yeah, his executive assistant had probably already left work for the day, but Oliver was the CEO and if he needed Bailey to work late, then Bailey worked late.

Then again, Bailey was always talking about his wife and the latest adorable thing their two-year-old son was doing and Oliver would feel bad interrupting his dinner. A man should spend time with his family. He should be involved in the lives of his children.

No, Oliver couldn't in good conscience bother Bailey after work hours.

Which apparently meant he was going to think about

Renee. She had looked so much better after her nap. Still tired, still worried—but she'd been softer. Not as brittle.

That made him feel good. He had given her that.

But that was all he could give her. It didn't matter how much his body responded to hers, how much it hit him in the chest when she smiled—or how much it killed him when her eyes watered but instead of crying, her whole face went oddly blank. What he wanted didn't matter.

He would repeat that sentiment until he got it through his thick skull.

Because it didn't matter that he had finally given in to his impulse and pulled her tight in his arms in the office. It made no difference when he'd felt the tension drain out of her body and it didn't matter that, a moment or two later, he felt the different tension begin to work its way through her. It had no bearing on anything that being around Renee was a slow burn of torture.

Oliver was no angel. He'd been caught up in the throes of lust from time to time. Those affairs had always burned white-hot but fizzled out after a matter of months, if not weeks. He and his lady friends had parted ways with a smile and a fond farewell.

So he knew this attraction wasn't just lust. His whole body was *not* on fire for Renee Preston-Willoughby.

Had he seriously told her that he wouldn't be back until maybe the weekend? That wasn't right. She was all alone in the middle of nowhere in a strange house. Yes, he'd shown her how to operate the stove and where the pantry was and walked her through the remotes for the televisions. He'd even left her with keys for his ranch truck, in case she needed to get to Mineola, the closest town.

But what if something went wrong? What if she had a medical emergency? What if someone figured out where she was—someone who did not think kindly of the Preston family?

He almost turned his Porsche around. He could stay the night and make sure everything was okay and then get up and…

Okay, getting up at four to slink out the house wouldn't help anyone. And she was a grown woman who could navigate New York City by herself. She wasn't a child or an invalid. She'd be fine.

At least for the night.

Maybe he'd go back out tomorrow night, after work. Just to make sure she was doing all right.

Yeah. He'd do that.

That's what friends were for.

Five

She was going to bake.

Renee stood in the massive kitchen at Red Oak Hill, surveying the row of copper pots hanging from a pot rack over a massive island in the middle of the kitchen with stools tucked along one side. The countertops were a cool gray granite and the cabinets were cream with an aged patina. A Subzero fridge, better suited to a restaurant than a house with only one person living in it part-time, commanded almost half of a wall.

She didn't know how to cook. Or bake. No one in her house had cooked growing up. On the few occasions they'd suffered through dinner as a family, either Rosa, the undocumented Guatemalan maid her mother had constantly threatened with deportation, had prepared a meal for them or they'd had food delivered in. Nothing good ever happened at those family dinners. She shuddered at the memories and absently rubbed her leg.

Otherwise, her parents ate out—separately, of course. Breakfast had been cold cereal to be eaten as quickly and quietly as possible before she and Clint made their escape to school because waking her mother up before noon was a surefire way to suffer.

Instead, she had happy memories of boisterous meals with the Lawrence family where everyone bickered and told jokes and only sometimes did she and Chloe switch out sugar for salt or drop peas in Clint and Oliver's milk. If anyone yelled, they were laughing when they did it and no one ever jabbed silverware into someone else's legs.

She had afternoon teas with Chloe and Mrs. Lawrence after they'd gone shopping or seen a show or even just because. She had fun afternoons with Mrs. Lawrence teaching her and Chloe how to bake cookies and cakes. Then Renee and Chloe and sometimes even Mrs. Lawrence would eat their creations with a big glass of milk while watching cartoons. Those times were all the more special because...

Because of Mrs. Lawrence. She'd been warm. Loving. *There.* How many times had Renee dragged her feet when it was time to go home? How many times had she prayed for Mrs. Lawrence to be *her* mother, the Lawrence family *her* family? Her and Clint's. They could've been happy there. They *had* been happy there, all the happier because it was such an escape from home.

Mealwise, not much had changed when she'd married and moved into her own condo with Chet. They'd eaten out most of the time, often separately because Clint was working late or entertaining clients or dating other women, probably. And Renee hadn't seen the point in cooking just for herself, so she'd gone out with friends. Everything else had been delivered. Cooking wasn't a priority, not with some of the best restaurants in the world just a short phone call away.

Renee Preston-Willoughby didn't do anything so menial as prepare food.

That was going to change, starting now. Besides, she was dying for some cookies. Giant gooey chocolate chip cookies, just like she'd made all those years ago with Chloe and Mrs. Lawrence. With ice cream. Did Oliver have ice cream? If he were here, she'd ask him. But she wasn't going to wait around for someone else to solve her problems. Even if that problem was just ice cream related. She'd check the freezer herself.

Besides, what else was she going to do with her time? She could sit around and feel sorry for herself, but that was self-indulgent in the extreme. In addition to her nap yesterday, she'd had a solid night's sleep. She'd eaten breakfast, lunch and dinner for the first time in…a while. Last night Oliver had made these amazing burritos that he had had seemingly pulled together out of thin air and there'd been leftovers. Marinated chicken and steak and a corn salsa that was possibly the best thing Renee had eaten in months, plus tortilla chips and cheese. Lots and lots of cheese. It wasn't true cooking, but she'd assembled her own food today and that was a start. A *good* start.

It helped that, for the first time since her husband's funeral, food tasted good. Suddenly, she was starving.

She scrolled through Pinterest, looking for a recipe that promised both delicious and easy cookies.

It took a long time to assemble the ingredients. She had no luck tracking down baking soda, but baking powder was close, right? They both had *baking* in their names, after all. And it said *1 tsp* of both baking soda and salt. How much was a tsp? She found a measuring spoon that had a *T* on it. *That must be it.*

At least there were chocolate chips. Really, that was all that mattered.

She wished Oliver were here. The peace and quiet of this big mansion out on the countryside was wonderful, but she'd love to share it with him. This morning, she'd walked around the small lake, watching Fred and Wilma as they cut gracefully through the water with two baby swans trailing after them. Oliver had a small dock on the far side, so she'd kicked out of her flip-flops and sat with her toes in the water, watching the breeze ruffle the leaves of the huge red oaks.

This afternoon, she'd sat on the porch with a big glass of iced tea and, surrounded by the scent of roses, watched dusk settle over the land. She'd watched a few episodes of her favorite TV show—the animated one about a diner Chet had thought was stupid. And she'd taken another delicious nap.

No one had yelled at her. No one had accused her of horrible things. No one had mocked her appearance or told her that her husband had got exactly what he deserved. All in all, it had been a nearly perfect day.

Except she wished Oliver had been here. Which wasn't fair. He had to work, she knew that. As she dumped the sugar onto butter, she knew she didn't need Oliver by her side. But she wanted to show him that she was doing all right. Better than all right.

She'd been fragile and shell-shocked when she walked into his office, exhausted with worry and drained from the flight. But that didn't define her. It bothered her that he might think that was all there was to her.

But then again, she had a hazy memory of him telling her that she was strong for her unborn child. So maybe he knew? Or maybe he'd just been polite.

No matter. He would be here this weekend and by

then, she hoped to have figured out the secret to perfect chocolate chip cookies.

The sugar blended into the butter—at least, she hoped that was what *creamed* butter and sugar was supposed to look like—she checked the recipe again. Dang, she'd forgotten to turn on the oven. The recipe said it was supposed to preheat—maybe she should crank it up? Would it preheat faster that way? It was worth a shot. She set the oven to five hundred and then went back to her recipe. It called for one cup of chocolate chips, but that didn't seem like enough. So she doubled it. One could never have too much chocolate.

There. She had something that reasonably looked like chocolate chip cookie dough. If she wasn't pregnant, she'd test it, just to make sure it tasted right. But raw cookie dough was one of those things that pregnant women weren't supposed to eat, so she resisted the temptation. She scooped out the dough and set the sheets in the oven.

It was ridiculous, how proud she felt of this small accomplishment. Putting cookies in the oven to bake barely counted as an accomplishment at all. But still. She'd done it. God, she hoped they were good.

"What's going on in here?"

Renee screamed in alarm as she spun, losing her balance and bouncing off the corner of the island. Seconds later, strong hands had her by the arm, pulling her against a warm, solid chest. Tingles raced down her back and she knew even before she got a look at his face that, once again, Oliver had caught her before she fell.

She shouldn't be this happy to see him. But she was anyway. "You're here!" she said, breathless as she wrapped him in a big hug. *Now* the day was perfect.

"I am," he said, as if he were just as surprised to find himself back at the ranch—and in her arms—as she was.

Oh. *Oh!* She was hugging him, feeling every inch of his hard body against hers. She took a quick step back and let her hands fall to her sides. "I didn't think you were coming back tonight."

He leaned against the island, his mouth curving into a smile that sent another shiver down her back. "I wanted to make sure you were doing all right."

Something warm began to spread in her chest. "You could've called." After all, it wasn't like he'd popped next door to check on her. He had driven a solid hour and a half out of his way. He wasn't even in his suit. He was wearing a purple dress shirt but he had on dark jeans that sat sinfully low on his hips today. God, he looked so good. Better than chocolate chip cookies.

"I could've," he agreed.

His dimple was back and Renee had an inexplicable urge to kiss him right there on that little divot.

"Is everything all right?" If there was bad news, she could see him wanting to deliver it in person because that was the kind of man Oliver Lawrence was.

He wouldn't hide from the unpleasant truth. But instead of lowering the boom, he said, "Everything's fine."

They were words she'd heard hundreds, thousands of times. Chet had said them constantly, including in those last months when their lives had begun to unravel, even though Renee hadn't known it at the time. But she'd been able to tell that things weren't fine. But that's all Chet— or her brother or her father—had ever told her, like she was a toddler who'd bumped her head and needed a simple reassurance.

Those words coming out of Oliver's mouth were different. She was pretty sure. God, she hoped he wasn't that good of a liar. "You're sure?"

He lifted one shoulder. "I have Bailey scanning the

headlines for any mention of you in the greater Texas area, but nothing's cropped up. A few New York headlines are wondering where the pregnant Preston Pyramid Princess has disappeared to, but it's more because they're sad you're not providing them with clickbait fodder. Your brother hasn't accepted a deal yet. Your soon-to-be-former sister-in-law gave an interview to the *Huffington Post* where she eviscerated Clint, as well as your husband and your father, but only mentioned you to say that she'd always thought you were sweet and she really hoped you hadn't had anything to do with the scam. She didn't think you had."

A breath Renee hadn't realized she'd been holding whooshed out of her lungs. "Really? That's…that's great. I should send Carolyn a thank-you card. That's the nicest thing anyone's said about me in months."

"I can think of a few nice things to say about you." His voice was low and sweet, like dark honey and, as he looked her over with something that seemed like desire, her body responded. "More than a few."

Sweet Jesus, she wanted to melt into him. The space between her legs got hot and sensitive and her stupid nipples went all tight again. Which was the exact moment she remembered she didn't have on a bra.

Oh, hell! She didn't have on a bra and she'd hugged him and now he was making her blush. She crossed her arms over her chest and hoped he hadn't noticed.

He lifted an eyebrow and her face got even hotter. Of course he'd noticed.

But he had the decency to refrain from pointing out the *pointedly* obvious. Instead, he looked around the kitchen. "Baking?"

She was not disappointed that he hadn't lavished her in compliments. She was relieved, dang it. "I thought I'd give chocolate chip cookies a try. But fair warning," she said, desperately trying to keep her voice light, "I haven't baked anything in years."

He began to round up the dirty dishes without protesting or anything. "And you wanted to get back to it?"

"I do." She took a deep breath, thankful to have something to talk about that didn't have anything to do with her nipples or their willingness to turn into hard points around this man. "I have these wonderful memories of your mom taking the time to bake with me and Chloe and sometimes it was awful and sometimes we actually made something good and it was always so much…fun. Do you remember?"

Because now that she thought about it, she remembered that although Clint and Oliver hadn't been baking with them, sometimes Renee and Chloe had shared the cookies or cupcakes with them. But only when they were feeling generous.

He paused in the middle of dumping the mixing bowls in the sink. "Yeah, I do."

"Good." It made her happy to know that he still had those shared moments in an otherwise-fraught childhood relationship. "I want to have fun again. I want to be the kind of mom who enjoys making cookies and won't scream if the cookies don't turn out perfect. I want to be the kind of mom my kid looks up to, who'll…" Her voice caught in her throat. "Who'll be there for her kids. And her friends' kids."

Not like her mom had been.

The bowls clattered in the sink and Oliver turned. He studied her with that smoldering intensity of his that sent flashes of heat down her back.

But he didn't say anything. "Yes?" she finally asked nervously. She kept her arms crossed.

"I know my mother loved you. She considered you another daughter."

The sense of loss that hit her was more painful than she'd expected, mostly because she hadn't been expecting it at all. "Oh," she said, her throat closing up and her eyes watering. "That's...that's sweet. I was..." She swiped at her cheeks. "I was sorry we couldn't come to her funeral." Her mother didn't look good in black and funerals were dreary. Which meant Renee hadn't got a chance to say goodbye.

Oliver nodded. "And then we moved to Texas right after that."

It had been a one-two punch and honestly, Renee wasn't sure she'd ever got over it. She'd not only lost the wonderful mother of her best friend, she'd lost the entire Lawrence family. She'd lost the feeling of home that day.

But she hadn't been a little girl anymore. When Mrs. Lawrence had died, Renee had been thirteen and better equipped to deal with her mother's insanity. She'd joined more after-school clubs, found new friends.

Nothing had ever replaced the Lawrence family.

"Hey," Oliver said, stepping forward and pulling her into his chest. "I'm sorry. I didn't mean to upset you."

"It's okay," she replied, her words muffled by his shirt. "Sorry. Hormones. It doesn't take much these days."

"No, I'd imagine not." He leaned back, stroking his hand down her cheek and lifting her face so she had no choice but to look him in the eye. "Renee..."

Her breath caught in her throat again but this time, it had nothing to do with a spontaneous overflow of powerful feelings. Instead, Oliver's one hand was tracing slow circles around the small of her back, pushing her closer to him. To his lips. His thumb dragged over her cheek, sending sparks of electricity across her skin.

"I'm so glad you came back," Renee whispered, even as she lifted herself on tiptoe, closing the distance between them.

"I'll always come back for you," he murmured against her mouth.

Dear God, please let that be the truth. She didn't want easy lies. She couldn't bear the thought of him lying to her at all. Not him. Not now.

His lips brushed over hers, the touch a request more than a demand. She inhaled deeply, catching his scent— spicy and warm, with his own earthy musk underneath and a faint hint of something burning.

Something burning?

She jolted as he asked, "What's that smell?" at the same time a loud beeping filled the air.

"The cookies!" She twisted out of his arms and raced to the oven.

By the time she got there, smoke was beginning to curl out of the oven door. "Oh, no!" She frantically looked around for the oven mitts or…something. Anything, before she set his house on fire! But she didn't know where anything was!

Oliver picked her up and physically set her to the side. Then, as cool as a cucumber, he turned off the oven and produced the missing oven mitts. In short order, he had the cookie sheet and the nearly black puddles that had once aspired to be cookies out of the oven, a fan running and windows open to clear the room, and he was…

Laughing?

He was, the wretch. He was mocking her failed attempt at baking while he pulled the battery from the smoke detector and for a moment, it felt like they were kids again, always poking each other until the other responded. She wondered if she could hit him with a water balloon—

and what he might do in retaliation. Renee tried to scowl at him, but she was suddenly giggling along with him.

"Why, in the name of all that is holy," he sputtered, dumping the ruined cookies into the sink, "was the oven set to five *hundred* degrees?"

God, she was an idiot. "Oh! I forgot to preheat it so I thought I'd turn it on high to make up for it and I must have forgot to put it back down to the right temperature."

He laughed so hard that he slapped his thigh. She had to wrap her arms around her stomach to make sure she didn't accidentally wet her panties. When she thought she had herself under control, she eyed the mud puddles. They clearly had spread beyond the ability of the cookie sheet to contain them—but now that they were charred, they weren't going anywhere. "I may owe you some new cookie sheets," she said, which set off another round of giggles.

"What did you do to those poor things?" He grabbed the spoon she'd used to scoop out the dough and poked at the closest mud puddle.

And then they were off again. God, when was the last time she'd laughed?

She couldn't remember when. How sad.

But she was laughing too hard to let self-pity take control. She sagged into Oliver's arms and he buried his head against her shoulder, which didn't do a whole lot to muffle the almost unholy noises of glee he was making. They both were making.

Eventually, the giggles subsided. But her arms were still around Oliver and his arms were around her and he'd promised he'd always come back for her and then he'd almost kissed her, and she still wasn't wearing a bra.

"It's a good thing I came out here to check on you," he murmured against the skin of her neck.

"It is," she agreed, holding her breath. Would he kiss her again? Or let her kiss him? She shifted against him, bringing her breasts flush against his chest again. "I'd feel really bad if I'd burned your house down."

"That would've been tragic." Then she felt it, the press of his lips against the sensitive skin right below her ear.

She exhaled on a shudder as his mouth moved over her jaw. Then his lips were on hers and this time, it wasn't a hesitant touch.

This time, he kissed her like he wanted her.

Even though she knew she shouldn't because *complicated* would never be a strong enough word to describe her life, she kissed him back.

Months of sorrow and anger drifted away under the power of Oliver's kiss. Because it was an amazing kiss, sweet and hot and a seduction, pure and simple. His hands circled her waist, his thumbs tracing a path along her lower ribs. All the while, his lips moving over hers, his tongue lapping at the corners of her mouth. She opened for him and his tongue swept inside, claiming her.

Branding her as his own.

Because he wanted her. Not because she was her father's daughter, but in spite of that, Oliver Lawrence wanted her.

God, it was so good to be wanted.

So Renee kissed him back. She looped her arms around his neck and lost herself in the rhythm of their mouths meeting and parting and meeting again. Her body went hot and soft and hard all at once and she wanted him with a fierceness that left her dazed.

She wanted this to be real. She needed it to be honest and true.

But the niggling doubts in the back of her mind

wouldn't be quieted. Because what if it wasn't? She couldn't bear another person lying to her.

She pulled away. Slowly, but she did—and just in time, too, as Oliver's hands had begun a slow but steady climb up her ribs and toward her aching breasts. She wanted him to touch her, wanted him to soothe the tension with his touch. With his mouth.

But she wasn't going to throw herself at him. She wasn't going to do anything until she was sure.

She had no idea what that certainty would look like, however.

He let her pull back, but he didn't let her go. Instead, he clutched her to his chest, breathing hard. She curled into him, unwilling to break the contact.

"We should…" His voice cracked and he cleared his throat. "We should do the dishes."

"Yeah."

Neither of them moved.

He stroked her hair. "I'll need to head back tonight. I have an early meeting tomorrow."

That was a good thing. Because if she knew Oliver was asleep right down the hall, she might do something stupid, like slip into his bed in the middle of the night and pick up where they'd just left off.

Funny how him leaving didn't feel like a good thing.

"You can't miss your meetings," she said, her voice wavering just a little. "Not for me."

He made a snorting noise. "I might be able to come back out tomorrow night. Just to see how you're doing. But I can't make any promises."

She smiled and hugged him tighter. "I'm going to try cookies again."

"Maybe this time, you could follow the recipe?"

"Maybe," she agreed.

They laughed and, as if by silent agreement, pulled away from each other. "Then we better wash the dishes."

She grinned. The ways she'd messed up those cookies... "And find the baking soda."

Six

He really didn't have time for yet another three hours in the car, round-trip, plus however long it took to make sure Renee was doing okay and hadn't set the oven on fire. He'd cut out of work an hour early today in an unsuccessful attempt to beat rush-hour traffic, which meant yet another meeting with Ritter had been pushed back. That wasn't going to make his father happy.

Oliver needed to be focusing on his job. His jobs—he needed to check in on Chloe and see how the negotiations with ESPN were going.

Funny how that to-do list wasn't stopping him from making the long drive out to Red Oak Hill again.

He pulled up in front of the house, grabbed the groceries out of the trunk and bounded—bounded!—up the front steps and into the house.

The first thing he noticed was the smell. Instead of burning, something that smelled suspiciously like chocolate chip cookies wafted through the house.

Oliver grinned as he hurried back to the kitchen. Hopefully, she'd followed the recipe this time. But he made up his mind—he was going to eat the damned cookies and tell her they were great, no matter what.

Well, almost no matter what. He wasn't eating charcoal.

He pulled up short when he walked into the kitchen. The place was an utter disaster. Flour coated almost every surface and the sink was overflowing with mixing bowls. Ah—she'd found the stand mixer, as well. Cookies covered every square inch of countertop that wasn't taken up with baking supplies.

Racks and racks of cookies. There had to be eight, maybe ten dozen in all. Some were noticeably darker and some were almost flat and a few looked like they hadn't spread at all.

That was a hell of a lot of cookies.

"If we eat all those cookies at once," he said, trying to find a place to set his bags, "we'll get sick."

"Oliver!" Renee popped up from where she'd been bent over the oven. "You're here!"

He grinned at her. "I am. You've been busy, I see."

She glanced around at all the cookies, her cheeks coloring prettily. "You're out of chocolate chips. Sorry about that."

For a moment, all he could do was stare at her. The longer she was at Red Oak, the better she looked. The shadows under her eyes were a distant memory now and the lines of worry at the corners and across her forehead had faded away. True, she had a smear of flour across her forehead, but that just made her look even more adorable. She was wearing yet another pair of soft leggings and a loose turquoise T-shirt that made her eyes shine. Her hair had been pulled back into a messy braid and all he wanted to do was mess it up further.

He didn't. All he did was look. Because for the first time, Renee looked like she was meant to be—a young, beautiful woman enjoying herself.

God, she took his breath away.

To hell with his restraint. The grocery bags hit the ground and the next thing he knew, she was in his arms and he was kissing her like she was the very air he needed and he'd been holding his breath for the last twenty-four hours.

"I brought more chocolate," he murmured against her mouth before he plundered it ruthlessly with his own.

He hesitated, but she didn't pull away. Instead, her body molded itself to his, her lips parting for his tongue, her fingers sinking into his hair as she tilted his head for better access.

"More chips are good," she agreed, but Oliver had already forgotten what they were talking about.

All he could remember was that this was why he had come. To hold Renee and discover her secrets one long, leisurely kiss at a time.

"Tell me to stop," he muttered as her hands slid down from his hair, over his back and down to his butt. She squeezed and what was left of his self-control began to fray. Badly. "Tell me to stop and I will."

She pulled away, her eyes closed, and he damn near fell to his knees to beg for her. Him! Oliver Lawrence!

But if she wanted him to beg, by God he would, because at some point, his best friend's irritating little sister had become a gorgeous young woman he couldn't walk away from.

He wasn't going to walk away from her.

"Oliver." His name on her lips was soft but he didn't miss the undercurrent of need in her voice. God, he hoped it was need.

"Yeah, darling?"

She opened her eyes and the force of the desire reflected back at him threatened to unman him right then and there. "Don't stop."

This was crazy. Worse than crazy. Dangerous, even.

She couldn't let Oliver sweep her off her feet and carry her up the stairs—again.

She shouldn't let him kick open the door to his bedroom and set her down on her feet. And under no circumstances should she let him kiss her as if she were his last chance at redemption.

There would be no redemption. Not for her anyway. It was selfish and shallow but she just wanted to feel good again. Even if it were just for an evening in Oliver's arms. Nothing permanent. She wasn't looking for another 'til-death-do-us-part. She'd done that already.

But was it so wrong to want to feel desirable? Was it bad to want a man to look at her with naked want in his eyes, to need her so badly that he kept driving halfway across Texas to see her?

Was it an awful thing to take what he was offering?

"Renee," he murmured against her lips as his hands slid underneath her loose tunic. The touch of his bare fingers to the skin at the small of her back made her groan.

How was he doing this to her? She was no innocent— she was almost five months pregnant, for heaven's sake. She'd known desire and want in her time.

But nothing had prepared her for *this*, she realized as Oliver pulled her shirt over her head and cast it aside.

"Oh, dear God in heaven," he said, his voice revenant as he stared down at her bare chest. Because she hadn't been able to bring herself to put a too-small underwire bra on again if she were going to be alone in the house all day.

She'd planned to put the blasted thing on before he got here. She'd had the best of intentions. But Oliver had shown up earlier than she'd expected and it was rapidly becoming apparent that the bra was pointless in more ways than one.

"They're not always this big," she told him. "In the interest of full disclosure." Because no matter what, she didn't want anything that happened in this bedroom to be a lie.

Then she waited. Really, she wasn't afraid of what he might think about her new and improved breasts. Men liked big breasts, after all. Chet certainly had.

But it was the rest of her that had her worried. Her belly had started rounding out by the time she was three months pregnant and, aside from her loose tunics and leggings, nothing fitted. Not even close.

"I've put on a lot of weight." She managed to say it in a level voice, without any of the hurt bleeding into that statement. But if he were going to say something…less than perfect, she wanted to be braced for the worst. She wouldn't let it hurt.

"Hmm." The noise rumbled out of his chest as his fingers trailed over her ribs, their destination unmistakable. "It suits you."

What the heck did he mean by *that*? But before the words got off the tip of her tongue, his fingers were skimming over the sides of her breasts, circling around her nipples.

Which were, of course, tightening to hard points. Of course they were.

His thumbs swept over the tips and Renee stopped thinking about her weight, about Chet Willoughby and how perfectly average he'd been in bed. Instead, her head dropped back and she had to steady herself as the sensation of being touched—tenderly, sweetly and oh-so-hotly—overwhelmed her.

Then something warm and wet swept over her right nipple and her eyes flew open just in time to see Oliver lick it again. "Okay to suck or not?" he murmured against her flesh.

Heat flooded her body, making her shift anxiously. The pressure between her legs was so intense that she could barely think. All she could imagine was his mouth on her. "I... Gently, I think?" Was she more sensitive because she was pregnant? Or just because this was Oliver and he was seducing her like she'd never been seduced before?

She watched in fascination as he fell to his knees before her, his hands around her waist to hold her steady. Then he looked up at her and, holding her gaze with his own, he took her right nipple in his mouth.

She couldn't have held back the moan if she tried—and she did try. But it was a pointless exercise because sensations crashed over her like waves breaking over a jagged shore.

And this was Oliver being gentle. In control. Cautious. She had a sudden urge to see him beyond all reason, wild with need and crazed with desire. For her.

As his mouth drew down on her, his thumb continued to flick over her other nipple and that pressure between her legs crested and then crested again. She dug her hands into his hair and held on tight.

She didn't want to think about all the times she'd faked this kind of reaction, nor did she want to think about all the times Chet had skipped the foreplay to get right to the sex.

So she didn't. She made a conscious effort to put those unpleasant disappointments into a box inside her mind and shut the lid tight. Chet was dead and she wasn't. She was here and she was coming back to life under Oliver's skilled touch.

"You taste like vanilla and chocolate," he murmured as he kissed the space between her breasts before moving to the other one. "God, Renee, you taste so damn good."

She sighed and gave herself over to him. It wasn't selfish if he was giving himself freely, right? He wanted her. She wanted him. They were both consenting adults. There wasn't anything wrong with any of this.

A thought in the very back of her mind tried to remind her that, if anyone put her and Oliver in bed together—or even near the bed—there would be many things wrong with this. Her toxic reputation might very well damage his own, which might affect his business and his family.

All those lovely feelings threatened to turn sour in a heartbeat and she almost pulled away from him. She couldn't risk hurting the Lawrence family and, selfish as it was, she couldn't risk tainting all those wonderful memories from her childhood with loathing and re-crimination.

But that was the exact moment that Oliver relinquished her breast and began kissing down her stomach. Renee froze, torn between the need to do the right thing, the urge to hide her belly or the marks on her legs from him and the unleashed desire still crashing through her system. "Oliver…"

He kissed the top of her belly, where it rounded out. And as much as Renee detested it, she was powerless to stop her mother's voice echoing through her thoughts.

Look at you. It's disgusting, how you've already let yourself go. It's embarrassing to be seen in public with you when you're this fat and ugly.

She moved to cover herself but Oliver caught her hands

in his. "Don't hide from me, Renee," he said, his mouth moving lower. "You have no idea how gorgeous you are right now, do you?"

"I'm not." Her whisper was shaky, even to her own ears.

"You *are*." He looked up at her, that intensity shining through the lust. "Let me show you how much I want you." Then, before she could stop him, he hooked his fingers into the stretchy waistband of her leggings and her panties and pulled down.

He had to work the fabric over her hips but he was making that humming noise that seemed to come straight from his chest as he bared her. She balanced herself on his shoulders as she stepped out of her clothes and then she was completely nude before him.

He stared at her in what she desperately hoped was wonder and not something less…savory. He hadn't noticed the scars yet, so she fought the urge to slap her hands over the tops of her thighs. Maybe he wouldn't notice. Chet never had, after all.

God, why was she like this? Why couldn't she let go? Why couldn't she get lost in Oliver's eyes, Oliver's touch? Why was her mother's sneering voice cutting through this moment? Why were memories of Chet lurking just behind that?

Why couldn't this be perfect? No, that wasn't the right question, she realized as she blinked back tears.

Why couldn't *she* be perfect?

Then Oliver leaned forward and pressed a kiss to her belly button, his hands stroking up and down her thighs before moving back to cup her bottom. He squeezed as his mouth moved lower and his teeth skimmed over the space just above the hair that covered her sex. Because she hadn't been able to bring herself to keep up with her waxing. Being naked on a table before a near stranger?

That was a gossip disaster waiting to happen, and besides, who was going to see her like this?

Oliver.

He crouched down a little more and nudged her legs apart. She should let go of his hair, tell him to stop. At the very least, she should insist they pull the drapes and turn off the lights. Then she would be able to hide her belly and her thighs from him and she might be able to let go.

Because she needed to let go. She needed to prove those voices in her head wrong.

She needed this. She needed *him.*

"Beautiful," he whispered and he seemed so damn sincere that she had to believe he meant it, had to believe this was real. That was when his hand slid between her legs, brushing over her core with such tenderness that she wanted to cry. Stupid hormones. Then he leaned forward and pressed a kiss right there and, miracle of miracles, her mind emptied of all the hurt and criticism and pain and there was only Oliver and his mouth and his hands and *her.* He wasn't in Dallas with anyone else. He was here because he chose her.

His tongue moved over her sensitive flesh and it was the same and it was different and it was everything all at once. Because she didn't remember all these sensations crashing over her in a flood that couldn't be held back. She didn't remember making these noises without being able to control them. And she sure as hell didn't remember being so swept away by the rising tide that her legs shook and she suddenly was in danger of falling over.

"Oliver," she begged, pulling on his hair. "I can't stand."

He looked up at her, one arm locked around her legs and that was when she saw it—the raw hunger in his eyes. It took her breath away.

Then he surged to his feet, catching her in his arms. When he kissed her again, she didn't taste vanilla or chocolate, but instead she was on his tongue and he was marking her as his own.

She couldn't think. All she could do was act. So she yanked at the buttons on his shirt and jerked at the zipper of his pants because if she was naked, she wanted him naked, too.

He kicked out of his pants as she hauled his undershirt over his head and then there was nothing between them. She stepped back to see what he looked like underneath his button-up shirts and suit jackets. She got the impression of broad and lean and muscled with a smattering of chest hair. But she barely had time to say, "Oh, Oliver," before he was kissing her again, his hands pulling her hair from her braid as he backed her up.

So she let her hands explore. His chest was hard and warm and he hissed against her lips when she caught his nipples with her fingernails. His stomach rippled with muscles as she moved her hands lower and then...

"Oh, *Oliver*," she moaned against the skin of his neck as she gripped his erection. He was rock hard under her touch and she could feel his muscles shake as her hand moved up his impressive length and back down to his base.

He stilled against her, his head on her shoulder, his breath coming hard. "Woman," he growled, skimming his teeth over the delicate skin where her neck met her shoulders, "if you don't stop that right now, you'll have to wait at least five minutes before I can be inside of you."

She did that. She made him react like that. It was powerful, knowing that she could bring him to the edge, just like he'd done to her. God, it felt good to be in control of something again.

She smiled and stroked him again. "Five whole minutes?"

He groaned against her skin and then he bit her. Not too hard, but it was primal in its own way. "Maybe only three." He grabbed her hand when she squeezed. *"Renee."*

Then he picked her up. But instead of throwing her down on the bed, he spun and sat hard on a sofa. Renee blinked. She'd been so caught up in her own thoughts and in Oliver that she hadn't even realized that his room was set up similarly to hers. There was a large—and inviting—bed done up in deep blues and a sitting area with two love seats and a simple coffee table between them.

They were on the love seat that faced the big mirror over a dresser. "I need to watch you on top," he groaned. He rolled on a condom—where had that come from?—and then lifted her up so she could put her knees on either side of his legs. "I need to see you come apart, babe."

His erection brushed against her center and she shuddered. "Awfully confident, aren't you?"

She shouldn't tease him. But this was Oliver, dang it. She'd been teasing him for as long as she could remember and she had a feeling that he wouldn't dare turn a hose on her right now. It was safe to poke at him, to smile and laugh with him. He wouldn't demand to know what was so funny or, worse, who else she was thinking of.

He caught her face in his hands and touched his forehead to hers. "Renee," he said and she didn't hear any anger or insult in his voice. "I promise you, I won't leave you behind." There was a touch of sadness in his eyes as he said it.

Her throat closed up and her eyes watered. But she put on what she hoped was a sensual face. "I know."

He pressed a kiss to her lips that, considering their position, was surprisingly sweet. "Don't tell me what you think I want to hear, babe. Tell me what you need. Because I won't leave you frustrated." His hips flexed, dragging his erection over the folds of her sex and instinctively, she lifted herself up. His tip lodged firmly against her center and she gasped, her legs shaking again. "One way or another," he promised, "I'm going to make you scream with need." And there was nothing sweet about *that*.

It was hard to breath. Because he meant it. He meant every last word and in that moment, she fell in love with him. How could she not?

She lost her half-hearted battle with gravity and sank down onto him. For a long moment, they both sat still, breathing hard. Renee couldn't think, couldn't feel anything but Oliver inside of her, Oliver filling her. He was a part of her now. He always had been, but this?

"Woman," he growled again. "I can't—I need—oh, God." His fingers dug into her hips and he lifted her up before guiding her body back down again. She moaned as he filled her.

"I had no idea," he ground out, the cords on his neck standing out as he held himself in check. Then he caught her left nipple in his mouth and tugged, ever so gently, while she rose and fell and rose again. Each pull of his lips drew an answering pull from where they were joined and she was helpless to hold on to anything but him. "That's it, babe," he growled, moving to her other breast. "Take what you need."

And she fell a little bit more in love with him because he was waiting for her. And even if he came first, he'd still take care of her. He wouldn't leave her behind. She wasn't just here for his pleasure. He was here for hers, and *that*? That made all the difference in the world.

She lifted his face and kissed him with everything

she had. He groaned into her and that sound of pure need was her undoing. Renee came apart in his arms, her body going tight around his as the wave crested and broke over her.

She collapsed against his chest, unable to do anything but breathe hard as he thrust up into her, his hips moving harder and faster. "Renee," he said, somewhere between a groan and a shout. "Babe!"

She clenched her inner muscles at the same time she bit him on the shoulder and he made a noise of pure animal pleasure, so raw and desperate that she came a second time as he gave her everything he had.

Legs and arms everywhere, they didn't move, except for the panting. "I had no idea," Oliver said, his voice shaking. He leaned back and looked at her. "Okay? Or do you need something more?"

How could she not love him? Because no one—not a single one of her previous boyfriends—had ever asked. And if she'd tried to ask for something else, they'd taken it as an insult to their manhoods. It was her fault if she hadn't come, not theirs.

But Oliver was a different man. A better one.

God, it'd be hard to leave him when the time came.

But that was still a ways off. Hopefully at least a few more weeks. She didn't dare look further ahead than that.

Right now, she was going to live in this moment for as long as she could.

"Better than okay," she said, kissing him again as she lifted herself free. "So much better."

Oh, she liked that grin on him. Then, because on some level, she was apparently still ten and he was still thirteen, she added, "But we might need to try that again later, just to be sure this time wasn't a fluke."

His eyes popped open in surprise and she tried not to

laugh, she really did—but that was a battle she lost. A second after she started giggling, he narrowed his eyes to slits and he would have looked dangerous if he hadn't been smiling. "Why, you little tease. You know what I'm going to do?" He caught her in his arms and she wondered if maybe he hadn't been exaggerating when he'd said five minutes—maybe even just three—earlier.

"What?" She barely got the words out because he took her breath away.

"I'm going to…" He cocked his head to the side. "Do you hear something?"

"What?" That wasn't romantic. Or seductive. That didn't even count as basic flirting.

But then she did hear something. A steady, insistent beeping. Then another beep joined in with the first one, louder. Closer.

Her mind was still sluggish from the climaxes, so it took her a second before the beeping penetrated. Oliver got there first. "The smoke alarms!"

"The cookies!"

Seven

Renee scrambled off his lap and grabbed her top, but Oliver didn't even bother with clothes. He went streaking out of the bedroom at a dead run, his legs still a little wobbly from the sex.

Dear God, if she burned the whole damned house down...

He went skidding into the kitchen. For the second night in a row, smoke was curling out of the oven and hanging in a low cloud against the ceiling—but no flames. Thank God for that.

Oliver moved fast. He grabbed the oven mitts and turned the oven off before he snatched the cookie sheet out of the oven. Still no flames. Just carbonized cookies. Again.

These smelled even worse than the ones from last night. He didn't want to dump them in the sink and there were still dozens of cookies covering every flat surface.

Thankfully, Renee came running into the kitchen.

"Door!" he barked, the oven mitts getting hotter the longer he held on to the cookie sheet.

Coughing, Renee turned and ran. Oliver had to wonder where the hell she was going—there was a perfectly fine door on the other side of the island that opened onto the backyard, but then she yelled, "The pond!"

Right—water would be good. Oliver's hands were growing dangerously hot despite the oven mitts so he took off after her.

She jerked the front door open and stood to the side while he ran outside and barreled straight into the pond. With a silent apology to Fred and Wilma, he threw the whole damn mess into the water before tearing off the oven mitts and letting them fall to the water. He bent over and let the water cover his hands. It wasn't cold because the day had been sunny and warm but compared to the hot cookie sheet, the water felt amazing.

A few yards away, the cookie sheet hit the water with a sizzle, as if he'd been forging iron. He looked up to see the whole thing floating, the hockey pucks formerly known as cookies still smoking.

On the far side of the pond, Fred and Wilma made a lot of noise and flapped their wings in displeasure at having their evening swim disrupted.

"Tell me about it," he muttered, turning his attention back to his palms. They were red but not burned. He didn't see any blisters forming, nor any white skin that signaled a severe burn.

He dunked his hands back in the water, just to be sure.

He heard a strangled noise behind him and he looked over his shoulder. Renee was standing a few feet up the bank. She'd managed to grab her T-shirt and it hung down to the top of her hips, the hem fluttering in the breeze. Backlit by the setting sun, he could see every inch of her silhouette outlined and that was when his brain chose to re-member that, less than ten minutes ago, he'd been inside her, feeling the shocks of her body releasing a climax upon his.

But something wasn't right. Her hands covered her mouth, her eyes were huge and her shoulders were shak-ing. It about broke his heart to see her like that.

They were just cookies. It wasn't like she'd burned the house down or scarred him for life. He didn't like her looking so fragile, so scared.

But then she asked, "Are you okay?" in a voice that was strangled—but it wasn't horror or misery that laced her words.

He recognized that voice. He'd heard it countless times back when they'd been kids and he and Clint had fallen for one of Renee and Chloe's pranks—he was think-ing specifically of clear tape strung across his bedroom door that Oliver had walked into it so hard that he'd been knocked off his feet, tape stuck in his hair.

And Renee had stood over him then, looking almost exactly like she did right now—trying so hard not to giggle at the raging success of her trick. Trying, instead, to look worried and she'd uttered the exact same words.

She hadn't succeeded then and she wasn't succeeding now. "Are you *laughing* at me?"

"No!" she answered way too quickly. "I'm…" She took a deep breath, visibly getting herself under control. "I want to make sure your hands aren't burned."

The smoke detectors beeped from deep inside the house. Fred and Wilma continued to express their dis-pleasure on the other side of the pond, with Pebbles and Bamm-Bamm joining in. But all he could hear was the barely contained amusement in her voice. "Fine," he said coolly, because it was the truth and he didn't want her to worry. "Just a little warm. No burns, no blisters."

"Good." Her gaze cut to his backside at the exact same moment a stiff breeze rippled over the surface of the pond. And his butt.

His bare butt. The one that was sticking straight up in the air because he was bent over at the waist. Everything was hanging *all* the way out.

"Do you think," she said, dropping her hands and trying to look serious, "that there'll be a full moon tonight?"

Holy hell, this woman. She was easily going to be the death of him, and quite possibly his house. But honestly? He was so damned relieved she was okay, that the same mischievous, hilarious Renee who'd driven him up a wall when they'd been kids was still in there that he wanted to laugh with him.

But this was Renee after all, and he wasn't about to let her off the hook that easily. Turning, he scowled at her as he walked out of the pond. "You think this is funny?"

"Maybe." She sobered and took a step back as he advanced on her. "Maybe not."

"This is the second night in a row you've nearly burned down the house, Renee. I don't think I'm going to let you bake anymore."

The light in her eyes dimmed as she paled and she crossed her arms over her stomach, almost curling into herself even though she didn't so much as bend at the waist. Shit, he'd taken it too far. He wanted to make her sweat a little but he didn't want to beat her down.

Fight back, he thought as he got nose to nose with her. *Fight for yourself.* "You, ma'am, are a menace to baked goods the world over," he intoned in the most pompous voice he possessed. "I'd even go so far as to say you're a monster to cookies everywhere, to say nothing of how you're terrorizing my kitchen, my swans and myself!"

Behind him, Fred—or maybe it was Wilma—whooped

from much closer. Involuntarily, he flinched because no one wanted to be bitten on the ass—or other exposed parts—by an angry bird with a six-foot wingspan. He looked over his shoulder. The swans and cygnets had swum over to investigate the now-sinking cookie sheet, so his butt was safe. For now.

He turned back to Renee. She stared up at him, confusion written all over her face. "Did…did you just call me a cookie monster?"

"If the shoe fits." He snarled. Well, he tried to snarl. But suddenly the effort of not laughing was almost more than he could bear.

She blinked at him and then blinked again before pointedly looking at their feet. "We're not wearing shoes."

"Fine. If the shaggy blue fur and googly eyes fit, wear them!"

Fight back, Renee.

Then, miracle of miracles, she did. She gave him a fierce look and poked him in the chest. "I've got news for you, mister." *Poke.* "You're not the boss of me." *Poke.*

"Oh, yeah?" It was not the snappiest comeback he'd ever uttered.

But it did what he wanted it to do. Her eyes lit all the way back up as she smiled and then tried to scowl and frankly, she took his breath away again. This was a game. Maybe not one she'd played in a long time, but she hadn't forgotten the rules. Thank God for that. She was going to give him everything she had and that, more than the explosive sex or the questionably edible baked goods, made him feel ten feet tall. She wasn't afraid of him. He was worth the fight.

She was worth the fight. It was high time she knew it.

"Yeah!" *Poke.* "If I want to bake cookies—" *poke* "—then I'm going to bake cookies. And furthermore—" *poke*

"—I'll have you know that I was doing just fine before you showed up, both nights." *Poke.*

"Ow," Oliver said, backing up a step. She wasn't poking him hard, but she was hitting the exact same spot over and over again.

"You're the reason the cookies got burned." *Poke.* "You distracted me with amazing kisses and the best sex I've ever had." *Poke.* "If you hadn't distracted me, we could be eating the perfect chocolate chip cookie right now."

Amazing kisses? The best sex? He wasn't one to brag but hell, yeah, that was good for his masculine pride. To hell with cookies. He'd have her back in bed. Or on the love seat. Hell, any semiflat surface would do just fine, as long as he could hold her in his arms and feel every inch of her body against every inch of his.

Oliver was grinning his fool head off but he didn't care. There was something so right about Renee defending herself and putting him in his place that it made him want to sing.

Sing! Him! Oliver!

He didn't burst into song. However, he did say, "Were they edible cookies?" just to drive her nuts.

It worked. "The last batch was!" *Poke.*

Stumbling backward, Oliver looked over his shoulder. The cookie sheet had sunk now, but a few hockey pucks formerly known as cookies floated on the surface of the pond. Fred and Wilma and the kids seemed mildly terrified of the things. He couldn't blame them. "The *last* batch?"

"You know what I mean—the batch before that!" *Poke.*

Oliver retreated another step. She was in fine form, his Renee. Her eyes blazed and the breeze molded the thin T-shirt to her body, highlighting her breasts and the gentle swell of her stomach and all he wanted to do was pull her into his arms and kiss the hell out of her.

"I swear to God, if I had a water balloon—" *poke* "—I'd throw it right at your head. But you know what?" *Poke*.

He grabbed her finger before she bruised him. "What?"

A victorious smile graced her face, making her look like an avenging angel. He wanted to fall to his knees and worship before her. She pulled her hand back and said, "I don't need a water balloon."

This time, she didn't poke him. She put both hands on his chest and Oliver had just leaned down to take that kiss from her lips when she shoved him. *Hard*.

He fell backward and the next thing he knew, he was sitting on his butt in the pond, wiping water from his face while Renee stood safely on the bank, staring at him.

"You..." he sputtered, wiping water from his face. The mud was squishing up his butt and around his important parts and, judging from the noise, the swans had declared DEFCON 1 behind him. "You pushed me!"

For a second, she looked just as shocked as he felt. Then her face cracked into a huge smile and it was like the sun breaking through clouds after days of endless rain.

"You. Pushed. Me," he said in his most dangerous growl and then he splashed as much water as he humanly could at her. He missed, of course. From this angle, he could see under the hem of her long T-shirt and, as she danced out of the way of the water, he caught glimpses of her bare body that made him hard all over again, despite the mud.

She laughed, loud and free, and clapped her hands in delight. "Don't move," she giggled, pointing. "I'm going to get my phone. I think Chloe needs to see a picture of this—the high-and-mighty Oliver Lawrence stuck in the mud!"

"The hell you will," he said, trying to get to his feet. But the mud was slippery and he lost his balance and splashed back down again. He couldn't even keep a straight face this time.

The sound of her happiness was worth it, he decided. He'd be cleaning mud out of his crack for a week but he'd take the fall for her again, just to hear her laugh as if she didn't have a care in the world. She wrapped her arms around her waist and bent forward, tears of joy rolling down her cheeks.

"You win this round," he yelled, aiming for his best villain voice—high-pitched and nasal. "But I'll be back!"

Then, just like she always had years ago, Renee jammed her thumbs against the side of her head, waggled her fingers at him and stuck out her tongue, yelling, "*Nyah, nyah na nyah*, you can't catch me!" before she spun on her heels and bolted back to the house. Her legs flashed in the dim light, her bottom peeking out from under the shirt with every step she took.

All he could do was watch her go, an unfamiliar lightness settling around him even as the sun sank behind the house and shrouded the pond in shadows. He hadn't felt this lightness back when they were kids. She'd driven him nuts and he'd done everything he could've to return the favor. But now?

They weren't kids anymore. Life had changed them both but he could still give her those moments of joy.

"Are you coming?" she yelled from the front door.

He rolled onto his hands and knees and made sure he had his feet under him before he stood. Pond water sheeted down his body, leaving muddy rivulets all across his legs. "Hell, yeah," he called back.

Because she wasn't going anywhere without him.

Eight

"These aren't bad," Oliver said around his sixth attempt to eat one of Renee's cookies.

"Really?" Renee ducked her head, a delicate blush pinking her cheeks. "That was the last batch. That survived anyway."

He wanted to cup her blushing cheek in his palm and kiss her again and again. But then again, earlier he'd wanted to pull her back upstairs and try out a few other positions with her, but he couldn't.

Just like always, Oliver had bowed to the demands of reality. Stupid reality.

Frankly, he was lucky he hadn't mooned half of Mineola. Because that's about how many people had suddenly appeared on his property.

While Oliver had been splashing in the pond and doing everything in his power to make Renee laugh and fight back, his housekeeper, Lucille, had called three times to see if the house was on fire or not. When she couldn't get ahold of anyone at the house, she'd called the fire department. The fire trucks had shown up about five minutes after he'd got his naked butt back inside the house, with Lucille hot on their tail. And then she'd scolded Oliver like he was a schoolboy and demanded to know why he'd installed a houseguest without telling her because she could have brought over some more food.

"Or at least some better desserts," Lucille had grumbled when she'd got a good look at the kitchen.

But Oliver had introduced Lucille to Renee and, after her initial shock, Lucille seemed to be warming up. She picked up a cookie from a different batch and took a small nibble. "Good heavens, you're not supposed to use that much salt!"

"Well, I figured that out," Renee said defensively—but at least she said it with a smile. "Eventually. Why would anyone label *teaspoon* and *tablespoon* so similarly?"

Lucille gave Renee a look that made it clear the older woman didn't know if Renee was joking or not.

Oliver snagged another edible cookie and handed it over to Lucille. "The important thing is she figured it out."

Lucille was not one for effusive praise, but even she nodded and said, "That's not half bad," which made Renee bust out another one of those luminous smiles. "Honey, I can teach you to bake, if you'd like." She eyed the mess again. "Might be easier. Or at least safer. When are you due, honey?"

"Oh." Renee turned a pretty pink and stared down at her belly. Oliver couldn't figure out if she was embarrassed by this question or not. "September 27."

Because of course she knew the exact date of conception. The day her husband took his own life. Oliver didn't like the way Renee seemed to pull back into herself. He shot Lucille a look that he hoped communicated *say something nice*.

And Lucille, bless her heart, did. She wasn't a grandmother of six for nothing. "Pregnancy suits you," she announced a tad too loudly.

"It does?" Clearly, Renee didn't believe her.

"You've got that glow, honey. Some women look tired or drained, but you?" She waved her hand near Renee's belly. "Some women were born to this. You're one of them, you lucky duck."

Renee looked doubtfully down at her stomach. "But I'm fat."

Lucille looked truly insulted by this. She patted Renee on the arm. "Oh, honey—who told you that? They were nothing but jealous. You're gorgeous." She turned a hard stare to Oliver. "Isn't she?" It was not a question.

"I already told her that. Multiple times—because it's true," he replied, watching Renee's cheeks color even more. Which meant he almost missed the look Lucille gave him, one that had him realizing that he might have overplayed his hand.

Thus far, he and Renee had attempted to stick with their original story—they were childhood friends and he'd given Renee free use of his ranch while she was hiding and he was working in Dallas.

But that story wasn't holding water, so to speak, and Oliver knew it. It was the middle of the workweek and yet he was at Red Oak Hill. And not only was he at Red Oak Hill, he'd also barely got out of the shower and got pants on before the place had been crawling with firefighters. At least Renee had located her leggings. They'd told the fire crew that he'd fallen into the pond trying to deal with the carbonized cookies—which, again, was true.

But it wasn't a huge leap to get from him naked in the

shower to him naked with Renee. He'd even caught two firefighters nudging each other with their elbows and winking at Oliver's story.

Yeah, no one was buying that half-truth here. Worse, he'd screwed up and used Renee's real name when he'd introduced her to Lucille within earshot of at least three firefighters and now there was no going back.

For all intents and purposes, Renee's presence at Red Oak Hill was now common knowledge.

Especially because Lucille was no idiot and it was clear Oliver had screwed up again. Damn it. This was all going wrong. Lucille, he trusted, but the firefighters? And now Lucille was giving him The Look?

To avoid Lucille's sharp gaze, Oliver snatched up another cookie and immediately regretted it. Coughing, he spit the too-salty one into the trash. "I think we can get rid of these," he sputtered, scraping the whole batch off the cooling rack and directly into the trash. "We're lucky no one else tried these."

"*You* were lucky you weren't caught with your britches down," Lucille said, dumping another batch into the trash and stacking the dirty dishes in the sink.

Oliver froze, the blood draining from his face. A quick glance at Renee told him that the opposite was true for her. She was turning an unnatural shade of scarlet. She shot him a helpless look.

Oliver wanted to bolt but he couldn't abandon Renee to Lucille's questioning. "You should ask Lucille for some tips," he said, ignoring the status of his britches. "She does most of the cooking for me. And she makes an amazing cinnamon roll. I know it's not a cookie but…"

Bless her heart, Lucille said, "You should try a sugar cookie, honey. Once you get the basic dough recipe down, then you can start messing around with it."

"I saw some recipes but they looked really complicated—lots of detailed icing," Renee replied. "I don't think I could do that."

"You only need that much icing if you've got a boring cookie." The older woman eyed the kitchen counters. "I don't think anything you bake could ever be boring."

Oliver could have kissed the woman. Renee looked relieved and that was the most important thing. "I did see some really cute things on Pinterest I wanted to try..."

And they were off. "I'll be in my study—Bailey is emailing me," Oliver mumbled, making a break for it. He didn't know if it was a lie or not. Bailey probably *had* been emailing him.

He dropped into the chair and put his elbows on his desk. He was tempted to yank his hair out of his head, if only to make sure he hadn't hallucinated the last two hours. Renee was right. None of this—the smoke alarms, the fire department, Lucille—would've happened if he'd been able to stick with the plan. He should've stayed in Dallas. Barring that, he should've kept his hands off her. And barring that...

He shouldn't have teased her in the pond. But he hadn't been able to help himself. A jumble of emotions churned in his chest. He wasn't thinking straight and he knew it.

He wanted Renee. One time with her wasn't going to be enough. If anything, he wanted her more now than he had before he'd stripped her bare and slid into her body.

He did not want her to burn his house down. Thus far, they'd had two close calls and he didn't want to find out if the third time would be the charm.

He needed to make her laugh again, to see that joy lighting up her face. He didn't want to see the shadows that hovered around her anymore.

And he'd completely failed her because people knew where she was now.

What a freaking mess.

So he did what he always did when things went sideways on him. He worked. He logged in and attacked the twenty-one emails that Bailey had sent him since 3:45 p.m. this afternoon with a fervor that bordered on possessed. He sent a message to Herb Ritter that he absolutely would make their 9:00 a.m. tomorrow morning. He reviewed the messages from Chloe summarizing how negotiations with ESPN were going. He ignored the ones from his father.

"Oliver?"

He jumped. How much time had passed? It wasn't enough. Seeing Renee in the doorway to the study, her head tilted to the side, light from the hallway settling around her shoulders—he was terrified to realize it might never be enough. "How's everything going?"

"Good. Really good." She stepped into the room, but not very far. He could feel the distance between them. "Lucille's going to bring over some recipes on Friday. I helped her with the dishes. There's a right way and a wrong way to wash dishes, apparently."

He knew that, but he said, "Who knew?" in a teasing tone.

She took another small step into the study. "I'm going to go take a shower. For some odd reason, I smell a little like a pond and charcoal."

"Do you now?" Oliver couldn't fight back the grin.

She nodded, putting together a reasonable appearance of innocence. "Will you…" She paused and straightened her shoulders, her chin coming up. Oliver didn't like that look on her. But he was starting to recognize it for what it was—Renee putting her armor on. "Will you be here when I get out of the shower?"

Screw this distance. Oliver was out of his chair before he could think better of it, crossing the room and pulling her into his arms. "I won't leave you without saying goodbye."

That wasn't what he wanted to say. Hell, he didn't know what he wanted to say. It wasn't like he was going to tell her he loved her. He cared for her, yes. He worried about her. He wanted her happy and well and safe. But that wasn't love.

The problem was, he didn't know what it was.

She looked at him, her eyes round with something that looked too much like fear. "Is this goodbye?"

This was *not* love. But it was definitely something more intense, more focused than he was used to feeling.

"No," he said, brushing his lips over hers. "It's not."

She exhaled against his mouth and he deepened the kiss, clutching her tighter so that her body was pressed against his chest. His hands moved down her back, cupping her bottom and pulling her against him. She gasped as the hard length of his arousal made contact with the soft flesh under her belly.

He lost himself in her. That's what this was. It wasn't love and it wasn't lust. He was simply lost to her.

God help him, he didn't ever want to be found.

He already had her shirt half-off when a loud clatter echoed from the kitchen, followed by some of Lucille's more creative language. Oliver and Renee broke apart, both breathing hard.

"I…" Blushing furiously, Renee backed away. "I need to shower."

Oliver begged to disagree. What she needed was to stay right here in his arms. Preferably with less clothing between them. But he didn't say that out loud. He needed to put more space between them. He needed to get his thoughts—and his dick—back under control. Hell, he needed to drive back to Dallas tonight so he could meet with Herb Ritter in the morning.

But he just might need Renee more.

So all he said was "Sounds good," as if that could've even begun to make things right.

He wouldn't have thought it possible but Renee blushed even more. "Okay."

"Good," he repeated dumbly, his arms beginning to shake with the effort of holding them at his side. But he fought those baser urges because the moment his control slipped, he'd do something foolish like pull her back into his arms and tell her to wait because he was absolutely going to join her in the shower. And then the bed. And everywhere in between.

With a smile, she turned and fled. It wasn't until he heard her steps overhead and the door to her bedroom shut that he exhaled and staggered back to his desk on weak knees.

"She's something." Lucille's gravelly voice made him jump again. "I like her."

Oliver pulled himself to attention. "Sorry about the kitchen. We, uh, lost a cookie sheet to the pond." He was real proud of the way his voice was level. Strong. Less...*shaken.*

Sitting in front of the desk, Lucille stared at him long enough that Oliver began to shift uncomfortably. Like the swans, the older woman had come with the house. She had been cleaning Red Oak Hill for almost twenty years. It had only made sense to keep her on when Oliver had bought the place six years ago.

He'd run a background check on her and got to know her, of course. He wasn't stupid. But the fact was, Lucille was so good at maintaining Red Oak Hill to Oliver's standards that he paid for her to come to Dallas one day a week and clean his condo, as well. And because he valued loyalty, he paid her well.

He was just about to open his mouth and tell her not to mention anything about Renee to anyone, but she beat him to the punch. "That's the Preston Pyramid Princess, right?"

"Right." He could feel himself deflating. "She was best friends with my sister when we were growing up. Her brother was my best friend. They were practically family."

"Darn shame about her husband. He shot his fool head off, right?"

"Right. She's had a rough go of it since then. I'm just giving her a place to lie low for a bit."

"That girl reminds me of me," Lucille announced.

"Really?" Lucille had three kids by three different fathers, but Dale was only her second husband.

Lucille gave him a smile that made it clear she knew what he was thinking. "Different circumstances, same story. Like recognizes like. I love my kids and I love my grandkids. I'm not saying I'd want to change anything because all of it—the good and the bad—gave me them. But I'm an old woman now."

"Hardly," he muttered. Lucille was all of fifty-five.

She ignored that interruption. "I can look back with a little distance. I had a rough childhood—my mom wasn't around much and my dad was a mean drunk. I spent years doing whatever the hell I wanted because who was going to stop me? No one. At least, that's what I told myself."

Okay, so maybe a picture was slowly starting to emerge of a less-than-happy childhood for Renee. But that wasn't anything comparable to what Lucille was talking about. However, discretion was the better part of valor, so Oliver kept his mouth shut.

Lucille went on, "But I didn't know what I wanted. I'd meet someone and suddenly, whatever they wanted was what I wanted. Drugs, alcohol, sex—did I ever really want any of that? Or did I just go along with it because I needed the approval? Who knows, if I'd met Dale earlier..." She let that trail off, her gaze getting soft.

He was about to argue with this assessment of Renee—but then he remembered something she'd said about her wedding. She would have been perfectly happy with something small and intimate but she'd wound up with something like ten bridesmaids and custom-engraved crystal and it was all wildly over-the-top.

Was that what Lucille was talking about? Hell, he didn't know. "As nice a guy as Dale is, I don't think he's Renee's type."

He didn't expect Lucille to scowl. "Do you know why she's been destroying my kitchen? Because she's trying to figure out what she wants. Not what her father, or I assume her mother, wants, not what her husband was willing to give her. Not even what you want, Oliver Lawrence. What *she* wants."

"Is that supposed to be difficult?" He didn't mean to sound flippant. But he didn't see how this was some sort of lifelong struggle. Okay, Renee was still in her midtwenties. And she was going through a rough time in her life. But most people got a handle on life by the time they got out of college.

After all, he knew what he wanted. He wanted to leave Lawrence Energies and his family behind and get back to his real life in New York and...

Didn't he?

Lucille leveled a look at him that, if he'd been a younger

man, would have made him drop his head in shame. As it was, he had to look away. "If you spent your entire life being told that what you want is useless and worthless," she said in a tone that walked a fine line between understanding and disappointed, "that what makes you happy is stupid, then yeah, it's difficult."

"I don't think she's stupid." In fact, he knew she wasn't. God knew he didn't tolerate fools. She was bright and charming and vivacious and gorgeous and... he wanted her.

"You know she's not stupid. I know she's not stupid. But does she know that?"

"Of course she does. Why wouldn't she?" But even as he said it, he had to wonder.

She *did* know, didn't she? That Oliver thought she was all of those amazing, wonderful things? That he never considered her stupid or worthless, not even back when they'd been children tormenting each other? She might've been a pain in his backside, but he had always known that she was smart and talented.

Lucille stood. "She can't stay here. Too many of those boys recognized her."

"You're the one who promised you'd teach her how to bake." The idea of sticking Renee in some soulless hotel where she wasn't allowed to wander around or even attempt a simple sugar cookie left him feeling vaguely ill.

"It's going to take me at least a day to put that kitchen back in order," Lucille grumbled, but she smiled as she said it. "Take her to your condo. I'll be there on Monday anyway. The building has decent security. They won't be able to sneak up on her like they would here."

Oliver had been worried about reporters but what if someone heard that the Preston Pyramid Princess was here and decided to take matters into their own hands?

What if someone came here looking not for a scoop, but for revenge? "You raise a valid point."

Lucille smirked. "Good. Tell her I'll see her Monday." She headed for the door but paused and looked back at him, a knowing smile on her face. "Besides, that would save you a lot of driving."

Yeah, Oliver wasn't fooling anyone.

"Tell her I'll bring my grandma's snickerdoodle recipe," Lucille called over her shoulder and then the door opened and shut.

Oliver dropped his head into his hands, trying to get a handle on the jumble of thoughts all clamoring to be heard inside his mind at the same time.

What did she want? What did he want? Well, he knew the answer to that.

He wanted to go upstairs and sweep Renee into his arms and fall into bed and spend the next twelve to twenty-four hours forgetting about cookies and firefighters and housekeepers and scams and family. He wanted to revel in her body and show her how good he could be for her. He wanted her with a fierceness that was a little frightening, if he were being honest.

Did she want him? Or did she want what he wanted?

He shook his head. None of that mattered, because neither of them was going to get what they wanted. Instead, they were going to get what they needed and right now that was to leave the seclusion of Red Oak Hill and head back to the anonymity of Dallas.

This was a problem. If word got out that Renee was here, then the only reasonable conclusion would be that Renee was with him. Even if she were safely tucked away in his condo, people might still try to get to her. And they might try to get to her *through* him.

He wanted to join her in the shower but he couldn't

risk being caught with his pants down for the second time in one night, so instead he composed an email to Bailey, updating him on the change in circumstances and directing him to order extra security for the condo and the office. Then, when Oliver had gauged enough time had passed that Renee was probably at least partially dressed, he went upstairs to break the news to her.

Damn it all to hell.

His father was going to find out sooner or later.

Oliver prayed it wasn't sooner.

Nine

This was not how she'd planned on spending her evening—making a late-night mad dash back to Dallas for the safety of Oliver's condo.

It wasn't like Red Oak Hill was hers. She'd spent the equivalent of a long weekend there. But she was sadder than she wanted to admit to leave it behind. She been able to breathe there and even though she was a born-and-bred city girl and should be relieved to be back in a big city, she wasn't.

It was true it was easier to hide in the city. But she hadn't had to hide for a few days. She'd been able to sit on the porch and take a walk around the pond and be herself. No worries about who was going to get a terrible photo, no thoughts as to what the next headline would be. Just…peace.

If only she hadn't ruined that.

"Did you enjoy baking the cookies?"

Renee turned her attention back to Oliver. His gaze

was focused on traffic. She didn't recognize where they were, but it wasn't like she'd spent a lot of time driving around. She'd had a taxi take her from the airport to Oliver's office. That was all she knew of Dallas. "I did. There was something soothing about mixing up the ingredients and hoping for the best. And when they were awful, I could try again."

God, she sounded pathetic. But that was the truth. Wasn't that why she'd come to Dallas and to Oliver? All she could do right now was mix things up and hope for the best.

She braced herself for a cutting comment, an affirmation that she wasn't capable of anything other than a Pinterest fail, a warning that cookies would make her fat—something. Oliver couldn't be happy that his house smelled burned. He couldn't be thrilled about bringing her to yet another home on such short notice. He couldn't enjoy the way she kept upending his life again and again.

So when he reached over and lifted her hand to his lips, pressing a tender kiss to her palm, her mouth fell open in surprise. "Then bake cookies. I won't distract you anymore."

Then he kissed her hand again. Sweet warmth spread from where his lips touched her bare skin and she wanted to revel in it.

Because underneath the worry and anxiety that had become her constant companion in the last few months was something new.

She and Oliver had made love. No, that felt too soft to describe what they'd done. They'd had hot, sweet, block-out-the-rest-of-the-world sex that had been a gift because he'd made her feel amazing and then, when it was over, he'd asked if she needed more. Because he was willing to give her more.

Oh, how she wanted to take him up on that offer. She'd wanted him to come upstairs and climb into the shower with her and pick up right where they'd left off before the fire department had shown up.

Instead, they were back in Dallas and any of those hot, sweet feelings had been put aside in the name of practicality.

"In fact," Oliver went on, "we should have a new rule—the moment we feel *distracted*, we have to turn off the oven before anything else happens."

Anything else? Did he mean wild, crazily satisfying sex, or did he mean an actual, full-fledged fire breaking out? Because it would've been tragic enough burning down Red Oak. It would be horrific to set fire to a high-rise building that housed hundreds of other people.

Good heavens, what would the press do to her *then*?

But that was the moment when Oliver tugged on her hand and suddenly his lips were skimming over the delicate skin of her wrists. "Or maybe you should just turn the oven off the moment I walk in the door. Just to be sure," he murmured and even though it'd been a long day, heat still flooded her body.

"Oh. Okay. Good plan." Renee knew she should say something grateful or appreciative. But there was a lump in her throat that made breathing, much less talking, difficult.

With a final nip at her skin, Oliver lowered her hand and laced his fingers with hers. "I can't promise that things won't get even crazier and there are certain realities we can't overlook. But I want you to be comfortable. If there's something you want to try, somewhere you want to go—tell me. I'll do my best to make it happen. Because I want you to be happy, Renee."

She took a long, slow breath. It wouldn't do to burst

into heaving sobs at that, even though it was one of the most beautiful things anyone had ever said to her. She was going to blame the hormones for all of this tearfulness.

On the other hand…what had that meant, if there was something she wanted to try? Were they talking about baking or…

Surely he wasn't talking about her fantasies. They were already making excellent headway on them. The knight in shining armor riding to her rescue? Yeah, that alone covered a lot of territory.

But before she could come up with any sort of reasonable response, she was saved by Oliver withdrawing his hand and turning into an underground garage. "We're here."

As he entered the access code and parked in his assigned spot, Renee felt old doubts creeping in. Oliver was being wonderful—there was no question about that. In fact, before he had come upstairs to tell her she was coming back to Dallas with him tonight and her baking lessons were being postponed because she wasn't safe at Red Oak Hill anymore—before all of that, she had been having the most wonderful day she could remember.

And it wasn't just the cookies.

She could *not* remember the last time she'd had a conversation with anyone that didn't involve the phrase "You should…" in one way or another.

Because everyone had an opinion. Of course her lawyers were going to say that—she was going into debt for their legal advice. But her parents? Her brother? Her husband? Her friends? It was for the best. Wasn't that what they all said? No one had said it louder than her mother. Her *suggestions* were thinly veiled orders she expected to be followed.

When was the last time anyone had asked her what

she wanted? Promised to make it happen? When was the last time anyone had gone *this* far out of the way for her?

When was the last time someone had done something as simple as make her laugh? Because she couldn't remember laughing as hard as she had at the sight of Oliver, butt naked, jumping out of the water while a pair of perturbed swans made menacing noises. For as long as she lived, she would never forget the sound of Oliver's laughter when he'd landed on his butt in the pond. And there'd been that moment when she'd thought he was furious that she'd nearly ruined everything—and instead he'd been teasing her.

Cookie monster, indeed.

She'd stood up for herself. She'd laughed so hard she'd got a stitch in her side. She'd come out on top—literally, she'd come on top of him. When was the last time she'd enjoyed sex so much?

Today had been magical. She hadn't climaxed like that in so long that she had almost forgotten what it was like. And then, instead of telling her she was getting fat, Lucille had told her that she had a glow about her. That she would get better at cookies if she kept practicing.

She hoped that, one day, she'd get back out to Red Oak Hill. Back out to that place out of time where she could be free, even if it were just another short visit.

Carrying her bag, Oliver led her toward a private elevator that required a key code to open. "The security here is good. The lobby is open, but all of the elevators are coded and guards are on duty twenty-four hours a day. No one should be able to slip in."

She nodded as the doors closed behind them. This was important information—necessary, she was sure. But she didn't want to hear about safety and privacy because that was a constant reminder that she was the pregnant

Preston Pyramid Princess and her family had hurt people and, even if she wasn't responsible, she was still at fault.

Her stomach lurched as the elevator began to climb. It'd been easy this evening to forget that simple truth that Oliver was risking not just his home but his reputation and his entire business by protecting her. It wasn't ruined cookies that drove Oliver out of his ranch house tonight. It was her.

Now he was bringing her here? This was a terrible idea. Why couldn't he see that she was a risk to him?

But he couldn't. "I'll request that you not leave the building without me. I know you can handle yourself, but I don't want to worry." He cupped her face in his palm. "I'm..." He took a deep breath. "I'm not used to worrying. I don't like it."

She leaned into his touch. "I'm sorry." Sorry for making him worry, sorry for setting off smoke alarms, sorry for upending his life. She was sorry for things that hadn't even happened yet but were still highly likely to occur.

"Don't apologize." His voice was deep as he lifted her face. "Not to me," he said against her lips.

She shouldn't lean into the kiss. She shouldn't want him and she certainly shouldn't take what he was offering. If she had half a brain, she would catch a ride to a nice hotel and spend the next week or so ordering room service and watching television. If she watched enough Food Network, she'd probably learn a lot about cookies.

But she didn't want to. It was selfish and greedy, but she wanted to kiss a man who wanted her—only her. So she did. She wanted to wrap her arms around his waist and pull him against her so that her breasts were pressed against his hard chest, so she did that, too. And when the elevator dinged to a stop and the doors opened, she didn't want to end the kiss.

But she had to when Oliver pulled away from her, his eyes dark with desire. "We should get inside," he said, but he didn't let her go. He slid his free arm around her waist and guided her down a short hallway with only three doors. "My condo is half the floor. Of the other two condos, one is an oil baron who only sleeps here when he's in town on a business meeting and the other family, I believe, is summering in Paris. So the only people who come off the elevator should be me or Lucille."

She suppressed a sigh. "All right." Like Oliver had said—there were certain realities that neither one of them could ignore. Oh, how she wanted to ignore them.

Wouldn't it be lovely to pretend that they were coming home after an evening out, just the two of them? That this was an everyday occurrence, kissing on the elevator and struggling to keep their hands to themselves until they were behind closed doors? Oh, how she wished that this were her real life instead of a brief, wonderful interlude.

He'd said that all she had to do was ask and he would do his best to give it to her. Somehow, she didn't think he'd been talking about the rest of their lives.

Because she couldn't ask that of him. Sooner or later, her family's scandal would catch up with her. Even if nothing came up about their misadventure with the fire department today, eventually word would get out. That was just the nature of scandals. She'd be called back to New York to testify, kicking off a fresh round of gossip and hatred, especially because she was more noticeably pregnant every single day. When that happened, it wouldn't be just her caught in the cross fire. It would be Oliver.

She shouldn't have barged into his life. If she were smart, she'd bail now.

But then he opened the door to his condo and ushered her inside. When the lights came on, she gasped. "It's beautiful."

The apartment she had lived in with Chet had been worth close to six million, but in reality it had been a smallish two-bedroom apartment. Chet had hated it, hated that they hadn't been able to get the place he'd really wanted, which had gone for ten million and had four bedrooms and a formal dining room. Renee had always considered their snug condo to be perfect and she'd known that, sooner or later, they would move out. But that had never been good enough for Chet. He hadn't looked at it as a starter home. He'd looked at the smallish condo with only four windows and no balcony and seen nothing but failure because it wasn't the very best.

Renee had always feared that he'd had the same feeling when he'd looked at her.

But Oliver's place? There were floor-to-ceiling windows that wrapped around a wall behind a dining table set for six and continued around the corner to another full wall of windows with plush leather sofas and chairs that was interrupted only by an elaborate fireplace and mantel. She glanced around, but she saw no signs that this place was occupied by more than one person.

The place looked...lived-in. Like his study out at Red Oak Hill. Everything in here was of the highest quality. She knew an expensive Persian rug when she saw one and there were three scattered around with various seats grouped around them. All that wealth was understated.

This was his home, on the top floor of a thirty-story building with a view that encompassed half of Texas.

Nothing could touch her here. No other windows looked down into his apartment because this was the tallest building for blocks. She was above the fray here—

literally. "You can see for forever," she said in a sigh, drifting to a window and staring out at the twinkling lights of the city. It wasn't as perfect as Fred and Wilma swimming in the pond but it was *amazing*.

Oliver came up behind her. Her breath caught in her chest when she saw the look in his eyes. Even the hazy reflection in the window couldn't blur away the desire in his eyes. And she was still in her leggings and a T-shirt. After everything that had happened today—and especially with her looking like she did—how could he still look at her like that?

"The view is always spectacular," he said as his gaze dipped to her chest. Her nipples hardened to tight points and she heard him suck in a deep breath. Then he stepped into her and rested his hands on her shoulders. "But it's even better now."

Oliver watched Renee's reflection in the glass as he rubbed her shoulders. He should be giving her a tour of the rest of the condo. He should be showing her to the guest room and giving her plenty of space. It was late and they'd had a crazy afternoon and she was pregnant and…and…

And none of it mattered when he touched her. Despite the air-conditioning and her clothes, he could feel her body's warmth under his touch. When she leaned back into him?

Yeah, this was what being lost felt like.

He wrapped his arms around her waist. "Tell me what you want, babe. I want to give it to you."

Her reflection smiled a saucy smile at him and reached up to lace her fingers into his hair. He went hard for her, harder than he'd ever been in his life. Which was saying something, considering it'd only been a few hours since he'd buried himself in her body.

"I don't want to talk about safety and security," she said, giving his hair a tug to pull him down to her.

"Done." He didn't want to deal with those realities anymore, either. He had her here now and he sure as hell wasn't going to let her go.

"I want to make cookies tomorrow."

He slipped his hands underneath her T-shirt. Bless these loose shirts and doubly bless her for going without a bra. Did she know how much it tortured him to watch her walk around, her beautiful breasts swinging freely? "I'll show you where the fire extinguisher is before I leave for work," he said, cupping her in his hands and stroking the undersides of her breasts.

She inhaled sharply, but he didn't want to rush this. Earlier, he hadn't been able to hold back, to hell with the consequences. But now? They had the rest of the night. If he was dragging at his meeting with Ritter tomorrow, that was a price he was willing to pay. As long as he had Renee in his arms tonight.

So he took his time fondling her breasts and teasing her nipples. He focused on listening to her breaths and watching her reactions in the glass.

When her body bucked in response to his gentle tug on her nipples, he felt it down to his toes. When she moaned as he rolled those nipples between his thumb and forefinger, he moaned with her. He couldn't help it. Her pleasure was his.

She was his.

"Look at you," Oliver breathed as he stared at Renee's reflection in the window. Her mouth was open as she panted, her eyes heavy-lidded. It had almost killed him to watch the light in her eyes die a little when, instead of taking her right back to bed, he'd told her they were leaving.

He wanted to see the Renee who managed to get the upper hand on him, who laughed at his corny jokes, who wasn't afraid of anything—she was the Renee he wanted back. He'd do anything to make her smile again.

The moment the thought crossed his brain, he was stunned by the truth of it.

He would do anything for her.

"You feel so wonderful," he told her as he let the full weight of her breasts fill his palms. "But I need to see these. I need to see all of you."

She inhaled sharply as he skimmed his hands down her ribs and over her hips to the hem of her T-shirt. But when he started to lift, she stopped his hands. "I don't… What if someone sees?"

"No one can see in these windows. That's one of the reasons I've bought this condo."

She didn't let him strip off her shirt. If anything, her grip on his hands tightened. "But…"

Oliver dragged his attention away from the reflection of her chest in the window and looked at her face. The sensual glaze of desire was gone, leaving her face drawn and tight. Then, somewhere far in the distance, a light blinked. It was probably a helicopter or something that was at least a few miles away, but Renee gasped as if someone had flown a drone into the window and started snapping pictures.

Right.

He kissed the side of her neck and then bent over, sweeping her legs out from under her. "Oliver!" she squeaked in alarm.

"I'm being a terrible host," he said, holding her tight against his chest. "I haven't even given you the tour yet."

"Oh?" She relaxed into him, her arms going around his neck. "I saw the living room."

"But not the kitchen," he said, walking right past the doorway on his left.

"It's lovely," she murmured and then her lips were against his neck. "I look forward to spending time there."

"Office," he ground out through gritted teeth as he carried her past the dark doorway on his right.

"It suits you perfectly," she agreed without looking. Then she began to suck.

His knees almost gave. "Guest room." Another fifteen steps—he could make it.

"Is that where I'm staying?" Her teeth skimmed over his skin with the barest hint of pressure.

Take what you need, he wanted to tell her. Hell, he wanted to shout it. "No," he groaned, all but staggering into his master suite. Dimly, he was aware this was supposed to be a slow, steady seduction where all the focus was on her. "For as long as you want, you're staying here with me."

"I…"

"Tell me," he all but begged. His body was on fire for hers but he didn't want to presume a single damned thing. "Tell me what you want."

She leaned back and gave him that smile, the exact same grin she'd launched at him seconds before she'd shoved him into the pond. It made him want to yell with victory.

"I want you." Then she bit him—not hard, but it sent a jolt of need through him unlike anything he'd ever experienced before.

He couldn't even make it to the bed along the far wall. He all but dropped her in front of the door to his walk-in closet.

The door covered with a full-length mirror.

He paused only long enough to reach over and flip on the light. The drapes were pulled and no one would be able to see anything he did to her.

And he was going to do it all.

When the lights flickered on, she gasped. But he was already pulling her T-shirt over her head. "God, Renee," he whispered, starting where he'd left off at her breasts. This time, he tugged on her nipples a little harder and was rewarded with a shudder. "You truly take my breath away."

"I do?"

It just about broke his heart to hear the doubt in her voice. She truly didn't see it.

This was a problem—but he had the solution. He'd make her believe she was the most beautiful woman he'd ever seen or he'd die trying. And given how much he was aching for her, she might be the death of him.

With the last of his control, he spun her around. For the second time today, he hooked his fingers into her pants and pulled, baring her. "Do you have any idea what you do to me?" Because the sight of her bottom begging for his touch really was going to kill him.

So he touched. He slid his hands down her full hips and then to her backside, where he dug his fingers into her generous flesh. She shuddered at his touch. Good. "I'm... I'm getting an idea."

"Not good enough. You need to know how badly I want you."

But when he looked in the mirror, he could see her struggling. "Oliver..."

"Babe." It was rude to interrupt her but he could see that she was going to do something terrible, like ask if they could turn the lights off and hide under the covers

and he couldn't let her think that there was a single thing about her he didn't want. "Watch," he commanded, falling to his knees so he could skim his teeth over the soft skin of her bottom. "Watch what you do to me. Watch what I do to you." Then he bit her. Not hard enough to bruise. He'd never hurt her. But he needed her to stop thinking and start feeling.

It worked. She sucked in a ragged gasp as he kissed the sting away and slid his hand between her legs.

Slow. He needed to take this slow. Because…reasons. Good ones, he was pretty sure.

But those reasons were lost to him as Renee shifted her legs apart for him. She put her hands on the mirror, her gaze moving from Oliver to where he was touching her and back again. He could see her surrendering to her needs—her eyes growing darker, her chest heaving as her breath came faster and faster.

He dug deep for words that were more than just *mine*. "Do you see how pretty you are?" he asked quietly, kissing his way up her back. "Do you see how luscious you are?" He cupped her bottom and squeezed. "God, I love your body."

"Even though…"

If she was trying to convince him that he couldn't want her because someone had told her she was fat, he was going to lose it.

He surged to his feet. "Renee. *Look*." He gripped her by the chin—again, gently—and turned her face so she had no choice but to look in the mirror. "I don't care what anyone else says. I only see you. I see your beautiful eyes and your delicate collarbone," he said, letting his hand drift down to that bit of skin. "And your breasts. God, your breasts." He cupped them again. Since he couldn't kiss them from this angle, he settled for kissing her neck—which he did without breaking eye contact in the mirror. "You are the sexiest woman I've ever seen."

"Don't tease," she said but at the very least, it came out as a breathy sigh. "I'm sorry I pushed you in the pond."

"I'm not." That moment when she'd fought for herself had been glorious.

That was what she needed to do right now—fight for herself. "This is the only way I'd tease you, darling." He slid one hand over the swell of her stomach again and down between her legs. "God, do you see how pretty you are? See how your eyes darken with want?"

"Yes," she moaned, her head dropping back on his shoulder. But she didn't look away as he tormented her nipples, her sex.

He thrust his hips against her backside, his erection chafing behind his pants. "Do you feel what you do to me?" This was where they'd been earlier at the window before she'd allowed doubt to crowd out desire. She sagged against him, bearing down on his hand, but he wrapped his free arm around her waist and held her up. "Look at you," he said, breathing hard as he stared at where he was touching her. "Look at us."

"Oliver," she said, her voice straining.

He pulled back only long enough to shove his pants aside. "Feel what you do to me?" he moaned against her skin.

Then she reached back and circled him with her hands. When she gripped him tightly, he had to brace himself against the mirror to keep from falling to his knees again. "Who else gets you like this?"

"You. Only you."

Her hand slipped lower to cup him. "No wife? No mistress or…" She squeezed and he made a noise that might be considered undignified, but he didn't give a single damn. "Or a girlfriend?"

He shook his head, trying to think. But what she was doing to him—there was no thinking. "Nine months— no, eight. Eight months since my last lady friend." Her grip shifted again and he was helpless to do anything but thrust into her hands.

"What am I, Oliver?" Her voice was so soft that he had to look at her. "What am I to you?"

Not a wife, obviously. But the moment that thought crossed his mind, he had to close his eyes against it.

He'd never wanted to get married. Never wanted to bring someone into his messy family life. He had enough responsibilities—how could he add a wife or children to managing his father and running Lawrence Energies and, who could forget, the damned rodeo? How much more did he have to give, when there was so little of himself left over?

But Renee was already a part of his family. She had been for years.

"Am I your mistress?" she went on and he heard an edge to her voice, one that made him want to weep with joy.

She was fighting back.

"No," he ground out when she gave him an extra-firm squeeze. Not that he wanted to think about her cheating, lying ex right now, but he realized on a fundamental level that she had to make sure. "Not a mistress. Not a... Oh, God," he groaned as she stroked him. "Not a girlfriend, either." That wasn't a strong enough word for what she meant to him.

"Then what am I?" Her voice was quiet but there was no mistaking it—she had him in the palm of her hand. Literally.

When she reached back with her other hand, Oliver's restraint cracked. He grabbed her by the wrists. "I can't wait," he growled as he pushed her hands against the mirror. "Don't move."

He grabbed the condom from his pants and frantically ripped it open. He nudged her legs apart and then slid into her warmth with one long thrust. They both moaned.

Mine. It was all he could think as he grabbed Renee by the hips and buried himself in her over and over again. It wasn't slow or sweet or tender. The way he took her was raw and hard and heaven help him, he loved it.

She loved it. Her hands on the mirror, she bent forward at the waist and thrust her backside up and out, just enough that she could see his face unobstructed in the mirror. And holding her gaze while he furiously pumped into her body was the singularly most erotic thing he'd experienced in his life.

She moaned and then shouted, "Oh, God—Oliver!"

"Renee," he growled, digging his fingers into her skin, fighting the urge to mark her as his.

She pushed back into his thrusts and cried out, her muscles clenching him so tightly that he couldn't hold anything back. Not with her. She would always push him past the point of reason, past the cold grip of logic.

He needed to do something. Something romantic, like whisper sweet words of promise in her ear. Something practical, like *take care of the condom. Something*, for God's sake.

"You destroy me, Renee" was what he came up with. "You simply destroy me."

Because Renee Preston-Willoughby had walked into his office and thrown everything ordered and planned about his life right out the window. His organized days of meetings? Gone. His long-term plans to grow Lawrence Energies—including the damned rodeo? Cast aside. His careful management of his family? Forgotten. His promise to his mother that he'd keep the family together? A distant memory.

All that was left was this fierce need to be with Renee and protect her—and her unborn child.

The destruction was complete.

Because she was his, by God. And he was not letting her go.

Ten

Renee focused on keeping her breath steady and even. Okay, it was a little heavy because sex with Oliver was proving to be so much *more* than she was used to.

That man had scandalously stood her in front of a mirror and made her believe—really believe—that she was pretty and desirable and worth the risk. He was worried about her and he wanted and needed her and he couldn't keep his hands off her and it was perfect.

Or it had been, right until he'd ruined it.

Oh, she knew he hadn't meant it as an insult or even a warning. But there was no mistaking that "you destroy me" for what it was—the truth.

Because she would. Sooner or later, she would ruin him. Not on purpose. Never on purpose. But it was inevitable, wasn't it? Either she was going to do something accidental, like set fire to one or more of his homes, or word would get out about their connection and his reputation would be dragged through the mud.

Knowing her luck, probably both. He thought he understood her messed-up family. But even if things went perfectly from here on out—the press left her alone or her baby's delivery was textbook or Oliver continued to be wonderful?

Her family would go on trial or her mother would find some way to ruin everything all the way from France because there was no way Rebecca Preston would approve of what Renee was doing. Preparing food? Doing the menial work of washing dishes? Doing something unladylike like pushing a friend into a pond and laughing out loud?

She hoped no one from that fire department went to the press. If her mother could find a way to ruin the little bit of peace Renee was struggling to hold on to, she would. Just out of spite.

She and Oliver were fogging the mirror up with their breaths. She didn't want to move. She wanted to pretend like everything was fine.

But she was tired of that, too. She'd spent years pretending and she wasn't going to anymore. At least, she was going to try to not do it as much. She might have to ease into this whole total-honesty thing.

But she definitely wasn't going to let thoughts of her mother into this room. Rebecca Preston had abandoned Renee long before she'd decamped to Paris. It was high time Renee returned the favor.

She pushed against the mirror and thankfully, Oliver backed up. She shivered from the loss of his body covering hers.

She turned to go to the bathroom just in case she fell apart, but Oliver caught her hand.

"Will you stay with me tonight?"

The smart thing to do would be to say no. He had a guest room. She was a guest.

But then he added, "It's whatever you want," and her resolve buckled because honestly, she wanted to spend the night curled in his arms. Whatever this was, it would end badly for all parties involved—she didn't have any doubt about that.

But the fact was it was going to end badly no matter what. Maybe it was selfish and definitely shortsighted, but she wanted to hold on to this little bit of happiness while she could.

So she brushed her lips against his and said, "I'll stay," because he'd done everything in his power to protect her. He'd made her feel good again. For heaven's sake, he hadn't even been that upset about the ruined cookies.

By the time she finished in the bathroom, Oliver had carried her bag in. "You're going to need more clothes," he said absentmindedly as he stared at the solitary piece of her luggage.

She didn't exactly have the money for new things, so she said, "It's not a big deal. I can do laundry."

Actually, she wasn't sure she could but that had to be one of those things that came with instructions. At the very least, Lucille should be able to walk her through the process while minimizing fire hazards.

Oliver looked up at her like she might be crazy. He must've taken advantage of the other bathroom because, while he had taken off his button-up shirt, he was still in his trousers and undershirt and she was completely nude. There was no missing the appreciative gleam in his eye but she was suddenly tired and feeling self-conscious. Her hands dropped to her thighs, covering the scars, but she thought she did so casually enough that he hadn't noticed.

If he wasn't naked, she wasn't going to parade about. The nightstand on the right side of his bed had the alarm clock, so she walked around to the other side and slid under the covers. She immediately felt better.

"You're just going to walk around braless? What happens when you need to leave the house?"

That was a good question. Suddenly, she had a feeling that Oliver was going to insist that she allow him to buy her clothes.

Because that's who Oliver was. If he saw a problem, he was honor-bound to find a solution. She had enough clothes for a week—but in another few weeks, she'd be pushing her luck with the underwear. She had a month, tops, in her yoga pants. Maybe another month in her loose tunic tops. And Oliver was right—eventually, she'd need a bra again. But if anyone caught wind of Oliver buying maternity clothes...

Destroyed. That was the only word for it.

To distract him, she arranged herself on the bed in what she hoped was an inviting way, making sure to suck in her stomach while the sheet fell down off her hips— but stayed above the scars on her thighs. "I thought you requested I not leave."

"You're not Rapunzel. I'm not going to lock you in a tower." His eyes darkened as he looked her over. "Although it's damned tempting to keep you all to myself for the weekend, at least."

Tempting. She liked that. She could still be tempting. And she could have him all to herself for the next few days. "What was that about the weekend?"

He made a noise that was part growl, part groan and all need. But then he paused. "Can I get you anything before I join you? Water? A snack?"

And that, in a nutshell, was why she was in Oliver's bed. "Just you."

She didn't have to ask twice. He flung his clothing

off and was between the sheets within moments. When he pulled her against his chest and pressed a kiss to her forehead that would've been tender if there hadn't been so much heat packed into it, Renee sighed with pleasure. As soon as she settled in his arms, though, her eyes began to drift closed. It had been a very *long* day...

When Oliver spoke, she startled back awake. "I have to go to work tomorrow and Friday," he said apologetically. "I've put this meeting off twice and there's no avoiding it. By Sunday we should know if anyone has connected you to Red Oak Hill. If not, I'd like to take you out. We've got museums or movies or the theater or—"

"Gosh, like a real city?" she couldn't help quipping. She ruined the sarcasm by yawning, however.

"Smart-ass." But as he said it, he began to stroke her hair. "There's a pretty park with a pond and ducks about a block away—we can just take a walk. Although I wouldn't recommend that at high noon, unless you enjoy sweating. Whatever you want—I'm yours for the weekend."

"I'll think about it." She was too damned tired to make any sort of decision right now. It was probably for the best that Oliver was going to work tomorrow. Today had been wild on about six different levels and she needed to recover.

But...there was something she wanted to do before Saturday. "Would it be all right if I called Chloe tomorrow?" So much had happened in the last week—which was saying something, because a lot had happened in the last five months. If she vented to Oliver, she knew he'd listen—but she also knew that he'd try to solve the problem. And she didn't want to be his problem.

She really needed a girlfriend, which meant Chloe. Frankly, there wasn't anyone else.

She felt the tension ripple through Oliver but as quickly

as it had appeared, it was gone. "I don't see why not. I'm sure if you explain the situation, she'll keep your whereabouts quiet. And she's launching a new clothing line, so she might be able to help with the clothes."

She smiled against his skin. Even when he wasn't solving the problem, he was still solving the problem. Men. *This* man.

Mine, her brain whispered as she yawned again. She was his and he was hers...wasn't he?

"I'll call her. But I won't tell her about us," she murmured against his chest. She wished Chloe were here, although...if she were, there would be no hiding the fact that Renee and Oliver were sleeping together. Or they were going to, shortly. Very shortly.

As she drifted off to sleep, she thought she heard him whisper, "I doubt that'll make much of a difference."

"You're *where*?" Chloe Lawrence squealed in Renee's ear.

"At Oliver's condo." Renee thought it best to leave out any mention of Oliver's ranch house. "It's a really long story, but I needed a place to lie low and you're... Where are you?"

"Omaha." Then Chloe's voice got muffled and Renee got the feeling she was giving instructions to someone. "Sorry. Oliver has given me a lot more control over the rodeo—which is great. But it's a lot of responsibility and combined with the Princess clothing launch..."

Renee exhaled in relief. "Which was exactly why I didn't try to track you down. I figured I would just hang out here until you came to Dallas and then we could catch up."

There was a long pause. "I told you not to marry that asshole."

"You were the only one," Renee said, trying to keep the bitterness out of her voice and failing. It wasn't Chloe's fault she'd been right—or that Renee hadn't listened. She deserved that *I told you so*. And probably a few others.

"Oliver would've told you not to marry him, too," Chloe said, because even as a kid, she'd never been able to let anything go.

Because this was a telephone call and not a video call, Renee rolled her eyes. "Tell me about the clothing line." Nothing like a change of subject to dance around the Oliver issue. "Couture or cowgirl?"

"Cowgirl," Chloe said so firmly that Renee had to wonder if she was insulted by the couture suggestion. "Why?"

So Renee laid it all out as quickly as she could. It was odd that Chloe was more up-to-date on the situation than Oliver had been. But she knew of Chet Willoughby's suicide—she'd sent flowers. She knew about the pyramid scheme and had sent emails—not a lot, but some—offering Renee support and help if she needed it.

What she didn't know was how the prosecutors had seized anything that was even remotely close to an asset.

"So all of the designer clothes are gone and even if I still had them, they wouldn't fit. I'm pregnant. I only brought two bras with me and neither works anymore." The words *your brother doesn't seem to mind* danced right up to the tip of Renee's tongue, but she bit down on them before they could escape. "Nothing's going to fit in a few weeks and I might be here longer than that."

"Man, I long for the days when I can wear nothing but yoga pants," Chloe said with a sigh. "But I understand the problem. I bet it's driving Oliver nuts that you're not in a suit or something. I hope he's not being a total butthead."

"He's...fine." Which was not a lie. He certainly wasn't

being a butthead. But that left a lot of room around what *fine* meant. "It's not like anyone will see me in his condo."

"Wait—why did he take you to the condo? Why didn't he take you to the ranch?"

Renee bit her lip. "He did. But I decided I wanted to bake cookies and there was…an incident. The fire department showed up."

"Did you burn Red Oak Hill down?" Chloe asked in a panic. "He loves that place! And those stupid swans!"

"No, no." Although just thinking about it—again—made her stomach flip. "It was only some cookies. The swans are fine. It was just smoke."

Unexpectedly, Chloe began to laugh. "Was Oliver mad? He's *such* a stick-in-the-mud."

That was the thing Renee kept coming back to—he had been upset. But he hadn't taken it out on her. Instead, he'd treated it more like she'd pulled off a successful, funny prank and he was impressed. She told Chloe the whole story.

Chloe hooted with laughter. "I would've paid good money to see that. I knew he was hiding something! If he'd told me you were there, I would've tried to get there, even if only for the day."

"Yeah? I'll admit, it'd be great to see you." Of course, Chloe was too smart by half. She'd take one look at Renee and know for sure that she was sleeping with Oliver. "But Oliver's taking care of me. So you don't have to worry."

Chloe made a humming noise and Renee realized she might have overplayed her hand. But then Chloe said, "Hey, the rodeo is coming to Dallas—well, Fort Worth, which is practically the same thing—in three weeks. I'll be in town for at least five days—longer if I can swing it. You, my friend, are going to spend a few days with me and we are going to catch up. I'm going to take you to the rodeo," Chloe said in a tone of voice that made it clear this was nonnegotiable. "A pitcher of sangria, unhealthy snacks and—"

"I'm pregnant." As if anyone could forget that small detail.

"I don't mind. That's more sangria for me." She was quiet for a moment. "Renee, are you sure you're doing okay? I know Oliver can be grumpy. And rude. And bossy. And—"

"It's fine," Renee interrupted. True, Oliver could be all of those things. But far more often, he was encouraging and kind. When he teased her, she could tease right back and feel safe that, instead of telling her she was wrong, he'd laugh with her instead. "And are you sure going to a rodeo is the best idea? I'm supposed to be lying low."

"It'll be fine! I'll send you some Princess clothes to tide you over but when we're at my place, we'll try everything on. We'll get you a fab hat and I'll tell Oliver to keep an eye on you." She sighed heavily. "As long as we keep you away from Flash, it'll be fine."

"Well…" She remembered Flash being an extremely irritating little brother. There had been lizards involved. But maybe he'd changed. After all, she wasn't the same little sister she'd been back then, either. "I'd actually love to go to one. I've never seen the Princess of the Rodeo in all her glory." Chloe snorted. "But only if Oliver agrees…" She was pretty sure he wouldn't.

"Oh, he will," Chloe said, sounding way too pleased with herself. "It's his damned rodeo, too. He doesn't appreciate how awesome it is. If we're lucky, Flash will get stepped on by a bull. But," she went on, apparently cheered by that thought, "in the meantime, try not to kill him. I know he's uptight but it's just because he never has fun."

"He doesn't?" The man who owned a pair of swans named after the Flintstones seemed like he had maybe a little fun at least some of the time.

"He wouldn't know fun if it bit him on the butt."

Renee smiled at the memory of Oliver jumping when the swans took offense to his invasion of their pond.

Chloe went on, "I worry about the butthead. All he does is work and micromanage. He argues with Dad constantly about the business. He orders me to keep Flash out of trouble—as if anyone could keep Flash out of trouble," she added under her breath. "And all he does with Flash is fight. Promise me you won't let him boss you around."

Renee let that thought roll around her head. If she hadn't spent the last few days with Oliver, she would've agreed with Chloe's assessment. Because that's who Oliver had been, at least in her memory.

Frankly, that was who he'd been at her brother's wedding and that'd been five years ago. Because she'd tried. She'd struck up a conversation with him and she would've asked him to dance, if she'd got to before he'd had so much to drink. Oliver hadn't tried to boss her around, but he had been the textbook definition of *grumpy.*

"He's been great," she finally said, hoping that wasn't giving too much away. "Really, I don't want you to worry about us. I'm more concerned about what to wear to your rodeo."

There was a moment when she didn't think Chloe was going to go for that subject change. But then she said, "What size are you?" And they fell into the familiar habit of discussing clothes and sizing.

"I'll send some samples out for you," Chloe said. "It's not what you'd normally wear, but you'll blend in. And they're *samples.* You can't pay me for them," she added.

Because Chloe was a real friend, bless her heart. It

shouldn't feel different, accepting this gift instead of one from Oliver. But it did. "Thanks, Chloe. I can't wait to see you in a few weeks."

"If Oliver gives you any trouble, call me immediately."

Renee almost defended Oliver again, but she decided that would only make Chloe more suspicious so instead she said, "I will. Promise."

She sat there for a moment after the call ended. Chloe's clothing line didn't make maternity clothing, but she was going to send things a size or two up, which would give Renee a couple of more months to figure out how she was going to afford everything else she needed. Which meant the only thing she needed to buy on her own was underwear, and she could afford a bra and a few pairs of panties.

She began to browse on her phone. But instead of basic white or nude underthings, she found herself looking at pretty bra and pantie sets. Because Oliver wanted to take her out and show her the town. But more than that, because *she* wanted to feel pretty. Leggings were great but they weren't doing much for her ability to look in a mirror and feel good about what she saw. She wanted to be *tempting*, damn it. And she had about two hundred dollars left in her bank account from the money the feds had allotted her to travel with. New panties it was.

She still heard her mother's voice, dripping with icy menace as she complained about Renee getting fat. But at least now, she also had the memory of Oliver telling her how gorgeous she was and how he couldn't keep his hands off her.

She had to choose who to believe. And her mother had never loved her.

Not that Oliver loved her. Of course not. He liked her and he worried about her and that…that was enough.

This whole situation was still a mess. Just like her life. But she couldn't stop thinking about what Chloe had said—Oliver never had any fun. That picture of him didn't mesh with him laughing and naked in the mud, or of him insisting that he show her the town.

It was high time they both started having more fun.

Eleven

"Are you sleeping with her?"

It took a lot of work to make sure Oliver's face didn't react to this bald statement. Obviously, Renee had talked to Chloe. He'd known there was no way Chloe wouldn't put two and two together. But he hadn't quite expected her to scream it in his ear. "One moment." He turned to Herb Ritter, praying the older man hadn't been able to make out Chloe's screech. "Thanks again for coming by. I'm sorry our meeting had to be pushed back."

The older man did something Oliver never would've seen coming in million years—he winked. "I hope she was worth it," Herb said in his gravelly voice. "But try not to let it happen again."

Oliver came *this close* to asking Herb to keep the revelation that a woman was involved to himself, but he managed to hold on to his tongue. At this point, he was neither confirming nor denying anything involving Renee to anyone.

Including his own sister. He waited until the door had closed behind Herb before he turned his attention back to his sister, who was humming the *Jeopardy!* theme song on the other end of the line. "Can I help you with something?"

"You are! You're sleeping with Renee! I *knew* it."

Was there anything worse than a little sister gloating? If so, Oliver couldn't think of what that might be. But he had all the plausible deniability in the world when Renee was the subject. "What are you talking about?" Maybe he'd missed his calling in the theater.

"She told me you were being nice to her and frankly, you're not nice to anyone. Especially not her. So clearly you and Renee have hooked up."

He knew better than to fall for the trick of making a blanket denial. Chloe had missed her calling as a lawyer. Instead, he focused on the first part of the accusation. "I am perfectly capable of being polite, as is Renee. We both grew up and are no longer whiny children. Unlike some people I know," he said, hoping that Chloe would take the bait.

She didn't. "Do you have any idea how big of a mess she's in? And you creeping up on her isn't helping anything! You should keep your damn hands off her! Just because she's vulnerable and needy doesn't give you the right—"

"Stop right there," Oliver growled and, to Chloe's credit, she did. "First off, I am not taking advantage of anyone. Second off, I know exactly how big of a mess she's—I spoke with Clint, the ass, over the phone."

"Really? *Whoa.*"

He ignored her. "Third off, whatever happens between consenting adults is absolutely no business of yours—"

"I knew it," Chloe muttered under her breath.

"And fourth off," he ground out through gritted teeth, "she is *not* vulnerable and needy. She is not a helpless damsel in distress or a lost child and it's insulting her to imply she is. She's a woman in a difficult situation doing the best she can to get her life back on track for her and her child and all I'm doing is giving her the space to decide what she wants to do and helping her accomplish those goals, whether it's attempting a cookie recipe or shielding her from the press. And furthermore," he went on, because he was on a roll and Chloe wasn't interrupting him and that was a rare thing, "I am not creeping on anyone. *Really*, Chloe? You know damn good and well that Mom loved Renee like she was one of the family and all I'm doing for her is what I'd do for you or Flash."

Except for the part where he stripped her down and lost himself in her body. But again—he was neither confirming nor denying that.

"Because that's what Mom would want and expect out of me—out of all of us. So don't insult me or Renee, *sis*, because she's had quite enough unfounded accusations and rumors to last her the rest of her life. Are we clear?"

There was a stunned moment of silence. Oliver wasn't sure if the stunned part was coming from him or from Chloe.

Because he might have just lost his temper. There may have been shouting involved—he wasn't sure. Hopefully, Herb had got out of earshot.

"Is Renee why you gave me the negotiations?" All of her righteous anger was gone.

Yes. But he kept that to himself. "The rodeo is yours, you know that. Just because Dad doesn't appreciate all the work you do to make it profitable doesn't mean I don't."

"Did you just compliment me?" Chloe let out a low whistle. "You did! Jesus, she's good for you. And before you yell at me again, I'm not insulting either of you."

He growled.

"There's the brother I know and love. Listen, I invited Renee to stay with me when I'm in town and I'm taking her to the rodeo."

"That is *not* a good idea." But even as he said it—all right, even as he *growled* it—he knew he was being ridiculous. Hadn't he offered to take her to museums and theaters and whatever she wanted? A rodeo wasn't that different, was it?

Then again, it was the rodeo. Ugh.

"Keep your pants on. I'm sending her a bunch of clothes and we'll find a hat. I could give her big hair. Ooh! We'll try new eye makeup. Trust me, when I'm done with her, no one will recognize her."

He would. He'd recognize her in a crowd in the middle of the night.

"Oliver? You know I wouldn't do anything to hurt her. Or you, I guess."

"Thanks, brat." But he let go of the breath he'd been holding all the same. "How are the negotiations coming along?"

The conversation thankfully veered off into business then, but Oliver couldn't get Renee out of his mind. When he ended the call, he couldn't do anything but sit there and stare at the pictures lining the far wall—all those artistic action shots of the rodeo that Renee had noticed the moment she'd waltzed into his office.

He hated the rodeo—the smells and dirt, the bulls, the young idiots who risked life and limb for a belt buckle—and that absolutely included Flash. Oliver hated the whole damned thing. But if Renee wanted to go see one and

Chloe could disguise her appearance…maybe they could pull it off.

He had so much he needed to do. He should have Bailey order some flowers—delivered to the office so that he could give them to Renee in person. And more baking things—he'd make sure Lucille brought plenty of supplies with her. He needed to find out who Renee's lawyers were and make sure they were doing their job. And he should get the name of a trustworthy doctor. He didn't know how long she'd be here, but if there was a problem, he didn't want to take her to the emergency room and hope no one recognized her. A private doctor who would be on call—for a price, of course—was the solution. And…

Well, she'd be here at least long enough to go to the rodeo in three weeks. And after that?

A vision of her rounding out with her pregnancy materialized in his mind. She absolutely glowed, damn it, and he had a powerful urge to tell her she wasn't going anywhere until after the baby was born. But it wasn't like she could just up and relocate with a newborn. She'd need help then, too. And that baby—Oliver would have to make sure that the media didn't descend like locusts and turn that innocent child into nothing but clickbait.

Would she want him to be there when the baby was born? Would she want him by her side, holding her hand and telling her how amazing she was? Would she want him to hold that whole new person that was the best of her? Or…not?

A sickening wave of loss twisted his insides at the thought of Renee giving birth without anyone beside her to fight for her and that baby. Even if it wasn't him, at least he could make sure Chloe was there. Just so long as Renee knew she wasn't alone.

He shook his head. He was getting ahead of himself

by months. *Years*. Doctors and lawyers were all well and good, but it wasn't like he was asking Renee to stay forever. Chloe was right about that, at least. Renee's life was too complicated for anyone to be thinking about anything more long-term. There were still trials and plea deals to work through and the media to avoid. He needed to focus on the next three weeks. After that, he'd focus on the next three weeks.

Right. He needed roses and chocolate chips. And more condoms. But those he was getting himself. Because, while he trusted Bailey completely, there was no way in hell Oliver was asking anyone else to pick up protection.

Because that's all this was. He was protecting Renee, damn it.

And if that meant he had to go to the rodeo, then he'd suck it up.

For her. Only for her.

"Can I ask you a question?"

Breathing hard, Renee managed to open one eye and peer up at him. "I'm going to need five minutes to recover," she wheezed. The man was simply the best—and most intense—lover she'd ever had.

At least this time they'd made it to his bed. There was something to be said for actual sheets and pillows. Plus, the air was scented with roses and the smell of them together.

He'd brought her flowers. It was a ridiculously sweet thing and if she thought about it too much, she might get teary.

He grinned. "Not that." Moving slow, he skimmed the sheet down her body. At first, Renee thought he was going for another seduction—right until he unveiled the scars. "These."

Renee's lungs seized up. How could she have thought that he wouldn't notice them? Oliver was the most attentive, thoughtful and observant man she'd ever know.

But old habits died hard. She felt her chin lift and her shoulders square, which was impressive considering she was sprawled out over at least three of the four pillows on the bed. "These what?"

"Renee," he said, giving her a look. "Don't do that."

"Do what?" But even as the words left her mouth, she winced. Stupid defense mechanisms.

"*That*. When you put on your armor. You don't have to do that with me. And these are…weird." He looked at her thighs, catching her hands before she could cover them. "I thought they were freckles but they're too regularly spaced and all grouped together. And your right leg has a lot more of them."

How, exactly, did someone say, *Oh, those? That's just what happens when you repeatedly jab a fork into human skin. What of it?* She had no idea.

But if she said, *I don't want to talk about them*, then Oliver would wonder. And he'd ask again. He wouldn't take the pat answer at face value because he was the rare man who actually wanted the truth instead of pretty little lies.

And she didn't want to lie to him. She wanted there to be truth and trust between them.

Funny how those things were easier said than done.

Then he leaned down and pressed a kiss to the rows of tiny scars. "You don't have to tell me, if you don't want. But if you change your mind, I'll be here."

Really, the man was too perfect. She exhaled slowly and then, when she was sure her hand wasn't shaking, ran her fingers through his hair. "All right."

He rested his head on her leg, staring up at her with something that sure seemed like adoration. She was just happy he could still see around her belly. Honestly, between the pregnancy and the cookies, she was impressed she hadn't got bigger than she already had. "Do you want to go to the rodeo?"

"Maybe." She relaxed back into the pillows and stroked his hair. "But you hate the rodeo."

He grinned and she almost wished she could take a picture to show Chloe and say, *See? He can have fun.* "I can be mildly inconvenienced for an evening if you want to see the Princess of the Rodeo in action," he said as he moved to lie down by her side again. She couldn't help but think he sounded resigned to the fact. "Who knows— maybe we'll get lucky and Flash will get stepped on."

She burst out laughing.

He notched an eyebrow at her. "What?"

"Chloe said the same thing. I'm sensing a theme."

"It'll be fine. We won't be in the stands—there's usually a separate seating section for the VIPs," he said, stroking a finger down her cheek. "Brooke Bonner is the musical act that night, too. We'll make a date of it. If you want."

She thought about that. "It can't be any riskier than going to a museum, right? And I do like Brooke's music. Country rockabilly or whatever—it's good girl power music."

"Then we'll go." He squeezed her tight.

Her heart ached with a strange sort of happiness. It was such an unusual feeling, knowing that someone was willing to do something they didn't want to just for her.

She curled back against his side. "Oh, I ordered a few things today to go with the clothing Chloe's sending."

"Hmm?"

"A new bra. And matching panties."

Oliver groaned, which made her laugh again.

She hadn't been able to spend the money on her usual brand—La Perla was not cheap. But she'd found some cute sets at a discount site for less than fifty dollars, which was as much as she could comfortably spend. Then she'd done her best to guess on sizes, erring on the side of caution. If they were too big right now, they'd fit eventually.

"I can't wait to see them."

"Well, you'll get to do that before me—I didn't know the address here so I had them sent to your office." It wasn't like she couldn't have found out the street address of this condo. But there was something to be said for upping their pranks to a more mature level. One that included a lingerie delivery to the office.

Oliver rolled onto her, pinning her beneath his weight. The man was amazing—five minutes really was all he needed. She giggled as they struggled to get the sheet out from between their bodies.

Then, holding himself over her, his smile faded and was replaced by a look of such intensity that it took her breath away all over again. "God, Renee, you destroy me," he said before he captured her lips with his and it was a good thing he was kissing her because she didn't know what to say to that.

Oh, what a mess. She couldn't bring herself to tell him about the scars, about why she and Clint had always been at the Lawrence house instead of their own. But the longer she kept quiet, the more he'd feel like she hadn't put her faith in him when he did find out.

And the longer this not-dating thing they were doing went on, the more time he spent with her, the bigger the implosion would be. She knew all of that and, sadly, she was too selfish to put a stop to it.

Because Oliver was the best thing that had happened to her in a long, long time. So she kissed him back and wrapped her legs around his waist and, after he rolled on the condom and plunged into her, she dug her fingers into his bottom to urge him on because she wanted him.

She might not ruin him. Not like she'd been ruined. But his personal life would become public fodder and his business would take a hit. Because of her. Because of *this*.

But at least he knew it.

Hopefully he'd never find out about the rest.

After two and a half weeks of playing house, Renee was more than ready for a change of scenery.

Not that she was complaining. She'd managed to produce not just a decent chocolate chip cookie on a consistent basis, but had also turned out surprisingly edible sugar cookies and even a batch of snickerdoodles. She was giving Lucille a solid 75 percent of the credit for that, but still. Oliver was taking cookies to work to share with his staff on an almost-daily basis. She had no idea how he was explaining that, but no one had died of food poisoning so it must be okay.

The amount of satisfaction she felt when she opened the oven and pulled out a sheet of nearly perfectly round cookies that not only looked right but tasted good was amazing. Even better was when Oliver came home and, after a kiss—okay, sometimes after a lot more than kissing—he'd try a cookie and tell her it was good. The first time he'd pronounced a snickerdoodle she'd made all by herself "really good," she was so happy she'd actually started crying.

Stupid hormones.

The day he'd brought home the underthings she'd ordered, they never made it to the cookies. Hell, they didn't even make it to the bedroom—not at first anyway. The only time Oliver had hesitated was to ask if the oven was off.

It was.

The day the box of clothes arrived from Chloe, Renee spent the whole afternoon playing dress up and video chatting with Chloe about what worked and what didn't, what Renee liked, what she might change. She got two tunic tops that might last her a few months and two pairs of super-skinny-leg jeans two sizes larger than she normally wore that fitted comfortably with the addition of a rhinestone belt. Chloe had even included a pair of boots— *because everyone wears them and you should break them in now,* she'd said.

Which is how Oliver came home one night to find her in boots and not much else.

They barely made it to the hallway that night.

She baked and learned how to wash dishes and do laundry and clean up after herself. She pestered Lucille for information about babies and pregnancy and also how to vacuum when the older woman came every Monday to clean the condo. Renee watched baking shows and kids' cartoons and whatever else struck her fancy, including a kung fu movie with subtitles.

And when Oliver came home from work, they had fun together. There hadn't been any breathless updates on the Preston Pyramid Princess being spotted in Texas so Renee didn't dread leaving the house. They went to late showings of movies and picked up carryout food—she'd never eaten so much barbecue in her entire life but it was glorious—and when she announced that maybe she'd like to learn how to crochet, he took her to a craft store.

He didn't ask about the scars again and she didn't tell him. But then again, he didn't ask about her former husband or her family and she wasn't about to taint their time together by bringing any of that crap up. She was surprisingly, amazingly happy right now. If only they could stay this way.

It wouldn't last. It couldn't. Renee knew this like she knew her name. The way she burned for Oliver was something white-hot and clear—but, like all raging infernos, it would burn itself out soon enough. After all, she'd once believed that Chet loved her beyond distraction, and see how that had turned out?

She knew Oliver wasn't the same kind of person Chet had been. She *knew* that. But it was hard to unlearn a lifetime of lessons. A few really great weeks didn't change things, not in the long term. Her family was still toxic and she might be called back to New York City at any moment and there was still a pregnancy to deal with. She had no idea how long she and Oliver could share a bed and a condo before things got awkward and even less of an idea of where she would go when it did. She couldn't imagine him relishing the idea of a crying newborn upending his world.

But that was months off. Right now, things were good.

And in a few days, Chloe was coming.

Then they were all going to the rodeo.

Twelve

He wasn't wearing a hat and that was final.

Oliver had no problem putting on the boots and the belt buckle, and jeans and a button-up shirt with a sports jacket were fine, but he drew the line at a hat. Yes, Flash looked decent enough in his black felt hat but Oliver was of the opinion—the correct opinion—that his father looked like a life-size Howdy Doody doll in his enormous Stetson.

No hats.

Oliver was fully aware he was being irrational. But he had barely seen Renee for the last few days. When Chloe had blown into town like a twister, she'd swept Renee up and together they'd decamped to Chloe's place for "quality girl time."

Which was fine. He was perfectly capable of entertaining himself. He'd been doing it for years.

But when he came home to an empty condo and no fresh-baked cookies, it bothered him and it had nothing to do with actual cookies. Renee wasn't there to breathlessly tell him about everything she'd accomplished that day. Whether it was successfully baking a loaf of bread or managing to crochet a small pot holder—at least, that's what they were calling that lopsided square of yarn— she did so with such raw joy that he couldn't help it if he wound up wrapping her in his arms before she'd even asked how his day was.

She *glowed*, damn it. Every day, her body changed a little bit and the haunted shadows under her eyes became an ever more distant memory and he was helpless to do anything but stare at her in wonder.

Because she was wonderful. And he'd missed her more than any reasonable man should miss a houseguest for the last two days.

But that was just it, wasn't it? She wasn't a houseguest, not anymore. She was…

His. She was *his*.

Wasn't she?

He was in a foul mood by the time he made it to the Fort Worth Stockyards. He was hours early, but he wanted to talk to security and make sure Renee wouldn't have any problems.

Plus, now that he was here, he was duty-bound to check in with the promoter and the stock manager about how Chloe was doing. The attendance numbers were good and her clothing line was selling well, as were the other souvenirs, but he wanted to hear it from the horse's mouth.

He gritted his teeth and grinned his way through handshakes and back slaps. Everyone had good things to say about Chloe's management, which was great.

Where the hell were she and Renee?

Then, like something out of a damned movie, the crowd of riders and horses and calves all parted and there she was. His breath caught in his throat as he stared. He barely recognized her, but he *felt* it when Renee looked up and their eyes met across the crowd. She gave him a little smile, one that sent a thrill all the way down to his toes, which were firmly wedged into his damn boots.

Chloe had worked magic on Renee. Her hair curled and artfully arranged under the brim of a straw hat, she was wearing a lot more makeup than usual. Her jeans clung to her curves and her button-up top sparkled with sequins. Her curves were more pronounced, her belly rounding out behind a ridiculous sequined buckle. He guessed that, if someone didn't know she was pregnant she might not look it. She looked like a cowgirl, one that could walk in this world.

Even though it'd only been two days, he could still see how much her body had changed and he was pissed that he'd missed a single moment.

Leading her over to where the calves for the calf-roping event were penned up, Chloe said something to Renee and they laughed.

This was how she should always be—laughing and having fun and no doubt making cooing noises to the calf that sniffed her hand.

God, he'd missed her. Too much. He'd done his best to focus on the last three weeks instead of game planning the next few months or years, but he couldn't help the fantasy that spun out of control in his mind.

He could marry her. He could adopt her baby and they could be a family. He'd grow old with her by his side, teasing each other while eating cookies and spending long evenings in bed and doing all those things parents did with kids—parks and soccer games and school plays. All those things that his parents had done with him—and her—when they were kids.

She could make him happy.

Then a thought jolted him almost completely out of his chair. All those happy scenes?

They hadn't been in New York. They'd been in Texas, at Red Oak Hill, here in his condo. His perfect life with her was *here*. Not thousands of miles away.

Reality barged in because, in that vision of happiness, he hadn't seen his overbearing father or loose-cannon siblings or even this stupid rodeo.

Besides, he didn't even know if he could make *her* happy. She was still getting back on her feet and it probably wasn't helping that they were sleeping together. Hell, she hadn't even been able to explain those strange marks on her legs. He was afraid it had something to do with her husband, but he hadn't wanted to push. She'd tell him in her own time. He hoped. And if she didn't...

Hell.

A big man came up to Chloe and, after a second, Oliver recognized Pete Wellington. Damn it, when would he learn that the All-Stars wasn't his anymore? The last thing anyone needed right now was for Wellington to cause a scene. But if he was here—and by the look of it, giving Chloe trouble—then things were about to go sideways. Fast.

Not that Renee knew it. She looked over at him again, joy on her face. She pointed to the calf, as if to say, *See?* He shot her a thumbs-up. Her whole face lit up and damned if that didn't make him stick out his chest with pride.

He began to work his way toward her and Chloe but a rangy cowboy beat him to it. *Flash.* Damn it. He grabbed Renee's hand and kissed the back of it—then startled and stared at her face. Crap, he'd recognized her. Oliver needed to get over there before Flash did something stupid. Well, Flash always did something stupid. All Oliver could do was hope that Flash took a swing at Wellington instead of making a big to-do over Renee.

"Mr. Lawrence? I need to speak to you. Right now."

Groaning, Oliver cast a worried look at the Chloe/Pete, Renee/Flash train wreck in action before he turned. Surely they could all keep from killing each other for fifteen seconds. "Yes?"

A man glared up at him. Next to him stood a young woman with huge hair and a skintight leather skirt that was so short every single cowboy—and a few cowgirls—were staring.

"Brantley Gibbons." When Oliver blinked in confusion, the little man said, "Brooke Bonner's manager? And this is Brooke Bonner?" in a tone of voice that made it clear he thought Oliver was an idiot.

Right. The up-and-coming country singer performing after the rodeo tonight. Oliver cast another worried glance back at his siblings and Renee, but the crowds had shifted and he couldn't see them.

He put on as welcoming a smile as he could. "Yes, hello. It's a pleasure to meet you both." He shook hands. "Welcome to the All-Around All-Stars Rodeo. We're thrilled you were able to be here tonight." The man's eyes narrowed. Oliver knew that look. Something wasn't quite right. "What can I help you with?"

"For starters," Brantley Gibbons drawled, "you could see to Ms. Bonner's dressing room. We very clearly stated in the contract that there was to be—"

"Why didn't you tell me Renee was here!" This shout was accompanied by a punch to the arm that was hard enough to knock Oliver a step to the side.

"Shut up, Flash," Oliver ground out. He spun to see his annoying younger brother with his arm around Renee's shoulders and the world—well, it didn't go red. But it went a little pinkish.

Flash, being Flash, did not shut up. "How long have you been hiding her?" He sidestepped Oliver's attempt to grab him—and in the process, knocked Renee's hat off her head. "I haven't seen Renee since we were little—but maybe I should've checked her out."

"Damn it," Oliver growled, trying to step between Renee and…everyone. Because everyone was staring now. "Flash, *shut up*."

Renee tried to bend over to grab her hat, but Brooke Bonner beat her to it. "You look familiar—have we met?" the singer asked, handing the straw hat back to Renee.

Brooke's manager made an alarming noise. The look of shock on his face wasn't good. And it only got worse when he said, "You're Renee Preston, aren't you?" in a way that made the hair on the back of Oliver's neck stand straight up.

Flash launched the grin that made him a favorite with the ladies. "She was. Got herself married a few years ago?" He had the nerve to look Renee up and down. "Missed my invitation."

"Knowing you," Renee said, her smile stiffening as she cut another glance at Gibbons, "you would've used the wedding to get even for that one prank when…"

Flash held up his hands in surrender, but at least he was laughing. "God, I've missed you, Renee. You never did play fair, did you?"

The only reason Oliver didn't break his little brother's jaw was because the man between them was staring up at Renee with something Oliver wished wasn't rage—but was.

"No, she doesn't," the manager said, menace bleeding into his voice.

Renee looked at him with panic in her eyes. *Shit.* He had to get her out of here before anyone started snapping pictures. At the very least, he needed to shut Flash up.

He moved toward her as Flash went on, "Damn sorry I missed— Ow!"

Chloe beat Oliver to the punch. "Mr. Gibbons, Ms. Bonner, hello. I'm Chloe Lawrence and—" she paused to grind the heel of her boot into Flash's foot again "—we're thrilled you're here. I see you've already met Flash, one of our featured riders and, unfortunately, my brother."

"Son of a— Damn it, Chloe, get off my— *Ow!*" He shoved Chloe aside and glared. "That was unsporting of you."

Brooke Bonner giggled and Flash's head whipped around. "Hello, Ms. Bonner." With an exaggerated limp, he stepped closer, whipped off his hat and executed a perfect bow, somehow managing to get ahold of her hand and kiss it, just like he'd kissed Renee's. "Flash Lawrence, at your command."

Bonner batted her eyes at him. "Why do they call you Flash?"

If there was one thing Flash was good for, it was a distraction. As long as his attention was on Brooke, no one but the manager was paying any attention to Renee. Oliver got between Gibbons and Renee and started backing up. Renee hooked her hand through his waistband and held on tight.

Chloe let out a long-suffering sigh. "Because that's about how long it takes for him to rub you wrong."

"Or right," Flash cut in. He still had Bonner's hand.

Another cowboy—Oliver didn't remember this kid's name—crowded up. "Brooke, baby—" But that was as far as he got before Flash had him by the shirt and shoved him back.

"You don't talk to her like that," he growled, then added in a louder voice, "None of you talk to her like that. She's a lady and you will treat her as one or I will personally make sure you live to regret it."

Normally, Oliver would be irritated by Flash's ability to make any situation about him. But he'd neatly redirected the crowd's attention away from Renee. Gibbons seemed to remember where he was. He pivoted and headed straight to Brooke's side, shooing back the crowd that had started to press in for a better view of the fight. "Brooke will not go on without—"

Oliver wasn't about to look a gift distraction in the mouth. He backed up another step and was beyond relieved when Renee followed his lead. "Chloe will be able to make everything right." She wanted the rodeo? This was her chance to prove she could handle it. Oliver gave his sister a look. "Mr. Gibbons says there's a problem with the dressing room." Chloe nodded and Oliver gave thanks he had at least one intelligent sibling.

"I'd be happy to see what I can do to make you more comfortable," Oliver heard Flash say, which was followed by something that, if Oliver had to guess, was the sound of Chloe punching their twit brother.

Oliver didn't care. He spun, tucking Renee against his side and all but dragging her away from the crowd. He glanced back over his shoulder to see Gibbons peering past people. Crap. Hopefully, Chloe would be able to communicate to Flash—either with words or fists—to keep his mouth shut about Renee if anyone asked questions.

Oliver was so busy looking over his shoulder that he nearly clocked into Pete Wellington. "Lawrence," the bigger man all but spit.

Jesus, what else could go wrong? "Not today, Wellington," Oliver growled, shouldering past the man.

"Your sister is ruining this—"

"She's in charge—take it up with her," he called over his shoulder as Renee crammed her hat back onto her head. "We're leaving."

If he'd expected her to shrink and cower, he was wrong. "Slow down."

"What?"

Still holding on to him, she pulled back, forcing him to take smaller steps. "If you run, they chase." She glanced up at him. "And for God's sake, stop scowling."

Confused, he slowed down. "Because…"

She sighed. "Because they're sharks, Oliver. If they smell blood in the water, they'll go into a frenzy." Somehow, she managed to smile up at him. "Trust me on this."

He damn near stumbled over his feet at that smile. It was warm and carefree and, if he didn't know her so well, he'd think she was just another cowgirl having a good time before the rides.

But he did know better. Her shoulders were back and her chin was up and she had every single piece of her armor locked into place. And she was right, he realized. She had a lot more experience dealing with unfriendly crowds than he did.

So he forced himself to go at a snail's pace. "I'm sorry you're going to miss the rodeo," he said, guiding her around a pair of cowboys making a beeline toward Brooke Bonner and her leather miniskirt. "I'll make it up to you, babe."

"It's fine," she lied. And it broke his heart because that lie rolled right off her tongue like he was supposed to believe that things would ever be fine again.

After what felt like a century but was probably only

about ten minutes of semileisurely strolling, they made it to where he'd parked his truck. He helped her up into the cab and then fired up the engine.

Anger boiled through him. He'd told Chloe this was a bad idea, although it wasn't her fault it'd all fallen apart so quickly. No, he had Flash to thank for that. His father was going to pitch a fit over this.

For years—*years*—Oliver had kept his promise to his mother that he'd take care of the family, because Trixie Lawrence had known then that her death would devastate Milt.

She hadn't been wrong. But he'd tried and tried and *tried*, for God's sake, to be the glue that held the Lawrence family together. He'd given up on his dreams of moving back to New York and working for anyone other than his father—because that was the truth. He wasn't going back to New York as anything more than a tourist.

He'd given up so much more than that. He dealt with the damned rodeo and he ran an energy company and he didn't like either one. His whole life had been in service to the Lawrence family name. Yeah, he had money to show for that. Money was great.

But it wasn't a life.

And he wanted his life back. More to the point, he wanted a life with Renee. He wanted to make those daydreams a reality. He wanted to do what he wanted, not what was best for the bottom line or his father.

Maybe he wasn't that different from Renee, after all. He wanted her for himself.

If he lost her because of his brother, so help him God, he would not be responsible for his actions.

They were silent while he navigated through traffic, but he was thinking the whole time. He could deal with his rage and his dreams later. Right now, he had a problem—

a huge one. The Preston Pyramid Princess had been confirmed at the All-Around All-Stars Rodeo by someone who'd probably lost a lot of money in the scheme.

Oliver was a man of means. He had options. He didn't have to put everything and everyone on lockdown. He didn't want Renee locked away. He wanted her to be safe—and free. And more than anything, he didn't want those two things to be a contradiction.

Once they made the roadways, he began to talk. "Here's what I'm thinking."

"Oliver..." she said softly.

He kept going. "I have a vacation home in Colorado—Vail. If I charter a flight, we could leave first thing in the morning."

"Oliver."

"But we could plant some rumors—be proactive. Say you were seen in Florida or something. I know a media specialist and—"

"Stop."

"I see the red light," he muttered as he braked. "If you're not up for flying, we can take a car, but it'll take longer. We should probably still hire the charter and send them in the other direction so—"

"*Oliver.*" Her voice was sharp, hard. It cut through the cab of his truck like a knife. "No."

"You'd rather fly?"

"Jesus, men," she said under her breath as the light turned green. "No, I'm not going to Vail."

"That's fine. Where would you like to go? I can—"

"Are you going to make me keep interrupting you?"

He almost didn't recognize the woman next to him. There was something so cold and remote about the way she spoke, the way she held herself...

It was exactly how she'd been on that first day when she'd waltzed into his office. Had it really been a month?

One month with Renee, watching her grow and change with her pregnancy. Watching her discover who she wanted to be and making sure she had the space to be that new woman.

This was a huge problem. Because there had to be a way to keep her in his life without telling his family to go to hell or resigning. There had to be a way to get what he wanted and still honor his promises. She had to let him fix this because if she thought he was going to hang her out to dry...

"Well," she began and instead of sounding upset or even worried, she sounded...amused? "I knew this would happen."

"Babe..."

She held up a hand to cut him off. "It's fine," she repeated again. Oliver decided that the more times she said that, the less *fine* it actually was. "It was lovely while it lasted. And I did learn how to bake cookies. So that was nice."

The hair on the back of Oliver's neck stood up. He didn't like how everything had suddenly become the past tense, as if the time they'd spent together was a chapter and Renee was closing the book. "It'll be nice again," he said, hating those pitiful words. *Nice* didn't cover waking up in her arms. *Nice* didn't cover laughing with her. *Nice* didn't come close to how he felt about her. "I'll—"

"No, you won't." She all but whispered the words. And then it only got worse because she turned to him and said, "I shouldn't have come and I shouldn't have stayed. I'm sorry, Oliver."

"This is not your fault," he ground out. That did it. Flash was a dead man.

She smiled. It didn't reach her eyes. "That's sweet of you, but we both know the truth."

"The truth? What 'truth' do you think you know? Because here's the truth, Renee—if I thought it'd make things better, I'd marry you today. Right now." She went dangerously pale but otherwise, she didn't react. Oh, hell. "I'd turn this truck around and head right back to the rodeo because there's always a preacher who gives the opening prayer and I'd marry you in front of God, my crazy family and a bunch of livestock because, even though it'd be a huge scandal, it'd be the right thing to do. It doesn't matter what your father or your brother or that ass of a husband of yours did, not to me—just like I hope it doesn't matter to you that Flash is a jackass and my father is lost in his own little world and I've given years of my life trying to help them only to have them fight me on every single damned thing. I don't care about them, Renee. I only care about you."

Her eyes glimmered and her armor almost cracked. *Fight*, he wanted to yell. *Fight for us.*

"I care about you, too." He took it as a good sign that her voice wavered just a little bit. "But I can't hurt you like this."

"Like what?" He stared at her, aware that his mouth was open. "How are you hurting me, Renee?"

She turned to look out the windshield. "Did you ever wonder why Clint and I were always at your house?"

So much for that crack in her armor. "Because we were friends and our house was more fun."

Her mouth moved into something that would have been a smile if it hadn't been so damned sad looking. "Fun. That it was."

When she didn't have anything to add to that, he said, "Renee?"

"Do you know what those marks on my legs are?" she said all in a rush.

"No." He looked at her thighs as if he'd magically acquired the power to see through denim in the last five minutes.

He hadn't. But he remembered those evenly spaced dots clustered together over a few square inches of her skin. They were too perfectly spaced to be random.

"She liked forks," Renee said softly. "Whenever we did something that displeased her, she'd smile that cold smile and insist that we sit on her left side. She was left-handed. But once Clint tried to stick up for me, she stabbed him in the other leg, just because she could."

Oliver blinked and blinked again. "Those are…stab wounds?"

"The scars of them," she said with a single nod.

"Who stabbed you?" He felt an odd sort of relief that at least it hadn't been her husband.

But that relief was short-lived. "My mother, of course."

Oliver let out a slow breath. "Your mother."

Another single nod. "She had these rules. No noise, no mess, obviously. Anything that might embarrass her was not a smart thing to do."

He reached over and covered the spot on her leg about where the scars were with his hand. "I didn't know."

"We didn't talk about it," she said, as if that weren't obvious.

Another long moment passed as traffic streamed past them in the direction of the Stockyards. All those people were putting down good money to see if Flash would get stepped on by a bull or not, and to see Brooke Bonner and her leather miniskirt bring down the house. They'd buy Chloe's clothes and the men would spend money on All-Stars merchandise—all of which also had Lawrence

Oil logos on it. People would buy nachos and beer, and there were games for the kids, who would buy stuffed horses and bulls. The rodeo was an evening of family fun.

He'd pay any price if he could give that to Renee.

He'd do anything to change the past. To do a better job of shielding her from an abusive, controlling mother and the scandals of her father. If he could go back, he'd give Clint a job, one that was legal and legit—one that would keep him out of jail.

"I need to leave," Renee said quietly.

"I'll go with you."

She made a huffing noise that might have been laughter or it might've been frustration. "No, you won't."

"But—"

"You don't get it, do you?" She pivoted in her seat and pinned him with a hard look. "I will ruin you, Oliver Lawrence. I'll ruin you and your business and everyone you love. And I won't do it. I…" Her voice cracked and she looked back out the windshield. "I can't do that to you."

His mouth opened but nothing came out.

"I need to pack," she said, her voice strong and sure again. "And then I need to leave before it all comes crashing down on you. I won't let my family destroy yours like they've destroyed me."

Thirteen

Oliver kept talking. One minute, he was going to charter a plane. The next, a helicopter. Then it was a private yacht leaving from Galveston and heading for open waters because "no one could follow us there," as if determined reporters wouldn't be able to rent a speedboat.

Renee listened with only half an ear as she packed because it didn't matter—whatever harebrained scheme he came up with, it wouldn't work. There was no quick, easy fix that would let everyone live happily-ever-after. Not this time. Not for her.

She knew that. She'd always known that. Funny how thinking it, however, made her heart ache.

She needed to leave quickly before Oliver got it into her head to *make* her stay or, worse, enlist his family. Renee knew what she had to do but if the entire Lawrence family showed up to plead their case, she might not be strong enough to do the right thing.

And the right thing was so obvious. Renee simply couldn't hurt any of the Lawrences. Not even Flash. After all, he hadn't done anything Oliver himself hadn't done. Oliver had just had the good fortune to blurt out her name in front of small-town firefighters instead of a desperate music promoter.

So her mind was made up. She was leaving—alone. She'd see if she could stay with her former sister-in-law, Carolyn, for a few days. It would be awkward and uncomfortable but then again, Carolyn had given that interview where she'd passed on the chance to destroy Renee. And she and Carolyn had always got along before the scandal and divorce and death.

Besides, it wasn't like she could do more damage to Carolyn's reputation. She'd already been married to Clint. In the ruined department, she and Renee were practically equal.

Renee and Oliver would never be equal. Good Lord, he'd proposed. He'd said he'd marry her in the middle of the rodeo and he hated the rodeo.

In another time, another life, it would've been something wonderful.

Except for the *but*. Because there was always a *but*, wasn't there? As sweet as that marriage proposal had been, Oliver had prefaced that declaration with, *If I thought it'd make things better...*

He'd marry her. He'd do his best to make her happy. He might even adopt her child, when the time came, and she knew he'd be an amazing father. It might be good. Great, even.

But it wouldn't be perfect because he couldn't live without her. He'd offer her the protection of his name and access to all his resources because it was the most obvious solution to a problem.

Her.

She might be hopelessly in love with him, but she wasn't his problem to solve. And she wasn't about to marry another man who didn't love her.

Leaving was the only option.

"...one of those big bus-sized RVs that rock stars travel in," he was saying when he growled and spun, pulling out his phone. He never kept the sound on and therefore, she was always startled when he'd answer it at random times. "What?"

She hadn't bothered to pack the funereal dress or shoes—neither fitted anymore. But her lawyers would most likely blow their collective tops if she were spotted walking around in Chloe's fancy rodeo clothes. But the only alternative was pushing her leggings past the point of decency, so sequins it was. Which left the problem of the boots. She couldn't exactly walk around in those things anywhere but Texas. If she showed up in New York in the boots and the sequins, the press would have a freaking field day with her. What a shame. She set them next to the closet door and then closed the zipper on her single piece of luggage.

"Renee?" There was something different in Oliver's tone instead of the desperation that had colored all his grand plans thus far.

"Yes?"

"There are some men here for you."

The way he said it made it clear that he wasn't talking about the press. Even as the bottom of her stomach fell out, she squared her shoulders and lifted her chin. Old habits never died, it seemed. Just because she hadn't had to fall back on them for the better part of a month didn't mean she'd forgotten how to protect herself. "Who?"

But she already knew because Oliver wasn't trying

to arrange a quick getaway in his zippy sports car. "The FBI. Security checked them out. They need you to return to New York with them."

Ah. They must have decided to turn the pressure up on Clint. At least, she hoped that was the case and not that they'd already caught wind of the disastrous rodeo outing.

Again, her stomach tried to turn at the thought of someone snapping a picture of her smiling and laughing—the very things her lawyers had informed her not to do. But Oliver had reminded her how to be happy and she'd almost forgotten what it was like to keep her real self locked deep inside.

She needed to remember. Quickly.

"I see." She tried to smile for Oliver, to show him that she wasn't scared or worried—that she'd be perfectly safe in the company of the Justice Department's best officers.

She didn't make it. "Don't do that," he snapped, throwing his phone down and closing the distance between them. He grabbed her by the shoulders. "Don't act like everything is fine when it's not."

She was leaving. Things might never be fine again. "You can't fix this, Oliver."

"The hell I can't," he said and slammed his mouth down over hers.

He meant it as a kiss of possession. Renee knew that. He wasn't going to let her go without a fight, fool that he was. But Renee knew the truth.

This was goodbye.

She wasn't going to cry.

Once upon a time, the Lawrence family had shown her what love was. They'd given her another life, one where people were sweet and loud and messy and loved. So, *so* loved. If she hadn't had that second childhood with Chloe, she didn't know how she'd have survived.

Oliver might not ever realize it because, knowing him, he'd look back at this moment and see nothing but a failure to fix everything just so. But he'd given her the same gift again. Love and happiness and a glimpse into a future she might one day have. He'd let her find her own way and made her laugh again.

She'd be forever grateful for this month.

But she couldn't tell him any of that without breaking down into sobs and she knew damned well that if she so much as wavered, he'd do something stupid like bust out the high-powered attorneys and call a press conference and all but announce to the world that he'd been sleeping with the pregnant Preston Pyramid Princess, and that?

That would be his downfall.

So, when the kiss ended, she pressed her lips against his cheek and gave him one final hug. "Goodbye, Oliver." Then she grabbed her solitary piece of luggage and hurried for the door before she changed her mind.

"Damn it, Renee, I can fix this! I just need more time," he said, sounding half-mad with desperation. "By the time the FBI is done with whatever they need you for, I'll have this figured out—I promise."

No, she couldn't be his problem.

So she kept walking.

She didn't look back.

Fourteen

Goodbye, Oliver.

Fuck that shit.

After nearly running over two photographers staked out by the garage entrance, Oliver stepped off the elevator. The door to his father's condo swung open seconds later, making it clear that Milt Lawrence had been waiting for him. Just when he thought the day couldn't get worse...

"Beer?" Milt said, holding up a longneck, and Oliver knew he didn't have much say in the matter.

He supposed this wasn't a surprise. Renee's brief appearance three days ago at the All-Around All-Stars Rodeo—brought to you by Lawrence Oil—in the company of Oliver Lawrence, head of Lawrence Energies, had made headlines less than an hour after Renee had been whisked back to New York in the company of the FBI's finest. The whole debacle was exactly the sort of thing that would draw Milt out of his hunting lodge and into the city.

Not for the first time, Oliver wished his father hadn't bought the condo next to his for those rare trips into Dallas. Being called in for a lecture had a way of making Oliver feel like he was twelve again and about to be grounded for another prank gone wrong.

Except this time, it wasn't an elevator and a bunch of balloons filled with shaving cream. This was the family business. Their livelihood. He'd risked an international energy company and his family's financial safety and well-being for...

For Renee. Who'd walked away without a look back.

God, it hurt.

It turned out that Brantley Gibbons, Brooke Bonner's manager, had lost a lot of money to the Preston Pyramid. In fact, he was under investigation because several of his clients claimed he'd inappropriately invested their funds with Preston's firm. Brooke had stuck by him because Gibbons was her uncle.

Family. Was there any bigger blessing and curse than that word?

"Here," Milt said, handing Oliver a beer and motioning for him to sit on the leather sofa overlooking the skyline. Unlike his hunting lodge, Milt Lawrence's condo was as impersonal as a hotel. Probably why he only spent maybe ten nights a year here. "Well, this is a fine how-do-you-do you've got yourself into."

Oliver gritted his teeth. "Do you think that, just once, we could cut the cowboy crap, Dad? Because I'm not in the mood to hear about how I look lower than a rattler's belly in a wheel rut." He took a long pull on his beer. It didn't help. "No offense." Oliver braced himself to be dressed down because with that attitude, he deserved it.

But that's not what happened. "I take it she'd been with you since you first asked if I'd heard about the scam?"

To Oliver's ever-lasting surprise, there was less drawl in his father's voice. Still a little bit, though.

It was enough. "Yeah. A month." A good month. One of the best he could ever remember having.

Because Renee had been there. For the first time in years—maybe decades—Oliver had done something more than look at the family business or his family as just problems waiting to be solved.

He wasn't able to go back to who he'd been before Renee.

"Do you know where she is now?"

"New York." She wasn't responding to his texts, beyond the bare-bones information to let him know she was fine. Everything, apparently, was fine.

He was *not* fucking fine.

"She said she had to leave because she'd ruin me. I think she actually believes that," he said before taking another long swallow of his beer. It still wasn't helping.

"Hmm," Milt said noncommittally.

"She said..." He had to swallow a few times to make sure his throat was working right. "She said she wouldn't let her family ruin mine or my business like they ruined her."

"Ah," Milt unhelpfully added.

"That's it? That's all you've got? *Hmm* and *ah*?"

"I was going to say something about rattlers but that didn't seem to be the way to go."

"Jesus, Dad, are you mocking me?" There were days when his father was every bit as irritating as Flash— and worse.

"Simmer down, son." He held up his hands in surrender. "I'm not here to fight. If you're looking to take a swing at someone, either find your brother or go punch Clint Preston. Doubt either would help in the long run, though."

They sat for a moment. The silence was getting to Oliver, which had to be the only reason why he kept talking. Either that or the beer was actually starting to work and he just couldn't feel it. "I asked her to marry me and not only did she not say yes, she said goodbye." All that armor had been so locked in place that he still couldn't tell if she would've said yes or not had circumstances been different.

If the FBI hadn't shown up, would she still be here—or there or wherever he could have safely hidden her away? Or would she still have walked?

"Did she, now? In general, women like a nice proposal," Milt managed to say without laughing.

Oliver drank some more. Had it been, though? A nice proposal, that was. He'd said...

If he'd thought it would help.

Shit.

"She said she wasn't my problem to solve," he admitted, feeling suddenly stupid.

"Ah," Milt said again.

Oliver didn't dignify that with a response.

But had he actually said those words to Renee? He'd been upset, yeah. Flash had blown Renee's cover and Oliver had been frantic with worry about the best way to keep her safe but...

It hadn't been a nice proposal. Hell, it'd barely qualified as such.

"Do you know," Milt began, and for the first time in years, Oliver heard New York in his father's voice, "what I would give to have another day with your mother?"

Oliver let that thought roll around his head as he finished his beer and got up to get another. "Everything," he said when he settled back on the couch next to his father. "You'd give everything to have her back."

"You're damn right I would. The company, the rodeo, the lodge…" Milt cleared his throat and Oliver made sure not to look because he didn't want to see his father wiping away tears. "*Anything* to have her back."

"I'm sorry it's not going to happen," Oliver said. His mother's death was a problem he'd never be able to fix.

"And you know why I'd give everything for her?"

Oliver did look at his dad then. "Because you love her." There was no past tense about it.

"You're damn right I do." He stood, knocking back the last of his beer. "Herb Ritter's in town and I've got to smooth his ruffled feathers. And don't think I don't know you gave Chloe those negotiations after I told you not to. But Oliver?"

Oliver unclenched his teeth. "What?"

His father stared down at him with love and worry in his eyes. "We aren't your problem, either." He put a hand on Oliver's shoulder. "I know what you promised your mother, and she'd be right proud of you and everything you've accomplished. But we can take care of ourselves." He sighed. "We always could."

Then he grabbed his hat and walked out of the condo, leaving Oliver alone with his thoughts.

He couldn't function without Renee. He loved watching her try a new recipe and sharing in her success. Hell, he loved her failures, too—because they were always hilarious and only occasionally a hazard to home and health. He loved watching her grow and change with her pregnancy and he absolutely hated that she wasn't next door, waiting to welcome him home with a kiss that became so much more.

Holy hell, he loved her. Scandal-ridden family, broke, pregnant with another man's child—he loved Renee exactly as she was.

He hadn't told her that. Instead of treating her like the woman he wanted to spend the rest of his life with... he'd treated her like a problem that he was responsible for solving.

Jesus, what had he done?

Because now she was thousands of miles away, facing lawyers and officers and, worse, her family without anyone to back her up while he sat here and got scolded by his father.

What the hell was wrong with him? She wasn't the problem. *He* was.

He loved her.

That was worth risking everything.

"And have you had any other contact with anyone in your family?" the bored federal prosecutor asked.

Frankly, Renee was bored, too. She'd been sitting in this conference room for the last three hours, answering the same questions she'd answered a few days ago with the same answers, which were the same questions she'd answered a few months ago. She was pretty sure the prosecutor was wearing the same suit.

"The friend I stayed with in Texas spoke with Clint, but only to confirm that I had nothing to do with the scheme."

That got the prosecutor's attention. "He did?"

"Oliver Lawrence was a childhood friend. He runs Lawrence Energies. He wanted to make sure I was being honest." Renee cleared her throat. It hurt to think of Oliver right now. "Trust but verify, right?" The prosecutor didn't so much as blink and Renee felt that old fear of having done something wrong roil her stomach. "I did get permission to go."

The prosecutor conferred with his secretary, who made notes as the prosecutor said, "Anything else?"

Renee unlocked her phone and called up the most recent text message from her mother. "I got this two days ago." She handed the phone over because there was no way in hell she was going to read that message out loud.

Someone had got a shot of her at the rodeo. Renee had actually thought it wasn't as bad as some of the paparazzi shots and she liked the way Chloe's jeans had looked on her. But her mother had, of course, felt it necessary to remind Renee how fat and embarrassing she was—especially in those clothes. Sequins were against her mother's rules, to say nothing of actual blue jeans. The horrors.

Renee hadn't even finished reading it. She was a grown woman, an expectant mother. She did not have to let her mother into her life anymore. Her parents had never loved her—or Clint. She owed them nothing.

The secretary made more notes and Renee forwarded a screenshot to the lawyer's email. "What else do you need from me?" Because no one had escorted her to Rikers or arranged for transportation. She was here to plead with Clint, wasn't she?

The bored prosecutor looked over his notes again and Renee fought the urge to roll her eyes. Finally, the man said, "Ms. Preston-Willoughby, Clinton Preston has accepted a plea deal in which he'll get a reduced sentence in exchange for testifying against Darin Preston."

"Oh." The word rushed out of her. "That's good. If I may ask…how reduced?"

"He'll plead guilty in exchange for a sentence of twelve years at a minimum-security prison with the possibility of parole. He might be out in seven." The prosecutor looked up at her. "I don't plan on letting your father out of prison in his lifetime, even if he pleads guilty to avoid a trial."

"Good." If the man was surprised by this, he didn't show it. "Will you be able to extradite my mother?"

That got her a faint smile. "If we do, will you be willing to testify against her?"

Renee thought about all those terrifying family dinners with forks repeatedly stabbed into her legs and being blamed for getting blood on her ruined pants and skirts. She thought about a lifetime of manipulation and deceit, of being made to feel small and hopeless and embarrassing.

Then she imagined her mother in the defendant's table, being forced to listen to Renee poke holes in her story of innocence one precise jab at a time. She smiled. Let her mother find out what real anxiety was like. "I'd be delighted to."

"I believe we have everything we need," the prosecutor went on. "If your father's case goes to trial, we'll expect your full cooperation." Renee nodded. That was always the deal. "Please don't leave the country and keep my office informed of where you are. Otherwise, you are free to go." He gave her that faint smile again. "Good luck, Ms. Preston-Willoughby."

She sat there for a moment, stunned. "I can go back to Texas if I want?"

Not that it was a good idea—it wasn't. She'd walked away from Oliver, after all. And he had paparazzi watching him now. She'd seen the pictures of him entering and leaving his building and Lawrence Energies's office complex. In every single shot, he was scowling. In all probability, she was probably lucky he hadn't punched anyone. But at least he wasn't running. He'd remembered that.

She'd done that. She'd taken away his privacy, not to mention Chloe and Flash's privacy. The Lawrence family was in the press in a highly public way.

"Of course. Get a job, move on with your life. We

won't be garnishing your wages or any wages of anyone you marry."

Renee's mouth almost, *almost* dropped open at that, but those old damned habits kept her face blank. The prosecutor was just as unreadable but she shouldn't have been surprised. The man was no idiot.

"That's good to know. Thank you."

She and her lawyers stood, as did the prosecutor. Everyone shook hands. "Good luck," the man said.

She almost laughed at that. She'd been born to privilege and she was lucky enough to have known the love of the Lawrence family. But beyond that?

She'd been lucky enough to have a good month with Oliver. To ask for more than that would be too much.

She said goodbye to her lawyers and then hurried to the ladies' room. Her bladder seemed smaller every day. Her baby was growing. She could focus on impending motherhood now. That would be enough.

Lost in thought about what kind of job she might be able to get—something anonymous would be great— she exited the elevators into the lobby and headed for the door. She could see the paparazzi milling around outside but she didn't care anymore.

"I thought you hated the paparazzi."

That voice. *His* voice. "Oliver?" Renee stumbled as she whipped around, searching for him. Please, *please* don't let her be imagining his voice.

"But here you are, about to walk right out into their waiting cameras." He guided her to the side so effortlessly that she wasn't sure her feet touched the ground.

"You're here," she whispered as he pulled her into a waiting elevator. His arm went around her waist and he pulled her against his chest. God, she'd missed him. The five days since she'd forced herself to walk away from him had been a new, different kind of misery. She threw her arms around his neck and held on tight as the elevator doors slid shut. "What are you doing here?"

"Looking for you." He hit the button for the garage level and they began to move. "I made you a promise."

"You did?" She searched her memories and her heart sank.

He'd promised Clint he'd look after her.

Oh, no. He wasn't here because he couldn't live without her. He was here because he had a promise to keep. This wasn't any different than him offering to marry her because it might help. Oliver Lawrence was the most honorable man she'd ever known. Even though she'd walked away from him, he was going to take care of her. Whether she wanted him to or not, apparently.

"You don't have to do this," she said, her voice too soft. She was too soft when it came to him. Because she'd walked away once with her head up and her shoulders back. She wasn't sure she could do it again.

"I do." He lifted her chin so she looked him in the eye. "I promised I wouldn't leave you without saying goodbye."

She reared back, but he didn't let her go. He *had* promised that, hadn't he?

"But..." she said, staring at him. "I said goodbye."

"I didn't." Her breath caught in her throat at the sound of his voice, deep and intense. Oliver's eyes darkened. "What do you want, Renee?"

Before she could come up with an answer, the elevator dinged again and people got on. Oliver shifted so that Renee was standing next to him but his arm stayed locked around her waist and, fool that she was, she leaned into him.

He was really here. He was warm and he smelled like

Oliver and he was wearing cowboy boots in New York with his suit, and if she wasn't careful, she was going to burst into tears.

Her brother had agreed to a plea deal. Her father was never getting out of jail and, with any luck, her mother would be locked up before too much longer.

Renee was free to do whatever she wanted.

So what did she want?

They rode in silence the rest of the way down to the parking garage. He led her to a chauffeured car. The driver hurried to open the back door for her and Oliver guided her inside.

It was only when the door was shut that Renee found her voice. "What…"

"You didn't really think I was going to let you walk into that crowd of sharks and try to hail a cab, did you?" He shook his head like he'd told a joke.

"Oliver," she said, aiming for a sharper tone. His eyes softened as he folded her hand in his. "What are you doing here?"

"Coming for you."

She blinked and then, when nothing changed—he was still staring down at her with those warm brown eyes, still looking at her like he was glad to see her.

How was any of this possible? She'd seen the headlines. The wild—and not always wrong—guesses about the nature of her relationship with Oliver. The firefighters telling how she'd almost burned down the ranch house. Hell, someone had even got Lucille to give a comment. True, it'd been "Private people are entitled to private lives. Now, get off my porch or I'll shoot," but still.

"You know if we're seen together again, it'll only make things worse for you."

Everything soft and happy about Oliver hardened in a heartbeat. "Renee, what do you want?"

Her eyes watered instantly and she had to turn to look out the darkened windows of the car. They were out of the garage now and slowly creeping past the paparazzi waiting for her outside the building. She wondered how long they'd wait. Hopefully hours.

"I don't want to cost you your business," she said because it was the truth.

He snorted. She jerked her head around to stare at him. "Renee. What do *you* want? In the next five minutes or the next five years. What you want. Not what you or anyone else thinks you should do."

Her throat got tight and somehow, a lifetime of training herself not to cry began to fail her now. Because Oliver was the only person who'd ever asked and actually listened to the answer. "I don't want to hurt you."

"Oh, babe." He moved, pulling her onto his lap. She curled into him. "You know what I want?"

She shook her head against his shoulder.

"I want to take long walks around the park and maybe trail rides on the ranch. I want to see first steps and hear first words. I want to come home to fresh-baked cookies and spend nights in bed with you and wake up in the morning knowing you'll be right there. I want to be by your side, in sickness and in health, in scandal and in quiet times—hopefully more quiet than this," he added with a chuckle.

"But why?" She sniffed. "Why would you risk everything for me?"

He tilted her face up and stared into her eyes. "Because I love you."

Her breath caught. She wanted that life, too. She wanted to raise her baby with him and know that he'd always be there for her. He'd never leave her and never cheat on her because he couldn't live without her. Not because she was a promise he had to keep.

"I *love* you, Renee," he repeated again, putting more force on the words. He tilted her chin up so she had to look at him. "And you know what?"

"What?"

"You're worth more than any business or house or even swans. I'd give all of it up in a heartbeat, just as long as you were by my side. My father, my siblings—they're all grown adults. They can take care of themselves. I don't have to do anything for them. I only have to do what I want. And what I want is to marry you. I want to love you for the rest of our lives. That's all I want."

She gasped. As declarations went, that was pretty damned good. Much better than offering to marry her if it'd help. But there was still one giant, huge problem. "I can't be your problem to solve, Oliver. I can't. That's not a life."

She braced for him to start a running list of why he could protect her, how he could take care of her—just like he'd done when she'd been outed at the rodeo. But instead, he touched his forehead to hers. "I'm always going to do my best to make things easier for you. Not because you're my responsibility but because that's what you do for someone you love."

When she didn't say anything, he cupped her face and kissed her. "Tell me what you want. Forget the cameras and our families. Just you and me, babe. We're the only ones who matter."

"I want it all," she sobbed. Stupid hormones. "I want to bake and crochet and take care of my baby. I don't want nannies or chefs or… Well, Lucille is okay. But I just want us. I want to know that you won't lie to me and

I won't lie to you. I want to know you'll come home at the end of the day and we'll spend the evening together as a family. I want to hang out with Chloe and be irritated by Flash. I want…" She was crying so hard she could barely talk. "I want to be a Lawrence. I've *always* wanted to be a Lawrence. I want a big, happy family where everyone is loud and messy and loved and no one hurts anyone. And I want that with you."

"Oh, babe." His voice sounded choked as he wrapped her up in a huge hug and let her cry. When she'd calmed down a little, he looked her in the eyes. His thumbs rubbed over her cheeks, erasing her tears. "Renee, I promise you—I will never lie to you or cheat on you. I will always be there for you and make sure you have the space you need to find your own path forward. I'm not going to give up on you and I'm not about to let a little notoriety drive me away. You know why?"

"Why?"

"Because you—both of you," he added, resting a hand against her belly, "will always be family. Because I love you."

"I love you, too. God, Oliver, I love you so much."

He kissed her again and again and she lost herself in his touch, his taste, his smell. God, he smelled so good. Renee had no idea how much time had passed before the car made a wide turn, startling her back to her senses. "Where are we going?"

Oliver gave her that smile that, had she been standing, would have weakened her knees. "We're going home."

Finally.

Home was with Oliver.

Epilogue

"Up next on ESPN, June Spotted Elk has an exclusive interview with the Princess of the All-Around All-Stars Rodeo, Chloe Lawrence, about how the All-Stars are about to break big."

Pete Wellington's head popped up from the report on cattle prices he was working on. Not that there were many cattle left—but even if there were, at these prices, he'd never be able to pay the mortgage off. "What the hell?"

He caught a glimpse of the one woman who could make his blood boil with nothing more than a smile. Because Chloe Lawrence was smiling at the screen and his blood hit boiling in 0.2 seconds.

The camera cut to June, the world-famous bull rider. "Bull riding brings in the big money. How can the All-Stars compete with the Total Bull Challenge?"

Pete's eyelid began to twitch as the camera cut back to Chloe. She flipped her rich auburn hair over her shoulder, the rhinestones on her shirt—unbuttoned just far enough to hint at the tantalizing curves of her breasts—sparkling in the lights. But nothing outshone her smile. That damned woman simply glowed. "For starters, I'm hoping to get you to ride on our circuit!" The women laughed. "We'll be introducing more women competitors," Chloe went on.

God forgive him, she was nothing short of perfect, which only made his ridiculous attraction that much worse. How many people tossed and turned at night because she haunted their dreams with that smile, those lips, that body? How many woke up hard and aching for her?

Probably too many to count. Pete took comfort that he wasn't alone.

But no one else saw her for what she was. The rest of the world bought into her stupid cowgirl persona.

He didn't want her. Hell, his life would be that much better if he never heard the names Chloe or Lawrence ever again. Pete's body might crave hers, but his brain knew the truth.

Chloe Lawrence was no cowgirl. She was nothing but a thieving, cheating liar, from a long line of cheats and thieves. The Lawrence family were little more than con artists and criminals. They'd stolen Pete's rodeo, his family ranch—his entire life.

Now she was ruining his rodeo. The one her father maintained that Pete's father had lost fair and square in a poker game. But Pete knew better.

When it came to Chloe Lawrence and her damned family, Pete Wellington had one goal and it had nothing to do with the way he ached for her.

He wanted his life back. And he was going to start by getting *his* rodeo back.

Even if he had to steal it out from under her nose.

* * * * *

LET'S TALK
Romance

For exclusive extracts, competitions
and special offers, find us online:

- **f** facebook.com/millsandboon
- **🐦** @MillsandBoon
- **📷** @MillsandBoonUK

Get in touch on 01413 063232

For all the latest titles coming soon, visit
millsandboon.co.uk/nextmonth

MILLS & BOON
MODERN
Power and Passion

Prepare to be swept off your feet by sophisticated, sexy and seductive heroes, in some of the world's most glamourous and romantic locations, where power and passion collide.